KERNOW & DAUGHTER

KERNOW & DAUGHTER

Malcolm Macdonald

St. Martin's Press ❧ New York

Library of Congress Cataloging-in-Publication Data

Ross-Macdonald, Malcolm.
Kernow & daughter / Malcolm Macdonald.
p. cm.
ISBN 0-312-13995-0
1. Fathers and daughters—England—Cornwall (County)—
Fiction. 2. Young women—England—Cornwall (County)—
Fiction. 3. Cornwall (England : County)—Fiction.
I. Title.
PR6068.O827K47 1996
823'.914—dc20 95-45792 CIP

First published in Great Britain by
Judy Piatkus (Publishers) Ltd.

First U.S. Edition: February 1996
10 9 8 7 6 5 4 3 2 1

to

Dick and Diana Lipsey

This tale of positive (and negative) economics

Contents

Part One

the Angel
Coinagehall St

The New Century

*I*t was a new century — the Twentieth Century. A new dawn, people said. A new age, full of new ideas ... new this, new that. Above all it was time for the New Woman. But to Jessica Kernow, standing at the drawing room window at Wheal Prosper that Sunday afternoon — the last of the old, fustian Nineteenth Century — it looked depressingly like the same old Cornwall, drowning in the same old rain, and suffocating under the same old ideas that had been around all her life.

In just over a month's time, on the fourth of February, to be exact, the tally of her years would exactly match the tally of the centuries: twenty. Twenty years and nothing done; twenty centuries and so little achieved, except on the surface. Actually, the affinity wasn't as precise as the bald figures made it seem. They called it the Twentieth Century but it would still be nineteen hundred and something for the next hundred years, whereas she would actually *be* twenty-something for the next decade. (Like all sensible people, of course, she ignored those pedants who had nothing better to do than fill the newspapers with the prissy observation that the new century didn't begin until 1901 came around. Apparently such people popped up every century and bored the rest of the world to death.)

The door opened and closed quietly behind her. It was Harry — her elder brother. She knew it without turning to look; no one else in this household came into the room so self-effacingly, not even the servants.

Harry came up behind her, put his arms around her waist, and rested his chin on her head. "Sunday!" he moaned.

She sighed in sympathy but told him that if he intended leaving his chin where it was, he'd oblige her by slipping a small cushion beneath it. He chuckled and heaved himself away from her, resting his hands against the transom of the sash. Harry always had to lean on something. He stared moodily out across the sodden fields to the village — Nancegollan — where wet granite walls and wet slate roofs gleamed soggily in the fading afternoon light.

"Penny for 'em?" she said with little enthusiasm.

"Trying to devise a poem," he replied. "You know how, when Sunday comes around, they lock up all the swings in the children's playground in the park? And the only toy the children are allowed to play with on the Sabbath is a Noah's Ark set? Park-Ark, you see? The rhyme is ready made but the rest won't come."

She turned from the window and went back to the fireside. Staring into the flames she said, "Perhaps it's God's way of telling you not to write poems on a Sunday, either." The flames put her in mind of hellfire and thus of Reverend Coulter's sermon that morning. Everyone had wanted some message of hope to launch them into the new century. Instead they had been given a dose of good old hellfire; you could have cut the disappointment with a knife. "Have you gone through the figures the old man left with you?" she asked.

He sniffed and cleared his throat. "Are you at all busy, little face?" was all he replied.

She picked out several lumps of coal with the tongs and placed them in the hottest parts of the fire. Then she sat down and stretched her hands toward the blaze.

"The old man would scalp you alive if he saw you doing that," Harry said.

"Warming my hands?"

"You know what I mean. A lady rings for a maid when she wants more coal on the fire."

"Where is Father?" she asked.

"Having a nap still."

He did not add 'with Miss Pym,' but she knew it anyway. He came and sat beside her. "Jessie?" he wheedled, running a finger softly up and down her forearm, like a lover pleading for a favour.

She gave out a little grunt of exasperation. "I shan't always be around, you know," she exclaimed. "One day you'll have to do it for yourself — and then you *will* be in a pickle. What then?" Her expression changed from a frown to a genial smile during this brief speech for she really felt a great warmth for her big, useless brother.

Useless? No, that was unfair. He was just useless at doing all the things the old man expected of him. But ask him to draw one of his fantasy pictures or dash off a little jewel of an essay on some utterly trivial topic — and my! You'd see him come to life.

"I suppose he'd kick me out." The tone was hopeful.

"You're incorrigible."

He nodded. "Can't change the old spots, I'm afraid."

"No." Her glum mood returned. "Nothing changes. Nothing will ever change, will it! We'll still be fighting the Boers in the Cape this time next year. It'll still be raining. We'll still be singing *God Save the Queen* — the same old Queen ..."

He laughed and, taking his cue from her, sang: "God save our same old Queen ..."

"*Shh!*" She struck him sharply on the arm and glanced fearfully over her shoulder toward the door.

"What?" Harry sneered. "D'you think he's lurking out there — just waiting for some excuse to pounce?" His tone strongly implied that their father had much better things to do, but he said nothing directly.

"He hardly needs any excuse to pounce, does he!" she said glumly. "We're a standing excuse, you and I." After a pause she added, "Have you got the figures on you?"

He nodded but made no effort to fish them out. Time never bothered him. Their father might come in at any moment — it was, after all, getting close to the hour for pikelets and china tea, the Sunday-afternoon ritual Miss Pym had introduced years ago, soon after she took up residence. But still he showed no urgency. "D'you know what nags him most?" he asked.

"Father?"

"Yes. He can't bear to realize that, in the nature of things, we're going to outlive him. We'll go our own ways in the end — and he won't be there to stop us. I'm the daughter he wants you to be, and you're the son he'd like to see in me! I think it's bothering him more and more with every week that passes. This dawning of the new century isn't going to help much. But you just wait till your twenty-first comes round!"

"Why? What's so special about ..."

"It's the Great Divide. It's when life gets *really* serious. You thought it was serious enough already? Believe me — the best is yet to come! If you're not married by February twelvemonth, or engaged at the very least, he's going to make life intolerable for you."

She didn't want to talk about these things. They might be true — indeed, they almost certainly were true, insofar as anyone could predict another's future behaviour — but she didn't want to face it just yet. "Show me the figures," she said abruptly.

He drew the papers from his breast pocket and tossed them contemptuously in her lap. His contempt was for the paper, though; toward her he felt nothing but gratitude.

She ran a quick tot, adding all three columns — pounds, shillings, and pence — in the same run of her eyes down the page. At the back of her mind a little imp exulted in this skill, even while she exercised it, for her father hated her to add up money in that unladylike way. When a lady added figures, she should roll her eyes in agony and her fingers should beat a surreptitious pitapat against the side of her thigh (oops — her *nether limb*) and she should perform this ritual three or four times and take the average of the three or four answers it provided. That, at least, was Miss Pym's way with figures, and she was the Kernow family's authority on all that was ladylike. Cressida Pym was a lady; the Kernows merely had money.

Jessie said, "D'you realize, Harry, that thanks to you I probably know more about our family business than anyone? Probably more than the old man, even."

"Really?" His expression became animated but she could see he was more interested in the amusing situation her knowledge might give rise to than in the simple fact of it.

"Don't you *dare* so much as *hint* at it!" She wagged a warning finger an inch from his nose.

"As if I would!" he replied with wounded scorn.

"You might — in one of your moods. I'm just saying don't!" She looked again at the figures and sighed. "One day he'll be caught out, you know," she said. "He leads a charmed existence. What does he do with these papers he gives you? Does he know you treat them so casually?"

He shook his head. "He takes them back and burns them."

Her lips compressed to a thin, angry line. "Why doesn't he just tell you? Why run this risk? People can piece together bits of burned paper."

"I don't suppose he can just come straight out with it. Not in so many words. He couldn't bring himself to do it, could he — you know him. You know *us!* We're that sort of family. We know lots of things we'd never *ever* talk about. Father and Miss Pym, for instance." He wet his lips with a nervous little dart of his tongue and waited for her to take up the point — for he had run with it as far as he dared.

Jessie, for her part, wondered why she didn't. It had been on her mind times without number to broach the subject of Miss Pym with her eldest brother — the 'Surface Angel,' as they called her. It was certainly not something she could discuss with Frank, though he was only a little more than a year her senior. And Godfrey, at sixteen, would just die of embarrassment; even when they called her the Surface Angel — or, more usually the sa — it made him snigger and blush. So why did she not now take up Harry's rather obvious offer?

Perhaps because it was rather too obvious. Or perhaps because she'd always promised herself she'd speak to him about it after her twentieth birthday — which was only thirty-six days away now. Somehow it was important not to be something-teen, not even a *nine-teen*, before embarking on such a thorny topic.

He saw she was once again going to duck the issue and so, to make it easier, nodded toward the papers and said, "Is it really so wicked? The figures, I mean?"

She shrugged. "By all we were taught in Sunday School, yes. But by the standards of the real world ... who knows? It's nothing like as bad as the scandals one sees in the national papers. But it would make one of those sad little paragraphs one sees in the Helston *Vindicator* — or even in the *Western Morning News*. 'I can't imagine what possessed me,' claims noted Nancegollan businessman!' So I don't know what scales to weigh it on."

"But is it against the law?"

"It's evading tax — which one hears smart people boasting of every now and then."

"Do you?" he asked in surprise.

She smiled. "When they believe I'm not actually listening, yes." She grew serious again. "Listen — don't go pumping Frank for information. Don't ask him, even in the most roundabout way, where the law stands and how close one could sail to it and all that sort of thing. He'd smell a rat at once."

"He'd never peach on the old man, though." Harry was shocked that she could seem to suggest such a thing.

But she laughed at his assertion. "Of course he wouldn't — you dear, sweet chump! Not while there was a chance of squeezing himself in there and carving a nice juicy slice off the joint! Aaargh!" She raised her face and hands toward the ceiling in her frustration.

He nodded grimly. "You're right, little face. Why can't Father see it? He and Frank are two peas from the same pod. Frank should be the one to inherit the business, not me. Don't you think he's much the best suited for it?"

She wanted to shout an even louder *Aaargh!* and shake her fists at the ceiling this time — but she had already devalued the gesture. Frank was nothing like their father. He was reserved, cautious, watchful, cool; the old man was outgoing, reckless, observant, fiery. But Harry was an artist; he remade the world the way he wished it to be. So, with a wan little smile and an air of resignation, she picked up the papers, clamped them in his hands, and supplied him with one or two perceptive remarks to try out on their father when it was time to hand them back.

*C*ressida Pym smoothed her blouse downward, chasing a minute wrinkle into hiding behind the waistband of her skirt; the blouse was white, the skirt, clerical gray. The gesture accentuated her bosom. She considered its shape in her looking glass awhile, but not long enough for her satisfaction to sink to frank admiration; she drew her new navy-blue woollen shawl over her shoulders to put a stop to any of that. She smoothed some imaginary wrinkles in the weave of it. Was she growing more statuesque? And would it be a good thing if she were?

Her shoulders had precisely the same slope as Queen Victoria's — the Queen in the bloom of her youth, of course, as painted by Winterhalter. But such a slope was no longer fashionable, alas; nowadays they all wanted to look like Elizabeth Siddall, with the square-shouldered Pre-Raphaelite shape. Though why any woman should wish to look as if she'd be a handy pal in a rugger scrum was beyond Miss Pym. 'An old-fashioned beauty,' Mr Kernow called her. She didn't mind the 'beauty,' even though she knew her face was really rather plain (also like the youthful Queen), but that 'old-fashioned' made it a bit of a two-edged compliment.

She smoothed further nonexistent wrinkles from her clothing, this time over her hips. 'Generous' was Mr Kernow's word for them — another two-edged commendation. Generous to *him*, all right! The gibe caused wrinkles on her spirit, which were not so easily smoothed away. She turned petulantly from the glass and went out to the stairhead. With impeccable timing Kernow opened his dressing-room door and joined her.

He did not take her arm as they descended the stair. They never touched in public, except as any two people might casually touch — in passing a plate or negotiating a corridor, for instance. He had once caught her arm when she missed her footing on the front steps — and with the whole of the Four-Borough Hunt drinking stirrup cups and looking on. He had almost had to *embrace* her to prevent her from falling; it had left her feeling ill for most of the day. They were always 'Miss Pym' and 'Mister Kernow' in public and they remained 'Pym' and 'Kernow' even in their most intimate moments.

"Our last Sunday tea of the century, eh," he said as they entered the drawing room.

Jessie and Harry rose to greet them. Miss Pym thought they had a furtive air but Kernow seemed not to notice. She rang for Clarrie, the maid, to bring their tea.

"And what plots have the two of 'ee been hatching, then?" their father asked jovially, rubbing his hands and stretching them out as he advanced toward the fire. "Sit 'ee down! We aren't on parade."

Jessie almost flung herself back into the sofa — and Miss Pym almost reprimanded her for it as she took her own seat beside her master. Harry, who had been sitting in his father's chair, returned to the sofa and sat beside his sister once more. Miss Pym eyed them, suspecting collusion.

"Oh, Dad!" Jessie exclaimed with cheerful weariness. "Everyone always has to be plotting something, according to you, don't they!"

"'Everyone' is singular," Miss Pym said.

"They would be if they were forever plotting," Jessie agreed amiably. "*Most* singular!"

Miss Pym gave up; life had been hard enough when she had officially been Jessica's governess. The memory of it was enough to discourage her from taking up those reins again, even over the status of a singular pronoun.

The maid must have had the tea things ready for she appeared with them almost at once. To Miss Pym's horror Frank was behind the girl, carrying the tray with the teapot and hot water. She looked to Kernow to upbraid his son but the man had eyes only for the pikelets. Clarrie, meanwhile, was signalling apologies with her eyes, trying to convey to the housekeeper that she had no power to stop the young master from committing this grave solecism.

Miss Pym decided to give her a public dressing-down nonetheless, knowing she would accept it in silence and without rancour because she, in her turn, would realize that the true target of the reprimand would be Master Frank — who, in *his* turn, would feel awful for having exposed the girl to such a stern rebuke. She drew breath to begin but Frank — who had been watching her coolly, knowing very well that he had transgressed her code and that she would not let it pass — called out, "Why, Miss Pym! I see you are wearing the shawl I gave you for Christmas. You transform it. I had no idea it would look so beautiful upon you."

Harry took advantage of her hesitation to get in with: "But Miss Pym has always made the *plainest* clothes seem elegant, Frank. You should know that by now. Are you going to toast these fellows or am I? I'm starving."

Miss Pym swallowed the words she had been going to utter. Insincere compliments from little Frank were water off the duck's back to her, but compliments from Harry, sincere or not, were more disturbing. It had been quite different when she had first arrived in this strange household, for she had been eighteen then, and Harry, the oldest boy, a pimply gawk of thirteen. But now he was twenty-five and she twenty-nine (for the second year running), they seemed almost contemporaries. She averted her gaze from them both.

Jessie had meanwhile answered Harry's question by seizing up the toasting fork and spearing the first pikelet, which she now held out toward the fire.

"Lay it down, maid," her father growled ominously. "That's work for a boy." He watched her whole body go rigid and wondered if she'd try to argue the point; she grew more like her mother, God rest her, with every day that passed. Stubborn wasn't the word. Part of him was proud of her spirit but most of him wanted to slip his fingers round that proud, elegant neck and strangle her.

Jessie contained her anger and passed the toasting fork to Harry with a cold smile.

Miss Pym, cheated of her argument with Frank — an argument he could not possibly have won — and, discomfited by Harry's compliment, turned upon Jessica, saying, "Have you finished that watercolour, Miss?"

"The light has been atrocious, Miss Pym," the girl replied as she resumed her seat. She just sat on her skirts in whatever way they fell. When she rose they'd be a mesh of creases. But one couldn't keep up a constant flow of criticism and reprimand or it became like a waterfall or the dawn chorus — a noise one heard without noticing.

"And your embroidery?" she countered.

"It was too atrocious, even for that, Miss Pym."

"No painting. No needlework. So what have 'ee done all afternoon, maid?" her father asked sharply.

"I copied all the receipts for dishes and salves — all the ones I've noted down this year — from my commonplace book into my household book. I do it every New Year's Eve." She smiled acidly.

It was Stella's smile, reincarnate. He grunted and returned his gaze to the fire.

Jessie thought, *Dear heaven! I'm not yet twenty and I can already say things like that — 'I do it every New Year's Eve!'*

Harry handed her the first pikelet to butter, but she offered it on to Frank. He, however, rejected it like some actor in a melodrama, putting up both his hands, leaning away, and rolling his eyes in torment. "Buttering pikelets is maid's work," he declaimed in as close a parody of their father as he dared.

"Buttering or buttering-up?" she asked as she accepted the rôle. He grinned. "Same difference."

"Where is Godfrey?" Miss Pym asked sharply. Then she bit her lip and mumbled, "Oh yes — I recall now."

Of course, Godfrey was at the extra choir practice for the special centennial service at midnight. He'd gone from treble to tenor with hardly a break. Mrs Coulter, who was in charge of the choir, said she wouldn't know what to do without him — but that was mainly to pacify Mr Kernow, who thought all his sons should, like himself, sing baritone or bass; he considered that tenors were a little suspect in the manhood department.

Clarrie returned and said, "If you please, sir, there's a man at the back door."

In any other household such a curt announcement would have provoked a flurry of further questions: What was the man's name? Did he seem respectable? Had he stated any business? Who had sent him? And so forth. But not at Wheal Prosper.

Kernow rose at once; it was almost as if he had been waiting for the summons. He was gone no more than three minutes and he returned smiling. Miss Pym and the youngsters made no inquiries as to who it might have been, nor what he wanted at half-past-four on a drenching Sabbath afternoon. Such unannounced visits had been the common-place of their lives for as long as they could remember; their father claimed he could, if he liked, put 'a fox in every hen-coop in West Penwith' — by which he meant the whole of Cornwall west of Truro. No one at Wheal Prosper doubted it for a moment.

The hot, buttered pikelets and the mildly astringent china tea caused a somewhat mellower mood to settle on the company. Harry stretched out his legs and, gazing at the ceiling, said, "It's odd about the changing of the century, you know. It's a purely man-made event. I'm sure the sun rises and sets without even knowing the day of the week, much less the month — and still less the year. And the same goes for the rest of the animal kingdom. It's only we humans who make a fuss about it."

"The days of the week are not casual. They are ordained in the Bible," Miss Pym pointed out.

"The existence of a day called Sabbath — yes," Harry replied without explicitly contradicting her. "But for the Muhammedans the

Sabbath is a Friday and for the Jews it's Saturday. So ..." He waved his hand dismissively.

"That is just God's way of showing us that Muhammedans and Jews live in error," Miss Pym pointed out. "If they can't even get the day of the Sabbath right ... well!"

Harry returned his gaze to the ceiling and closed his eyes tight. "Actually, I was making a slightly different point," he said. "I woke up this morning and wondered what day it was. And then I thought: Suppose the days had *no* names! Suppose all we could say was 'daylight' and 'night'! And they just followed each other forever. Wouldn't it be terrifying? I'll bet one of the first things primitive man did was to give the days names."

Miss Pym was going to point out that Adam named the days as soon as the world was created, which was in 4004 BC; so the days had always had names.

But Frank got in ahead of her with: "Poor old Harry! He gets ideas that even Socrates would find hard to express. No wonder his poor old brain-box just sinks under the weight! Go and lie down in a darkened room, old fellow!" He gave his brother a kindly pat on the knee.

"Jessica, my dear," Miss Pym said. "I'd be most obliged if you'd hand me my embroidery. I find this illumination perfectly adequate to the task."

Frank, who was closest to the work-basket, obliged. "Jessie's ashamed to admit she needs glasses," he explained as he returned to his chair. "Also she's too vain to get some made up."

His sister flashed him a weary smile. "Bad sight or not, I spy with my little eye something beginning with FB," she said. "And I'll give you a clue — it's so teeny-tiny small, most people would never so much as notice it."

Harry laughed and said at once, "You've given it away — FB. Frank's Brain!"

It was Frank's turn with the weary smile.

"I just thought that — while we're trading insults — I oughtn't to be left out," she told him.

"Why *must* you trade insults?" Miss Pym asked, looking to Kernow for support. "Why can't we just be ..." She was going to say 'a nice, normal family,' but realized that she, of course, was hardly the one to put it like that. "... friendly?" she concluded instead.

Mr Kernow rose and said he had to go out on a little errand of mercy. On the Sabbath it was always 'an errand of mercy.' Weekdays were more interesting. Then his little outings were 'to see a man about a dog ... to mend a fence ... to see why beef's gone up tuppence a pound ...' and so on.

A short while later Miss Pym said she thought the light might be better in her boudoir. Frank and Harry offered to carry her sewing box up for her but she said Clarrie could manage it.

The moment they were alone Jessie clenched her eyes and fists and let out a quiet scream.

"What now?" her brothers asked.

"I'm *bored!*" she answered vehemently. "We must be the most boring family in the world. If there were championships in boring at the Royal Cornwall, we'd carry off all the rosettes. We'd put even Reverend Coulter in the ha'penny place."

Harry exchanged a slightly puzzled glance with his brother. "What would you rather be doing?" he asked.

She shrugged disconsolately. "Hoeing turnips? Gathering cockles and mussels by starlight? Anything thrilling in that line." She turned to Harry. "Just before you came in I caught myself wishing the train would leave the rails on the curve out of Nancegollan. Wouldn't it be exciting? We could all dash down over the fields and help them back here and fill the house with people, all in a state of shock. Wouldn't it be fun? D'you think it's possible to derail a train *gently*? Not to hurt people but just to unnerve them, so they'd need tea and calming down and things like that?"

Harry, pretending to take her seriously, looked at Frank and said, "Know any helpful railway engineers?"

"Never mind 'helpful'," Jessie put in. "D'you know one with a chip on his shoulder against the Great Western — someone who'd advise us for free?"

Frank looked at her sharply. "That's not exactly a ladylike observation," he said. He wasn't joking, either.

It put an end to their fantasy.

"You mean the Surface Angel would never say such a thing," Jessie grumbled. "Is that your measure of gentility?"

"I mean she'd never even *think* such a thing," he responded. *"That's* my measure of gentility."

Harry weighed in on his sister's side. "How d'you know *what* the SA would think?" he asked scornfully. "How would anyone ever know what that woman would think? I doubt if she even knows it herself. I'm sure there's a little demon in her mind that spots the ideas as they boil off the top of that cauldron she calls her 'mind' and bats back the ones she shouldn't be allowed to realize are festering away inside her

— so that only the sugary-spicy-all-things-nicey thoughts are allowed to emerge."

A slow smile spread across Frank's lips and a distant light filled his eyes. "Miss Pym a seething cauldron, eh? I wonder ..."

Jessie rose. "This conversation sounds as if it will soon become unfit for a lady's ears." She added pointedly at Frank. "I must show I can be ladylike in *some* things, eh!"

But Harry tugged at her dress from behind. "Stay," he begged.

She hesitated, for she wanted nothing more than to stay. "Why?"

"I don't know. We only ever discuss Miss Pym by way of significant glances and rollings of the eyes — and the odd clipped phrase. We're all masters of evasion. We ought to face it squarely."

"Face what?"

He looked away awkwardly. "Whatever it proves to be. We'll never run it down if we keep on as we have been. There's no point in giving days names and having years and centennials if they don't push us into ... clearing the decks, so to speak."

Jessie sat down again.

Silence followed.

"Fire away," she said hopefully.

"Yes, Harry — fire away!" Frank rubbed his hands with cruel glee. "Tip out some of the unseen contents of this cauldron for us — there's a dear fellow."

Harry did not rise to it. He stared into the flames and said, "The poor woman is ..." He licked his lips and darted a nervous glance at the other two. "She's in a pickle," he concluded. "I feel we should help in ... some way. In whatever way we can."

His patent earnestness prevented his brother from persisting with his flippancy. "Help?" he echoed.

"How can we?" Jessie asked. Her heart was racing suddenly. She knew they were talking about forbidden things — things she ought to push to one side, or to the back of her mind, or anywhere out of sight. And yet she felt compelled to stay and join in.

"Whatever we do, it must be done for *her* sake. For her own good."

Frank had one last shot at humour. "You mean it should hurt us more than it hurts her!"

They saw the humorous reference; they even accepted the implied warning against pomposity; but they did not outwardly respond to it. Harry replied, "I mean things simply cannot go on as they are — and if the dawn of a new century doesn't give us the chance to *do* something about it, then ... well, what's the point of anything?"

After a further silence Frank said in his best lawyer's voice, "Define the problem as you see it, then."

Harry crossed and uncrossed his legs. "The problem is that she came to this house at the age of eighteen, twelve years ago, to take the humble position of governess to Jessie here — who was then ..." He frowned at her. "Eight or nine?"

Jessie nodded.

"God knows why she did it," he went on. "Have *you* ever asked her?" His eye was still on his sister. "Has it ever croppped up in conversation between you?"

Jessie shrugged awkwardly. "Usually girls become governesses because they need the money."

"Yes, but we know that certainly wasn't the case with her. The Pyms have oodles of oof. The question remains."

"Perhaps her trouble is that she's lost her place?" Jessie suggested. "I mean, I'm too old to need a governess any longer — and I'm too young for a companion — and confidantes went out of fashion centuries ago."

"No they didn't," Frank said quietly. "They turned into chaperons."

"Yes, well, chaperons are going out of fashion, too. But amn't I right? She's lost her purpose in being here."

Harry scratched his head and stared awkwardly at his boots. Frank stared at her with an odd blend of amusement and scorn, as if to say, 'Are you *really* so naïve?'

It annoyed her because she truly did not wish to discuss the truth about Miss Pym and her real function in their household. Something in her wanted to find the words that would make it all untrue — or unimportant. She knew that 'something' was the remnant of her childish self; she knew Harry was right and that too much had gone unsaid for too long; but it made no difference. Why couldn't they talk about it tomorrow? Or when she'd turned twenty? Why did it have to be now?

Harry shifted his feet again. "Perhaps you're right," he said insincerely. "She's just lost her purpose." He glanced at his sister and saw her eyes were not on him.

But they were a split second later, just in time to see him look away and wink at Frank. "Must put on our thinking caps, eh?" he said, dismissing the whole topic.

Jessie felt awful. She had betrayed him in some obscure way. Even worse, she had betrayed herself.

*C*ressida Pym came bustling into Jessie's room without knocking; she never knocked. It was one of several little habits and traits that were beginning to annoy Jessie though she had been quite tolerant of them earlier — indeed, several of them she had only lately begun to notice. For instance, there was her tendency to organize Jessie's life in the smallest detail, from her calendar to her person; what had seemed right and proper when she had been sixteen was now, almost four birthdays on, becoming daily more irksome. Soon it would become intolerable. She gritted her teeth and waited to hear what the woman would say.

Cressida had intended to remonstrate with the girl for not being ready; when she found her not merely ready but sitting on the end of her bed with that especially annoying look of impatience — the one she adopted for almost all social functions these days — she changed her mind and said, "But you can't possibly be ready, child!"

That 'child' was the twist of the knife in a never-healing wound — and the smile that garnished it was the salt in the same gash.

"Before you start, Cressida ..." Jessie said.

"Start what, dear?" Miss Pym steeled herself *not* to respond to the flagrant use of her first name — a recent habit of Jessica's and one she heartily deplored.

Jessie ignored the interruption. "There is a confession I must get off my conscience: I freely confess I have not poisoned myself with Deadly Nightshade in honour of tonight's earth-shaking Centennial Ball. There now!"

Miss Pym's lips almost vanished in a thin line of disapproval. When they reappeared they were as pale as milk. Jessie was tempted to offer her a touch of lipstick from her hidden hoard but managed to resist; she didn't shrink from an argument over lipstick but would prefer to stand on firmer ground. The bodily poison of Deadly Nightshade was, she felt, much firmer than the moral poison of lipstick.

"In the first place," Miss Pym said, "it's not Deadly Nightshade, it's belladonna — a purified infusion."

"*Pure* poison, then," Jessie said as if in wholehearted agreement.

All the while Miss Pym spoke she plucked at portions of Jessie's clothing, without producing the slightest change; when she was not plucking she was smoothing out wrinkles, which sprang back as soon as her fingers had passed on. "And its purpose," she continued evenly, "is to enhance our beauty in a natural and moral manner — such beauty as the Lord has seen fit to grant us, that is."

"In what way is it natural and moral?"

"It is sanctioned by usage. Don't start this tiresome ..."

"But that still doesn't ... I mean, why should we wish to enhance our beauty at all?" Jessie persisted.

"Why — in order to make ourselves look ... beautiful," Miss Pym replied in a baffled tone.

"So! We enhance our beauty to make ourselves *look* beautiful?" Jessie summarized. Then, adopting her ex-governess's manner in a way she knew the older woman found especially annoying, she added, "The statement is tautological, surely? One might as well say giraffes grow taller in order to *look* tall. Or that ..."

"Thank you, Jessica, that is quite enough of that. You know perfectly well what I mean. We enhance our beauty in order to make ourselves *seem* attractive. Does that satisfy the pedant in you?" She pinched the girl's cheeks in order to improve their colour.

Jessie backed away swiftly, hoping the woman wouldn't notice that some of the existing colour had transferred itself to her white gloves during the pinching. To distract her she continued the argument, which she had intended to drop at that wearying point. "Attractive to whom?" she asked belligerently. "To men, you mean."

"To gentlemen," Miss Pym corrected her. "But I have neither desire nor intention to open up that Pandora's box again." She took a pace back, surveyed the girl's ballgown critically, and added, "Did Clarrie tie your corset laces?"

"So, we may poison our bloodstream and assault our flesh for the sake of these *gentlemen,*" Jessie rattled on — hoping to bury the latest question — "but we may not ..."

"*Did* she?" Miss Pym insisted.

"It is a new kind of corset," Jessie explained in a bored voice, "called the *Health* corset."

"Health?" Miss Pym echoed, as if the word, when coupled with 'corset', were morally dubious.

"Devised by Doctor Glénard and Madame Gaches-Sarraute." She spoke as if quoting from a pamphlet. "It supports the abdomen while leaving the thorax free."

Miss Pym jibbed at the word 'free'.

Jessie revised the statement. "It permits natural breathing. If you unbutton my bodice at the back, I'll demonstrate."

"I think I'd better," Miss Pym said. "Where did you obtain this ... this article? I don't seem to recall ..."

"Maisie Pask bought them in London. Two for her and two for me. See!" She turned about as the bodice slipped off her shoulders. "It's a straight-fronted busk. It doesn't curve in upon the abdomen like the old-fashioned wasp-waister. It supports and raises the abdomen without compressing it — which, in turn, leaves the diaphragm unhindered, so it can get on with breathing or whatever it is that unhindered diaphragms actually do. Best of all, Cressida" — she glanced fearfully over her shoulder and lowered her voice as if to share an important secret — "it obviates chronic disturbance to the vital female organs."

A weariness overcame her. All she really wanted to say was that it was vastly more comfortable than any other corset she'd ever worn; but such an argument would be incomprehensible to Miss Pym. It would be like saying one should choose one's medicine entirely by how nice it tasted.

But her highfalutin puff for the new health corset, with its solemn medical footnote, won the older woman over. She turned the girl round and round, like a milliner's dummy, examining it from every angle. "And yet I believe it will pull in a little tighter, dear," she said, slipping the knot before Jessie could complain or twist out of her grasp. A moment later she had her knee in the small of Jessie's back and was straining like a full tug-o'-war team at an assault-at-arms. But for the fact that her knee was well padded by her ballgown and two petticoats, the pain of it would have been unbearable to Jessie.

As things were, it was merely excruciating. Jessie felt as if some giant beetle had seized her in its jaws and was slowly, relentlessly, pinching her in two. She gasped and raised her hands heavenward, as if seeking escape that way; unwittingly she assisted her tormentor's apparent purpose, which was to crush the last breath of life from what Dr Glénard would have called her thorax.

"Yes!" exclaimed a delighted Miss Pym when she saw the result. "So *that's* how they do it! I've wondered and wondered." She swiftly knotted the drawstrings before all her good work could be undone by a single inhalation. "You clever girl!"

"Do what?" a panting Jessie just managed to ask.

"The S-shape, of course. You see it in all the ladies' magazines nowadays — but no one bothers to tell you you must have these new health corsets to achieve it. Just look at you!" She plucked the girl's blouse up around her shoulders again and arranged its lace trimmings to drape from a bosom that now projected like a vast, tilting slab over the sheer cliff of her transfigured frontage (or 'abdomen' in Gérard-speak). She spun Jessie sideways-on to the glass so that she could see how the savage drawing-in of the straight-fronted busk had, perforce (and with the stress on the 'force'), thrust out her posteriors to a degree that seemed quite indecent in Jessie's eyes.

But Miss Pym was delighted by it. "Every inch a Gibson Girl!" she enthused. "You're the image of that one in last month's *Cosmopolitan*. If you don't come back with at least a brace of proposals under your wing, my girl, then there's something rotten in the state of Cornish manhood. That's all I can say."

If she hadn't mentioned *Cosmopolitan* and the image of the Gibson Girl, Jessie might not even have bothered to look at herself. But it was just enough of a compliment to make her do so, and with unbiased eyes. And the vision in the looking glass was, she had to allow, really rather alluring — as breathtaking in the metaphorical sense as the corset itself was in the literal one.

Jessie's own imaginary self-portrait was of a no-nonsense girl who avoided all extremes. She sneered at the demands of fashion and beauty and at those friends who gushed endlessly about new babies and wallpapers and dress materials; but she was equally scornful of women who ran to the other extreme — the no-corsets-at-all brigade, the Dianas who'd spend every waking hour at the saddle or in the butts, and the black bombazine and fustian harpies who made such an obsession out of churchgoing and who wanted religion to burst its natural one-day boundaries and flood over all seven. From the middle ground, she had discovered, you could snipe at almost everyone else in perfect safety.

Unfortunately for her, nothing she had learned in that zone of eternal compromise had prepared her for the shock of facing such a magnificently statuesque and fashionably perfect creature as now smiled back at her from the glass. It was a transformation — indeed a transmogrification — so wildly beyond anything she might ever have dreamed of achieving that she had no defences against it. The regal, stately creature captivated her at once.

"Is it *very* uncomfortable?" Miss Pym asked solicitously, afraid the girl's silence might presage a fainting fit. *Cosmopolitan* had printed dire warnings of such a possibility.

"Not at all," Jessie replied. "Well … a little, perhaps. But I'm sure …" Her voice trailed off as the sublime and majestic vision overwhelmed her disbelief once more. "Nothing one could not quickly get used to, I'm sure."

Reluctantly she turned full-face to the mirror; the amazing S-shape was so captivating to see. And to think one could achieve it so easily — and with a corset designed for *health!* And it really wasn't too, too uncomfortable once the initial shock wore off.

The pinching-in of her waist made the swelling of her hips seem shockingly generous. The pert derrière could be rationalized away as 'mostly bustle' — though, in fact, her bustle was of the very smallest pattern. But the bounteously swelling hips were, indeed, *hers.* It made her feel disgracefully provocative. She wanted Cressida's reassurance but could not think of a delicate way to prompt it. Instead, she said, "You don't think it rather exposes the bosom?" She tweaked the lace up half an inch.

Miss Pym shook her head vigorously. "Not for a ballgown, dear. It's what an attractive bosom and a fine ballgown are for." She tweaked the lace down three-quarters of an inch and gave a nod of satisfaction. "They complement each other to perfection."

Glancing down at the result, Jessie was shocked to see that the pearly aureola of each nipple was *just* visible. Miss Pym read her mind and said, "Remember, dear, the gentleman will stand no closer than here. *His* line of vision has its *terminator* — to borrow a term from the astronomers, who also (come to think of it) gaze at objects out of their reach — *here!*" Her fingernail rested delicately above the nipples. "So the effect you were trying to achieve just now — from your point of view — will, in fact, be the one you achieve from *his.*" She smiled benignly at her own achievements. "We do not, after all, dress to please ourselves."

Jessie pulled a glumly humorous face and said, "On that point, Cressida, we are in absolute agreement."

"If it's too tight, dear, I could loosen it off a fraction, I believe — without marring the effect, you know?"

"No, no! It shall stay as it is now. I'll just grin and bear it."

Miss Pym looked at her sharply, to see if she were making an indelicate pun on 'bear it' and 'bare it.' When it appeared that the girl was quite innocent of any such *double-entendre,* her own suspicion became embarrassing. To mask it she stared at Jessie's exposed bosom and said, almost under her breath, "All the same, I think we'll dust it with a little light powder, don't you? Come to my room a moment."

"Powder?" Jessie was scandalized.

"Shh!" Miss Pym glanced guiltily about them. "Just the teeniest dab of it. I see one or two little blue squiggly veins here and there, which stand in the way of the perfection we *know* is there."

"D'you realize, Cressida," the girl asked as she followed her across the upstairs landing, "you haven't called me 'child' once, this evening."

Miss Pym made no reply until she came to dab a few discreet touches of powder on Jessie's bosom. "After tonight, maid" — she adopted the Cornish idiom with a self-conscious smile — "I think no one will ever again call you 'child'."

s the two women appeared at the stairhead, Barney Kernow and his three sons cheered ironically, implying that theirs had been a long, tedious wait. Jessie was still feeling rather dazed, not simply by her own metamorphosis from unremarkable young woman to glossy fashion plate but also by Miss Pym's shocking revelation of the contents of her dressing-table drawer. What an armoury of powder, rouge, *and* lipstick had been hidden there — and for how many unsuspecting years, too? True, the woman had passed the lipstick off as 'a salve to stop my lips from being chapped,' but the merest roguish glint in her eye had made it clear she did not expect to be believed. Jessie had the first intimation that the woman might become something more interesting to her than an ex-governess and present housekeeper ... or whatever her precise rôle in this household might be.

As a family the Kernows were used to amateur theatricals of the domestic kind. They knew what burned cork and coconut-fibre wigs could achieve in the way of disguise. In short, they could tell you a dozen ways to make an ordinary sort of person appear comical, ugly, or grotesque. But nothing of that experience had prepared them for the shock of seeing their sister — or, in Barney's case, daughter — transformed in the opposite direction. She was Cinderella on her way to the ball. The ironic cheers died in their throats and she completed that last dozen steps of her descent in an awestruck silence.

"Jess?" Harry was the first to recover — being the most artistic of the three brothers and the one most disinterestedly interested in feminine charms.

Poor Jessie was sure — wrongly, as it happened — that the tips of her ears were beetroot red but she said airily, "Anyone would think you'd never seen me in a ballgown before."

"Never like *that*," Frank said fervently. "Never on you. What have you done to yourself?"

Godfrey just stared at her and blushed as hotly in fact as Jessie had in fancy. At sixteen he was too young for the ball, so he was still in tweeds. He had not minded his exclusion until now, when the sight of his sister, looking so radiant, made him realize what bevies of feminine pulchritude (as he would have put it) he would be missing.

"Come-us on!" Barney growled, being unable to express his delight at how beautiful and stately his daughter appeared. He turned his back on her and stumped off toward the front door, where Clarrie, the maid, was waiting to see them off.

"Now there's a hot pasty if you want it," Miss Pym told Godfrey. "Or some cold brawn. Don't wait up for us — and don't burn too much coal."

"Yes, Miss Pym," he replied wearily. This was only the third time she had told him.

The housekeeper leaned toward Clarrie as she went out by the door. "He has a full coal scuttle there and that's all he's to get," she warned the girl.

" 'Tis all he'll get from *me*, missis," Clarrie replied, implying she had no power to prevent him if he wished to refill the scuttle himself.

Miss Pym smiled but said nothing; she knew the coalshed was padlocked but she thought Godfrey might as well discover that for himself. She saw him smirking in the corner of her eye.

In fact, the youth was smirking not at the thought of purloining an extra scuttle of coal but at Clarrie's certainty that he'd get nothing from her while the rest of the family was out; he had plans of his own in her direction — though, in the sort of fiction the girl liked to devour, they were more often called 'designs' than 'plans.' He changed his smirk to a frank, honest smile and favoured them with it, impartially.

The party stepped straight into the waiting carriage and set off down the drive at a smart trot, being already a little behindhand.

Clarrie, who had a very good notion of the young master's designs, took a wary step away from him as she closed the door on the departing revelers. "Shall I bring 'ee supper now, Master Godfrey?" she asked.

On a sudden impulse — and before he had a chance to regret it — the lad replied, "No. Bring me my hat and coat, quick!"

"Are 'ee going out?"

"Just do it!"

The maid took three steps to the hall stand and three steps back, bearing his inverness cape and cap.

"I'll be gone about forty minutes," he said as he raced out by the door. "Perhaps an hour."

An abrupt silence settled on the house. The astonished Clarrie required a moment or two to take stock of her situation. Mrs Hodgson, the cook, had just gone home; Becky, the other maid, was having her regular evening off; Shaw, the coachman-gardener, was now driving the family into Helston; and Mrs Shaw had earlier gone to see her sister in the infirmary in Camborne. So she, Clarrie, was now sole occupant of Wheal Prosper — mistress of the entire household! For the next forty minutes, anyway.

For one of those forty minutes she stood irresolute at the foot of the stairs — resisting the temptation to climb them to Miss Pym's room. She was not a weak character, so it says something for the strength of her temptation that it took a full sixty seconds to overwhelm her scruples, propel her feet up the staircase, carry a lamp into that holy-of-holies, and set it down behind one of the triptych looking-glasses, where it would both light her countenance and shield the windows from its direct rays. Then at last, with racing heart and trembling fingers, she dared to open the Aladdin's cave, the Pandora's box of that drawer in which her mistress hid (or fondly imagined she hid) her perfumes and cosmetics.

Godfrey wished he had had the sense to put on his galoshes before he raced down over the fields, across the railway line, then over one more field, arriving at the main road rather spattered with mud but just in time to waylay the coach carrying his family to Helston. He timed his emergence from the hedgerow perfectly, so that he remained invisible both to the blinkered horses and to the inside passengers. Only Shaw, sitting outside, saw him; Godfrey uttered a quiet, "Only me!" in time to prevent his crying out in surprise. Instead he asked, "What's the game?"

"Just thought I'd ride into town with you," the youth replied. "You are coming straight back again, I hope?"

The coachman assured him he was — not that Godfrey had doubted it for, as all the world knew, Shaw was building a model of Truro Cathedral in matchsticks and begrudged every hour away from this great labour; other drivers might congregate at the Blue Anchor and sup the evening away but Shaw would turn about at once and snatch a couple more hours with his beheaded vestas and the reeking pot of horsehoof glue.

They chatted in a desultory fashion until they reached the old toll house at St John's, at the foot of Sithney Common Hill. There, picking a moment when the carriage lurched on the turn, Godfrey leaped to the ground and crouched low until it had passed on by. He followed it at a cautious distance up into Cross St, all the way to its junction with Church St. There, however, the throng of coaches was so great that the family decided to get out and walk the last hundred yards or so to the Assembly Rooms above the Corn Market.

This threw Godfrey's plans into confusion for he had assumed Shaw would stay in town half an hour or so, swapping gossip with the other drivers before returning home — and here was the man returning at once. On his way back down Cross St he slowed down to let Godfrey jump aboard but the young fellow waved him on. "I'll catch the eight-ten from the station," he explained. "Tell Clarrie I'll be home about half-past."

The hour was just short of seven so he had plenty of time. He sauntered along Cross St, thinking that the others would have arrived at the ball by then. But no one was able to get through to the Assembly Rooms from this part of town. They were being held up by a grand scrap in progress between two women, rolling about in the mud at the bottom of Church St; in fact this, rather than a general thronging of coaches, was the cause of the traffic jam. Godfrey slipped into the grounds of the house on the corner and ran tiptoe across the lawn to where he hoped a gap or two in the privet might furnish a grandstand view of the combat without giving him away.

At first he could see nothing but a throng of frustrated patrons of the ball. Respectable folk, they turned their noses up in disgust at the brawl — but could not take their eyes off the excitement for all that. Then a shift in the locus of the fray created a gap in the crowd immediately beyond the hedge and Godfrey was able to make the two women out at last.

The taller of them was a strapping redhead in her thirties. She wore a torn blouse and an oft-patched skirt, both in the style of the seventies — which was probably when they had first become cast-offs. Now, at fifth-or sixth-hand, they had little wear left and offered no resistance to the assaults of the other, younger woman. Smaller and nimbler, she could have been anything from pale blonde to mid-brown — depending on your estimate of when she last washed her hair. At that particular moment they appeared to have reached a point of mutual exhaustion, for they were standing a couple of paces apart, staring balefully at each other, with the steam curling off them — and both breathing great clouds of vapour upon the dank night air.

"I never 'ad no trouble with my feller afore you come 'long, you scadger!" shouted the large woman.

"That molly-cuddle!" the other sneered. "I'd grudge a farthing for 'n. You tell 'e to leave I be. Sniffin' round I day an' night, the fudgy-faced ol' gawpus!"

"Ha! Little Madam Nice-guts now — but you wasn't so choosy in Ma Wilks's wash-house last night — was you!" The redhead squared up again like a pugilist. "I seen 'ee."

"Why, you gurt galliganter!" The other sprang at her, all ten talons unsheathed. She buried them in the older woman's face and raked down hard, drawing blood at once.

The redhead screamed and, grabbing a handful of the other's hair, jerked her head back with a fearful snap and then bit her in the neck.

An appreciative groan went up from the crowd. The more genteel spectators protested verbally; it was the onlookers of the rivals' own class who physically separated them and made them promise to fight fairly or not fight at all. The brawl moved about twenty paces back toward the town centre, to where the road was a little wider. This cut them off altogether from Godfrey's view; it also allowed those who were genuinely disgusted by the brawl to squeeze past on their proper business; the rest of the respectable onlookers, who wouldn't have minded staying to see the thing to its finish, then realized they had no choice but to follow suit. Godfrey saw his own family leave before he made his way back to the street. There he turned up his collar, pulled down his cap, and hastened past the brawlers, up the hill, past the Assembly Rooms, past the Coinage Hall and over the street that bears its name; and so at last he reached the relative darkness and obscurity of the yard behind the Angel Hôtel. There, he reckoned, he had about twenty minutes to wait before he could safely return to the Assembly Rooms and carry out his original design.

He chose an out-of-the-way spot beside the kitchen door, for the yard was almost as busy as the street. Ostlers and coachmen came and went to the stables with their horses, or fetched them fodder from the haylofts above. Bar-boys carried crates of empty beer bottles to padlocked outhouses, which they, like keyholders everywhere, opened and closed with a certain degree of self-importance; they returned indoors, weighed down by crates of bottles that had yet to be lightened. Outworkers delivered pasties, tarts, and mince pies direct to the kitchen door and sauntered off with a whistle, happily jiggling coins that, Godfrey guessed, would not long remain in their pockets tonight.

In between these distractions his gaze kept returning to the single scullery maid whose task it was to wash every pot and pan and dish, every knife, fork, and spoon — and everything else beside — that came out of the kitchen and dining room. She looked about fourteen, as thin as a starveling sparrow. Her lank, mousy hair was all gathered up into a straggly, lopsided bun, half of whose contents had fallen back down again, much of it over her face. Every now and then she lifted a wet, greasy hand and wiped it back over her shoulder, where it never remained for long.

Her dress consisted of two sacks, saturated with greasy water — and, no doubt, sweat as well — and clasped to her skeletal frame by several lashings of binder-twine. Behind her was a filthy deal table, which she would almost certainly have to scrub spotless before retiring exhausted to her bed in seven or eight hours' time. And, Godfrey realized, she had probably started work twelve hours ago, washing up the breakfast dirties. On a normal day she might have been given two hours off in the afternoon, but not today — not on this brilliant dawn of a new millennium!

The table was littered with saucepans, roasting dishes, baking trays, gravy boats, knives, ladles, cutlery in heaps, and piles of plates of every size. The room was windowless and would have been quite airless, too, but for the open door; on a cold, stormy day she would have no choice but to suffocate or freeze. And all for what? For five measly pounds a year — and two clean sacks at Michaelmas, no doubt! It made him want to seek out Walter Blackwell, proprietor of the Angel, seize him by the throat, and shake the life out of him until he agreed to treble her wages and give her the rest of the night off.

He was so sympathetic to her plight that he tarried ten minutes longer than he had intended. Also, the sacking was slipping from the binder-twine at the back and he could already catch exciting glimpses of the lower half of her lean, slender legs.

Three times during that half-hour vigil a scullion came down the passage bearing a large kettle of boiling water, which he set down outside her door with a cheery, "Billy-ho!" — whatever that might mean. To the maid it meant she paused in her unremitting washing-up, let a gallon of water out of the sink, replaced it with the freshly boiled supply, shook in a cupful of soda, and resumed her toil. Her hands were those of an Egyptian mummy, all shriveled and cracked.

On the third occasion she spotted him and, after a swift glance up the passage toward the kitchens, came to the back door with a smile, saying, "Hello, Charley!" She hitched the falling sacking back under her belt.

And he could think of nothing more sensible to say than, "Actually, the name's Godfrey." He was just so amazed that the poor little drudge had managed to preserve any capacity for cheerfulness at all.

"I shall finish here in a half-hour," she told him hopefully. "My sister do come on then, see." Her pinched little face was almost pretty. "Ah." In fact, it *was* pretty; but she had no bosom to speak of. "That's if you was thinking of asking I on."

"On to what?"

She laughed. "My dear life! On to a dance, o' course. To a kiddley-wink. 'Tis the new century in case you gone and forgot!"

"Ah, no — I'm afraid I'm going to the ... to a ball already — thanks all the same."

She gave a shrug and returned to her labours, calling back over her shoulder, "Suit thyself, Mister Godfrey Whossyername. There's more fish every Friday."

Still amazed at her cheerful resilience he drifted away from the scullery door, back across the yard and up the alleyway to Coinagehall St. To an equal degree his mental turmoil at that moment would have amazed those of his acquaintance who thought of him as a young man born for the outdoor life — a youth whose thoughts were as far removed from human affairs, especially female human affairs, as possible. But in fact, his thoughts were lately becoming obsessed by all things female.

At its most concrete, of course, there was a fascination with the female form in all its exciting digression from the male; but the thing went much wider than that and into areas far more abstract. Vaguest of all was what he could only call a female *principle* at work in the universe. Even at the most exciting climax to a foxhunt, say — or when a vigil beside a particularly dense thicket of withies rewarded him with a rare glimpse of a cirl bunting — his awareness of this new obsession was ever-present.

Until quite recently the 'female principle in the universe' could have been very neatly summed up in the single syllable: *No!* The female principle was the Absolute Negative. Females were those creatures who stopped you from doing exactly what you wanted, when you wanted, and to whatever degree of perfection or slovenliness might suit you at the time. True, they could also be affectionate and indulgent on occasion, but he had never been deceived by that. Those melting occasions were always of *their* choosing, and the kindly indulgence suited *their* purpose — never his, unless by chance.

It had been a wonderful, simple world, for it had only one law — to evade *them* and get away with it.

But lately it had all gone awry. Last month, for instance, he had woken up, after sleeping for barely an hour, filled with a profound sense of discomfort. What about? He had had no idea. He had racked his brains but its cause remained a mystery. Then, after trying, and failing, to get back to sleep, the truth had suddenly struck him: He stank to high heaven!

He hadn't had a bath for over a week, and somehow Miss Pym hadn't noticed. Anyway, she hadn't harried him outdoors to the laundry outhouse and fished down the old tin bath in her usual angry fashion. Normally such a discovery would have filled him with delight; he would have lain in bed giggling to himself and thinking *I've got away with it for once!* And he would have positively relished his own stale odour with every rise and fall of the bedclothes. But on that night it had made him so nauseous that he'd been compelled at last to rise and give himself the chilliest and most uncomfortable flannel-bath of his life — and then, dear God, he'd been unable to return to his bed, frozen though he was, until he had changed his sheets! His entire universe was shattering to pieces around him.

The smile with which Miss Pym had favoured him the following morning, after Becky had whispered something in her ear, was unprecedented, too. It was not the usual smile of a housekeeper to a naughty young lad who must be encouraged in whatever good actions he may accidentally perform; he'd been favoured with that sort of smile on the odd occasion — often enough not to mistake it for this new, knowing kind, which was like a smile of welcome to some new club. The fact that he himself had, by rising and washing of his own free will, applied for admission to that same club was no comfort. Clubs have rules; and rules hint at underlying principles. That was his first intimation that a specifically *female* principle was at work in the world around him and that he was beginning, in obscure ways, to become its pawn.

Now, some months later, he realized it was not merely 'at work in the world,' it was running riot in his very blood, playing havoc with every fibre and sinew. Even the little tatterdemalion in the scullery could have bent him to her will — if he hadn't already formed plans of his own for that evening. And yet those very plans involved *other* females and showed him up in varying degrees of enslavement to them. His spirit recoiled at the thought that, simply for the 'privilege' of being with her — the little angel of the Angel — he might have hung around the scullery door until she came off at eight and then have taken her on to dance-hall and kiddleywink, precisely as she had suggested. Despite her rags and lowly station in life, something within him felt profoundly unworthy of her — vile and unclean in her presence. He shivered at the closeness of his escape. But even then some opportunistic little imp at the back of his mind reserved the right to go back to that scullery door on some future evening and take her up on her suggestion.

A short while later he slipped into the Assembly Rooms by the rear entrance and, choosing moments when no one was around, made his way by back stairs and fire escapes to where a little hatch opened among the rafters. Intended for electricians to mind the lamps and for janitors to drive out nesting pigeons, it now afforded him a lordly view of the entire glittering company assembled below. He remembered this hatch as the starting point of several boyhood adventures of do-and-dare. He had remembered it again the moment he saw Miss Pym and his sister departing Wheal Prosper in their ballgown décolletage — when Clarrie had asked about bringing in his supper. In that moment, too, he had realized that he would probably never again have such an opportunity: to gaze down from this sublime concealment at so much near-nakedness of bosom, so much twirling female flesh, so many exquisitely bare and rounded shoulders ...

And here he was, heart pounding, limbs weak and trembling, belly hollow with desire ... actually doing it. Oh, that time could stop upon this hour! The world was one foaming sea of rounded white breast and shoulder ... so many happy, laughing females!

The fact that one of those enticing creatures was his own sister did not trouble him unduly. For a start, the chances were about two hundred and fifty-to-one against his gloating over her at any given moment; and in any case he was not lusting after any *individual* female down there, at all. He could probably name most of them if he were actually among them, but from this vantage he could hardly recognize one. No, his was a pure, almost impersonal adoration of femininity in general. A dumb, masculine homage to that infinitely desirable entity — the human female form.

And would they complain if they knew of it? They'd have little right to. After all, why else were they taking the trouble to expose so much of their delectable persons if they did not wish to excite the adoration of men? No, he had no qualms of conscience over his present thrilling business. He stood there in unclouded raptures until the clock told him he'd have to break all sprinting records if he was to catch the eight-ten to Nancegollan, there to carry out the rest of his plans — or, rather, designs — for the evening.

*J*essie's card was half filled before the first set was over. She had been to numerous balls before, of course, so the procedure was second-nature to her now. What was quite new upon this occasion was the tone in which she was asked for the privilege of a cotillion, a polka, a turkey trot, or whatever — so different from anything she had experienced in previous years. Miss Pym's admonition to her brothers was still echoing in her mind: "Remember you are gentlemen. The plain girl's heart will bruise more easily than her pretty sister's. Look to the wallflowers!" It was with the same spirit that, in earlier years, the governess had insisted on their always eating a slice of plain brown bread with their blancmange or jelly trifle at children's parties; her one great fear was that pleasure, freed from all sense of duty, would sap the moral fibre of the soul. Jessie could see the result in the way the young men, all of whom had been similarly admonished, now approached the Plain Janes and wallflowers at the Centennial Ball.

To a man they were oleaginously charming to any young miss whose looks fell below what they would consider an adequate standard; and each young man would get his name down with three or four of these Plain Janes before he dared approach those Venuses whom only cads bagged first.

The girls, meanwhile, died of mortification and only wished they could curl up inside their puppy fat and hide there till 'Carriages, please!' was called.

(The one exception was her eldest brother, who ignored the pretty girls entirely. In fact, Miss Pym would have done better to advise him not to ask so many matrons for a dance, to say nothing of ladies of uncertain age, who had gathered dust on the shelf for so long they were clearly beyond marriage by now. Miss Pym often commented upon it to Jessie, saying it was very *good* of him but not at all *wise*, but something more than simple delicacy prevented her from confronting the young man directly.)

Jessie knew the dance-programme conventions very well for, in the two years since her own coming-out, she had been the butt herself of those cruel civilities. But now, thanks in large part to Dr Glénard and Mme Gaches-Sarraute — and, to be sure, Miss Pym's muscle and determination — she was transferred to the other pan in beauty's scales. The first three names on her programme were howling cads to a man — and great fun, too. Usually she looked forward to a ball so keenly that, even thus early in the evening itself, she was consumed by disappointment and only wished it all to be over; tonight, however, though she had anticipated it no less ardently, she was by now wishing it could go on for ever.

The fourth name on her programme, Cornwallis Trelawney, represented an enigma, however. One could hardly wish for a more Cornish name than Trelawney:

And shall they scorn Tre-, Pol-, and Pen-...?
And shall Trelawney die?
Here's twenty thousand Cornish men
Shall know the reason why!

And yet Jessie, who, through her father's multifarious dealings, knew every titled, landed, or professional family west of Truro — including a smattering of Trelawneys — could not place him. And nor could Miss Pym, whose knowledge of Cornwall's gentry was even more encyclopædic. She could only guess at origins somewhere north of Bodmin, where her mental maps became sketchy and even, in some parishes, quite blank. Mrs Tresidder happened to overhear their musings and came to their rescue.

Cornwallis Trelawney (wasn't he handsome!) was, indeed, originally from Launceston in the very north of Cornwall, practically on the boundary with Devon (or the border with England, as she and all true Cornish people would put it). His family had once owned a large estate up there — the name of it would come to her in a moment. They'd made *oodles* in tin early in the century just gone — and, better still, had got out of the business before it vanished, when the country started importing the alluvial muck from Malaya. They had moved north and were now in mining machinery. They had several factories or smelters or something — not sure where. Lancashire? Sheffield? They were 'up North,' weren't they? Well — somewhere like that, anyway. She had heard — now mind you, they weren't to breathe a *word* of this to another living soul — but she had heard he'd fallen out with his father lately ... something connected with the business. Probably very dull. Anyway, he was staying at the Angel while he looked for somewhere more permanent. Wasn't he handsome! She'd not been introduced to him yet — but it was only a matter of time, of course. Mrs Chinnor knew him, or knew the family, because she'd grown up at Bolventor, which was on the right side of Bodmin Moor for Launceston. He'd be an asset to local society if he managed to find a congenial house near by.

Miss Pym thanked Mrs Tresidder for passing on so much information, which would help Jessica no end when Mr Trelawney's dance came round. The moment the lady had gone, however, she vented her anger at being given so much half-digested knowledge, which was worse than no knowledge at all. While Jessie enjoyed the first set of dances, Miss Pym sought out Mrs Chinnor.

It turned out that this second lady knew very little more about Cornwallis Trelawney than had the first. She knew the *family* quite well, of course, and confirmed that they had an iron and steel works in Sheffield — or was it Bradford — and a factory that made all kinds of mining machinery in Leeds — both being cities in Yorkshire. She knew of nothing in the neighbouring county of Lancashire. The rest of her information concurred with what Miss Pym had already heard. The only extra nugget was that Cornwallis was rumoured to be an amusing conversationalist.

Jessie's spirit sank at this last intelligence; amusing conversationalists always left her tongue-tied and feeling dreadfully inferior. It fell even lower when, on looking once more at her programme — which was almost full by now — she saw that he had put himself down for the one-step, which immediately preceded the break for supper. It meant that she would have to measure up to this 'amusing conversationalist' not just for the five minutes or so of the dance but for the subsequent half-hour as well. By the time the one-step was called her heart was doing its best to leap out of her throat. She had brushed past Trelawney during several earlier dances; sometimes he had noticed her, sometimes not, but whenever their eyes *had* met he had given her the warmest smile, somehow managing to suggest that all these other dances were just killing time, for form's sake, until their one-step came round. And here it was at last. Half of her prayed she wouldn't make too much of a fool of herself, the other half told her that was the worst possible attitude she could adopt. And the little censor that sits in final judgment on each of us, especially when we are as divided as that, said it was now too late to worry about such matters, anyway.

"Miss Kernow!" He reached forth a hand to her. "How many centuries since I asked for this dance?"

Replies teemed in her mind but wedged one another tight in her throat. Centuries? Time. Hunger. Food next. Talk about empty tummy? For God's sake! Say the hours have dragged for you, too? Too forward.

Comment that the pause coming up in four or five minutes will be most welcome? No — implies the four or five minutes themselves will be wearying. For heaven's sake say *something* — if only goodbye!

"Your name intrigues me," she said.

Who thought that? His name hadn't really done anything except flit across the surface of her mind about fifty times since he spoke it first; you can't call that *intriguing*.

"Trelawney?" he asked, slightly surprised.

"No — Cornwallis." She was committed now. "It's usually a surname, isn't it?"

They took to the floor and joined the swirling throng. Conversation was impossible until they reached the nearest corner, where he said, "D'you feel in energetic mood, Miss Kernow?"

"Not in the least!" she assured him, and truthfully.

He smiled with relief and said, "Would you think me ungallánt if I suggested we simply sway in time with the music and move in a little sort of eddy in this corner? I doubt if people will notice."

She assured him she could think of nothing more pleasant, which was also true.

"Cornwallis," he said. "It *is* usually a surname. There was an earldom, I think, but it died out after the fifth in the line. The second earl was the man who lost America for us. Almost lost us Ireland, too. What a hero he'd have been if he'd only managed to rid us of both! Every town in England would have had a Cornwallis Square."

Jessie laughed. "That doesn't explain how you come to bear the name, though."

"Oh, I don't think my parents knew the first thing about the noble Cornwallises. They picked the name out of the blue in a fit of Cornish patriotism. And a touch of guilty conscience, I shouldn't wonder. They were just about to get out of tin, you see — move all the family assets out of Cornwall and into Yorkshire. A blaze of patriotism at the font came in very handy. And cheap."

This brand of conversation was so far removed from the sort of thing required by etiquette that Jessie decided — if anything so rash can be called a decision — to cast aside the rules of conversation herself and take the plunge into his swiftly flowing stream instead. "I expect every girl you've danced with tonight has asked you all the usual boring questions, Mister Trelawney. In the very nature of things I shall get to hear all the fascinating answers you gave them anon. So may I ask you the one question that is uppermost in all our minds — and which, I'm quite sure, not one of them has so much as hinted at?"

"Fire away," he said guardedly; his pace was already slowing for, though he knew what she meant, he did not believe she'd have the nerve to come out with it.

"Are you looking for a wife?" she asked simply — and in precisely the neutral tone she would have used if the word 'wife' had been 'house,' instead.

He stopped. For four whole beats (of the band, not her heart, for that had stopped, too) he held his breath and stared at her, jaws slack, lips agape. Then he broke into the most genial smile and said, in a tone as calm and quiet as hers, "As a matter of fact, I'm not, Miss Kernow."

She let out her breath in a huge sigh of relief — partly that he had not exploded at her question but mainly at the answer he had given. They began dancing again. Not shuffling as before, but not with the full vigour the music demanded, either; conversation was still possible.

He laughed, trying to recapture her attention, for she was now eagerly checking that no one around them had overheard her asking so shocking a question.

"I'm glad you have enough humour to cover such an awful gaffe," she said.

"Oh, I'm not laughing at that — and by the way, I think it was the very opposite of a gaffe. I'd have walked from Yorkshire just to be asked that question — and above all by you, Miss Kernow. No, I was laughing at my own vanity."

"Vanity?" She frowned.

"Yes. When I heard you sigh with relief at my reply, my unthinking response was: *How dare she! She has no right to feel relieved like that!* Now if that isn't vanity, this isn't the twentieth century. Was that your brother I was speaking with earlier? Harry Kernow?"

"One of them. My eldest. My eld*er* brother, Frank, is also here — though I don't see him at the moment."

"Shall we drop out of this dance now and get to the watering hole ahead of the main herd?" he suggested.

She agreed gladly.

"I look forward to meeting Frank — if he's anything like Harry, whom I ..."

"He's not," she assured him at once.

"Ah. No — I imagine all three of you are quite individual."

"Four," she told him, "My younger brother, Godfrey — being only sixteen — is staying at home tonight. Though, curiously enough, I imagined I saw him here in Helston, earlier in the evening — staring down at us from that little hatch among the rafters."

"Is that likely?" They stepped off the floor and began threading their way among the onlookers, some of whom were also intent on beating the main herd.

"One never knows with Godfrey. He's actually quite a solitary and secretive young fellow."

"When you say 'actually' you mean beneath the surface? He doesn't appear solitary?"

"No, I'm sure most people think of him as a budding sort of huntin'-shootin'-fishin' man — bluff and hearty, you know. But it wouldn't surprise me if he turned into a poet, instead."

"Really?"

"He's just starting to feel the tug of romance, I believe."

"Ah!" His tone was laden with insincere compassion. "Poor lad! But, from that huge sigh of relief you heaved just now, I take it you're rather glad that — in your case — those dreadful days are over?"

She hugged his arm a little tighter to her side and said, "Glad? I have even more cause for gladness than that, Mister Trelawney — for in my case they have passed me entirely by."

Their eyes met — and sparkled with the hints of many gladiatorial contests yet to come.

*T*here was something subtly different about Clarrie that evening; Godfrey noticed it the moment he arrived home — and she was not a girl at whom even a young fellow like him, in the dawning of his ardour, would normally look at twice. And as far as most people were concerned, she was the sort of maid who gets noticed merely as a maid rather than as any sort of real person at all. Her figure was solid, well built, and rather dumpy. She had a plain, open, honest sort of face with deep-set eyes and a loose mouth that usually hung open a fraction of an inch. Her hair was mid-brown, short, and straight; it had been cut back to her scalp eighteen months ago to cure a bad attack of ringworm and had not yet grown back beyond the nape of her neck. Until then she had been a rather effervescent little character but the mutilation (and by her feelings that was not too strong a word) had changed her; she had become taciturn and slightly withdrawn. Miss Pym said it made her a better and more attentive servant but inwardly the whole family would have welcomed the return of the earlier, slightly scatterbrained Clarrie.

There was, indeed, a hint of that vanished maid when she came running down the main stair, just as Godfrey let himself in at the front door. But he would not have noticed it if she had not explained, rather breathlessly, that she had just been drawing the curtains in the bedrooms; then the fact that no such explanation was necessary made him wonder — briefly — why she bothered to give it. He became rather more talkative with her than he might otherwise have been.

"I love being in a house all alone," he said as he struggled out of his overcoat and kicked off his muddy boots. "Don't you? It happens so rarely, though. Even if the family's out, there's always a servant or two. Real loneliness is to be found only in haunts of coot and fern."

She passed him his slippers and picked up his disgraceful boots by their laces. Holding them at a fastidious arm's-length, she said cheekily, "I'll go out for the evening, if you mind."

He laughed and, rubbing his hands in anticipation of the fire and his delayed supper, crossed the hall to the drawing room, saying, "Go out where?"

"Dunno," she replied. "On the razzle. 'Tis New Year."

His heart dropped a beat. If she had not used that vague but emotive phrase, 'on the razzle' — which can mean anything from you-know-what to enjoying a few twirls around the dance floor — the evening might have taken an entirely different course.

His grand 'designs' had, in fact, been rather timid in scope, not to say downright furtive. He had intended to begin by looking through the artistic books in his father's study, where *The Greek Slave, The Odalisque, Les Baigneuses,* and — a recent find — King Cophetua's *Beggar Maid* were all hiding in wait to ambush his passion. Then he thought he'd send Clarrie off for the night, knowing she'd go straight to bed and read one of her penny-dreadfuls for hours and hours. Behind this early dismissal lay the fact that he had lately come across (and enlarged) a knothole in the paneling that separated the maid-servants' room from the back staircase; and if he took a precarious foothold, straddling the banister and a wainscot ledge, he would be able to watch her getting undressed. Tonight, with no one else in the house, would be an ideal time to try it out. He would not be able to stick it for long because the hole was right under the slope of the roof and even a short vigil would give him the most painful crick in the neck. But still … needs must when the devil drives; and no man was more devil-driven than he, he thought in his ignorance.

Such, then, had been the full scope of his dastardly designs on Clarrie that evening — to catch the odd, thrilling glimpse of her *en deshabille.* But the phrase 'on the razzle' was a key that unlocked doors in his mind, doors that until now had borne such legends as 'laughable,' 'out of the question,' and 'don't even think of it.' He unlocked the first and said, "We can go on the razzle here, Clarrie — if you like." He laughed to show he didn't really mean it; and she laughed to show she understood it was just a joke, really.

"Don't bother to lay a place in the dining room," he said. "I'll have it on a tray by the drawing-room fire."

But the drawing-room fire, he discovered, was almost out. What on earth had she been doing all the time he was away? He determined to tick her off about it but then realized that her neglect had, accidentally, preserved the entire scuttle of coal — which, in turn, would enable him to prolong the evening. Time was all he needed. And that gave him a further idea. He left the room at once.

He passed a rather surprised Clarrie on her way from the kitchen; she was then bearing his tray of supper to the drawing room. "Be with you in half a jiff," he called over his shoulder. "Don't stir up the fire yet." And, true to his word, he was soon back with as big an armful of logs as he could carry. "At least she couldn't padlock the woodshed!" he chuckled.

"Yes," she murmured, "there's always a way round."

He threw the driest and smallest of the wood on the glowing embers and stepped back, brushing bits of moss and sawdust from his jacket. "See what you can do with that," he told her as he seated himself in the fireside armchair and took up his supper tray.

She knelt in the hearth and raked the poker among the ashes. The cherry-red coals soon flared to bright orange. She went forward on all fours to blow at them and encourage the wood to catch fire. But it was nothing to the incandescence this little scene ignited in Godfrey's mind. Shame urged him to look away but powers far more ancient kept his eyes fixed on the kneeling maid and her stocky, pneumatic body. He only managed to get down his meal because *that* appetite, too, was running throttle-open. By then the discomfort of her situation had made Clarrie squat on one knee and use the bellows as they were intended. Only when the wood was well ablaze did she pick up the tongs and start building the lumps of coal upon it.

"There's more art in that than people think," he said, laying aside the tray.

She rose to her feet and stared in quiet satisfaction at her handiwork. "Can I bring 'ee anything else?" she asked, picking up the tray.

"Yes." He grinned. "Go and fetch a bottle of wine."

She laughed, thinking he was joking again, and carried the tray to the door.

"Seriously," he called after her.

"She'd notice," she replied scornfully. "You'd be whipped for it and I dismissed."

"There's a bottle in Frank's room. In his riding boots."

"Gusson!" she exclaimed scornfully, but he could already hear a tinge of doubt in her tone.

"See for yourself. He won't dare complain. Anyway, I'll tell him. I'll own up. He won't grudge me one bottle — not if I promise it'll only happen once every hundred years."

She laughed again but left without giving any sign she'd obey. However, she returned a few minutes later with a bottle of '95 Barsac — plus a corkscrew and wineglass. These she placed on the whatnot beside his chair, giving him a brief smile of complicity. "Will that be all, then?" she asked hopefully.

"No," he replied, having had time to think it out. He rose and, without touching her, ushered her back toward the door. "You wash the dishes and I'll lay the breakfast and bring down the lamps for trimming, and then you can bring another glass in here for yourself, and fetch down one of those books you enjoy reading so much, and I'll get one of my books, too, and then we can sit by the fire, and enjoy a long, lazy evening of it, reading to our hearts' content. And on the stroke of midnight we'll drink a little toast to the baby century."

They were out in the passage by now, on their way to the kitchen.

"My gidge!" she exclaimed. "I can't do that." But there was more speculation than prohibition in her tone.

"Why ever not?"

"Because. That's why."

"*Because* isn't a reason. It's just a word. A preposition."

"A conjunction, actually," she said.

He stopped and hung his head in mock shame. Then, brightening, he continued, "Actually — talking of conjunctions — tonight offers a perfect conjunction of all sorts of things: warm fire, lamplight, working day done, no one to boss us around ... D'you think an evening spent reading in my company would be so dreadful?"

" 'Tin't that." She gave a hopeless, trapped sort of smile.

"That attic of yours will be freezing cold, Clarrie. I can't believe you'd rather spend the whole evening up there on your own. And what about ghosts?"

Her eyes raked the ceiling; she knew she was going to give way.

The advantages he had listed were just too tempting, quite apart from the flattery that he actually preferred her company to his own.

"How long have you been with us?" he asked lightly.

"Six year an' a half. I come to 'ee on me fourteenth birthday."

"Well, Clarrie — you're practically family, then. Come-us on. We're wasting time. I'll help with the washing-up. I'm quite the expert now, you know."

As she filled the scullery sink from the kettle on the hob she asked him how he worked that one out. He told her of his visit to Helston and how he had spent a few minutes hiding in the Angel yard and had watched the scullery maid there.

"How did 'ee go to Helston at all then?" she asked — meaning not 'how' but 'why?'

He shrugged awkwardly. "To see the ball, I suppose. Not that it was very interesting, mind. In fact, it was pretty dull. But it was just being excluded, you see — being told I was too young to go." He laughed drily. "If I'd been ordered to go, I'd have spent days scheming how to get out of it. Human nature. I'll bet the Queen must sometimes long to slip down to the Windsor Castle kitchens in the middle of the night and make herself a cup of cocoa."

"She can do anything if she's Queen."

"Oh no she can't. She couldn't go cockle-gathering on Wherrytown beach, for instance. She couldn't shy for coconuts at Ram-Buck Fair. Nor sit with the likes of you and me on a cherry-bang outing with the Band of Hope. All the ordinary little pleasures of life — she's barred from them for ever. I was thinking, you see, watching that little skivvy in the Angel — she might envy my sister Jessie, but she has no idea how confined Jessie's life is. She has a hundred times more freedom than my sister. A thousand times. An infinity of times — because she's *absolutely* free, you see? Put a thousand pounds in that skivvy's pocket and there's nothing she couldn't do."

"Oh yes!" Clarrie said sarcastically. "That would change things a bit, I must say."

"It wouldn't for Jessie, though. That's my point. Put a thousand pounds in Jessie's pocket and she'd still be as hedged about with restrictions as she is now. Can you honestly not see that, Clarrie?"

The girl sniffed, unwilling to admit that she could, if only just; in her mind, a thousand pounds would compensate for scats and scats of restrictions.

He made the point, anyway: "She'd still be confined to doing only those few things a respectable, unmarried lady of her class is permitted

— which isn't much when you add it all up." There was a thoughtful silence and then he asked, "What would *you* do with a thousand pounds, Clarrie?"

"Dunno," she lied.

"Come on!" He cajoled her with a nudge.

"Leave service," she said hesitantly.

"Of course."

"Take a lease on a little shop."

"Splendid! A sweet shop? Haberdasher's? What?"

"A village shop — bit of everything. Like Ma Bucket in Nancegollan. She do know everyone — and everything they do get up to, and all. Just me and ... a helper. Nothing big, see."

"A husband?"

She glanced at him sharply to see if he were teasing. Then she said, "The shop'd be mine, not his."

"He'd be the helper, then."

She grinned happily. "That'd do me very nicely." She threw the washing-up mop in the air and caught it nimbly. "Where's that thousand pounds you promised, then?" she asked as she pulled the plug on the used water.

He dried the last item and hung the damp teatowel over the rail on the kitchen range. "It's what we're all looking for," he said.

"A hundred would do it," she added more soberly as she slipped off her apron and hung it beside the towel. Then, taking up a clean glass she said, "I'll gather the lamps and lay the breakfasts tomorrow morning. They won't be up and about too early."

Five minutes later they were settled at the fireside, each with a favourite book. He saw with surprise that hers wasn't a penny-dreadful at all, it was *Tess of the d'Urbervilles*. It made him wish he'd picked something a little more intellectually challenging than *Stonehenge's British Rural Sports, Illustrated*, fascinating though it was.

Clarrie refused to sit in a chair; she said she'd never settle comfortable if she did. Instead she sat cross-legged on the floor, leaning against the chair with her skirts pulled tight across her knees to make a sort of shelf for her novel — in which she was soon completely absorbed.

Glancing at her from time to time, Godfrey could not help being aware of what an enormous change had come over him — at least in his attitude to her — during the past hour. He realized that, although they had lived under the same roof for six and a half years, as she had pointed out, he hadn't really known the first thing about her until tonight. It changed everything. He tried to imagine her sitting there without her skirts but with her limbs in that same attitude. An hour earlier it would have been a scene to gloat over — something to carry up to bed and use as the basis of some incandescent fantasy of seduction; but now he was furious with himself that he could even think of using her so basely. And as for that knothole in her panelling ... well, you could take out a whole panel and sit him in front of it in an armchair and with a bag of jam doughnuts and he'd clench his eyes tight rather than risk seeing her taking off her clothes.

What had happened? Why this change in her — or in him? What was the change, anyway?

She was a person now, not simply a maid — not a handy surrogate for a girl who would otherwise exist only in his fantasy, and only for very specific purposes.

Was it love? He was on the *qui-vive* for signs of it lately.

He gazed surreptitiously at her, ready to avert his eyes the moment hers looked like rising from the page, and he tested himself.

Did he wish to caress that neck?

Actually it was rather a delicate neck, seen obliquely from the side like this.

Did he want to run his fingers through her hair?

And her ears were ... endearing ... fetching? Something like that. Attractive! Yes. She had very attractive ears.

As he ran the gamut of things they might *properly* do as lovers he became increasingly aware that, pleasant though each little action might be, what he most wanted to do with her was what he was, in fact, already doing: just sitting together by the fireside, not touching, not talking, not necessarily looking at each other even — simply *being* together like this.

So it probably was love!

But was it the shallow kind or the deep kind? The shallow kind was all physical attraction and seeking after pleasure. The deep kind appreciated people for what they were, not for the stimulation they could provide.

In the end, he decided to come to no very firm conclusion — yet. If it was love (which was still a big if), then it was *probably* of the deep kind. One would just have to see.

After about an hour she mumbled that her foot had gone to sleep. She stretched out on the carpet, rolled onto her tummy, leaned the book against the fender, propped her chin on her hands, and continued her reading. But after only a minute she giggled and shook one boot violently, saying it was full of stars and that her blood had turned to lemonade. He thought it the most wonderful description of pins-and-needles he'd ever heard but he said nothing for fear of seeming to patronize her.

The gesture had accidentally displaced her skirt, leaving the lower part of her calf visible. He merely averted his gaze and smiled in amazement at the profundity of the change in him — the change *she* had wrought in him. It proved that women were morally superior to men in every way for, though she was only a servant, she had achieved that with him — she had taken a callow, evil-minded youth ... (Was 'callow' the same as 'evil-minded'? Never mind. Youth was always 'callow' — that much was certain.) She had taken him, an evil-minded youth whose waking hours were consumed with thoughts of — and filled with ill-informed images of — female anatomy, and, simply by the purity of her example, she had transformed him into a parfit gentil knight who would rather sit with her all evening than even glance at a carelessly displayed calf.

Just before eleven o'clock she finished her book. She gazed at the page through brimming tears, thinking how monstrously unfair life was and yet what a good tale it made in Tess's case and you wouldn't want it to end all happy like a fairy story.

Then, when the hour began to strike, it bore home the realization that, contrary to all her earlier fears, poor Master Godfrey was too terrified to try anything with her. Before the family left her alone with him this evening her greatest worry had been that she might have to spend it literally fighting him off; he had certainly given the impression of a young man all *hurrisome*, as they call it. She would have hated that. She had no desire to ... well, play Tess to his D'Urberville or anything like that. But a little light couranting with a handsome young lad like him — too young to take seriously but old enough to know what was wanted — that was another matter. That was why she'd put on the merest hint of Miss Pym's cosmetics. And it had seemed to work well enough to begin with; he'd flirted with a will and said all the right things.

"Sad sort of story, is it?" he asked, laying aside his own book.

She nodded and sniffed back the remnant of her tears. "Lovely!" She chuckled. "If I was on my own, I'd weep buckets."

"Well, that's no mood in which to start the new century." He glanced at the clock. "An hour to go. Shall I open the wine bottle? We could have a sip now — see how we like it."

She rose to her feet and stretched with evident relief. "And if we don't like it?"

"I don't know." He peeled the lead foil off the neck of the bottle with the tip of the corkscrew, which he then began screwing into the cork itself.

"Well then, we shall just have to find something we *do* like, shan't us!" she said archly.

He blushed. "Sit down. I'll serve you. That's what the Romans did on the Lupercal, you know. Slaves became masters, masters slaves."

He hadn't intended for her to sit on the floor again, much less at the foot of his own armchair — but that seemed to be her interpretation of his command. With a glass in each hand he lifted one leg carefully over her and sat down, thighs wide apart so that his knees avoided contact with her shoulders.

"Isn't that nice, now?" She stared briefly into the fire and then smiled up at him over her shoulder. Her deep-set eyes seemed to smoulder darkly in the glow of the fire; her generous lips were adorable when she smiled like that; he could not think how he had ever thought her plain. Nor ignorant. She knew a conjunction better than he did — and she read a higher class of book, too. As for her face, there was a simple, honest beauty shining out of it, just waiting for him to grow up sufficiently to appreciate it. He stared at her, transfixed — appreciating it now.

"Don't I get a drink, then?" she asked.

"Oh, sorry!" He set his own glass down and leaned forward to hand her hers.

But she lifted her face to him rather than her hand. For a bewildered moment he wondered if he was expected to pour the wine directly into her mouth.

Then he realized what she was doing.

Then it seemed the most natural thing in the world to lower his lips to hers.

It was the first time he had ever kissed a girl — other than in a giggling fashion during party games and the like. The first time he had ever seriously kissed one. It was ... he fought to find the word but the sheer sensuous pleasure of it overwhelmed him. The sweetness ... the softness ... the warmth ... the yielding ... the tenderness ... joy ... delight ... the ecstasy of it all! He seemed to be melting away inside. Most of his innards turned hollow — and the rest of them just fell into that vast space ... and fell ... and fell forever. And then, out of that huge, misty, rosy, glowing blur of sensations came something sharp — a sensation sharply focused in one vibrant point. It took a moment or two before that point resolved itself into the tip of her tongue, questing up between her soft, loose lips ... on between his lips ... and on and on until the whole of her tongue was wriggling, squirming, writhing against the whole of his.

It was a novelty so far beyond any pleasure he had ever known that he possessed no scale on which it could register. It was as if she had discovered a new sense, furnished with its own nervous pathways directly into his brain. The curious thing was that his brain continued to function with an almost inhuman calm; it knew that the lovely softness in his mouth was a girl's tongue — something he had never experienced before, nor even imagined, come to that. But the knowledge was abstract ... remote. The only reality was that glorious marshmallow warmth there.

Her fingers touched his. She relieved him of the wineglass and set it carefully down, all without breaking the contact between them. She raised her hands again and carried his fingers to her face. Her darling face! He cradled it in his hands and began to caress her cheeks, her ears, the slope of her shoulders, her neck.

She let out a low moan — but only through her nose. Her lips she kept fastened tight to his so that when, as now, she began to withdraw her tongue, his had no choice but to follow. It was an invasion he would not have dared initiate, but once she began it, he followed her lead with a will.

The moment he had invaded her mouth she pursed her lips to an O and somehow rolled the sides of her tongue into a tube — forcing his into movements so blatantly symbolic of a different invasion that it raised him to a fever of longing and self-disgust, equally mixed. Fortunately, before the symbolism became apparent to her, she experienced a sudden need to breathe openly — indeed, to gasp and pant and fan her cheeks and cry, "Oh!" and "My life!"

"My darling," he said, panting a little himself. Staring deep into her eyes, he started once more to caress her cheeks with the very tips of his fingers. He could see that she was not the most beautiful woman in all the world — not as the world judges beauty, anyway. But by *his* lights she was the fairest of the fair; she was unique — she was herself — she was Clarrie; how could one judge her against others? The scales did not exist.

So many new thoughts and sensations clamoured for his attention now. He realized he had never been as close as this to any other person. Family didn't count, especially if you were the youngest, because you grew up with them always around; you were close to them even before you realized what 'close' and 'distant' meant. But

Clarrie was from that vast region labeled 'distant' — indeed, being a servant in his household, she could hardly be more distant. Yet somehow, tonight, some magical power had woven a web of feelings — of tenderness, longing, understanding ... of wordless empathy — and cast it over them like a great protective cloak against a cool, indifferent world ...

No! That was wrong. He was already beginning to poeticize it, to see it in the conventional terms of what little verse he had been forced to read at school. It was more like discovering that an old, familiar house had a room he had never noticed before — not a new room, simply one he had never been aware of — a room that, now he had trespassed over its threshold, proved full of wonders ... a room he wanted to stay in forever.

They sipped their wine, toasting each other shyly. She wrinkled her nose and said actually it wasn't as bad as some she'd tasted. She said it must be because she was with him. He said nothing tasted as sweet as her lips. She blushed and rubbed the back of her neck, saying any more of that and she'd get a permanent crick. He suggested she should sit on his lap, instead. She required no second bidding.

She sat in his lap, leaning against him with her dear head resting against his collar bone, and gazed into the fire. Occasionally she would look up at him and say, "Innit nice!" And he would see the firelight dancing in the huge dark pools of her eyes, and his heart would stop once more, and his innards fall away inside him, until he wondered how his body could possibly withstand the exquisite torture of loving her so tenderly — and knowing how hopeless it was — and wanting to protect her from all the cruelties of the world ... How he didn't burst was a marvel.

Now they drank from the same glass, first hers, and, when that was finished, his. To him it symbolized the fact that he and she had somehow flowed into a single *us*.

"Innit nice," she said again, wriggling against him and giving out a happy sigh.

"When I grow up, Clarrie, I want to marry you — if you'll wait for me. Will you? Dearest girl!"

She chuckled. "That's silly talk, master. Don't spoil it now. We'm just dollymoppin', that's all."

"Oh, don't call me 'master'! How can you be so cruel?"

"We'm just playing kissey and cuddley. Just canoodling, because it's nice. That's all. So don't you spoil it with high-quarter notions of marrying and stuff like that."

"I can't stop myself, Clarrie. Oh, if only I could tell you one tenth of all I feel about you ..."

She sat up and stared at him in alarm. "Since when?"

"Well ..." He tilted his head awkwardly, reluctant to say it had only really started about an hour ago.

"I never seen 'ee look twice at I."

He corrected her: " 'I never saw you look twice at me.' You can talk like that perfectly well if you'd only try — a girl who reads Thomas Hardy! You're only doing it to point up the difference between us — in social place, I mean."

"Which is something one simply ca-ahn't ignore, my de-ah," she said in a comic, high-falutin voice. Then she giggled at herself and, nudging him playfully, said, "Come on, Master Godfrey. There's limits to everything. You know that and so do I. So ..."

"There's no limit to what I feel for you, Clarrie."

She gave up and snuggled against him again before reaching up her lips for more. "Give us another kiss and a cuddle then," she said. "Work away like a man — I'll soon let 'ee know when you do reach one of *my* limits!"

*T*he argument lasted all the way home from the ball, though, since Miss Pym did not permit arguments on matters of taste and decorum — once she had laid down the law on the subject — she would have called it a family discussion. Argument or discussion, the labels did nothing to inhibit the to-and-fro of words.

The trouble was that Colette Beckerleg had overheard Jessie's shocking question to Cornwallis Trelawney; what is more, she had caught the first glimpse of his astonished reaction, before the general swirl of the dance carried her beyond the slower moving pair. Then all she could see was the back of Cornwallis's head, so she missed his delight. Understandably, then, she assumed Jessie's answering smile was a vain attempt to brazen it out and win over his aggravation at her impertinence. It was quite in character for her to brazen things out like that, so Colette's mistake was pardonable.

Less pardonable was the way she promoted Cornwallis's aggravation to fulsome annoyance when she told Jane Matthews of the incident, which she did at the first opportunity. But in that she was no less culpable than Jane, who promoted it further to indignation when she told Frances Stour. And when Frances told Fenella Compton, indignation was raised to the rank of outright anger — which, in its turn, became a towering rage when Fenella passed the tale on to her mother. By then the fire was well alight and the ballroom was buzzing with the authentic tale of poor Mr Trelawney's seething fury ... his apoplectic outrage ... his absolute paroxysms of wrath ...

True, the fact that the gentleman himself had, apparently, snapped up two of Jessie's still-unclaimed dances and engaged her in jovial and animated conversation throughout both of them, required a little explanation; but it was not beyond the combined powers of the matronry of West Penwith. The condescension of Cornwallis Trelawney in claiming two further dances with such an impertinent little madam simply revealed him for the impeccable gentleman he was. Realizing that the silly girl had blurted out her dreadful question from sheer gaucherie, he had extended his civility like a shield to protect her from the consequences of her folly. Well, it was a noble act, but he didn't fool them — by which they meant they weren't going to allow an inconvenient fact like his obvious enjoyment of Jessie's company to rob them of the choicest bit of scandal of the entire ball.

"It really makes no difference that Mister Trelawney was amused by your question, child," Miss Pym said after the opening speeches for the prosecution and the defence were made. "If his *amusement* was genuine, which I beg leave to doubt, then it diminishes him. It does nothing to augment you in the eyes of others. Any empty-headed little flippertygibbet can ..."

"Flibbertygibbet," Jessie corrected her.

Harry saw a chance to come to his sister's aid by apparently taking Miss Pym's side but really deflecting the argument from the big canon of Good Form to the little popguns of good pronunciation. "I think 'flipperty' is right," he said. "From 'flippant,' don't you know."

"Hold your tongue, boy," his father growled. "I'll give you flippant!"

Miss Pym tried again. "Any empty-headed little minx can build a cheap reputation for herself these days by mocking the accepted conventions of society; it doesn't even require much wit."

Frank put in his pennyworth: "Looking at it dispassionately," he said, "that does rather suggest that the conventions themselves are witless, too. I mean ... to be so witlessly demolished, if you follow?"

In the feeble light of the two small carriage lamps Miss Pym stared across at the three youngsters — painfully aware that the description fitted them less and less with each month that passed. Thank heavens

Godfrey, at least, was still a child; when he matured, her already threadbare cloak of respectability as 'governess' at Wheal Prosper would wear right through. Who could blame her, then, for wishing to maintain the rôle long after good sense (and the self-will of the three young people now facing her) warned her to lay it aside?

"What's got into 'ee all?" Barney grumbled at his brood. He was as baffled as Miss Pym. Unfortunately, they gave him no real peg on which to hang his anger. Their opposition was always so polite, so reasonably phrased, so 'dispassionate,' as Frank had just put it. Perhaps it had been a mistake never to permit full-blooded arguments within the household; Cressida had always insisted on diverting all anger and frustration into calm and reasoned debate. And now that the young folk were in their twenties — or rising to them in Jessie's case — they could turn that edict to their own advantage, conjuring specious justifications out of thin air. If only Cornwallis Trelawney had flown off the handle at Jessie's impertinence! This journey home would be the emotional equivalent of those violent thunderstorms that shake the earth but leave the air calm and sweet behind them. Instead the young man had laughed his head off — and he'd even seen Jessie out to the carriage and handed in his card, asking for leave to call upon them soon. The sheer perversity of young people nowadays! There was no accounting for it.

Jessie smiled. The hesitation of the two elderly antagonists sitting opposite them was brief — but long enough to reveal their uncertainty. She spoke in a most conciliatory tone. "I accept that in your opinion, Miss Pym, I have behaved badly, and for that I am truly contrite ..."

"And in the opinion of many others," Miss Pym put in.

"Ah, but that was the point I was about to make. Are they really in any position to cast the first stone? I don't know who overheard me, but I do seem to remember Colette Beckerleg go swishing by with that look of a panicstricken weasel she imitates so perfectly, and ..."

"Frightened ferret, surely?" Harry suggested.

"Startled stoat?" Frank offered.

Jessie, sitting between them, buried a sharp elbow in each. "She, or someone, heard the question and simply *assumed* that Mister Trelawney responded with anger. And surely to go spreading a desperate slander on foot of such a false assumption is at least as reprehensible as anything I may have done? By so doing they rule *themselves* out of court. Therefore it follows that *anybody* who passed — or continues to pass — a derogatory comment upon my question to Mister Trelawney is simply a pot calling the kettle black. If not worse."

"I rest my case, m'lud." Frank took off his hat and pretended to mop his brow.

"Well done, Portia!" Harry patted her arm.

Bristling with annoyance Miss Pym leaned forward and said, "When you've quite finished preening yourselves on your all-round shrewdness and wit, you'll permit me to point out that you are — all of you — entirely wrong. Mister Trelawney's response is quite immaterial. The *only* point to establish is did Jessica or did she not ask the man if he was, like Mister Rochester, in need of a wife."

"Which one was Rochester?" Barney asked; the idea that there was yet another unknown bachelor moving into the locality without his getting to hear of it first alarmed him.

His merciless offspring began to tease. Frank said he was the tall one with bushy eyebrows who'd come with the Visicks. Harry said he was sure Rochester was the short, bald fellow who'd come with the Gilberts. Before Jessie could speak, though, Miss Pym patted his arm and told him that Mr Rochester was someone in a famous book.

"Anyway," Jessie said, "it was Mister Bingley 'in need of a wife,' not Rochester. And I didn't ask if he was *in need* of a wife, just whether he was looking for one."

"You're splitting hairs, child. There is absolutely no difference ..."

"Oh, really? Ask Harry."

"You leave me out of this," her brother muttered in alarm.

"Ask Harry what?" Their father spoke menacingly.

She was delighted to shift the spotlight onto someone else for a change. "To *need* a thing implies a certain degree of personal desire for it. Harry does not *need* a wife but — on your instructions, Father — he is looking for one."

Miss Pym's patience snapped at last and, in a manner quite uncharacteristic of her, she gave a throttled cry of rage and mimed the tearing-out of her hair by the roots — her own hair, of course, though Jessie's would have made a most acceptable alternative. "It makes no difference whether you asked him was he needing a wife, or looking for a wife, or wanting a wife, or ... or *hunting* for a wife. It doesn't matter! *All* such questions are equally reprehensible. A well-brought-up young girl has no right to go asking anything of the kind — and especially not to the most eligible bachelor to come into the district for many years." She paused, breathless and still shivering with anger.

"Why?" Frank asked calmly. When she did not reply he answered for her: "For fear of putting him off? Because he'd give her the cold shoulder and resolve he'd never have anything more to do with her?

Good reasons, I think we'd all agree?" He gazed around as if summing up the feelings of a united family. "But good yields to better. What if the very outrageousness of her question so intrigues him that, at the end of the ball, he feels impelled to single her out from all the dozens of hopeful spinsters there ... to follow her to her coach and there present his card in the hope of being asked to call? What then, eh? Are we to judge our poor fallen sister by results? Or by some vague, abstract canon that may no longer be appropriate to the new century?"

"Is our etiquette utilitarian or absolutist?" Harry summarized.

"Gosh! I wish I'd said that!" Frank exclaimed.

Jessie fought hard not to giggle. There had been many moments in her life when she had wept bitterly at her elder brothers' neglectful and unfeeling behaviour toward her; tonight they were making up for all of them.

Miss Pym breathed stertorously for a moment or two, trying in vain to find an argument to squash this clever but specious bit of pleading. Then, to mark time, as it were, she said, "Well, Mister Trelawney gains no points from me for presenting his card like that — as if to say he couldn't be bothered to drive all the way out to Wheal Prosper and leave his card properly."

"Or," Harry put in — still managing to make it seem they were discussing the strange behaviour of remote peoples on the far side of the world — "one could also claim that he was obeying the very highest demands of etiquette. By the end of the ball he must surely have heard the absurd rumours then in circulation. Some damnably good-natured friend is bound to have told him of them. In the circumstances it takes the very highest calibre of gentleman to realize how important it is to show the rumour-mongers how wrong they are — even at the risk of bringing down upon himself the wrath of every right-thinking matron in West Penwith for leaving his card with us in such a disgraceful, corner-cutting way." He leaned forward and patted Miss Pym's knee, making her start in alarm. "I agree with you, Miss Pym. To leave his card like that was thoroughly reprehensible. Why, he has probably barred himself from every decent household this side of Plymouth."

"Oh, you may mock!" she interrupted furiously.

"Believe me I do not," he said earnestly. "And nor do I think we should mock such a noble sacrifice — when his only reason for making it was to save our fallen sister's honour."

"Stop calling her *fallen!*" Miss Pym was trembling all over. She had often had her differences with one or other of the 'children' but never had all three ganged up on her like this before. And never had they turned all her good reasons so cleverly against her. Why, they even had her doubting her own convictions now! Never, never, never would she have conceded that etiquette was a simple, utilitarian affair; to her it was one of life's absolutes. And yet if these three youngsters were right, and if Jessica's outrageous behaviour had started a process that ended with her walking down the aisle on Cornwallis Trelawney's arm ... well, could anyone *absolutely* condemn her for it?

"Stop calling her anything!" their father put in suddenly. "I've heard enough." He pointed an accusing finger at his daughter. "You, maid, behaved like some betwattled li'l giglet tonight — and that displeases me. But judgement's suspended, thanks to Mister Trelawney. No thanks to you. Your only way back out of my displeasure is to get that man's ring on your finger." He reached out and squeezed the third finger of her left hand. "There!"

He glared at his sons but neither risked any further flippancy. Frank, the most indiarubber of them all, said, "I thought the band played particularly well this evening, didn't you? The first requirement of a good dance band is a constant, almost imperceptible, *variation* in the rhythm. It keeps everyone on their toes."

Fortunately they were by then passing through the gates and starting up the quarter-mile drive to Wheal Prosper, so there was no time for this new line of rather brittle conversation to get out of hand.

When they were indoors at last, Jessie was the first to enter the drawing room. Her attention had been attracted by the lamp, which — she supposed — Godfrey must carelessly have left burning. And in a way she was right, but what its light revealed put all thought of *that* trivial offence right out of her mind.

Harry noticed her frozen stance, her gaping jaw, and swiftly joined her — whereupon he, too, was immobilized in dumbstruck amazement. Moments later the mood had claimed Frank as its third victim.

Miss Pym, seeing the tableau they formed, went bustling in to investigate. What she saw there robbed her not merely of speech but of the power even to scream. The strangled little bubbling sound that emerged from her throat did nothing to rouse Godfrey and Clarrie, fast asleep in each other's arms upon the sofa.

It was Frank who noticed the *two* empty wine bottles first. He picked them up and held their labels toward the light. "Barsac 'eighty-nine," he murmured, staring furiously at the sleeping couple and only just managing to stifle the self-incriminating oaths he might so easily have uttered.

*H*alf an hour after the rumpus had died down, when a tearful Clarrie had gone to her room, still begging not to be dismissed, Miss Pym slipped through the connecting door to Mr Kernow's bedroom and sank gratefully into the warmth of his welcome. It had been a most distressing start to the new year, never mind to the new century. It was all horribly inauspicious.

"Oh, Kernow, what is happening to this household?" she asked. "We used to be so ... so *good* together."

Barney recognized that tone. She wanted to talk. So he knew what would *not* be happening in this household — or that part of it where he slept — for the next ... however long she needed in order to lift these worries off her mind. He turned on his back and, linking his fingers behind his head, said, "I don't believe anything happened down there tonight — beyond a bit o' kissing and cuddling."

"But that's the water running over the top of the dam. The rest follows inevitably: The dam continues to resist for a while but the water wears a groove, then a gully, then a mighty channel, and then ... floods." Her voice trailed off; she wished she had not hit upon such a liquid analogy. "It's a forest fire," she concluded.

"Flood or fire, there's no fighting it," he remarked. "Civilization has been trying for God knows how many thousand years. Channel it! That's the answer. Divert its energy into productive ..."

"We've set a bad example, you and I," she interrupted miserably.

"Bad?" he queried. "Bad nor good doesn't come into it, surely. We aren't above the struggle. We're part of it. Or it's part of us. I've seen stallions kick the whole stable to fletters if there's a mare giving out the marching orders two fields away. And cows who'd burst through thorns that'd stop a steam roller, just to find a service from a bull."

She considered this in silence awhile before saying, "Well, I'm sure *I* never gave out any marching orders to *you*."

Chuckling, he reached out a hand and fondled her breast through the heavy flannel of her nightgown, murmuring "You don't hardly need to, maid. Just being there's enough."

She felt the familiar stirrings of lust in her blood. It filled her with self-loathing but she knew that, if he went on just a bit longer, she'd yield to it. And then, afterwards, he wouldn't want to talk at all. "Are you saying our very existence is a bad example, then? That's dreadful."

He sighed and withdrew his hand. It was going to be one of those start-stop nights of mind-versus-body — where body would have to sneak up on mind if it was to stand any chance of winning. "We shouldn't ought to have left just the two of them alone," he offered.

"I'm not just talking about Godfrey and Clarrie — bad enough though that is. It's also the way the other three teamed up against us. There can't possibly have been any collusion among them. It happened quite spontaneously. What do you think? Am I completely out of touch with modern manners? Is it quite in order nowadays for a girl like Jessica to make an impertinent joke out of what ought to be the most important question in her life?"

He took an enormous risk and said, "Marriage? Maybe she sees it isn't the most important question in someone's else life!"

He felt her stiffen. She breathed in and out through her nose, several times, rather rapidly. "You might be right at that," she admitted. "Perhaps I should explain to her."

"About us?" he asked in surprise. "Surely she knows?"

"No!" She was horrified he could even think she'd say a word to Jessica about his and her ... doings. "About my money — how it all goes into trust if I should marry."

He chuckled. "You'd better explain how your grandfather wrote his will afore I came out of short trousers — or she'll think 'twas to keep *my* thieving hands off it!"

She took up his hand and kissed it. "These aren't thieving hands," she murmured. Then she pushed it away before he could get any untoward ideas.

He, knowing her workings well by now, bided his time.

After a silence she said, "D'you really think Jessica knows about you and me?"

He cleared his throat awkwardly. "Depends how much you told her about ... you know — storks and gooseberry bushes and that."

Miss Pym was suddenly awkward, too. "I'm sure girls inform each other about such things — as we did in my day."

He laughed. "'In my day'! You aren't but ten years older than she."

"Well then," she snapped. "Things can't have changed all that much — can they!" Then, more amiably, she said, "Perhaps I ought to have a word with her, nonetheless."

"And Clarrie."

"What?" Miss Pym was horrified. "Let that trollop talk to Jessica about ... you know?"

"No!" He laughed again. "You talk to Clarrie about *you know!*"

"Ha! The devil I will — begging your pardon! Servants know all about that sort of thing. They always do. Their whole idea of morality is quite different from ours. If any impropriety did take place tonight, *she's* the one to blame, not Godfrey. And if there are any consequences, she can jolly well fend for herself. I shall certainly make *that* much clear to her." Then, aware that her talk of improprieties taking place that night might give him the opening he was undoubtedly hoping for, she quickly added, "I think there's something more important than all that, though — namely Harry's behaviour. He did it again tonight, despite my specifically warning him."

"Did what?"

"Danced mostly with the dowagers and girls who are quite obviously on the shelf. Girls! I mean some of them are almost my age! But I can't read the riot act to him any longer. He's twenty-four — past heeding anything I may say. Can't *you* have a word with him?"

Barney grunted sourly. "That's all I *do* have with that young man lately: words. He shows no interest in the business at all. I sent him out to call on farmers round Gulval, show them the new catalogues, come back with a few orders. The sort of thing anyone could do in their sleep. Just afore Christmas, it was."

"And?"

"Gulval's only four or five miles from Saint Ives — so that's where he goes instead, of course."

"Calling on his artist chums!"

"What else! I gave him the ledgers to look at over Christmas, and I don't suppose he's ..."

"The real ones?" she asked in amazement.

"No, no! The Sunday-best ones. He must walk afore he runs. Anyway, when he put them back they were full of little sketches in the margins. Said he couldn't make head nor tail of the figures but it was good quality paper."

"Tskoh! He does it deliberately, I'm sure. Perhaps we could shock him out of it?"

"How?"

"Stop his allowance. Tell him to go over to Saint Ives, if that's what he's set his heart on, and struggle like the rest. Tell him Frank is going to take over the business."

Barney chuckled at this fantasy — but it was sheer fantasy. Frank was the very last person he'd let into the business. From the moment he was born, that boy had only ever been interested in himself. If Frank took over the family business — or businesses, if you included the ones that were not entirely above board — the rest of them would end up as pensioners, living at his grace and favour.

"Or Jessica?" Miss Pym suggested, even more lightly. "She has a very sound head on her shoulders."

He merely laughed at that. "No, by heaven," he replied, "Harry's the eldest and the business is his whether he likes it or not. And he shan't defeat me in this. I'll make him master of it if I have to break every knuckle in his artistic hands in order to secure his undivided attention. He will ..." He sought for a strong enough phrase and then said, with a chuckle, "He will *knuckle* under, or I'm not Barney Kernow. And as for Jessie, she'll learn her ladylike accomplishments and find a husband — or she'll be on a diet of bread and water before too long."

She yawned, to signal that the conversation had only a few minutes left to run, and said, "What about this Cornwallis Trelawney, then? I know it's absurdly early to start building one's hopes — added to which he has an unfortunate disregard for the conventions of good society — but all the same, if the Trelawneys live up to everything one heard about them tonight, he would be quite a catch."

Barney spoke more cautiously. "I should want to know how he's left his people up Yorkshire and come to settle here. Is the parting amicable or what? If not, how sound is he going to be on his own?"

"Quite," Miss Pym agreed. "But if he's still the heir apparent to the Trelawney fortune, I take it you don't mind Jessica's becoming involved in business matters — as long as her part is of the dynastic rather than the ... how shall I put it? Of the dirty-fingernails kind!"

"Making dynasties is proper woman's work," he said approvingly. "Paying for them is best left to men."

The clock over the stables struck two.

Miss Pym sighed, knowing he would not hold back much longer. "Meanwhile," she said, "we have a much more immediate problem to deal with."

"Clarrie," he said tersely.

No words were needed between them as to why the expendable maid rather than the dearly beloved son was their main problem. They could both think of a dozen other houses in the district who would snap up the girl, even without a written character. She was well known as a hard worker, respectful, quiet, and neat in her person — an ideal maid these days, when servants more often interviewed their prospective mistresses than the other way about. So she would have no difficulty in finding another place. But the real reason she would be so eagerly snapped up would be for the tales she could tell of the domestic arrangements at Wheal Prosper, especially those between the master and the ex-governess-turned-housekeeper.

"We've made a rod for our own back there," Miss Pym said gloomily.

"We know it — the question is, does she?"

"Can't risk it," he replied.

"Can't risk too much anger against her, you mean?"

"Can't risk any anger at all. Besides, she'll be expecting anger, see — why, I daresay she's lying up there now, churning over in her mind all the harsh things you might be saying to her tomorrow ... and thinking up one or two choice replies of her own. Can't risk it. Once a single word is spoken, the glass is shattered and there's no mending it."

"What, then? One can't simply ignore it."

"Guilt," he said. "Work on her guilt."

"If she has any!"

He snorted. "She's a woman, isn't she! You're born with guilt in your bones — all of ye! You know that. So make use of sorrow — not anger. Bitter, bitter disappointment. She's let us down — after all our kindness to her, too. How *could* she? Dear, dear, dear! It's made you feel quite ill. And what's to become of her if she doesn't mend her ways now, afore it's too late. You can do that, surely? She'll flood that kitchen with her tears before you've done with her."

"And then?"

"The old preacher's trick. When you've brung her to her knees and her heart is full of sorrow and repentance, offer salvation! Say *we'll* never-ever desert *her*. Put the boot on the other foot. Pile obligation on guilt. Make her see we're her only hope. You can do that — like I say. No one better."

"You mean no one understands the workings of guilt better than I do!" she said dourly.

He made no reply.

"Come on then," she said, turning on her back and plucking up the hem of her nightdress.

In all the years she had been coming to his bed she had never once lain naked with him. She always wore pantaloons and bedsocks on her nether half, and her upper half was shrouded in a voluminous nightdress, flannel in winter, cotton in summer. Whatever the material or season, she never lifted it above the waist band of her pantaloons — which were furnished with the usual arrangements to facilitate calls of nature. And it was those same arrangements that allowed Mr Kernow to 'have his way with her,' as she liked to express it. The phrase laid all the blame upon him.

The fact that she came to his bed rather than he to hers (because that was how they had begun their affaire) … the fact that he often had to stifle her mouth with the pillow to prevent her cries of ecstasy from rousing the entire household — these could be glossed over and forgotten when the fever of her passion had died. But the fact that the only bare skin of hers to touch bare skin of his was on their hands and faces (apart from the unfortunate bits 'down there,' of course, which was unavoidable) was something she never let herself forget. It helped enormously to assuage her guilt.

In fact, her ravished conscience had usually healed again by morning, which enabled her not merely to face the world again but to insist that those parts of it under her direct management should be ordered along lines of impeccable morality and irreproachable propriety.

*ortunately for Clarrie it was her morning *not* to serve break-fasts. She and Becky took it by turns, one of them cooking the eggs and bacon, or kedgeree, or whatever was on the menu, the other serving and clearing up. When Frank entered the kitchen she was spooning hot fat up over the master's fried egg to make the white of it live up to its name; today, she was resolved, the master and Miss Pym would have everything *exactly* the way they liked it.

"That smells good, Clarrie," he said.

"Don't 'ee go distracting me now, Master Frank," she replied. "I got no time for cooze and coursey today."

"I wonder why!"

She shot him a guilty smile but did not pause in her work. "Now! That's just 'bout ready. Out my way!" She stuck out an elbow and nudged him aside as she turned to pick up the flat wooden spatula. "Becky!" she sang out. "Egg and bacon up!"

She slipped the spatula beneath one of the eggs and tilted it to drain before transferring it to the plate, which already held two lightly cooked rashers of bacon. "That's Miss Pym's," she said, passing it to Becky. To Frank she added, "She do like it without fat, see." The other, drooling with melted lard, she put straight on top of three rashers, fried to a crisp.

Frank said, "And so you see, between the two, they licked the platter clean!" He laughed. "Have you got a kiss for *me*, Clarrie?"

Ignoring him, she pushed the frying pan off to one side of the hob and pulled the kettle back onto it. It began at once to sing. When he took a step toward her, she turned on him, jokingly menacing him with the spatula.

He stepped back and held up his hands. "Pax!" he cried. "This suit is due in court at ten. All the same, pet, you shouldn't go cradle-snatching like that."

"That's my business — and his."

"No, love. It's family business — and today, I hardly need remind you, you need all the friends you can get in this family."

"At a price, no doubt," she sneered. "Well, that's a price I'm not willing to pay."

She carried the spatula to the sink; as she walked past him she tried to bump him aside with a swipe of her hips, but he, imitating a matador, nimbly avoided her, saying, "So — you didn't 'pay the price' with dear little bro last night. Just as well, really. The Favour would be wasted on him. He's only just turned sixteen, you know. You should be ashamed of yourself — especially when there's something much better available."

He followed her to the sink and reached over her to turn on the tap.

She smacked his hand out of the way. "You don't have to pump that water up every morning," she said. "We don't let it run to waste like what you do."

"Ah, but we pay the man who does. That's the way of the world, isn't it. Get what you want and pay for it."

"Very interesting," she said coldly. "But like I said — I got no time for cooze."

She measured two tablespoons of beans into the coffee grinder, which was bolted to the wall beside the dresser, an operation that required both hands. He raced across the kitchen, intending to take advantage of the situation but she was too quick for him. She snatched up a fork from the dresser and, still with her back to him, completed the grinding with one hand while holding the weapon poised in readiness against him.

"That's not what I mean by being friendly, Clarrie," he said in a sad voice, now with an edge of menace.

"I know what you do mean by 'being friendly'," she sneered, turning to face him but keeping her arms up defensively. "If you don't leave me in peace, I shall complain to Miss Pym. There now!"

"Where now?" He laughed. "You know very well what she'd think of *that*! What? There she is about to bend you over a chair and give you six of the best for canoodling with the baby of the family, and you come whining to her with a complaint about me! A complaint that I shall deny with all the wounded innocence at my command! My dear girl — she'd laugh you out of court!" He gave her his most genial and sympathetic smile. "I don't think you understand the full implication of what you and little 'Godfwey' did last night, my dear. It isn't just a simple matter of saying you're sorry and taking your swishing like a Trojan ..."

Clarrie licked her lips uncertainly, eyes filling with alarm. She lowered her arms. "She's never going to bend I over and give us the cane!" she said.

Frank's smile became even more sympathetic. "What do you think! That's the *least* she can do. But, as I was saying, it's not a simple matter of taking your punishment and that's that ... all forgotten — oh no! In the minds of Miss Pym and my father you have stepped across that merciless line which separates the good, pure, chaste young girl from ... the other kind. It's merciless because there's never the slightest hope of stepping back across it. In fact, it's not a line, it's a precipice. One slip and you're in the abyss for ever. You could spend the rest of your days singing hymns and falling to your knees hourly, but there'd always be that little thorn of suspicion in their minds."

Tears were brimming in her eyes by now. " 'Tin't fair!" she said.

"I know, pet. But that, too, is the way of the world. They'll hang you for a sheep, though you know — and I know — you didn't even touch the lamb."

It was true. She did know it. Every word he spoke was true. A girl couldn't slip even once. The mud would stick for ever. She couldn't even afford to let people *think* she'd slipped.

What to do now? The thought that Miss Pym was going to cane her — six of the best — something that had never happened to anyone in this household, and never in her life to her — had her terrified. Where could she turn?

She was within an ace of throwing herself into Mister Frank's arms and begging for his protection when, over his shoulder, she saw Miss Jessie standing in the kitchen doorway.

How long had she been there? How much had she heard? She closed her eyes and felt sick of everything.

"Frank," Jessie said quietly. "Miss Pym saw you come downstairs ten minutes ago. She is beginning to comment on your absence."

Smiling calmly, but inwardly cursing his sister's sense of timing, he patted the maidservant's arm and murmured, "Remember, eh?"

As he passed his sister on the way to the dining room he said, "Aren't you coming?"

"In a moment," she replied firmly.

He continued to smile though he cursed her even more soundly now, for he knew that, by the time Jessie had finished with the girl, he'd have to start all over again.

Jessie crossed the room and took the fork from Clarrie's nerveless fingers; the maid still seemed in something of a daze. "I don't know what nonsense he's been pouring in your ear, Clarrie," she said, "but I can easily imagine. I wouldn't pay the slightest attention if I were you."

"She isn't going to cane us, is she?" the maid asked.

Jessie's eyes raked the ceiling. One could never quite rule anything out where the Surface Angel was concerned, of course, but all the same, the likelihood of a caning was very remote. "Of course she isn't," she replied contemptuously. "And if she tries anything so stupid, *I'll* put a stop to it."

"You?" Clarrie asked in surprise — tinged with disbelief.

"Yes — me," Jessie insisted. "I'll physically stop her. I'm stronger than she is, you know. Anyway, what can she do to me? She can't dismiss *me!*"

Clarrie wet her lips again, all her uncertainty returning. "Well, Miss, if it's a choice between a caning and being dismissed, I think I'll take the caning and say no more."

"Well, it *isn't* a choice, so put it out of your mind. That's what I want to talk to you about. Isn't there some work you could be doing — in case Miss Pym comes out here?"

Becky came out with a stack of empty plates. "They'm asking where's the coffee," she said.

"The stove is slow, tell them," Clarrie replied. "Mrs Hodgson mentioned it to Miss Pym two days ago. The chimney do want a good sweeping. Tell them I'm only now wetting it."

Becky left with the toast. Clarrie put the grounds in the can and covered them with near-boiling water. Jessie went on talking to her. "I don't mind telling you, I've been awake half the night thinking over your situation, Clarrie — ever since I saw you and Godfrey lying there like that."

She giggled. The maid tried hard, but not too successfully, to keep a straight face. "Nothing happened, Miss — honest. We read our own books till gone eleven. We never even touched the wine till that. And even then we just talked — and talked and talked. That's all we done."

"And put down two bottles between you!"

"We never gulped it. Just one sip and then another. I don't rightly know how it went so quick — nor how we felt no effect of it till we went off to sleep."

She carried the can to the tray and brought a jug of cream from the pantry. Carefully avoiding Jessie's eye she said, "Still, I don't hardly think she'll dismiss us, either."

"Why not?" Jessie's tone was provocative rather than curious.

"Well ..." The maid shrugged awkwardly. "She wouldn't hardly dare. You know ... the way it is."

Jessie drew a deep breath and said, "Yes, Clarrie! I do know. And that's what kept me awake half the night — the thought ... no, the *fear* that you might blurt out some such threat as that to Miss Pym today. It would certainly save your bacon but can you imagine what life would be like in this house following such an outburst? Not just for you but for all of us. I'm sure that before January was out you'd be begging to be let go — and the rest of us would be envying you that miserable degree of freedom."

"Well ..." Clarrie said again, giving the same hopeless shrug.

"I know. You think it's the only weapon you've got. Like that fork with Frank just now ..."

"You seen that, did 'ee?"

"I saw enough. Pay no heed to Frank. He's only after one thing — and he'd cast you aside the moment he got it. But if you'll follow my advice, you may brush him off like a piece of lint. You deal properly with your main problem — Miss Pym — and Frank's threats will evaporate like summer rain."

For the first time since Nemesis had fallen on her last night the maid's eyes shone with hope and a smile split her countenance. She swiftly checked it and bit her lip in a proper show of repentance, but the smile continued to twitch at the corners of her mouth. "How?" she asked and bated her breath.

"I said just now — you think that threat is the only weapon you've got. But it's not! There's a much gentler one to hand and, better still, it'll prove even more effective."

The self-satisfied smile faded as her lips hung slack; now the girl would have listened with a hundred ears if she'd had them.

"The fact is, you're not the only one in this house with a little bit of a brain up top there. The threat that occurred to you has almost certainly occurred to Miss Pym. And, indeed, to my father, as well. Don't you think that's likely?"

Clarrie nodded. "But if I say nothing as to it ..."

"I know, dear! You're afraid they'll think it hasn't even crossed your mind — so they'll have carte blanche to dismiss you, and without fearing any repercussions."

The maid nodded earnestly.

"But just follow my reasoning one step further," Jessie went on. "If *you* can think of it, and *they* can think of it, then surely Mrs Compton will think of it. And Mrs Stour. Mrs Gilbert. Miss Grylls ... Why, there must be several dozen ladies in the area who've been wondering about the ...er, intimate domestic arrangements in this house for the past dozen years — ever since a sweet little eighteen-year-old governess named Cressida Pym came to stay."

Clarrie smiled to hear the gorgon of the Wheal Prosper household so lightly dismissed.

Jessie continued. "So, even if it hadn't occurred to you, it will most certainly occur to those bright ladies. You'd be met at the gate by their carriages! And then the fat *would* be in the fire!"

Clarrie nodded fervently; all this was so true — and yet it suggested no positive action on her part. "So what should I *do*, Miss?" she asked.

"Nothing, my dear. Do nothing. Say nothing."

"And when she do send for us?"

"Well now — that's my real purpose in coming out here and spending rather more time with you than this simple project requires. I propose to go at once to Miss Pym and tell her that I've had a heart-to-heart chat with you ... that you've had the fright of your life, and fortunately ..."

"That's the God's truth, anyway," Clarrie said fervently.

"Good! I hate telling *unnecessary* fibs! Fortunately, as I was about to go on, Godfrey proved too inexperienced. And you are, in any case, too virtuous for anything improper to have taken place between you. It was an act of thoughtlessness but nothing worse. And it has left both of you the wiser. That's all! If you agree to my suggestion, I think you'll find the whole thing will be buried and forgotten — and with great relief all round, too."

Becky returned with more washing-up and went back to the dining room with the coffee tray.

"You won't say nothing about ... you know?" Clarrie asked as she set about her next chore, the trimming of the lamp wicks.

"Of course not!"

"Not even a hint, like? So she understands the threat is there even if I never uttered it myself?"

Jessie stared hopelessly out of the window. "But that would be only slightly less disastrous than coming out with it directly. Can't you see, Clarrie? We're all walking on eggs in this house. I can't blame you if you don't see it — I only realized it myself while pondering your situation, and Godfrey's, last night. The only way we can continue with life as we know it here is to say absolutely nothing — not even the teeniest tiniest hint. Is that clear?"

Clarrie nodded. "I s'pose so," she said as she set a glass chimney gingerly aside.

Jessie was about to leave her when the maid added, "And what about Master Godfrey, then?"

"He's your problem," was the laughing reply. Then, more seriously, "But you're a big girl now. It's not going to be too difficult, is it — keeping him in his place?"

Speaking carefully Clarrie replied, "He promised to wed with I if only I'd wait for him."

Jessie laughed again. "Yes, well you wouldn't be the first maidservant to have to listen to such tosh from an over-enthusiastic young puppy like Godfrey. Nor would you be the first to be laughed to shame for repeating it in any serious manner."

Clarrie was forced to join her laughter. Jessie patted her on the back. "Not that I blame you for trying — but do try to pick battles you can win." She became serious again. "One more thing before I go — just in case you think I'm the kindest, wisest, most generous-hearted miss you could possibly meet — the truth is I have a rather selfish reason for doling out all this wisdom. I'll let you into the secret." She lowered her voice and added, "Between you and me, I have a feeling I may need an ally in this house quite soon — a female. Someone I can trust implicitly. This trifling favour I'm doing for you today is just my way of cementing that trust in advance. D'you see?" She held out her hand.

The maid wiped hers in her pinafore and shook it, smiling broadly. The world was back at last on a recognizable course.

*T*wice Becky was sent up to Master Godfrey's room to remind him that breakfast was not an infinitely movable feast. The youth, for his part, hoped to delay for as long as possible his arrival at a board he knew would be somewhat less than festive — and at least until his father had departed. Not that he relished the prospect of facing a solo Miss Pym. The uncertainties were just too great.

If only he could see Clarrie for a moment and learn how much, or how little, she had told them. No doubt they'd been up at crack of dawn, hauling the poor girl over the coals, giving her such a tongue-lashing she might have confessed to anything. He did not doubt she'd have told the truth; she'd have explained that what they did might have been socially ill-advised, but they had never strayed into regions of moral danger, let alone actual turpitude. Nor did he doubt but that he himself would shoulder all the blame. That was not the question. The question was *how much* had she said — and how much blame should he, correspondingly, shoulder? For he saw no good reason to accept more than was absolutely necessary. Least said, soonest mended.

He opened his wardrobe door and surveyed himself in the looking glass. "You're a dashed handsome fellow, Godfrey," he told himself hopefully. "Can't blame the girls for falling for you!" He gave a blackhead on his upper lip a tentative squeeze before deciding to let it ripen a little longer; he'd had them in that pit before and if he squeezed too early he only made his lip look as if it had met a hornet and come off worse.

He practised several kinds of innocent look, some with wide-open eyes, for surprised innocence, some with the lids half closed, for haughty, how-dare-you innocence, and some with a sidelong look, for wounded, how-*could*-you innocence.

Surprised innocence was out, he decided; he outgrew it two years ago without quite realizing it at the time. It would have to be something between the aggressive how-dare-you and the long-suffering how-could-you. They would be the easiest to sustain because, when you got down to it, they were actually justified in this present situation. How *dare* a man and a woman who lived in such flagrant violation of society's codes turn upon him for so small a breach? How *could* they rise from their unchaste bed and sit all prim and proper at the breakfast table, scolding him for the most innocent of snatched kisses? (He must remember that phrase about 'unchaste bed' — and never again would he moan at having to read the Bard at school.)

Lost in admiration of his manly good looks, he enjoyed a fantasy in which he calmly admitted that he had begun the evening filled with the basest designs on young Clarrie's virtue but that her moral superiority and invincible chastity had made a convert of him for ever. And now all he wanted was to kiss her sweet lips and hug her delightful body daily — and thus daily forge a new link in the chain-mail of his armour against the dragon of moral turpitude. And Miss Pym smiled fondly at him, saying, "Oh, well, if *that's* all you want to do, you and she may sit for an hour together each evening, as long as you do not shut the door." And his father blinked back tears compounded of remorse and pride, and pressed a guinea into his hand before turning away to blow his nose.

Or I could run away and live among the creatures of the wild, he thought, giving himself a more heroic and manly rôle. He could visit the house at night and sup the food Clarrie put out for him. And he'd build a secret place where they could live together after he was twenty-one, far beyond all the codes and cares of the world. The contradiction between living beyond worldly codes and yet waiting until he was twenty-one to do so collapsed that pleasant daydream. And in any case, that was when Becky came with the second reminder about breakfast not being an infinitely movable feast.

Wondering why his boots had doubled their weight overnight, he made his reluctant way below.

"Good evening," he called out a fraction of a second before appearing in the doorway. "Happy New Year — once again." He helped himself to porridge, which was thick enough by now to stand his spoon in.

His salutation stole the wind from his father's sails for he had been about to bid his son good evening, too. Miss Pym was more resilient. "I must say, Godfrey, we had hoped to find you in a more contrite spirit this morning — and believe me, you have much to be contrite about."

"I'm sorry I'm late," he replied in a conciliatory deference. "I did not sleep well last night, but ..."

"Understandably!" his father interjected.

Godfrey accepted the rebuke with a dip of his head and continued, "... but I had so much to ponder over, you see." Actually his main trouble had been with the bed — indeed, his whole room — which had possessed the extraordinary ability to tilt and tilt and tilt for ever at its southwestern corner without once turning turtle.

"And are we permitted to share in the results of so much cogitation?" Miss Pym asked icily.

He smiled wanly at her; by God, he'd make her smile back before this day was done! "It was more soul-searching than cogitation, Miss Pym," he said softly.

This was a Godfrey they had not met before; and even though he was at that age where, every few months, he presented them with a similar change of character or personality, it still left them at a slight disadvantage. After all, if the soul-searching had been deep and the contrition were genuine, it would be more fitting to encourage that than to continue baying for blood.

"Well?" Miss Pym said, still rather sharply, but with an uncertain edge to it now.

He chewed a mouthful of porridge before saying, "It's rather embarrassing, actually."

She stirred uneasily and glanced at the master, who said, "I'd like to know how it even started, boy."

Godfrey bit his lip; again the question nagged him — how much had Clarrie blurted out? "Didn't she tell you?" he asked as if surprised.

"We haven't spoken to her yet," Barney said before Miss Pym's exasperated glance could halt him.

Godfrey's relief was short lived, for the shoe now pinched the other foot — it was now up to him to decide how much, or how little, to tell. He decided to scavenge along the farthermost shores of the Sea of Vagueness for a while. "If sincere repentance is that which wipes out shame," he said solemnly, "then I have done naught of which I now feel ashamed."

"Humbug!" his father exploded.

Miss Pym briefly laid a calming hand upon his wrist before turning to the youth. "That is a very encouraging development in you, Godfrey, my dear, and one which we heartily applaud. All the same, your father and I should like to be informed of those ... indiscretions, shall we say? — of which you have so sincerely repented." She smiled then, but too coldly, too triumphantly for him to count it a victory.

He began to wish they *had* confronted Clarrie first for then he could spin his 'confession' out so long that sheer impatience would force them to blurt out something at least of what she'd told them. "It was all my doing," he said.

"*What* was all your doing?" Barney roared, thumping the table and making the crockery dance. "By thunder, speak plain, boy, or I'll lock you in the coalshed till you do!"

"Yes!" Miss Pym joined in. "Talking of locked coalsheds — when I gave orders that only one scuttle was to be allowed you, I assumed you'd understand that the ration applied to fire logs, too." Then, realizing she'd let herself be sidetracked from her main anxieties, she added, "But let it pass. It is the very least of ..."

Godfrey saw his chance. "How right you are, Miss Pym," he confessed. "It *is* the very least of my transgressions. And yet it is where I began to go wrong. I thought I was so clever, you see, to have got round your edict. Oh yes, it was I who went out and fetched that firewood. I see now how childish I was to think ..."

"Get on with it!" Barney growled. "Fine words butter no parsnips with me. We don't give a fig about your coals or your firewood. Get to the bones of it."

Miss Pym stared at her master in wounded pride while Godfrey continued: "Well, one transgression borrowed another, you see. After Clarrie had brought me my supper, and removed the remains, and built up the fire, and built it again ..."

"What were *you* doing meanwhile?" Miss Pym asked.

"Reading *Stonehenge's Rural Sports*. Funnily enough, that's the very question I asked Clarrie — what was *she* doing meanwhile — in between washing up and tending the fire and so forth. And she told me she, too, was reading a book."

"Oh, was she, indeed!" Miss Pym exclaimed. She had once been heard to say that teaching the menial classes to read had been a grave error; she was convinced that most of the fires that devoured big houses were started by maids reading secretly in bed and falling asleep when the candle flame had consumed the oxygen under the sheet and blankets.

"*Tess of the D'Urbervilles*, actually," he added.

The housekeeper's lips shrank to a thin, bloodless line; the trouble was that one could not find a single *respectable* domestic these days who was not literate.

"So," the youth concluded, "what with it being New Year, and me being all alone, and Clarrie being all alone ... well, I suggested she should come and sit by the fire and we could each read our books and keep each other company."

"Keep company!" Barney exploded yet again.

Godfrey frowned and shook his head. "Not 'keep company' in *that* sense — though I admit I did attempt to kiss her on the stroke of midnight, as we drank our toast to Auld Lang Syne, you know. Just a quick peck on the cheek."

"And?" Miss Pym's eyes were like saucers and she sat on the edge of her chair.

He smiled ruefully and rubbed his cheek as if it were still tender. "She gave me cause to regret it."

The housekeeper glanced uncertainly at the father, who did not quite know how to take this confession — for he, recalling his own youthful indiscretions, knew that a young man hanged for merely eyeing a lamb will then think nothing of returning to steal the whole sheep. "That's not what we'd have guessed from the way we found the pair of 'ee," he said. "Drunk as lords on two bottles of wine. And where did *they* come from we'd like to know?"

So they had counted their own cellar — and Frank had not added his own private indictment to the general list. While he was wondering how to explain the two empty bottles, without incriminating his elder brother, his eld*est* brother walked in, clasping the firm's ledgers under his arm. "Evening all," he said pleasantly, not understanding the glowering looks he received in return. He wiped aside the toast crumbs and placed the books at his father's side. "Ask me any queston you like now," he said proudly.

Becky appeared with a fresh pot of coffee; Jessie was behind her.

Barney, distracted from his hounding of Godfrey, turned his suspicions on her. "Have *you* anything to do with this?" he asked, tapping the ledgers.

"I've been seeing Frank off, Father," she replied, then, smiling at Miss Pym, she added, "I'd appreciate a little chat with you, Cressida, sometime this morning — if you could see your way?"

Miss Pym could not understand why she did not immediately protest at this familiarity; nor did any of the others — but they did not catch the stony glance in Jessie's eye, which, fleeting though it was, sufficed to warn Miss Pym off trying. "Very well, dear," she replied warily. "I shall be doing a little marketing in Helston this morning. Perhaps you will accompany me?"

And at that the breakfast table broke up. Godfrey, who had taken advantage of the interruptions to bolt his kedgeree, now gulped down his coffee and made a demonstrative exit — and a great deal of noise in ascending the front staircase. Ten seconds later he made a much quieter job of going down again by the servants' stair and tiptoeing into the kitchen, where he found Clarrie engaged as Jessie had left her, trimming the lamp wicks. Two she did with a patent trimmer supplied to fit them; the others had to be shaved more carefully with an old cut-throat razor.

He watched her for a while, thinking he had arrived unnnoticed — until she said, without turning to look at him, "I got nothing to say to you, Master Godfrey."

"Clarrie!" he replied in a wounded tone. "Don't be like that, please! It's not ... it's not ..."

She faced him then and repeated: "Nothing!"

Gazing into those eyes, which had been so wise and limpid in last night's firelight, and watching those adorable lips, on which he had hung with such ardour not twelve hours since, he felt his adoration of her return in a flood that numbed the senses and drowned out all speech. She became aware of it, too, for her gaze grew troubled and she looked away, saying, "It's best you go."

"I love you," he murmured. "You're the star in my life." And then, feeling very stupid — for she made no reply to his outburst — he turned on his heel and left as silently as he had come.

She's naught but a maidservant! he told himself angrily as he went back upstairs. *And you're naught but a fool!* But — oh! — the exquisite misery of that great hollow feeling inside him and the mournful ecstasy of knowing their love could never be!

Whether he'd have felt any happier — in the long run — if he had seen Clarrie's delayed response to his declaration is doubtful. At that moment she was cursing her hands for being all soaked in lamp oil, and wiping one small tear off her cheek with the knuckle of her wrist, and sniffing heavily to drain off the rest before they could fall, and telling herself he was naught but a little boy, really — just feeling the stirrings of manhood and picking on the first available thing in skirts to practise on.

All the same, she could not help remembering that Godfrey Kernow's late mother, Stella Cartwright, had been no better than a parlourmaid at Clowance, one of the nearby big houses, and Barney Kernow had only been a clerk in the estate office there — and *his* father had been apprenticed at the blacksmith's forge in Nancegollan to *her*, Clarrie's, grandfather — so, if this was the year for miracles in love, they'd have no cause to get all high and mighty.

*M*iss Pym and Jessie took the 11.17 train into Helston; thanks to deep cuttings and a splendid stone viaduct it reduced a rambling, roundabout coach journey of half an hour to one lasting under ten minutes. The branch line, which ran eight-odd miles between Helston and Gwinear Road on the main London line, carried seven trains daily in each direction. Jessie had turned seven when it opened in 1887 and so she could well remember the former tedium of marketing in Helston — indeed, it was something her mother had attempted no more than once a month. The line had still been building when she died. Nowadays Nancegollan people — and those from Praze-an-Beeble, the next station up the line — would often 'pop in' to Helston on the merest whim. The second-class return fare was only threepence.

The compartment was crowded that morning and so was the horse bus that plied the half-mile between the station and the town, so Jessie had no chance to speak her piece until their marketing was completed; then they went to the Angel for a light, early luncheon before catching the 1.30 home again. They were shown to their place by the proprietor, Walter Blackwell, in person, for he knew Barney Kernow as a good customer who had concluded many a business transaction over a meal or a glass under his roof. By way of conversation Blackwell said, "I believe I almost fed young Master Godfrey here last night, Miss Pym."

"I beg your pardon?" she asked in surprise — though, with her crisp manner, it sounded more to the poor landlord as if she found his remark offensive.

Jessie, recalling her fleeting glimpse of someone who looked like Godfrey among the rafters at the Assembly Rooms last night, smelled danger at once and, taking advantage of the fact that she was momentarily outside Miss Pym's field of view, shook her head warily at the landlord.

He cottoned on at once and, laughing, said, "I mean, of course, that I mistook someone else for him — a young man hanging out by the pantry door. I'll bring you a menu." And he was gone before she could quiz him further.

Jessie said, "Mendicants hang out there in the hope of getting scraps off the plates. I think he was trying to make a joke that one of them resembled the dear boy."

The explanation soothed Cressida a little. "Well, he has a very strange sense of humour," she said. "Actually, all I want is a bowl of soup and perhaps a sandwich. You?"

"I could eat a horse, but we haven't time. Soup and a sandwich would be wiser, perhaps." She almost added, 'remembering the torture of my corsets last night,' but thought better of it. Cressida was lost in thought, anyway. Jessie said, "But talking of Godfrey — are you still worried about that brouhaha with Clarrie? I don't think you need to, you know — nothing happened."

Miss Pym looked at her former charge in considerable alarm. "What d'you mean, my dear — nothing happened? What, may I inquire, d'you know about ... well, about *things* that may or may not happen in those circumstances?"

Jessie gazed back wearily. "Oh, come on, Cressida! I'll be twenty in four weeks' time. Give me some credit."

"Well, you never heard of it from *me.*"

Jessie glanced swiftly all about them and, although they were alone in the dining room, she lowered her voice as if to suggest Miss Pym had been shouting; she said, "I'm sure the Recording Angel has already noted the fact, Cressida — though on which *side* of the ledger is a moot point."

The older woman bridled again. "I can't think what you may mean by that, Miss!"

Jessie remained unruffled. "I mean, in the balance of right and wrong, it may not be seen as a wholly admirable thing to have left me — as far as you knew — in total ignorance of what they call the Facts of Life."

Miss Pym patted her hair, rather flustered. "Oh, you girls nowadays!" she muttered.

"How did *you* learn them, then?"

Miss Pym stared at her in horror — that she could even *dream* of asking such a question, much less come right out with it like that, and in a public place, too! Then suspicion clouded her brow. "Are you *trying* to provoke me, Jessica?" she asked. "Calling me by my Christian name ... raising unsuitable topics ... and now this impertinent question. I tell you — if you are not trying to provoke me, then I begin to dread the day when you do!"

"I am putting my father's precepts into practice, Cressida," Jessie said calmly. "I am looking to my own interests — because no one else will. Isn't that his creed?"

"How dare you say such a thing!"

The girl ignored the question. "And I'm putting my cards on the table now, all open and above-board, so that you — and therefore he — will never be able to say I was the least bit underhand about it, or went behind your back, and so forth."

"But your father and I have *always* had your best interests in mind," Miss Pym protested. "You know what a vexation you have been to him, yet he never ceases to fret about ..."

"My father has in mind *his* best interests ... concerning me. And concerning you, Cressida, come to that. And Harry. And Frank. And Godfrey. *His* interests, his interests, his interests — they rule our entire world ..."

"Jessica! I simply forbid you to talk in this fashion! May I remind you that ..."

Blackwell returned at that moment to say that his wife was still writing out the luncheon menus but the soup was onion or beef consommé. They chose the consommé and fresh Porthleven crab sandwiches. Jessie thought of telling an indelicate story about consommé and consummation, which Lorna Gilbert had told her last evening — but she thought better of that, too. It would have been a rather juvenile way of showing how grown-up she now was. Instead, when Blackwell had withdrawn, she said, "You were about to remind me what a drain I am on the Kernow finances until I can lure some poor simp into asking for my hand."

"And so you are!" Miss Pym exclaimed. "You seem to think it a matter of some levity, but let me assure you ..."

"Let *me* assure *you*," Jessie interrupted, "that if the situation makes *you* unhappy, it makes *me* utterly miserable."

The other stared at her in bewilderment. "But the remedy is entirely in your hands, dear child! Get a diamond on that finger and your days of subjection are over."

"No they're not!" Jessie had to force herself to breathe in and hold it, counting out her anger. "They are not," she repeated with disciplined calm. "I would merely be transferring my subjection from my father to my husband."

"Oh!" Miss Pym closed her eyes and folded her gloved hands as if in prayer; a seraphic smile played about her lips. "Is *that* your difficulty!" she murmured.

Jessie was nonplussed; just when she seemed to have gained the upper hand — in compelling Miss Pym to take her seriously as a grown-up — she played this old trick of pretending she understood it all and if only her darling Jessica could outgrow her present charming naïveté, she would understand it, too. The trouble was — it usually worked! That simpering smile, which had once greeted so many slips in French grammar, or slipshod stitches in embroidery, or water-colour washes that had bled into areas that should have remained dry, or B-naturals when B-sharp was scored, still had the power to make Jessie feel all wrong and in need of correction.

But this time she knew she was not wrong. The kindly domination of a husband would, indeed, be no less lethal to her spirit than the well-intentioned tyranny of her father and Miss Pym. A mild sort of panic gripped her as she felt her confidence being nibbled away at the edges; she could stand pat in the middle of it and tell herself she was right, but the nibbling went on all the same; and it would continue for as long as the woman wore that smile, which seemed to say, 'How can I put this so simply that even *you* will understand me, child?'

Blackwell returned with their soup and wished them bon appetit.

When he had gone, Jessie, still rankled by Miss Pym's superior smile, was tempted to say something so outrageous that their relationship could never again return to that of ex-governess and pupil, or all-wise mother-surrogate and simpleton-child. It was on the tip of her tongue to blurt out: 'Why have you and my father never married?' — and then those bits from the prayer book about marriage being a remedy against sin and to avoid fornication. That would shatter everything! They'd have to begin again on a new footing after that. She drew breath and said, "Cressida?" — more to test the evenness of her voice than to press her monstrous question.

But Cressida Pym had a furrow of her own to plough. "Listen, dear," she said gently, taking her first sip of the soup. "Mmm! Good! But listen — it is understandable that a young girl brought up in very necessary ignorance of certain matters must look at marriage from the outside and see it as nothing but an extension of her tutelage to her father. Out of the skillet and into the flames, as they say. But believe me, it is not so." She nodded confidently but then corrected herself. "At least, it is so only if you are unwise enough to choose a tyrant for a husband. Girls do, you know. There is something in them — in many women — that is thrilled by a masterful, domineering sort of man. The strong, silent hero of so many tales. How he flutters the dovecotes at a party or a ball! Did you see that young cavalry officer last night — Walter Richards's boy? He's the very type — charming, attentive, courteous ... But just wait until after his victim is safely in the net! Then he'll turn out just like his father: a martinet and a bully. Unless ..." She paused and stared at Jessie as if sizing her up.

"Unless?" the girl prompted.

"Well, such men can eventually be tamed. They can't be beaten head-on — any more than you could beat a fighting bull by standing four-square in its path. But a woman who 'knows her onions,' as they say, can play the matador with such a man and have him head-down, trailing at her hem at last."

"How?" Jessie asked. It crossed her mind that, even without the provocation of that shocking question, Miss Pym was, in any case, introducing subtle changes in their association.

The proprietor brought their sandwiches and removed the empty soup bowls.

"How?" Jessie repeated when they were alone yet again.

The woman smiled at her now, and this time there was no condescension. "I could easily tell you, but I don't think it would mean very much to you just yet, Jessica. It will one day — when you have a closer alliance with some particular young man. You *are* old enough now — as you have made pointedly clear lately! — but your life still lacks any context in which you could set such ... what can I call it? 'Information' sounds so cold, 'teaching' so formal ... Actually, the real word for it is lore." She spelled it out to avoid confusion with 'law.' "Women's lore. There are ways of flapping our capes at all those bulls out there. There are ways of bringing them to heel. These suffragettes have entirely the wrong end of the stick — all that screaming sisterhood have. It's so unnecessary — and dangerous — the game they're playing. It's like standing smack in the path of the bull. You're not thinking of doing anything like that, are you?"

Jessie had the distinct feeling that she had just played the part of the bull to Miss Pym's matador. "No," she said, wondering quite what she was denying.

"Good. Then let us look to our assets. Let us see what bulls are presently in the market." From her bag she produced Jessie's dance programme from last night. "Which of these fellows seemed to you to have staying power?"

"Staying power?" Jessie echoed warily as she accepted the card back. How unexciting it looked now — like an empty champagne bottle after a lively wedding feast.

"Yes, which of them could you imagine yourself staying with for the rest of your life?" She laughed.

"None," Jessie replied immediately.

But Miss Pym saw a furrow appear on her brow. "You don't look quite so sure as you sound?" she prompted.

"Well ... I must confess I found Mister Cornwallis Trelawney quite interesting. Mind you, it's a long way from sharing an entire life with the man — but he was certainly the most interesting one there."

"What did you talk about? I saw you cut the last dance and go out to supper together. I meant to ask — it certainly *looked* very animated."

Jessie hesitated. "We spoke of love, actually."

"Love?" Miss Pym frowned. "That was rather forward of you — and certainly injudicious."

"I didn't start it." She frowned, too, trying to remember how it had happened. "Nor did he, really. It just sort of ... arose spontaneously."

"Spontaneous combustion," Miss Pym murmured.

"Oh, it wasn't heated. I can't remember much of it. We were both affecting to be very cool and ... what's the right word? Modern. Yes — very modern."

"*Soignés?*"

Jessie laughed. "If you like. But I remember one thing he said — which struck me as rather profound. We were both agreed that love will *always* disappoint — that lovers cannot help betraying each other — because its demands are impossible." She could see a tolerant sneer beginning to gather on Miss Pym's countenance but she pressed on. "He was the one who said they were impossible and I asked him why. And he said, 'Just think where we get all our ideas about love from in the first place. Our first love is with our mother. She's an ever-flowing fountain of warmth, comfort, food, and protection. This is before we're born, of course. When we're still ...'" She patted her stomach.

"Well, really!" All Miss Pym's earlier alarm returned. "I cannot think that that was a suitable ..."

"He didn't *say* so," Jessie assured her. "But I knew that's what he meant — and he knew I knew. Anyway, just listen, because I think it's so *true!* The problems start when we're born, because until then all that comfort, warmth, et cetera, has been quite unconditional — day and night, month in, month out. But from the moment of our birth it becomes sporadic. We can't *absolutely* rely on it any longer. And it turns capricious, too. Sometimes we cry and are comforted, but other times we cry and get smacked."

"That's called learning all about life, dear." Miss Pym relaxed a little when she realized the conversation had been less biological than she had at first feared.

"Of course! That's the side of the coin we *all* see. But look at the other side — which is the hidden part, the buried part, the bit that's always at the back of our mind. That's where we remember we once lived in paradise. We all know what the Garden of Eden was like because, like mankind itself, it's where each one of us started."

Miss Pym found herself sitting up and taking a reluctant interest, suddenly. There was a slight prickling at the back of her neck and she had one of those hallucinations where you feel quite sure you know what's coming next.

"Cornwallis says we never give up looking for that personal bit of Eden. Never. After our parents let us down we throw all our hopes on our schoolfriends. I suppose I avoided all that because I never went to school, but it's true, isn't it — boys and girls do go in for passionate friendships — blood-brothers, gangs, cliques ... you know? They do expect *absolute* loyalty ... that sort of I'll-defend-you-with-my-life friendship. 'Greater love hath no man than this ...' you know? That sort of love. And yet sooner or later even the best of friends will let each other down. And so then we come to the final, desperate attempt to return to Eden — which is through the gateway of love and marriage. You call it 'learning about life' — but we don't! We never learn that we're barred from Eden for *ever!* We rely at last upon love to get us back there. And it can't. It *has* to let us down in the end — because it's human. D'you see, Cressida? That's what Cornwallis said last night."

Miss Pym realized she had not drawn breath for some time. She made good the deficit now.

Jessie misinterpreted her agitation. "D'you still think it was a shocking thing to have talked about?" she asked.

Miss Pym shook her head. "In fact, I envy you," she replied. "In my young day there were certain ..."

"Oh Cressida!" Jessie interrupted, jovially cross. "I'll be twenty before you're thirty. Only by a month, I know — but for a whole month we'll both be in our twenties! When you first came to Wheal Prosper you were about double my age then. But when *I* reach thirty, you'll only have lived a quarter as long again as me. And if you keep talking about 'in my young day' and 'when I was a gel' like that, you'll turn all gray and wrinkled and your teeth will all drop out before then." She glanced at the clock over the mantelpiece and added, "We must make tracks."

Miss Pym left the money on the table and they went to collect their cloaks. "To put it another way," the older woman said, "as recently as ten years ago — is that acceptable, Miss? As recently as ten years ago it would have been quite unthinkable for young people to have held such a conversation as you claim to have held with ..."

"It would have shattered your illusions?" Jessie teased.

"Do not mock illusions, dear. One cannot live *entirely* without them." She thought of adding something to the effect that she'd sooner have gray hair than inhabit a gray world but, as she had lately discovered one or two gray hairs among her gold, the jest would have cut too near the bone.

"Well," Jessie replied, "Cornwallis and I agreed it was best to try — to live with as few illusions as possible, I mean. Perhaps one can't do away with them altogether, but we can at least try."

Cornwallis Trelawney called at Wheal Prosper the following Thursday for tea. There was great excitement because he came by motor car — one of the first in the district. It was a little Renault voiturette, which looked like a bath chair to which someone had bolted a motor — roughly where, in a real bath chair, you'd expect to see a gout-stricken and massively bandaged foot. He was supposed to have a man with a red flag walking out in front but he decided to risk the fine instead; the law was often lax until the numbers of cars grew to the point where it was worth enforcing. On the downhill stretch from Crowntown he got up to twenty miles an hour.

As soon as he arrived at the house he took Miss Pym for a brief ride, just to the bottom of the drive and back. But when, on their return, he saw Jessie jumping up and down excitedly and getting ready to claim her turn, he made clandestine signals for her not to, and she was quick-witted enough to comply.

Miss Pym enjoyed her first taste of motoring but she remained uneasy that his visit had come so swiftly on the heels of the ball. The letters she had dispatched to all her friends in north Cornwall, inquiring particularly into the young man's antecedents and circumstances, had not yet been answered. She called those few who were connected to the telephone system but, of course, with all those wretched girls listening in at the village post offices — at both ends of the line — there was little point in trying to elicit any really useful information. She would have to rely upon direct inquiry and instinct, instead; fortunately for her, the ability to place a person socially to within one percent of his or her correct niveau, and to gauge income to within five percent, is an inherited trait among the English middle classes. Like hæmophilia, it passes down the female line but does its damage chiefly among the males of the species.

Cornwallis, as an apparently eligible bachelor, was a seasoned sparring partner in that friendly yet lethal game — which was very fortunate for him.

"I believe your family has connections with this part of Cornwall, Mister Trelawney?" Miss Pym began. "You take milk, do you?"

"And two lumps of sugar, please. We once owned quite a few mineral rights up around Wendron and Porkellis — which we had the good fortune to sell off before the market dropped out of tin. As a matter of fact, it was a great-uncle of yours, Miss Pym, who advised my grandfather to sell. Oswald Pym."

His hostess smiled ruefully. "It is a great pity he did not follow his own advice. Madeira cake or caraway seed?"

"That is often the way of things." He chose the caraway.

"I hope you're not thinking of buying the rights back," Jessie said. "Even though they are so cheap at the moment."

He smiled at her, not condescendingly, as so many other young men might have done. "Where would you advise a young fellow to put his money these days, Miss Kernow?" he asked.

"Really, Mister Trelawney!" Miss Pym was both flustered and determinedly jolly. "A lady will always tell you to invest in Consols. It is not really seemly for her to know more than that."

"Well *this* lady," Jessie said, "would advise *that* gentleman that the future will see more profit on the surface of Cornwall than beneath it."

Miss Pym glowered at her but Cornwallis tried to push the business further. "D'you mean the profit is in farming or in building, Miss Kernow?" he inquired.

Jessie, who knew she had strained Miss Pym's tolerance far enough, merely smiled and said, "The Delphic utterance is free of charge, Mister Trelawney. But for a detailed commercial analysis there is a small fee. I hear you've joined the Gilbert and Sullivan Society?"

"Yes — under the mistaken impression that they performed Gilbert and Sullivan. Apparently they want to do Rustic Chivalry this year — *Cavalleria rusticana*, you know."

And so, for some time, the conversation drifted amiably along in those uncontroversial waters. In the course of it the two women learned that he sang a moderately good tenor and had played the lead in several productions by his college dramatic society. He had been at King's in London. He gained a degree in natural history, honours. He had thought of teaching — and then thought better of it. He had thought of writing a book on natural history but his enthusiasm for that was waning, too. Now he really didn't know what he wanted of life, though he was quite sure of what he did *not* want, which was to return home to Yorkshire and work in any of the family businesses up there. No, that did not please his family but it was his observation that people who devoted their lives solely to pleasing their families seldom had a very happy time of it; he did not wish to put this theory to a test in his own life. At which point Miss Pym considered that Jessica had heard quite enough seditious talk for one day and she turned the conversation to neutral matters. His further views on the treacherous nature of human love were not canvassed.

On his departure he turned to Jessie, as if it were an afterthought, and asked if she wanted a quick trip to the gates and back — since he had not been gentleman enough to offer her the chance immediately after Miss Pym's little jaunt. Only when she was actually climbing in beside him did he look toward Miss Pym for approval. She gave a shrug of annoyance and said they were to go straight there and back. She suspected he had deliberately chosen to drive a two-seater — and she was certainly not going to perch on the wretched little dickey-seat at the back. On their way down to the gate he coasted out of gear, so that they could talk above the futta-futta of the motor.

"A formidable young lady," he commented.

It made her realize that Cornwallis, though only twenty-two, was mentally much older — in that he could refer to a woman of twenty-nine as a 'young lady' still. For her own part Jessie imagined she'd have to reach her forties or even fifties before she felt that sort of equality with Cressida Pym.

"Surely you realize that the whole of West Penwith is bristling with questions and bustling with rumours concerning you!"

He laughed. "What are they saying? Please don't answer if you'd rather not."

"I don't mind. They're saying you've quarreled with your family and they've cut you off without a bean. Alternatively — because, of course, gossip always has an alternative ready — you own so many shares under the family trust that you can put a gun to their heads whenever you like. Though how an individual can control shares held in trust, I don't understand. I don't think they do, either."

He eyed her shrewdly and said, "You seem to take rather more interest in commercial affairs than most girls of my acquaintance, Miss Kernow. May I ask which of these rumours *you* subscribe to?"

"None, I'm afraid," she answered reluctantly.

It seemed to please him. "Could it be that you have no real interest in my circumstances, one way or the other? Please, Miss Kernow, I beg you be as blunt as you like."

"I shall be very blunt, Mister Trelawney. I should be quite interested in becoming your friend. But I have no romantic interest in you whatever. I have no romantic interest in *anyone*. I have never felt the slightest tug at my heartstrings in that direction and I do not understand its hold over people who are so ..."

"Afflicted?" he suggested.

She nodded. "I now feel entitled to ask the same of you."

"I reciprocate the sentiment, Miss Kernow: friendship, yes — romance, no! I wish we did not have to discuss this in so hasty and dangerous a fashion."

"Dangerous?" she queried.

"Absolute tiger country! The smallest misunderstandings can get blown up into huge causes. I would so welcome the chance to talk to you at leisure."

"About what, may I ask?"

He clenched his eyes tight and shook his head. They rolled to a halt between the gateposts, where he began to turn about. "I sense in you a certain ... what may I call it? Ambition? Am I right? Your lack of interest in romance is no mere whim, I think? It's connected with ambitions in other directions?"

"And?" she prompted him warily.

"And if I am right, then it is because I'm in the same boat, Miss Kernow. And if we *are* in the same boat ... well, we might take an oar each and pull in the same direction, don't you think?"

"I don't quite follow," she told him, though in fact she was just beginning to catch his drift.

The car was facing the house once again. As he let in the gear he said, "We could misdirect the world without posing the slightest danger to each other. Do think it over."

He pressed the throttle and sustained conversation became impossible over the roar.

"What did he say to you?" Miss Pym wanted to know as soon as silence returned.

"She has a one-and-three-quarter-horse-power engine, single-cylinder and water-cooled, by de Dion Bouton," Jessie replied. Godfrey had told her these facts as soon as they heard of the car.

"She?" Miss Pym echoed.

"Cars are feminine, didn't you know? They permit men to enjoy the illusion of being in control — very much the sort of thing you were telling me at the Angel the other day." She smiled sweetly. "I didn't tell Mister Trelawney that, though."

"I should hope not!" the other exclaimed, though she seemed happy enough with Jessie's answers.

That evening, when Clarrie was helping her to prepare for bed, Jessie said, "Did you ever think of going on the stage, Clarrie?"

The maid giggled and said, "Oh my gidge, no!"

"You've got quite a good singing voice, too, haven't you?" Jessie went on. "I've heard you in the kitchen."

Clarrie admitted she did enjoy a hearty sing-song.

"I'm thinking of joining the G-and-S in Helston, you see, and I can't ask Miss Pym to give up a whole evening a week to chaperoning me — dear, kind soul though she is. Nor you — unless you were actually interested …?"

"Gusson!" The maid raised her eyes to the ceiling at this nonsense. "They'd never take in the likes of me!"

"They'd have to — if they wanted the likes of me. Which they do. They're desperate for good female *ingénues*."

It was the truth, too. Spinsters did not dare join anything connected with the stage — even an amateur drama group — until they were, by general consent, on the shelf. It had once been the same all over England but the last two decades had seen an increasing relaxation; the old notions lingered in Cornwall thanks to the strength of the Methodists in the county. The Kernows were Anglicans but Barney always took care not to offend the other crowd.

"Remember poor Miss Waters!" Clarrie said. "Playing that schoolgirl in The Little Minister — talk about mutton dressed as lamb!"

"So what d'you say? Would you be interested?"

The maid's eyes gleamed; there was no doubting her interest. But she was of the kind that can never say yes to anything until all obstacles to it are removed. "What's your father say?" she asked.

"He doesn't know yet, but I know exactly what objections he's going to throw up — one of which will be this ridiculous business of chaperonage. And I want to be able to answer them before they grow thorns. You would be interested, wouldn't you — I can tell."

"They'd have to rehearse our bits first," Clarrie said dubiously. "'Cos eight-ten is the last train out of Helston."

"Well …" Jessie waved a hand as if such details hardly mattered. "Perhaps we could persuade some young fellow with a motor car to drive us home!"

*I*t took Jessie almost three weeks to overcome all objections and wear her father down to the point where he gave his reluctant consent for her to join the Helston G&S. Her impatience fanned her anger to the point where it included Cornwallis, too; after all, the scheme had been his, yet he seemed to be leaving everything to her. *He could at least do something to goad Miss Pym,* she thought. For Miss Pym, once goaded, would make short work of her father.

Then, around the middle of January, word filtered through to Wheal Prosper that Mr Trelawney had taken tea at the homes of several hopeful spinsters of nubile years and had spoken warmly of the G&S on each occasion — to the point where the hopeful spinsters were trying to talk their mothers into permitting them to join. Miss Pym then saw that further resistance was pointless; she could either yield now or wait until all the other girls had their feet on the starting line, too. And Jessie, for her part, saw that Cornwallis Trelawney's mind ran along very similar lines to her own — especially when his opening words to her as they all gathered for the first rehearsal were a murmured, "Don't worry if you miss the last train."

The rehearsals were held in the ballroom of Liston Court in Cross Street, which had lately been bought by Jimmy Troy, the American grandson of a Cornish emigrant. He had inherited a small rock-drill manufacturing company and turned it into a world-wide enterprise; he and his wife, Elizabeth, were presently on an extended tour of all their agents and factories in five continents, so Liston Court was untenanted and its staff on board wages. But Michael Vestey, a friend of the Troys and the producer of the G&S, had permission to use its magnificent ballroom. Or rather, one should perhaps say, its *once-*magnificent ballroom, for the house was beginning to show its age and the surfeit of owners and tenants it had suffered during the previous century. Vestey had covered the floor with a cheap coconut-fibre matting to protect its parquet, but the men who had laid it wondered why he bothered; and the absence of furniture, curtains, and paintings made the decay of the fabric even plainer to see. In short, whereas Liston Court in its noble heyday might have overawed the amateur thespians and singers of the Helston G&S, its present condition laid no *extra* social restraint upon them. It was a relaxed and easy gathering.

Jessie's arrival, chaperoned by Clarrie, caused something of a stir in the normally cooing dovecote on the female side of the cast. As a newcomer, she ought to have served her apprenticeship in the chorus. But to place her there might, among those not versed in the ways of amateur theatrical groups (such as Miss Pym and Barney Kernow, for instance), seem rather insulting, especially when one considered her father's importance in the district. Also there was the uncomfortable fact that she had the finest soprano voice among them — which she demonstrated from the first auditions, which formed the main business of the evening.

But that, in turn, led to a further complication, for the soprano role in *Cavalleria rusticana* is Santuzza, a Sicilian village maiden, or ex-maiden, rather, who has been put in that 'interesting condition' by Turiddu, a farmer (and tenor). The idea of casting a virtuous Cornish maid as a ruin'd Sicilian one, was abhorrent, no matter how suited her voice might be to the part. True, if Miss Kernow had not joined the company, the rôle would have gone to another virtuous Cornish maid, Miss Cissie Bagnall; but, since she 'could very well pass for forty-three in the dusk with the light behind her,' any objection would have been absurd.

The alternative was for Jessie to sing mezzo-soprano and play the part of Lola, wife of Alfio, the village drover and baritone. But that was almost as bad, for it was Lola's seductive beauty that had caused Turiddu to desert poor Santuzza in the first place. So even the legally married Lola was not a suitable rôle for a virtuous maid, either. If only these hot-blooded Italians could learn to be a little more like our own dear Gilbert and Sullivan!

And then, to confound matters still further, the part of Turiddu would clearly have to go to Cornwallis Trelawney, whose tenor was quite outstanding. But just think of the local furor that would erupt when it got out that Jessie had been cast in *either* rôle — his seduced victim *or* his adulterous seducer! No wonder poor Michael Vestey wrung his hands and contemplated a return to those safer waters where one might encounter nothing more hazardous than a few pirates from Penzance.

The two singers in question took the matter out of his hands, though. Jessie, knowing very well what qualms were troubling the rest of the company, slipped over to the piano and, taking up the music, began softly to play *Ah! lo vedi*, in which Santuzza makes her last, desperate appeal to Turiddu not to desert her — an appeal he dramatically rejects. At first she merely hummed the melody to her own accompaniment. Cornwallis joined her and hummed Turiddu's responses. On the other side of the ballroom the obliquely phrased debate continued, but a small group of chorus-fodder formed around the duo and began encouraging them with nods and smiles.

Cornwallis now started to slip in the odd word, whenever he could decipher the Italian without losing his place in the melodic line; Jessie followed suit. The nods and smiles encouraged them to yet bolder efforts, so that, by the time they reached the climax of the duet, they were in full La Scala mode and the rest of the company had fallen to silence — envious in a few cases, appreciative in the rest, and astounded universally. When they reached the final chord and held it in perfect harmony to the last flourish, the ensuing hush compelled even the envious to a burst of spontaneous applause.

Amateur productions usually rehearse for months before they produce even one or two moments of such quality. To achieve that standard before the piece is even cast was so rare that Michael Vestey would have needed the training of a saint to resist its seduction. He did not actually announce that the two principals were cast but he answered the unspoken objections to the arrangement by saying that, after all, it was only a piece of fiction ... and one could hardly be blamed for what the Italians wrote ... and the opera *did* win Sonzogno's competition for one-act operas in 1890 ... and anyway he had just laid out eighteen shillings and sixpence of G&S money on new recordings by Desfourches and Zigarda of *Addio alla madre* and *A voi tutti salute* among others.

And so the die — and CR, as they off-handedly called it — was cast.

The half-dozen principals were given their music and banished to corners of the room to make a preliminary study of their parts. Vestey gathered the chorus around the piano and, since the society was too poor to afford individual scores for each singer, began teaching them their parts by rote. With amateurs, as with the great stars of opera themselves, the music was all; the acting that linked the melodies was of no significance whatever.

As soon as Cornwallis and Jessie were in the safety of the ballroom's farthest window seat he asked, "Have you thought over what I said a few weeks ago?"

"Of course," she replied and, pointing to their score, added, "If anyone approaches near enough to overhear us, this is the bit we're singing, all right?"

"Very good!" He beamed with approval and then said, "Well? What conclusions did you reach?"

"I concluded that I should like to hear something a great deal more specific from you, Mister Trelawney, before ..."

"Cornwallis, please?"

"Cornwallis ... before I venture the smallest opinion."

His smile faded and she saw that there was an impatient — possibly intolerant — side to his character; even so, she made no move to soften her request for him to say more.

A degree of warmth returned to his expression and he said. "Very well, Miss ... er ..."

"Jessie." She smiled.

"Very well, Jessie. I imagined I had made myself plain, but — obviously not. I think I pointed out that the matrons of West Penwith are intent on making my life a misery until I yield to their combined pressure and announce my engagement to one or other of their ghastly daughters?"

"Why ghastly?"

"Figure of speech. It's the matrons who are ghastly, really. However, since 'all girls grow up like their mothers,' and all Gwendolens turn into Lady Bracknells, to call them 'ghastly' now is merely to state a truth prematurely."

Jessie laughed. "You think *I* shall turn into a Lady Bracknell then?"

"No!" he replied emphatically. "Because, as you yourself told me, you are *out* of that whole contest. Miss Pym may not be, but you are. That is the whole point of my approach to you. I wish to stop the ghastly matrons harrying me. The only way to do that is either to commit some dreadful social crime — which, believe me, I had seriously contemplated before I had the luck to meet you — or to announce my engagement. And you, for your part, wish Miss Pym to stop goading you into all the usual pre-courtship rituals of our ..." He sought for an alternative to 'class' and settled reluctantly for "... milieu. You know what I mean, anyway — the dances, the teas, the flaunting of bright water colours and pretty piano pieces. You *do* wish to leave all that behind you?"

She nodded fervently.

"Well," he concluded, "the only sure way to do that is either to commit the sort of social crime I mentioned just now, or ... to announce your engagement, too."

He passed his tongue rapidly over his lips and, smiling, waited for her to draw the last few threads of his argument together.

To lick one's lips after a longish speech can hardly be called an extraordinary act, yet the sudden and brief appearance of his tongue so startled Jessie that she was lost for words. She continued to stare at his lips, thinking, at first, that she was waiting for a repeat performance. Slowly it dawned on her that she was actually looking at them for their own sake — as if they were two living creatures, each with a life of its own, that merely happened to be fastened to his face.

Lips! They really were the most extraordinary appendages when you looked at them in isolation like that! Appendages? Organs? Organelles? Whatever they were. No matter. They were fascinating. People put them together and 'kissed' as they called it. She had kissed boys at birthday parties and so on, and it had always seemed a faintly disgusting thing to do. But somehow — and this was a new sensation for her — she did not imagine it would be like that if she were to kiss Cornwallis's lips.

"Well?" he prompted. "Has the majesty of my logic stunned you?"

"No," she replied with guilty haste.

"So?" he continued. Then, losing patience again, said bluntly, "Shall we announce our engagement ... soon? Next month, say ... or sometime in the spring?"

"I suppose we shall have to kiss?" she mused.

"Eh?" He frowned. "Oh, you mean in the opera!" He chuckled then. "I suppose we shall. Well, people won't be able to make much of it if they know that in real life our troth is plighted." He spoke the last three words with an amused irony.

"What are your objections to marriage, Cornwallis?" she asked, surprising herself almost as much as she did him. The question welled up out of nowhere.

He stared back at her suspiciously. "You're not going to trap me?" he asked. "I'd have to be very sure of your own opposition to the state of wedlock before making any public announcement — or even taking a single step with you toward it."

She realized then that she was not in love with him. A few moments earlier, fascinated by the inexplicable strangeness of his lips, her assurance had wavered; but it had been an exclusively *physical* fascination, entirely devoid of any romantic or spiritual interest. She felt sure of it now. Otherwise how could she stare back at him so calmly? And how could her heart remain so unfluttered?

"And don't you think I need *double* the assurance that you require?" she responded. "You could tire of our subterfuge, ask me to release you, and marry any one of those ghastly daughters you now affect to despise ..."

He interrupted. "I do not *affect* to despise them, believe me!"

"Not at this moment, perhaps. But no promise is easier to make than one that is not yet called!"

His eyes dwelled in hers, first in her right, then her left, as if he suspected he'd find a difference in their message to him. Finding none, he dipped his head in acknowledgement. "Very well, Jessie. You're right — and I'm the impetuous one."

She laughed again.

This time he asked why.

"You see the irony? Most people delay the announcement of their betrothal until they are absolutely sure of their love for each other. With us it is precisely the reverse!"

He frowned. "Not hatred."

"Oh no. Hatred is the shadow of love, not its opposite. Indifference is its opposite."

He thought that over awhile and then murmured, "And yet ..." but said no more.

"And yet what?" she asked.

He scratched the side of his neck diffidently. "Well, I've often thought we — our whole society, I mean, not ..." He wafted a hand at the people in the ballroom generally. "I've often thought we make a sort of god out of love. Without being too personal, d'you know of many marriages where love persists?" He did not embarrass her by pausing for a reply but continued, "It is, I believe, a form of temporary glue that holds a couple together until the real bonds take over."

"Children, you mean?"

"Everything. Shared interests, finances ... all those dynastic things ... a place in the larger community. You know! They're the real glue of a marriage. If love persists as well, so much the better, but it's not necessary. Straightforward affection will do just as well."

"Why then," she said, "our loveless engagement — if we ever decide to announce it — is just as great a threat to our celibacy as the most passionate romance would be!"

He nodded and smiled bleakly. "You have a wonderfully nimble mind, Jessie. I sometimes think you take my meaning before it is even half clear to me! However, I believe it is best not to leave such things *half* said. If we are to take this difficult course together, for the sake of the peace it will grant us, we should also be aware of the many pitfalls along the way."

"Amen to that," she said.

*E*aster in that first year of the new century fell on the fifteenth of April. The three performances of *Cavalleria rusticana* were booked into the Assembly Rooms for the Thursday, Friday, and Saturday of the following week, so the times were tight. Normally there would have been four performances, with a schools matinée on the Saturday; but the elements of adultery and bastardy in CR ruled that out. However, word of its unsuitability for tender minds spread very swiftly among the populace and promised three packed houses for the evenings.

The two stars were so keen to shine that they held a number of private rehearsals at Wheal Prosper, in addition to the regular Tuesday and Friday evenings with the whole company at Liston Court. Actually, to call their rehearsals 'private' is something of a misnomer, for nothing could have been more public than the phut-phut and clatter of Cornwallis's Renault as it scattered the hens down Crowntown hill, stampeded the cows in the fields beside the Nancegollan road, and even awakened the porters at the railway station.

Naturally, those mothers who had hoped their unwed daughters might attract young Trelawney's attention were greatly put out that the Kernow girl seemed to be making so much of the running. Miss Pym felt a certain discomfort, too, though hardly for the same reason. She expressed her misgivings to Jessie one morning in early February, after Cornwallis had paid some half-dozen clattery visits to the house. It was the week after Jessie's twentieth birthday; so, for the next five weeks, as Jessie had once pointed out, they would both be in their twenties. It made such a conversation less awkward, somehow. (And in any case Cressida intended to remain at twenty-nine for at least one more year, until March, 1901.)

"I quite understand, my dear," she said, "that your parts in this opera require the two of you to pass a great many hours in each other's company ..."

"We are scrupulous to keep the drawing-room door open always," Jessie hastened to point out. "And Clarrie is usually with us, for we rehearse her, too, you know."

Miss Pym looked at her wearily, for she not only knew of these arrangements, she had insisted upon them from the beginning and had taken care to entertain friends during young Trelawney's visits so that they could carry reports the length and breadth of West Penwith, telling of the absolute propriety of his association with Jessica.

"If I may continue?" she asked. "I was about to point out that the time you pass in each other's company is equal to that which, for instance, a betrothed couple could decently spend together."

"I daresay it is," Jessie replied uneasily, guessing where this point was leading. "But, short of standing and rehearsing in the rain on Helston Bowling Green, I don't see any alternative."

"If you *were* a betrothed couple, of course, it would be quite different."

A hope-filled lift of her eyebrows prompted Jessie to respond: "It's out of the question, surely — to become engaged after so brief an acquaintance?" And then, as if the notion had just crossed her mind, she added, "Unless ... no."

"What?" Cressida's hope was fanned to a blaze. "What were you going to say?"

But Jessie shook her head. "Pure nonsense. Stupidity. It's even more out of the question."

"But what?" Miss Pym's voice was almost a shriek.

Still in tones that dismissed the very thought, Jessie replied, "I was going to say that Cornwallis and I could announce an engagement that would be entirely genuine as far as the populace at large were concerned — but which he and I knew to be quite factitious, a mere cloak for our being so much in each other's company. And then later in the year, at some mutually agreeable time, we could announce an amicable parting — a mutual release by a couple who found they preferred companionship to romance." She laughed dismissively. "Absurd, as I say."

She had floated the notion out of curiosity, to see how Cressida would respond. She knew, however, that if she herself had shown any enthusiasm for it, her former governess would have dismissed it at once; a scornful tone, on the other hand, made the woman less eager to take that line.

"It would be very wicked," Cressida said; but already her tone was more thoughtful than dismissive.

"Wicked!" Jessie was, by contrast, vehement.

She retreated further. "Well, perhaps wicked is going too far. But certainly ill-advised."

Jessie nodded in eager agreement, murmuring, "Especially in my case." She patted the flowers she had been arranging all this while, stood back, and said, "There!" with a finality that seemed to close the discussion, too.

Of course it made Cressida more eager to continue. She reached out and plucked at Jessie's sleeve, just as she was turning toward the door, and said, "Why *especially* in your case?"

Jessie sighed. She was no longer playing a game with the Surface Angel. By skirting the real situation in this fashion she had come to the brink of a genuine revelation about herself — and one she was not sure she wished to make just yet, and certainly not to Cressida Pym. She'd much prefer to talk it over with Harry first. However, she could not pass it off with a girlish, 'Oh, nothing!' So she offered a diluted version of her worries: "I meant it would certainly be ill-advised in *my* case, since I honestly believe I shall never fall in love with anyone. I don't think it's in my nature, you see."

"Nonsense!" Cressida was panicked into exclaiming. "Every young girl has that capacity — even if she sacrifices it to God and takes the veil. You wait! It'll happen." Aware that she had reacted a little strongly, she smiled and patted the girl's arm, chiding her playfully. "Anyway, you're much too young to go saying things like that!"

"I'll have you know I'm *twenty* now," Jessie said with mock hauteur.

There was a tinge of sadness in the older woman's eyes as she said, "Yes. I know." After a brief silence she added, "And it does make some indefinable difference, doesn't it — I don't know why. It's quite stupid, really. D'you remember Harry's bit of buffoonery when we returned from the ball — when he said the sun doesn't know whether it's Monday or Friday ... something like that?"

By chance the sun came out and filled the drawing-room as she spoke those words, forcing them both to shield their eyes for a moment. They laughed and Cressida said, "Shall we take our constitutional? It seems a propitious moment."

As they pulled on their galoshes and helped each other into their raincoats, Jessie said, "Why d'you always call it a constitutional, Cressida? Why not simply a walk?"

The other gave a slightly baffled laugh. "There's no difference, dear. Constitutional ... walk — they're the same. We call it a constitutional because it's good for our constitution."

"Ah!" Jessie rounded on her, grinning and holding an accusing finger aloft. "Exactly! It's *good* for us! Whereas a walk is merely enjoyable. Heaven forbid that we should seek mere pleasure — rather than doing something *good!*"

Cressida laughed lightly as she stepped outdoors where, despite its being a February morning in Cornwall, the sun was *still* shining. "An amusing play with words," she said.

"Perhaps," Jessie replied. "But perhaps not. Don't you notice that you hardly ever say, 'Let's do such-and-such — it'd be such *fun!*' Even if we all know we're doing it for fun, you always say it'd be instructive, or good, or beneficial, or 'expected of us,' or healthy ... you know? Can't *fun* be its own justification just once in a while?"

She closed the front door and they set off at an ambling pace down the long drive to the highway — or, rather, the byway that led from Nancegollan to the wild, stony hinterland around Porkellis.

Cressida was silent awhile and then said, "We are piling up unfinished conversations. You were going to tell me why a feigned engagement with Trelawney might be especially dangerous to you — I mean, I see no connection between that and your delusion that you'll never fall in love, anyway. And also I was saying something about Harry's remarks after the ball. Oh yes — I remember what I was going to say! All about growing up. The difference between last Thursday and this is that you've turned twenty in the meantime. But it's quite artificial. The difference in your maturity is no greater than between *any* two Thursdays in the year, really, *n'est-ce-pas?* And yet I feel I can talk with you in ways that would have been 'not quite on' this time last week, when you were a mere nineteen! Absurd, but true. D'you feel any different?"

Now it was Jessie's turn to be silent awhile. Then she said, "I suppose I feel I can talk *with* you now — instead of just *to* you."

Cressida chuckled at the aptness of the distinction and, taking Jessie's arm, said, "Tell me, then — about why you think you'll never fall in love."

Jessie took a deep breath and, before she could think better of it, said, "Were *you* ever in love, Cressida?"

There was a sudden tension in the woman's arm; she exhaled as if the question had winded her. Yet her voice was quite calm as she said, "You certainly believe in plunging in at the deep end, Miss!"

"Well?" Jessie prompted.

"I was barely eighteen when I came to Wheal Prosper," she pointed out. "And I've been here ever since — so how can you ask?"

Jessie said nothing.

After a pause Cressida went on, "Oh, very well! It should come as no great surprise to learn that I'm in love with your father." She clasped Jessie's arm tightly and, feeling no sudden stiffening of her muscle, added, "I gather it comes as no surprise at all! I hasten to add that he reciprocates the sentiment — in his own rather brusque and diffident fashion, of course."

Jessie gave an involuntary laugh, and instantly apologized. "Brusque and diffident so exactly describe him," she explained.

Cressida glanced over her shoulder, back toward Wheal Prosper. The gesture was more apologetic than furtive; her attitude suggested she had postponed these revelations for as long as was humanly possible but time had now caught up. "And the question you are too well mannered to ask," she continued evenly, "is 'Why, since we love each other, are we not man and wife?' After all, there is no legal prohibition to our union."

When Jessie once again kept her peace, Cressida said, "Perhaps you'd rather not inquire any deeper?"

The other smiled back ruefully, as if to say, 'You know me better than that!'

"Hasn't Frank ever spoken of it to you?" Cressida went on. "Or Harry, perhaps?"

"Harry tried to — a few weeks ago. But I'm afraid I snubbed him rather. I don't know why. I thought I ought to talk to you about it before ... No, I don't know why. Do they know? Have you explained it to them?"

"In fact, no. But I thought Frank might have guessed — or worked it out. After all, my grandfather's will is available to any lawyer — or anyone who goes to the Public Record Office. He could get a copy for half-a-crown."

"And what would it tell him?"

"That I inherited forty thousand pounds when I was sixteen, or, rather ..."

Jessie let out a whispered whistle of astonishment.

"Wait!" Cressida warned. "There's a sting in the tail."

"At sixteen, though!"

"Well, nobody told me of it until I was eighteen — and even then it was only because I announced my intention of seeking a place as a governess. They were horrified, of course — well, you can imagine how such a bombshell would go down in *my* family!"

"No," Jessie said. "I can't."

Cressida shrugged. "No, I suppose you can't."

"I know *of* your family, of course. But ..." She left the rest unsaid.

"Yes." Cressida's tone was regretful. "We have well and truly parted company."

Jessie gave a baffled little laugh. "Come to think of it — you're actually a *rebel*, aren't you! That never struck me before — Cressida Pym, a rebel!"

"Not on the surface," Cressida said. "On the surface I'm a regular angel!" She laid no particular stress on those words but, a moment later, she chuckled and, touching the tip of Jessie's ear, said, "Why, my dear, you're blushing!"

"I didn't know you knew," Jessie stammered.

"You'd be surprised at all I know — about what's said and done at Wheal Prosper! Frank thinks he's so clever, keeping secret bottles of wine in his riding boots!"

Jessie giggled. "And Harry? And Godfrey?"

But Cressida shook her head. "That's enough revelation for one day. As I was saying — no one breathed a word to me of my inheritance until I made that sudden announcement. And even then they said nothing about the restrictions my grandfather had placed on the use of it. I had to find that out from the lawyers."

"Restrictions?"

Cressida nodded grimly. "I'm like the Little Match Girl looking in through the frosty windows at the feast within. I can see it but I can't touch. It's all in trust. Grandfather lived in the days before the Married Women's Property Act — when half the legal battles in England were fought by howling cads who'd married heiresses and then fought the law — breaking entails, undoing trusts, and gaining absolute ownership of property and wealth. He didn't believe there wasn't a trust that couldn't be broken. So, quite simply, he devised a trust that would vanish if I ever marry — and the money along with it."

Jessie was aghast. "You mean — you lose the *lot?*"

"To a dogs' and cats' home! Every last farthing. He was a romantic, you see!"

"How can you say that?"

"Obviously he was. If I marry anyone, it *must* be for love — it certainly won't be for money!"

Jessie did a quick calculation. Forty thousand pounds, conservatively invested in Consols at between two and three percent, would still yield a very handsome thousand a year, which was four times the salary to which most professional men aspired — and probably more than her own father made, despite all his financial subterfuges. She was on the point of asking about the income when an awful thought occurred to her: Perhaps Cressida had been eager to marry her father and forgo her inheritance; and perhaps her father, with his eye on that money, had persuaded her to live in sin, instead! It was so shocking that the question shriveled on her tongue; and the most shocking thing of all was that she found this explanation of the unconventional arrangements at Wheal Prosper by far the most plausible. And her thoughts were only partially stilled at the notion that Cressida and her father might have married in secret — perhaps by post through one of those odd tabernacles in America — so as to keep on the right side both of the Recording Angel *and* of Grandfather Pym's ridiculous will.

"So!" Cressida said at last. "Now you know."

"Now I know," Jessie echoed grimly.

"Which is more than I can claim," the other continued.

Jessie frowned in bewilderment.

"Well — you were going to tell me why you never can fall in love."

"Oh, that!" Jessie waved her one free hand in a hopeless circle. "I don't know *why* I can't. I only know it's a fact."

"And you were also going to tell me why it would be dangerous to have this mock-engagement with Trelawney."

"Cressida! That was just a joke. You'd never seriously consider it, would you?"

"No," she agreed, still hesitantly. "But that doesn't mean the idea isn't worth exploring. If only for idle amusement."

Jessie stopped dead and stared at her, exaggerating her surprise to a comical degree. "Idle amusement!" she echoed. "Is Miss Pym speaking of idle amusement with approval?" She added to her revenge by touching the other's ears and saying, "Now who's blushing!"

In fact, Cressida wasn't blushing at all, but she was flustered enough not to realize it. "Come on!" she said. "You're proving to be a passed mistress of procrastination. Let's assume this is a serious notion — to still the gossips of West Penwith by cloaking your friendship with Trelawney in the rosy glow of betrothal, knowing it to be *quashable*, or however you want to express it. Retractable, perhaps? Why would a retractable engagement pose especial dangers to *you*, who can never fall in love, or so you now believe?"

"So I now *hope*," Jessie corrected her.

But this time she refused the bait. "Why?" she insisted.

"Isn't it obvious? If I ever marry, it can't be for love. It will have to be because I admire the man, enjoy his company, envy his intellect, relish his conversation, feel I can rely upon his support, grant him confidences he will not betray ... you know. It'll be for all the things that marriage is still *for*, even when passion may have withered and gone."

She had no idea how she expected Cressida to respond to her well-rehearsed catalogue (for she and Cornwallis had discussed these ideas several times since that evening at Liston Court), but she certainly would not have expected a dumbfounded silence. At last, in a small voice, the woman said, "How odd that we have never discussed such things before!"

"Odd?" Jessie echoed nervously.

"Yes. To find your thoughts so ... so mature, so well advanced. I presume — since this 'joke,' as you call it, has only just flitted through your mind ... I assume you've given it no prior thought?"

"No, of course not!" Jessie could not possibly admit to having discussed it several times with Cornwallis!

"Well then — there you are! I think it'd take anyone else half a morning to assemble such a list as the one you've just trotted out, almost without thinking." She laughed self-deprecatingly. "D'you remember when you got hold of one of Frank's textbooks and asked me to explain quadratic equations? Me — who cannot add two and two without breaking out in a sweat! And you ended up explaining it to me so lucidly that I think I could still solve one if you put it in front of me."

"The formula is ex squared plus two-ex-why plus why squared ..." Jessie began before Cressida put a gloved thumb across her mouth.

"I notice you still haven't said why it would be so perilous," the older woman remarked.

"Because I already _do_ admire Cornwallis. I already enjoy his company, his intellect, his conversation ... grant him confidences he will not betray ... you know — all those things I said just now. Don't you see?"

arney Kernow's principal business was in agricultural machinery. Village blacksmiths might make up the odd chain harrow to fill out a slack time and they could all make a plough to order, but if you wanted to see the very latest in _everything_, from a hand-pushed wheel-hoe to a mighty steam traction engine, Kernow's Farm Machinery — now Kernow & Son — in St John's was the place to go. Jessie was always happy to be sent there with messages; St John's was the part of Helston she loved the best — the industrial and commercial foot of the town.

No part of Helston stands on level ground — except for the bowling green, which had to be especially engineered on the remains of an ancient castle, immediately above St John's. From the new railway station at the crown of the slope, some three hundred feet above sea level, the land falls southwestward, gently at first and then with increasing severity, to the valley of the River Cober, less than a dozen feet above the sea, which lies a couple of miles away at the farther end of the lagoon-like lake known as the Loe.

The normal flow of the Cober would sooner justify the name of brook than river. But it drains the hinterland around Pallas, Gwavas, and Mellangoose and farther still, up through Trevarno to Nancegollan — an area measuring several thousand acres. So, during heavy rains, when the land loses its thirst and can swallow no more, the Cober swells to a mighty torrent that overflows its banks and floods the whole valley. In deference to its uncertain temper, the houses down there are built with a knee-high slab of stone between the jambs, like a doorstep stood on its side.

But the land around the gasworks was purposely raised above the level of the floods. Barney Kernow's father, 'Old' Barney, who had passed on to his reward in the early nineties, had been a blacksmith and horse dealer there before the gasworks came; in fact he exchanged one of his two and a half acres for shares in the plant, the profits of which had become the basis of the family's fortune. On the remaining acre and a half 'Young' Barney now displayed his stock of reapers, binders, swath-turners, mangold-wurzel choppers, ploughs, potato ridgers, and harrows (or 'harves' as the Cornish call them) of every description — disc, fixed-tine, spring-tine, and chain.

Jessie liked to descend from the pony-trap at the entrance to the yard and walk among the stock on display, relishing each one as others might relish sculptures. She especially liked the reversible four-gang plough and would always walk around it a couple of times to admire the functional perfection of its eight curved mould boards. She could not look at them without imagining the ploughshares nosing through the topsoil like implacable steel moles — and the broken sod rising, tilting, turning over in a long band of gleaming tilth, rough-polished by the fi steel blades that shouldered them aside with such unfussy strength.

Best of all were the great steam engines at the top of the yard, next to the offices. One was a road roller on almost permanent hire to the county council; the rest were traction engines — two or three for sale and two or three for hire, along with their crew. Few farms in West Penwith were large enough to need their own engine; the sales were mostly to breweries, stone quarries, tin mines, and so forth; indeed, few farmers could afford even to hire an engine for routine field work like ploughing. But for mole drainage, tree clearance, and the breaking-in of old croft land there was no substitute, and there was enough of that sort of work to keep the engines on hire at least a couple of days a week. And, to be sure, in harvest time all the engines and threshing machines worked around the clock.

On the day Jessie called with a message from Wheal Prosper, the largest of the traction engines, a mighty, one-cylinder Marshall, was being steamed up for hire work. Its boiler was already mewing and pinging like some leviathan kettle and, in the chill, damp, March air Jessie could feel the heat it radiated before she got within twelve paces of the monster.

"Where's she going, Jack?" she asked the driver, who was bending away from her, peering into the firebox.

But when he rose and turned she was amazed to see, not Jack Miller, who had driven for Kernow's all his working life, but Cornwallis Trelawney! He wore an engineer's cap and boiler suit and had obviously been mopping his face with an oil-stained wad of shoddy. "I'm bankrupt!" he called out. "Lost every penny at cards last night. Starting a new life today. Your father's been very kind."

His smile gave the leg-pull away but just for a moment her heart quickened with joy at the thought that it might be true. This unguarded response surprised her — and her surprise, in turn, alerted him to the fact that, just for a moment, she had entertained the possibility quite seriously and that her face had not fallen in sorrow at it. He said nothing of it at the time, however.

"Seriously," she chided. "What on earth are you doing dressed up like that?"

"Dressed *up?*" he echoed, staring at his soot-and oil-stained boiler suit. "Most people would call this dressing down."

"Not me." She grasped his sleeve and shook it roughly — both as a substitute handshake and to relieve her annoyance. "I envy you. How I'd love to dress up like you and mess about with one of these engines!"

He hopped up onto the driving plate and reached a hand into a shelved recess beneath the canopy, from which he drew forth a spare set of dungarees, not new but fresh from the laundry. "Welcome aboard then," he said, offering them to her.

Seeing they were at least clean she took them and called his bluff. "Turn your back," she told him, "and keep cavey."

He snatched them back hastily and laughed. "By heavens, you would, too!"

"Like a shot! Are you going to explain yourself properly?"

As he returned the dungarees to their niche he said, "Wheal Dream — you remember?"

For a moment she thought he'd said 'we'll dream.' Then she recalled the farm, which was about half a mile up the lane from the entrance to Wheal Prosper. It was one of the places on his list of possible homes. "You've bought it?" she asked excitedly, for the other houses were all on the far side of Helston from Nancegollan.

"As good as," he replied. "We exchanged contracts yesterday, so I feel justified in starting on the place — pulling out the dead trees and clearing the drive, at least. Your brother doesn't agree, of course."

"Frank! He wouldn't get into a rowing boat unless it had a Lloyd's certificate. What can go wrong?"

"Barnicoat could get a better offer — Frank says."

"On Wheal Dream!" Her hoot of laughter showed how likely she thought that might be. "Anyway, you've signed a contract, you said."

He gave a sigh. "It's the one contract in English law that has no legal force, apparently — the contract to buy a house. It's just a sign of good intentions."

"Still, Barnicoat's *not* going to get a better offer. He's been waiting ten years to get any sort of offer at all." She jumped up and down on the spot and clapped her hands. "Oh, Cornwallis — I'm so pleased you decided on Wheal Dream, rather than that lovely house and beautiful farm at Saint Martin. You're insane, of course, but I'm glad."

Jack Miller came out of the office at that moment and trotted over to the engine. He tapped the gauge and said, "Just about ready, boss."

"Off we go, then," Cornwallis replied. As he climbed onto the plate beside the driver he turned back to Jessie and said, "Are you doing anything this afternoon?"

"Unfortunately, yes." She grinned. "I've just this minute decided to visit Wheal Dream."

After lunch, as good as her word, she had the pony harnessed to the trap again and set off for the deserted farmhouse, which was a mile away down the drive and up the lane but less than half that distance over the brow of Trelavour Hill — the hill that rose eastward behind Wheal Prosper. The farmhouse lay concealed in a hollow on a lazy bend before the three sharp bends that led to the hamlet of Releath. A two-storey granite dwelling, it was an exact twin to Wheal Prosper — the original Wheal Prosper, that is, before Barney added the Georgian-style façade in 1876, just after Harry was born. From the road, a distance of a furlong or so, it still appeared quite habitable but Jessie knew it had been dilapidated for some time. Not so very long ago, she and Frank had come raiding its apple trees and tried to make blackberry-and-apple jelly on its rusting old range.

She did no more than glance at the house, however, for the Mighty Marshall, with Cornwallis at the wheel, was at that moment drawing out onto the road, hauling behind it the bleached and barkless trunk of a long-dead sycamore. He gave her a wave of recognition but turned the engine away, facing up the slope, and dragged the trunk past two others in the verge before he came to a halt; by then Jessie was level with the entrance gate, only one of whose granite piers was now standing. There she saw Godfrey, marooned in a patch of furze and withies that had once been a creditable lawn.

He came forward to hold the pony while she leaped down with unladylike agility. "It's all wrong," he complained.

"What?" she asked stoutly. "You're here to chaperon me. So's Jack Miller. What's wrong?"

"I didn't mean you," he explained. "I mean this." He waved a hand at the places where the fallen trees had lain until today.

"Go on!" she chided. "By the time the lawn is restored you won't see any of those ruts."

"Aargh!" He tore out imaginary handfuls of hair. "*That's* what's wrong — restoring the lawn. Why must he do it at all? Has he any idea of the number of birds that now depend on those fallen trees and all this undergrowth — not to mention the mammals, the insects, the plants? He's sentencing literally *millions* of living things to death, you know — and all for what?"

"For a nice croquet lawn?" she suggested.

He turned from her in disgust. "There was a green-spotted woodpecker here last week. I'll bet we never see her again."

A year or two ago Jessie would have continued her playful mockery of his pet enthusiasm but they were both getting a bit too old for it now; suddenly she regretted their loss of the honest, unpolished rudeness of childhood. She had a fleeting vision of Wheal Dream as it would be if Cornwallis simply left the trees to rot away where they lay and let the furze and other regrowth come as it liked. A fine secret place it would be, safe for wild creatures of every kind. All at once the picture of a croquet lawn full of shallow, laughing players seemed a poor exchange.

"Well, well, well! It's been absolute ages!" Cornwallis advanced toward them up the shambles of the drive, smiling broadly and wiping his hands on that same bit of shoddy, which was by now several degrees dirtier. "Want to come and look at the house? Miller can get the chains round the next one by himself."

Brother and sister exchanged amused glances.

"Silly of me!" Cornwallis admitted. "I'll bet you've played every known childhood game under that roof. When exactly did Barnicoat's nephew last live there?"

"It wasn't his nephew, it was his cousin," Jessie told him as they started to pick their way among yesterday's thistles and tomorrow's trees. "Harry says he can just remember him farming here. He had a frock coat and a top hat always — even when hoeing turnips. It must have stood empty twenty years."

"Look!" Cornwallis stopped and pointed to a whole row of prostrate elms, some showing signs of budding for the coming spring's growth. "That's really just one tree, you realize? It suckered and suckered all round but the traffic kept it down on the drive and the scythe on the lawn. So it ended up as a single file of apparently separate trees. But when the storms came last winter the lot blew down in one. We must sever their roots before we can pull them out."

"What are you going to do with them, Mister Trelawney, once you've hauled them all up by the roadside?" Godfrey asked with a politeness that sat oddly beside his previous outburst.

"Cornwallis, for heaven's sake!" The older man punched him playfully on the biceps. "I'm going to turn it all into firewood and I'll have a fire burning all day in every grate for two months before I move in. I can't bear a damp house — it's like a clammy handshake."

The front door swung drunkenly inward, held only by its upper hinge. "Familiar?" Cornwallis asked as he ushered them into the hall. "When I first stood here last week, you know, I had a sort of daydream — like in H.G. Wells's *Time Machine*. Did either of you read that?"

They both nodded.

"I thought, here I am, standing in the hall at Wheal Prosper in some future century — when it's no longer inhabited. It'll be just like this." He touched the plaster, which flaked and fell, and he lifted a flap of rotting linoleum with the toe of his boot.

"Except that it took only twenty years to decay to this," Godfrey pointed out.

Cornwallis gave a dour laugh. "And I fear it'll take just as long to get it all back in order again."

Jessie gazed uncertainly at the holes where plaster had fallen from the ceiling; it was a year or two since any of them had played here and she could see that the place had deteriorated greatly since then. "Is it all still safe?" she asked.

"Oh yes," Godfrey assured her. "I was up here only last Saturday. D'you know there's a barn owl in the hayloft over the old stables?"

Another thought struck him. "I suppose I shall have to ask your permission now."

Cornwallis laughed. "You have carte blanche, young 'un," he said as he led them on into the house. "Actually, you can come up and help me anytime. I can always do with an extra pair of hands."

"Help you do what?" they both asked.

"Put on a new roof, to start with. That's the first job to tackle."

"Oh, but John Tregembo will do that in no time — timber and slatework. He's the best in the whole district. And he only lives down the road in Nancegollan."

But Cornwallis merely smiled and said he was rather looking forward to doing it himself.

For a moment neither of them understood. "Put the roof on all by yourself?" Jessie asked, as if she were searching the very words for meaning — never mind applying them to anything out there in the actual world.

He held out his hands toward her. "With these," he said. "You may come and help, too, if you like."

She laughed, not daring to think he might mean it — and in any case not believing he meant to do the work himself in the literal way his gesture had implied.

"As you wish," he said with a faint air of disappointment.

She realized he had meant his words quite literally, both of himself and in his invitation to her. She was about to try to retrieve the situation when he turned from them and led the way to the back of the house, saying, "The servants' staircase is a little less rickety than the one for the gentry." Smiling over his shoulder he added, "Rather symbolic, what?"

As they climbed the last half-dozen steps Godfrey could not help a surreptitious glance toward the panel that matched the corresponding panel at Wheal Prosper, where he had first enlarged and more recently plugged a spyhole into Clarrie's bedroom. To his amazement there was a knot a mere inch or so from the expected spot; true, it was not yet a hole, but a little push would be all it needed to become one.

Cornwallis observed his curious interest in that dim, dusty corner of the partition and raised an inquiring eyebrow.

"It's creepy," Godfrey said. "The similarity between this house and ours. I've felt it before but never so strongly as this. D'you suppose it really is an omen of the house of Kernow, fifty years from now?"

"The Fall of the House of Kernow!" Jessie said portentously, as if it were the title of a melodrama. Then, more conversationally, to

Cornwallis: "You know why they *are* so nearly identical, I suppose? They were built about eighty years ago — around eighteen-twenty — by the miller who had the mill beyond our place in Saint John's. Not the Trevoses in the modern mill — but the old one that's now a potato store. It belongs to Mrs Troy. Anyway, his name was James Polgray and he had twin sons, Peter and Paul, identical twins. And he bought them identical, hundred-acre farms and built identical houses and outbuildings, here on Trelavour Hill. Wheal Dream here on the east side, and Wheal Prosper back there on the west ..."

"We'll dream and we'll prosper!" Cornwallis laughed. "I never thought of it that way before. *Did* they dream? And did they prosper?"

Jessie shook her head. "Everyone made a joke of it, of course, but the farms were named the wrong way round. Peter Polgray of Wheal Prosper proved to be the idle dreamer. In eighteen-fifty-something he sold out to my grandfather — Old Barney Kernow — who was just starting to do well out of the gas company. Paul did much better here at Wheal Dream, even though, by general reckoning, the land is hardly as good. He lasted fifty years and then sold to old Josiah Barnicoat — the frock-coat farmer, who left it to his cousin."

"You've bought the land as well, have you?" Godfrey asked. "Or is Barnicoat going to continue farming it and living in Helston?"

"He'll stay on, rent-free, until Michaelmas," Cornwallis told him. "It suits me. I'll be busy on the house at least until then. Actually, I can have the ten acres of permanent pasture ..." His voice trailed off and he led them to the window to point it out. "There on the northern slope. I can have that portion at once. It'd keep two draft horses, a couple of milch cows, and a few pigs to fatten for Christmas. Except" — he shrugged — "I don't know. It's a lot of labour. And a distraction from my main purpose."

"I'll milk the cows for you!" Jessie said suddenly.

Godfrey laughed.

She rounded on him. "I can milk a cow — which is more than you were able to do, if you recall."

His playful scorn did not falter. "You were able *once* to produce milk from a cow. But that's a far cry from the business of *milking*. Milking means getting up at six every morning. *Every* morning. And not finishing until after seven at night. Anyway, it's absurd. You know Dad would never let you."

He had been staring vacantly out of the window while he spoke. All at once he went rigid and, leaning forward, wiped one of the panes with his sleeve.

"What's up?" Cornwallis asked.

"I just saw a fox cross the lawn — stalking something, I'll swear it. Excuse me. Be back in half a tick."

They heard him take the stairs three at a time; Cornwallis winced. "Perhaps I'll restore the staircase first," he said.

There was silence outside and they realized the traction engine was no longer turning. Cornwallis, annoyed that Godfrey might have distracted Miller, crossed to the window — only to see the man drawing off some boiling water into his billycan. He laughed. "He's a good worker, old Jack Miller, but he does like his cup of tea. His excuse is he sweats two pints a day and he needs to replace it somehow."

Jessie became aware then that the faintly pungent reek in the house was not some kind of fungus, as she had thought, but Cornwallis's sweat. It was somehow different — fresher and manlier — than the body odours that had so often repelled her at dances and afternoon tennis parties.

"The peace of it all!" he mused.

"Are you really going to do everything yourself?" she asked. "Absolutely everything?"

"No. I'll have a labourer to help me. One can't erect a roof entirely on one's own."

"I didn't mean that. I mean ... what'll people say?"

He laughed again. "A great deal, probably. Does it matter? Can I ask you a question, now?"

"Yes?" she answered in a guarded, inquiring tone.

"This morning — when I joked about going bankrupt — remember?"

"Mmm?" She was even warier now.

"Just for a brief moment you wondered if I were telling the truth — and it didn't shock you. D'you really think I'm the sort of fellow who could gamble everything on the turn of a card?"

She saw then that she'd have to tell him the truth. "Not for a moment," she replied. "I just had a fleeting thought that it'd be wonderful if it were true. Don't be shocked. Wouldn't it be splendid to lose everything and have to start all over again from nothing. Haven't you ever had that wish?"

"Have you?" he countered, not answering her directly. "Apart from this morning, I mean?"

"Oh, Cornwallis! Often and often! Only with me it's not so much losing money — since I don't have any in the first place. It would be losing my ..." She hunted for the word. "My ladyhood? Ladyness? Ladyship? What can one call it?"

"Your status as a lady?"

She laughed and clapped her hands. "Perfect — *les mots justes!*" She waved a hand toward his boiler suit and oil-smeared features. "Just as you've thrown off your status as a gentleman today — except that you can take it up again just by having a bath and putting on the right clothes. It's not so easy for a lady."

"What if you *did* have money?" he asked, tilting his head to one side and eyeing her speculatively. "What if you lost your status and gained …" He hesitated.

"A fortune?" she suggested.

"Let's say enough money to do anything you really wanted to do? I suppose that's what I really want to know — what would you *really-and-truly* like to be if you weren't so beastly constrained by the need to be a lady?"

"My father," she said at once.

It disappointed him.

She hastened in with a correction: "I don't mean I'd wish to be *him!* I mean I'd like to take his business and …"

"And what?" he asked when she failed to complete her sentence.

She realized then that if she pursued this line much further, she'd have to explain that her father used Kernow & Son as a cloak for numerous other activities, all of them more profitable and most of them a few points on the weather side of the law. "… and run it ten times better," she concluded rather lamely.

He accepted that but did not think it final enough. "Since it's an impossibility — unless you emigrated to some other county and set up there — let's rub the lamp again and grant you one more wish." He stooped and picked up an ancient brass bedknob from among the leaves and rubble on the floor. Polishing it elaborately on his sleeve he intoned, "Genie, genie, of this, er, lamp, remove this young person's status as a lady, and grant her enough oof to let her become …" He raised his eyebrows at her. "Quick! You say!"

She gazed desperately about her for inspiration. "A … er … an …" She clicked her fingers and shook her hands violently in exasperation but no thoughts came. "It's no good," she said at last. "I love those … all that farm machinery. That really is the only business I'd *ever* think of going into."

*I*t all began innocently enough — and who would have thought that an opera set in a poverty-stricken village in peasant Sicily could so divide a wealthy family living in modern England? It happened at Wheal Prosper, at dinner one Friday evening in the middle of March, when Godfrey, having supped early, was at choir practice. The meal had barely begun when Harry turned to his sister and asked how 'Cav rust,' as it had become known among them, was coming along. Before she could answer he went on, "I had an interesting talk about it with Trelawney today. I've been reading the original play by Giovanni Verga, which is full of wonderful themes and insights. It's amusing to observe that the so-called 'art' of opera finds it impossible to deal with them. Opera, it appears, cannot help trivializing, vulgarizing, and sentimentalizing the products of true art."

The others all knew, of course, that Harry used such words as 'themes, insights ... true art' simply to annoy their father.

It never failed. "How did you meet Trelawney, then?" Barney growled. "You were supposed to be over to Falmouth all day."

"Oh!" Harry feigned surprise that his father took an interest in such small details. "I finished up rather early, so I came back by way of Wheal Dream, just to see how he's getting along. He's jolly lucky with the weather."

"He's got half the trusses up already," Jessie put in proudly, though she did not add that she had helped with one or two.

Their father ignored the diversion. "So you 'finished up rather early'!" He sneered. "Did you call on Peter Mollard down Penryn? Or Jim Simons up Ponsharden?"

"We've had no order from Mollard's for the past ..."

"'Zackly, boy! *How* hasn't he sent in no orders, eh? Who's he getting his stock from nowadays? You ..."

Harry shrugged nonchalantly. "Well, if you *want* me to call on him, I will. I'll probably have to go back to Falmouth next week, so ..."

"How? I thought you said you finished up there?"

"Oh yes. I've finished the *business*. Fullerton paid me every last penny off his debt — and gave me a good repeat order, too." The softening of his father's attitude did not survive the rest of his explanation, however: "But old Bullock said he thinks he knows where he can get a first edition of Byron's *Don Juan*, so ..."

"First edition!" Barney exploded. "I'll tell you what comes *first* in your life, my lad — Kernow and Son! First and last! If we don't sell each new edition of *The Plough* by Trevithick Foundries and *The New Three-Tonner* by Wallace and Stevens, there won't be *any* edition of *Don Juan* for anybody. You shouldn't need me to tell you to call on the likes of Mollard's when they've gone dead on us."

"Sor-ree!" Harry said for the thousandth time — and in a tone which underlined the fact that it *was* for the thousandth time. "Anyway" — he turned back to his sister — "the theme of the original play is a clash between two types of authority, you see — the ancient Sicilian idea of justice, which is all about personal honour and vengeance, and the new Italian justice being imposed by the centralized authority of the state."

"How interesting!" Jessie glanced nervously at her father — who hardly needed such a cue.

"Authority!" he cried. "There's but one thing you need know about authority, boy! Authority says you work for Kernow's twenty-four hours a day — and *then* put in another six before bedtime. Authority says you think Kernow's, breathe Kernow's, eat, sleep, and dream Kernow's. That's authority for 'ee! Why, that maid there" — he pointed contemptuously toward Jessie without looking at her — "could run circles round you. And she's naught but a maid! You should ought to be 'shamed of yourself!"

A startled silence greeted this outburst. Never had the old man even hinted at such a comparison, let alone used it as a stick to beat his eldest son with. Realizing what he had done, he rounded angrily on Jessie, saying, "And that's as little cause for pride on your part, maid, as Harry's neglect may be on his."

The silence persisted, but now it was more pregnant than startled. Brother and sister exchanged inspiring glances; one thought was uppermost in both their minds — *It's now or never!* Their hesitation was merely as to which of them should speak first.

In the event — to the surprise of all — it was Frank. "It's beginning to look as if you've backed the wrong horse, Dad," he said laconically.

"How?" Barney asked, his tone a perfect blend of suspicion and pugnacity. An intervention of that kind was quite uncharacteristic of Frank, who had always held aloof from anything that touched on family passions.

"Isn't it obvious?" he replied.

"I'd sooner hear it from you," his father told him. Despite his irritation with all his rebellious brood, he was aware how rare an intervention this was from his middle son — and therefore not something to be lightly squandered.

Frank said, "You know that artist over in Mousehole — George Ivey? Used to be a solicitor in Helston with Coad and Coad? He showed me a drawing the other day which Elizabeth Troy had given him once. She wanted him to use it on his letterhead — during that endless litigation over the Pallas Estate. It depicted two peasants fighting over a cow — one pulling at the horns and the other heaving on the tail. But there in the middle, sitting on a three-legged stool and milking the poor cow for every last drop, is an old-fashioned country lawyer in frock coat and wig and tricorn hat."

Harry and Jessie laughed. Cressida, who had kept her thoughts to herself so far, wagged a reproving finger at them. Harry ignored her, saying, "She has a wonderful sense of humour, Elizabeth Troy. How we miss her!"

"Never mind your lawyers and cows," Barney snapped. "What's all that to do with us?"

"Simply this. The two peasants fighting over the cow have allowed their emotions to run away with their reason. Whenever that happens — in a family ... in a business ... and most especially in a family business — the only beneficiaries are third parties. The contenders in such struggles will *always* do better to stop fighting and calm down, then spread their assets out on the table and examine them dispassionately so as to draw reasoned conclusions." He smiled drily at them all. "I only say this because, from next week on, I shall no longer be around to help you resolve your differences. You'll all have to learn to manage without me, I'm afraid. I'll be moving into my own set of chambers in Helston."

"Frank!" Jessie and Cressida cried in unison.

"I say, really?" Harry asked, grinning broadly.

Frank nodded and went on staring at his father, who merely said, "How?"

The son sighed. "To be honest, Dad, I've reached that point in my own advancement where I feel it would be more appropriate if the world — or West Penwith, at least — were to see me in a slightly more independent light."

It was a plain hint that his father's commercial ventures were of such a dubious nature as to threaten his own business as a lawyer; but, since it was merely a hint, and phrased in such an oblique manner, too, his father could not respond to that hidden rebuke. "Suit yourself," he said gruffly.

"I'm afraid I have to," Frank replied evenly. "I did what I have just recommended you to do — I spread out my assets, examined them calmly ..."

"Yes, yes!" Barney waved away the unwelcome repetition.

"What *are* our assets, then?" Jessie dared to ask.

"You, mainly," he replied.

"That's enough now!" Barney told him.

Frank stared at him evenly for a moment and then said, "How high would you mark Harry as a book-keeper, Dad? What sort of score would you give him out of ten?"

Barney sniffed, sensing a trap. For among the wisdom Frank had passed on since taking up the law was the maxim: 'Never ask a direct question in evidence unless you're sure the answer will be in your favour.' He glanced unwillingly at Harry and mumbled, "Last year — nil! But you should see the improvement he's made lately. I'd give him seven or eight out of ten now. So put that in your pipe and smoke it!"

He rose when Frank drew breath to respond and said, "I think we'll retire to the drawing room. The servants will want to be off."

If he hoped to disrupt Frank's argument he was disappointed, for as soon as they had settled with their coffee — in the small demi-tasses that Cressida had introduced a couple of years ago — he continued, "And would you relate Harry's improvement as a book-keeper to the intense coaching he has been receiving from dear Jessie?"

"Frank!" This time Jessie almost screamed.

A stunned Barney glanced rapidly from her to his eldest son, who was trying with little success to suppress a mawkish grin.

"Didn't you realize?" Frank asked innocently. "Oh, come! You didn't honestly suppose that this great, amiable lump of humanity" — he punched his brother playfully — "could raise the slightest flicker of interest in anything other than 'the humanities,' as they call them?"

Barney set down his cup carefully before he asked, with ominous calm, "Is that the truth, Harry? Has that maid been a-helping of 'ee?"

"You had no right to say such a thing!" an anguished Jessie shouted at Frank.

"She's pointed out one or two ..." Harry admitted before yielding to Frank, who was saying, "On the contrary, my dear sister, I believe I have every right to reveal the truth of what's going on in this household. After all, it is the constant humbug and hypocrisy — the dissembling and the prevarication — that have combined to drive me out of it."

"I'd have twigged it all myself, given time," Harry offered. "But Frank's right. I have no natural aptitude for ..."

"Natural aptitude!" Barney echoed contemptuously. "There's no such thing. You're a Kernow, aren't 'ee? You're my eldest boy." He wagged a finger in his son's face. "Your only natural aptitude is laziness. You'd 'twig it yourself in time,' would you! Well, let me put you on notice, boy — the time is *now!* D'you follow?"

The rest of his homily was interrupted by a light but despairing laugh from Frank, who turned to Cressida and said, "One is taught to believe that this sort of thing only ever happens in Greek tragedy — the grand old patriarch brought down in ruin by his own noble defects of character, especially his inability to see what is plain to all the world. Can't *you* talk sensibly to him, Miss Pym? You know very well what I mean, I'm sure."

The wagging finger moved in his direction. "And as for you, boy — you can go to your 'set of chambers' now — this night — for all I care." He repeated his son's grandiose phrase with a muttered contempt: "Set of chambers! A back room with lino on the floor in some cheap digs down Five Wells Lane, I shouldn't wonder!"

"Actually," Frank told him, "I have taken a rather elegant suite of rooms in the de Lisles' house in Cross Street. Lovely garden. I'd hardly do better in Albany."

"Next to Miss Grylls?" Jessie asked excitedly. "You're practically across the road from Liston Court. Now you'll have no excuse to stay out of the chorus!"

"Just a minute — if you please!" Barney sought to re-establish his authority. "This young ..." He hesitated.

"Whelp?" Frank offered. "Whipper-snapper?"

"*You!*" his father exclaimed. "You have leveled a serious accusation against your brother."

"Me?" Frank responded.

"It's as good as saying he cheated in an examination."

A broad smile spread on the young man's face. "Oh, Father! Don't you realize what you've just admitted?"

Barney licked his lips nervously. "I know full well what I ..."

"When one cheats in an exam one takes the answer not from one's own repertoire of knowledge or skill but from some fountainhead of the stuff — some generally accepted authority. If you say Harry cheated, then ..."

"Not me!" Barney pointed out triumphantly. "'Twas you! You said he cheated."

"Did I?" Frank's smile did not waver. "I think I merely said that whatever correct assessments he gave you, he got them from Jessie. It

was *you* who interpreted that as cheating — which, as I pointed out —
is like saying Jessie is the acknowledged authority!"

Trapped, Barney merely stared at his son and breathed furiously
through his nostrils.

Frank knocked home the final nail: "You'd hardly have accused
him of cheating if he'd consulted Clarrie now, would you!"

"Confounded lawyers!" his father mumbled. "You can twist a
man's words to mean anything you want."

Frank spread his hands in a gesture of appeasement, like a priest
offering benisons. "I'm honestly not trying to score any points at all. I
merely wish to show you that — in your innermost heart — you
already know what I've been driving at, Dad. You already know
where the *real* commercial brains in this family lie. You already know
that to try and make Harry fit into Kernow's Farm Machinery — to
make it Kernow and *Son* — is as impossible as fitting the piston off a
Marshall into the cylinder of a Wallace and Stevens. They're just not
made for each other."

"Have a care, boy!" the old man warned. "Are you saying that a son
of Barney Kernow can't be anything he wishes to be? Isn't that the
way I brought you up? Isn't that our motto — *Quod volo sum!* — 'What
I wish, I am!' Are you saying my eldest boy, the firstborn brother,
couldn't be what I wish him to be — if he wasn't so bone idle?"

"*Quod volat sum!*" Harry murmured, adding a translation for his
father's sake, whose little Latin was all by rote: "What *he* wishes, I am!"

"I think we should speak of other things," Cressida put in. "Frank
may give himself the airs of a detached outsider, but I'm more qualified
than any of you for that rôle, I believe, and what I say is ..."

Whatever she had in mind, she got no further for Barney had the bit
between his teeth by now and was not going to drop the subject for
anyone. "I hold that any man can make anything he likes of himself.
Your grandad wasn't but a village blacksmith when he was your age."
His gaze took in both his elder sons. "Yet he owned a good bit of Saint
John's before he handed over to me. And you all know what I've done
with that inheritance. So now are you telling me that if that great
amiable lump of humanity, as you call him, wanted — really wanted
— he couldn't take it as far again — what with all his fine education?"

"Yes."

Barney, who had expected a long lawyer's ramble, was taken aback.
"What do 'ee mean — yes?"

"I mean yes, he couldn't — no matter how desperately he wanted
to. Just as" — he turned to Jessie with a smile — "I couldn't sing two

notes in tune, not if you were to offer me a million pounds. It isn't in him. And that's the choice you're having to face, Dad. You can put up the nameplate Kernow and Son — and watch the firm mark time. Or Kernow and Daughter — and watch with pride while that one takes the business as far beyond your reach as you took it beyond Grandad's. Justifiable pride, too, I'd say."

"Frank!" Jessie whispered, touching his arm as if she doubted he was really there.

"Viper!" Barney shouted at him. "Go to your room. And that do go for all of 'ee! Go to your rooms. It's a good thing you've found a place of your own — else I'd turn 'ee out for this impertinence."

They hesitated until his repeated cries of "Out! Out I say!" assured them he meant it. Then they set down their cups with dignity and made for the door. "Anyway, as I was saying," Harry remarked as they crossed the room, "the operatic form inevitably vulgarizes and coarsens the story."

"Out!" Barney continued to shout after them, even after they had made their exit.

And Harry continued calmly, too, while his siblings grinned and gave him free rein: "In Verga's original play Santuzza does *not* return at the finale. She's not simply a passionate but foolish girl who's been dishonoured — which is all the opera makes of her — she's also a wicked, scheming temptress who brings about her lover's death by exposing Lola's adultery to Alfio. It's much darker, you see — and much too strong for the shallow sentimentalists who keep breathing life into the alleged 'art' of the opera."

"Lovely tunes, though!" Jessie laughed and began to sing *Tu qui, Santuzza?* with operatic exaggeration as they ascended the stairs.

"Don't push him too far," Frank warned her, tilting his head in the direction of the drawing room.

She stopped. "What got into *you*, suddenly?" she asked. She was all at once aware that the atmosphere between them was unusually warm and loving; they had not felt so close for years — not that they were quarrelsome as a rule, but they could not have denied that a certain go-it-alone individualism had long been their chief characteristic.

"It seemed the right moment for home truths," he said.

They reached the landing, where none showed the slightest inclination to part. Jessie opened her door, which was the nearest, and the two brothers needed no more than the jerk of her head to follow her. Frank pulled out a packet of 'gaspers' and, murmuring, "In for a penny ..." offered them round.

Jessie, who had not smoked since she was thirteen, and had been made thoroughly sick by it then, took one hesitantly. She watched how her brothers lit up, drew on the glowing tubes, and breathed deeply of the smoke; she liked Harry's technique better, for he let the smoke escape slowly from his mouth and drew it back in by way of his nostrils. The merest attempt to imitate Frank and inhale it all at once brought on a fit of coughing.

"D'you suppose it'll do any good?" Harry asked in a tone that expected a negative. "Those home truths?"

"In time — who knows?" Frank replied. "It's like the dripping water that wears away the stone."

"Kernow and Daughter," Jessie mused. "D'you really think ... you know?" Even now she could not put it into words.

Frank grinned accusingly at her. "Don't pretend you haven't thought of it!" He turned to his brother and added, "Nor you! I'll bet it's crossed your mind, too."

Harry's nod confirmed it but Jessie said, "No. Honestly not that."

"But ...?" Frank prompted.

"Well, I have thought from time to time that it's jolly unfair. Why *can't* a woman take up business? I don't mean widows and people who *have* to. I mean why can't it be a proper choice, instead of marriage, you know?" She laughed awkwardly. "It's funny. I've been talking about this a bit with Cornwallis. Has he mentioned it to either of you?"

Their denials were genuine, and she saw it, too.

"What's his view?" Frank asked.

Looking back later on that conversation Jessie realized that the question might equally well have come from Harry. But because Frank had asked it, and because his altruistic outburst that evening was still too recent to overcome her almost lifelong assessment of him as the cool, calculating, self-interested, and ultimately untrustworthy one among her trio of brothers, she withheld the truth from them both. Had Harry asked it instead, she might very well have told them all. Instead, she said, rather more vaguely, "He thinks people should simply go ahead and do whatever they truly want."

"Well, *he* certainly practises what he preaches," Frank replied. "Have you told him what it might be in your particular case?"

She realized then why he was regarded as such a good courtroom lawyer; he carved each slice to the bone. And, as so many of his victims had done before her, she panicked mildly and said the first thing that came into her head: "Electricity."

In that entire evening of stunning revelations, this took the *palme d'or*. The brothers stared at each other, then at her, then at each other again. "Eh?" Harry said.

Jessie, having had a second or two to think it over, decided not to turn it into a joke but to brazen it out. "Electricity — you know! Crackle, crackle! The Kernows gave Helston its gas supply. Why not its electricity supply, too?"

It nipped in the bud any tendency to mock her ambitions — once the initial shock of their revelation started to recede.

"That's a very good question," Harry said, turning to his brother.

"Dad's right," Frank murmured. "It must be in the blood. He's wrong about *whose* blood, mind. It ought to be yours." He nodded at Harry. "But" — turning to his sister — "it's certainly in yours!"

Harry suddenly burst out with: "Is *that* why Trelawney's installing this electric plant up at Wheal Dream? For you to practise on!"

She thought she concealed her surprise at this news rather well. "Oh, it's come at last, has it?" she asked.

Harry nodded. "He was uncrating it today. Second-hand. It's the one that burned down Pallas House about six years ago, so it comes with an excellent pedigree!"

The hair bristled on Jessie's neck. Where the idea of *electricity* as a business came from she had no idea. It had never crossed her mind before. Now, though it was still barely a minute old, it already carried the oddest sort of credibility for her — a sense of rightness that few other notions had ever achieved in her restless and rarely satisfied mind. And now this news that Cornwallis — who had never said the word 'electricity' to her, nor she to him, as far as she could recall — was actually installing a domestic plant up at Wheal Dream ... it was incredible. If ever there was an omen, this was surely it!

"I'll amble up and start playing with it tomorrow," she said. "From little oaks, mighty acorns grow!"

*T*here is an old Chinese legend about a single raindrop that fell on the very highest peak of the Tanghla Mountains in Tibet, one day when the world was young and easily scarred. There on that knife-edge it split into two half-drops, one on the northern side, one on the southern. Each, in its brief moment of life before it evaporated in that high, dry air, dislodged a grain of sand.

But the southern drop, being on the side that was warmed by the sun, evaporated first and so the grain was displaced less than the one on the less hospitable northern face. And so it was that the next drop which fell found a slightly longer run toward the harsh, inhospitable deserts of the north than to the warm, sun-secured south — and so it was able to dislodge two grains of sand on that side; and the next drop managed four; the next, eight ... and so on for each of the myriad drops that followed. And that is why today the mighty Yangtse River flows northward from the Tanghla. But if that first drop had fallen at midnight when conditions to the north and south were equal ... who knows? The Yangtse might now be entirely swallowed up in the Bramahputra. So at least runs the legend.

As a piece of geographical history it may well be somewhat shaky, but as a pointer to human affairs it has a certain power to illuminate. For every enterprise is, in its earliest moments, vulnerable to the tiniest influence — little buffetings that, in some later, more robust phase, would not even be noticed.

And so it was with Jessie and her impromptu scheme to continue the family tradition by serving Helston with electricity as her grandfather had done with the gas undertaking. It had slipped her mind when she awoke the following morning; all that remained was a sense that something earthshaking had taken place the previous evening. She felt herself enveloped in a sort of aura of novelty. This day, she just knew, was not going to be like any other; it was destined to bring something of vast importance into her life. But what? She felt the beginnings of panic stirring within her. How could she be so sure of this feeling of greatness — no, of grandeur — and yet know nothing of its source?

She remembered an argument — no, an 'animated discussion' — last night, but there was nothing unusual in that; they were one of those families that thrived on the clash of strong wills. But this was more than the usual ... oh yes — Frank had told them he was leaving — going to set up — a 'set of chambers' — yes — and Dad had sneered that it was just a back-room down Five Wells Lane ... yes!

Bit by bit the fragments returned, until her conversation with Harry and Frank on the upstairs landing returned in a rush.

And at last she recalled how she had flung out the word 'electricity' ... and *her brothers had not laughed!*

That small, seemingly insignificant omission was enough to roll some metaphorical grain of sand in her mind a little farther toward the harsh, inhospitable world of commerce rather than to the warm, secure world of female domesticity. *They had not laughed!* They took her seriously. She sang as she rose and dressed for breakfast.

Further omissions from her two elder brothers did more to assist her purpose — for neither of them spoke of it at the table that morning, either. It would have been so easy to have had second thoughts, to see her notion as one of those late-night ideas thrown out in a fit of bravado but quite unable to stand up to the cold light of the following day. How mercilessly they could have pulled her leg if they had meanwhile revised their judgement! So their silence was equivalent to the second drop of water in the sequence that, so legend claimed, had eventually carved out the Yangtse Kiang — it made the next step easier still.

And that next step, for Jessie, was to spend the morning with a piece of embroidery ready to hand — in case Cressida should surprise her — while she read through Godfrey's *Physics for the Fifth Form,* by F.A. Fisher, A.M.Inst.E.E. — especially the section on dynamos and motors. She wanted to be able to make intelligent noises when she approached the generating set Cornwallis had bought from the old Pallas Estate. And actually, the more she read on the subject, the more she was amazed to find how much sense it all made — how the ideas clustered logically together, and how simply one notion led to another. It was so neat, so elegant.

This was such a wonderful discovery that she wanted to tell someone about it at once. She considered passing on her discovery to Cressida, who had always fought shy of teaching her any science; chemistry made unpleasant smells, she used to say, while physics dealt with powerful and dangerous forces, and as for biology ... well, much of it was quite unsuitable for young ladies. But it was Clarrie who had the misfortune to enter the room — and thus the firing line — first. Jessie could not resist the chance. "D'you know, Clarrie, here's the most amazing thing. If you move a bit of copper wire between the north and south poles of a magnet, you make an electric current flow along it? Along the wire, that is."

"I'm sure, Miss." The maid eyed her warily.

"That's all there is to it!" Jessie continued in the same eager vein. "And if you move the wire in one direction, the current flows toward one end of the wire. But if you move it in the opposite direction, the flow is also reversed. Isn't that amazingly simple!"

"Indeed, Miss." Clarrie chewed her lips uncertainly. "Miss Pym said I was to take the antimacassars down for washing if they need it. D'you think they do?"

"The point is, you may look at the most complicated generator in the world and be absolutely sure that those two simple principles were working away at the heart of it!"

"My gidge! I think I'll take them, just to be on the safe side." She gathered the linen and fled.

Jessie, heartened to discover that even Clarrie, distracted as she was by her duties, could grasp those simple precepts, returned to her studies; she was still not quite sure of the difference between volts and amps. And in the corner of her eye she had seen mention of 'joules' and 'coulombs' and 'gauss'; there was clearly some way to go.

But by lunchtime she felt she had mastered the rudiments to the point where she could make at least one or two intelligent comments about Cornwallis's new toy. Besides, she had enough loose theory swilling around in her mind. Before she added any more she wanted to anchor it all in something she could touch and explore. So, after lunch — and somewhat to Cressida's surprise — she suggested a walk over Trelavour Hill to Wheal Dream; until now Jessie had been reluctant to take Cressida on her visits in case her sharp senses twigged that there was far more friendship than romance in the air — indeed, there was no romance at all.

As they strolled across the fields in the crisp March air, Jessie wondered why she had broken the unwritten rule on this occasion. The premonition that this would prove to be an important day in her life had not waned, so perhaps it was all tied in with that — perhaps she required a witness with more standing than Clarrie or Becky, her usual chaperons on visits to Wheal Dream?

They spoke at last of the 'warm discussion' of the previous evening, a topic that had conspicuously failed to arise at breakfast that morning.

"D'you suppose Frank is in earnest?" Cressida asked.

"You know him!" Jessie replied. "He'd let the ink dry a couple of weeks on his lease before he even dropped a hint about a thing like that. Oh yes — the first fledgeling will soon flee the nest, all right."

Cressida took her arm briefly, ostensibly to steady herself over a patch of pockmarked turf. "And I wonder who will be the second to take wing?" she asked coyly.

"That will surely depend on how tight its wings are clipped," Jessie replied.

Naturally Cressida took this personally. "Do you think *yours* are clipped too hard?" she retorted. "In my view you are given a great deal of freedom — certainly more than young girls were accorded in my day."

"Hah!" Jessie raised her face to the sky and gave a scornful laugh. "How old are you, Cressida?" she asked. " 'In my day' — for heaven's sake! You'll talk yourself into a premature grave if you go on like that. Can't you see that I'm the late morning and you're no more than the early afternoon of one and the *same* day?"

"You may think so," she replied coldly.

But, Jessie noticed, it was not the coldness of the one-time governess, the disciplinarian who had to lay down the law in black and white; rather it was the chill of despair, of one who now glimpses a farther boundary to what had once been an infinity of days, and opportunities grow sparse that were once like the daisies in this pasture they were now traversing. It moved her to a certain compassion. "I do think so," she said in a much gentler tone. "And I do so wish you could think so, too. You frighten me when you try to make yourself out like that."

"Like what?"

"Like a grandmother to me. Heavens!" She laughed. "You'd think it'd be harder for the ex-pupil to feel kinship with her mentor than the other way about. If I can feel more of a friend to you than a ... what's the word? Not menial — someone under tutelage? Tutel-ee? Is there such a word?"

"Certainly not menial!"

"Anyway, you know what I mean. If I can feel more of a friend to you than *that*, surely you should find it easy, too?"

Cressida took her arm again and hugged tight; this time there was no uneven ground by way of excuse. Jessie looked at her and saw with surprise that her eyes were rather watery; she turned swiftly away, embarrassed that her words should have produced such an effect.

Cressida swallowed hard and said. "Is that what you want, dear? Who will guide you, then?"

Answers occurred to Jessie at once but she let them rest awhile so as to ease their mutual embarrassment. Then, when she did at last speak, it was to give an answer that had not occurred to her in that first flush. "If you have not already given me the grounding to navigate my own way from now on, then it's too late, don't you think?"

Now it was the older woman's turn to keep silent awhile. Then, calm and collected once more, she said, "I hope it's *not* too late — and yet I fear we ... that is, *I*, have failed to give you *all* the maps you might need. A compass, yes, and all the large-scale charts of the major oceans. But there are shoals and reefs where many an innocent vessel has come to grief ... and I fear I have not charted them sufficiently well for you."

Suddenly Jessie's heart began to pound. She had no very clear idea what Cressida might mean and yet she knew very well what it was about. She was referring to ... well, to those things that made biology an unsuitable science for young ladies.

The whole business was quite ridiculous in a way. Fenella Compton had told her years ago how men and women make babies — or did *It*, in Fenella's words. As a child she had bathed naked often enough with her brothers, so she knew very well the difference between them. She had seen bulls and cows in the fields and dogs and bitches in the streets, so, unlike her knowledge of electricity, it was not a flotsam of theory with no clear image to anchor upon. So, by plucking gossip and observation from here and there and putting it all together, she *knew* practically all that Cressida might tell her on the subject; and in the private calm of her own mind she could consider it — or It — in a serene, unflustered manner. Yet the very thought that Cressida might now start *talking* about It out loud was enough to make her heart flutter and her knees turn to jelly! If that wasn't ridiculous, what was?

She had come so often to this point, not just with Cressida Pym but with Harry, too, and always she had shied away from it in this frightened, girlish fashion. Now, suddenly, because this was earmarked already as a portentous day in her life, she took a deep breath and forced herself to say, "I think I know what you're talking about, Cressida. And, if it's any comfort to you, I believe I know more about it than you might suppose."

"Ah ..." Cressida was taken aback. So often she had wondered how this dreadful duty was to be accomplished; in her imagination she had held this conversation in a dozen different forms yet never had it started like that. In one mortified outburst Jessie had set all those hours of careful preparation at naught. "Er, how ... may I ask ... that is ..." she floundered.

"Well, what I mean is I know *nothing!*" Jessie exclaimed almost angrily. "I know the facts but they mean nothing."

Cressida was surprised to find herself suddenly relieved. The *facts* of the matter had been her chief anxiety — the need to use all those unpleasant words and so on. But the *meaning* was something she felt much more qualified to speak about. However, as Wheal Dream was by now a mere furlong or so away, and as the subject had much in common with crossing Niagara Gorge on a tightrope — that is, one could not break off half way and do something else for a while — she said, "Let us conclude our visit to Mister Trelawney as soon as politeness allows, my dear, and then I think I may tell you at our ease on the way back what I understand of the *meaning* of this thorny and difficult subject for a woman."

If Jessie had not spent all morning studying electricity, and if she had not been able to hear the exciting rumble of the generating engine already running, she would have suggested turning back on the spot; for, having screwed her courage to the sticking post, she did not want it to snap on account of being held there too long. "Very well," she said, stepping out eagerly. "We'll just say hallo and thank you very much but we can't stop today."

However, as they drew nearer the former stable where the set had been installed, it soon became clear that all was not well. It did not need a loud cry of, "Hell and damnation!" to confirm it. The two women exchanged glances and got their smiling over and done with before, straight-faced again, they leaned over the stile at the top end of the old farmyard and shouted, "Coo-ee! I say, anyone at home?"

A doubly red-faced Cornwallis appeared at the side window. "My profoundest apologies, ladies!" he called out. "If you heard, that is. But just come and look at the provocation I'm having and you'll forgive me entirely, I'm sure."

They helped each other over the stile and picked their way cautiously down the side of the old stables until they stood hesitating on the threshold, peering in and letting their sight grow accustomed to the interior gloom.

"It sounds sweet enough," Jessie said. She sniffed deeply, relishing the fumes of burned petrol and hot oil.

"Oh yes," Cornwallis agreed. "The motor's fine — now. It took all morning to get her running but she's sweet now."

"What's wrong then, Mister Trelawney?" Cressida asked.

"Just watch!"

He put his hand to a switch — a large ebony knob connected to what looked like two knife blades — and swung it gingerly down until the blades sank into the springy embrace of two metal jaws. The engine laboured for a second or two, then there was a bright flash from a device beside the ebony switch handle, followed by a puff of smoke, and then the engine raced again before the governor cut in and throttled it back to a quiet, even purr.

"She charged the accumulators perfectly for about a minute," he complained, "and then she tripped out — just like that." He pointed to a vast bank of electrical cells. "They were all fully discharged when they came — naturally. They can't *possibly* have recharged in a single minute. I don't understand it."

Jessie was the first to venture into that temple of a new age. As her eyes naturalized to the dim light and each new feature of the generating set became clear her heart sank to her boots. It was vastly more complex than she had feared — and so big and busy and dangerous-looking, too. Where were the north and south poles of the magnet? Where was the simple bit of copper wire? She stared in dismay at the array of cables, levers, taps, gauges, dials, coils, and switches — not one of which bore the slightest relationship to anything she had learned that morning.

But wait! One of the gauges said *Volts*. And another said *Ampères*. At least the ocean of her ignorance had two little islands with familiar names. She bent and peered more closely at the dials; both needles registered zero, of course. The volt dial went up to a hundred and twenty-five; the ampères to no more than ten.

"What?" Cornwallis asked hopefully. "Have you spotted something wrong with it?"

Cressida, thinking he was joking, laughed a tinkling giggle and said, "Really, Mister Trelawney! As if *we* might notice something that has escaped *your* notice!"

"A hundred and twenty-five volts," Jessie said. Then, drawing a bow at a venture: "How high did it register before it trapped out?"

"Tripped out."

"Yes."

Cressida repeated her giggle. "Really, Jessie, dear — don't be such a tease to the poor man!"

But Cornwallis took the question seriously. He had been so astonished by the violence of the trip on the first occasion — and so fearful of its discharge on all subsequent ones — that he had paid scant attention to the behaviour of the two gauges. "Out of the mouths of babes and sucklings, eh!" he said. "D'you know, I didn't think to look."

"Can you do it again?" she asked. "You throw the switch and watch the ampères and I'll keep an eye on the volts."

"I say!" He leaned forward so as to look her in the eye. "Are you pulling my leg or do you really know something about it?"

Unwilling to admit that the latter was truer than the former, she just tapped her forehead and said, "Let's find out."

For once Cressida said nothing; she merely stood and watched in baffled amazement.

He said, "One, two, three — now!" and threw the switch. Again the engine strained for a second, then the trip cut out with an even brighter flash than before. The reek of electric sparks — or rather of vaporized copper — filled their nostrils. Cressida jumped back with a little shriek but Jessie was proud she had stood her ground without flinching one bit.

"The volts hardly moved," she said.

He touched the glass above the pin beyond the figure ten on his gauge. "The needle hit this fellow with a thwack and tried to push it over until the trip cut out," he told her. Then he frowned. "Why is there such a huge current when there's hardly any voltage?" He peered into the whirring mass of machinery. "Has somebody connected something wrong? I didn't touch anything in there — that's just how it came."

"That must be what caused the fire at Pallas House," Cressida said confidently.

"What *did* you connect?" Jessie asked.

"Only the accumulators." He pointed at a large array of wet cells against the opposite wall.

A vague memory stirred in the back of Jessie's mind — vague because it was in a part of the textbook she had not studied that morning, merely glanced through. Something about accumulators ... different ways of connecting them. There was a picture showing it. A couple of three-volt cells. You could connect them one way and have six volts or another way and still have only three volts but the charge would last twice as long. That was logical and elegant, too — which was why she remembered it.

But what were the connecting systems called? Parallax and something? No, parallax was about how stars move.

Parallel! That was it!

Before her courage could desert her she said, "Did you connect them in parallel?" She kept the tone of her question neutral because she wasn't sure whether that method was right or wrong. Also because if she hinted he'd done wrong, he might ask her about it — and she couldn't for the life of her remember the name of the other method of connecting the things.

"Yes," he said. "Of course ..." His voice trailed off and he bit his lip. Then his frown changed to a grin and he pulled a playful punch on her arm — which surprised Cressida even more than the fact that Jessie had asked an intelligent question about something she had never seen in her life before. "You absolute genius!" he crowed. "Of course! They just soak up all the current this poor old girl can push into them. No wonder she keeps tripping out — wouldn't you?"

Jessie laughed. "Naturally. I'd switch off and rewire the whole lot if I were you."

He reached out and raised the exhaust lift on the motor. She coughed and died over about six revolutions. The silence that followed was profound, broken only by the ping of the red-hot exhaust as it cooled and the mewing of the water in the radiator circuit. "Miss Pym," he said. "I don't know what your educational system was, but you have produced a second Michael Faraday here!"

Cressida smiled modestly, hoping to imply that she had expected nothing less of her former pupil.

The word for the other connecting-up system came to Jessie then, as sought-for words often did, once her urgent need to recall them had passed "You'll rewire them in *series*, of course," she said.

He laughed with relief. "Thank you. For an awful moment I thought you'd ask me the opposite to parallel — and I couldn't find the word. Why not don overalls and help?"

Jessie looked at Cressida. "It'd be rather fun, wouldn't it?"

The other waved dismissively. "You put on a smock by all means. I'll go and make a pot of tea." She could not imagine a world in which the word 'series' was an opposite to the word 'parallel,' but she did not wish to display her ignorance, especially when her encyclopædic grasp of these matters had only just been singled out for praise.

"There's a bag of scones on the draining board and a pan of clotted cream on the hob," he called after her. "And damson jam in the larder." Under his breath to Jessie he added, "I hope." He tied the strings of her smock behind her while she rolled up her sleeves.

"Careful not to get any acid on your skin," he warned her. "If you do, dip it in that pail there — that's clean rainwater."

He gave her a spanner like his own and they approached the banks of accumulators gingerly. He hung back more than she, saying, "Let me see, now ... I'm not quite sure about all this. If this is parallel, how does series go?"

She knew him well enough by now to know he was teasing her — or testing-teasing her. But, having half-bluffed her way thus far she wasn't going to give up now. So, assuming an air of nonchalant confidence, she bent over the accumulators and tried to make head or tail of what looked like a spaghetti of heavy cables. Each accumulator had a couple of studs sticking up, she noticed. A moment later she found herself on very familiar territory — familiar since that morning, anyway — for one stud was engraved with a plus sign and the other with a minus.

"Positive ... negative," she said judiciously.

"Ah," he replied — and continued to hold back.

It did not take her long to notice that the cables connected all the positives together on one side and all the negatives on the other. *Parallel,* of course! That's what it meant. She only just managed to suppress a tell-tale cry of triumph at the discovery. The real world and the world of theory *did* match up perfectly if you only looked for it diligently enough!

From then on it was downhill all the way. She slipped her spanner round one of the nuts and said, "It'll be easiest to remove them all first, I think."

"And then?"

She turned to him with a sigh of exasperation. "Then we connect the positive of the first cell to the negative of the second, and the positive of the second to the negative of the third ... and so on all the way down. Really, Cornwallis! People like you shouldn't be allowed near delicate machinery like this. Don't you realize you could have wrecked it?"

*T*he electric lighting extended Cornwallis's working day by so many hours that, toward the end of March, he had all the roof trusses in place and half the slating battens fixed, too. Passing workmen no longer proffered jocund advice about not sneezing in case it all fell down; and John Tregembo, the Nance-gollan carpenter, who had come to sneer, or at least to shake his head sadly, was impressed enough with the work to offer Cornwallis a handy tip about how to sink the bearing boards for the valley leads. The no-longer-quite-so-eligible bachelor felt he had arrived.

The drop in his eligibility was directly related to his self-abasement to the status of building labourer, of course. Few mothers with unattached daughters of nubile age could believe that a gentleman would willingly undertake such work. "He must be doing it to save money," they told each other — and blessed the sixth sense that had led them not to thrust their darlings too prominently into his field of view. The Kernow girl was welcome to him as far as they were concerned. Their opinion of hard work was the only opinion they shared with the Communists: If it was really so good for one, the rich would keep it all for themselves.

These developments, in turn, removed the pressure on Cornwallis to become 'engaged' to Jessie in the conspiracy he had earlier proposed. Unfortunately, however, the very opposite was true of her. The more time she spent in his company — even though she was scrupulously chaperoned by Cressida or one of the maids, and at weekends by Godfrey — the greater was the pressure upon her to announce a formal engagement. The frustrations grew throughout March and early April; nor did it help that rehearsals for 'Cav rust' were at their most hectic.

Michael Vestey, the producer, was of the avant garde when it came to the staging of operas. Until the eighteen-nineties 'grand' opera had always dealt in aristocrats. Even those with low-life themes, like *La Traviata*, were dripping with marquises and barons. Operas about common people were invariably comic. There were thus only two acting styles for the singers: oafish buffoonery for comic opera and courtly bel-canto for the grand stuff. But the new 'truth' operas like CR, which showed the dramas of ordinary peasants with all the passion and seriousness that had until then been reserved for the aristocracy, demanded a new style of acting — the 'truth' style.

As far as Vestey was concerned this 'truth' involved a great deal of eye-rolling. And heavenward-stretching of the arms. And clutchings at the heart. And the running of distraught fingers through the wig. And there were the vocal equivalents of these passionate extremes, too — cries, oaths, sobs, and whimpers — all of which were to be delivered bang on whatever note the score indicated. To whimper in C-sharp while a partner howls with rage in F is a skill that does not come easily even to professionals. So, though the rehearsals themselves did not live up to Vestey's ideals in 'truth' acting, the private comments that followed them most certainly did — in the whimpering and howling-with-rage departments at least.

What with one thing and another, then, it was not the most satisfactory period in Jessie's life. One feature alone made the stresses bearable. Since her initial triumph with the generating set she had become its keeper. She wrote to Ransome's, the original manufacturer, and got a copy of the maintenance manual to replace the one that had been lost in the Pallas fire. Cressida knew of it but Jessie forgot to mention the fact to her brothers and Cornwallis, whom she was soon able to astound still further with her uncanny understanding of engineering mysteries.

In normal circumstances she would have felt a little ashamed at taking such undue credit but she soothed her conscience with the knowledge that *she* didn't consider herself any kind of a genius. Any man would take the work in his stride if only he had the manual, too; so she set herself no higher than that. But she also knew that if she revealed the secret of her surprising knowledge to the men, they'd immediately pooh-pooh any skill she might show. And that was not mere guesswork; once, when she had cooked a particularly difficult soufflé to prove to her father that she was not neglecting her domestic and feminine duties, only Cressida had truly complimented her upon it. The others had damned with faint praise and Godfrey had voiced the general opinion by saying that cooking involved very little skill, really — all you needed to do was buy good ingredients and follow the recipe.

So her seemingly uncanny skill at coaxing the best out of the generating set at Wheal Dream, and the genuine praise she received from Cornwallis and Godfrey, among others, was the one cheery element in a life of increasing pressure and frustration. It came to a head in the week before Easter, on the afternoon of Ash Wednesday.

Godfrey, whose school had gone down for the hols, accompanied her up the lane to Wheal Dream and helped her adjust the belt between the motor and generator — a tricky job involving a very slight realignment of the flywheel. That, in turn, involved fiddling with 'shims' and 'splines' and such-like, none of which she had ever heard of before that day. But she had spent the morning reading the manual and practising it all in her head so that, when she came to the machine itself, she wielded the calipers and tapped the splines with a certain calm nonchalance — and even managed to suppress her amazement that it actually produced the required (one could not honestly say 'expected') result.

Godfrey watched her with amazement for, though he had heard of her mystical way with the machinery, this was the first time he had seen it for himself.

"How d'you know those things, Sis?" he asked. "I wouldn't have the first idea where to start."

She gave a modest shrug. "Remember we used to watch old Baker taking the steam engines apart and mending them? And how he'd let us help if he was in a good mood?"

"But that was years ago."

"I suppose something of it must have filtered down through the brain cogs and stuck to them on the way. Anyway, it's all very logical. There's no magic in machinery. It's not like *cooking* — which really *does* call for a bit of art and magic."

She produced these comments with a certain sarcasm but it was entirely wasted on him; he had even forgotten making his derogatory remark that time.

"Take your word for it," he said. "I'm sure I couldn't make head or tail of all this!" He waved a hand at the bewildering intricacies before him. "What's that, for instance?"

"The trip. It measures ..."

"Last trip round the lighthouse, eh!" He interrupted her with a laugh, so as to cut short any solemn tutorial.

But she was determined to make him see her point and so pressed doggedly on. At first he just stood there, miming a village idiot with his jaw open and his eyes rolling all over the place. Bit by bit, however, her words penetrated and began to make sense and he stopped his clowning and listened; and then, to his further amazement, he found he actually understood not only how the trip worked but why it had to be there at all — and what a terrible stink of sulphur there'd be if it ever broke down.

"What are you going to *do* with all this knowledge, then?" he asked when she had convinced him. "I know! You could mend people's cars. Doctor Watts made an awful hash of doing up his. They say his back wheel came off and raced him down Sithney Common Hill last week." He laughed. "I'd love to have seen it."

"You wouldn't!" she assured him. "Tom Roberts was carrying the red flag in front of him and he said it was the most frightening thing he ever saw. Anyway" — she eyed him suspiciously — "haven't Harry and Frank told you?"

"Told me what?"

She knew him well enough to distinguish his true innocence from the put-on variety; her elder brothers really had kept her secret ambition to themselves — probably because they thought it would come to nothing and they'd only look like fools if they openly supported her. Briefly she wondered whether to let Godfrey in on it, but the heady wine of his admiration was too sweet to let her abstain from a further sip.

She started the engine and left it to run until the trip cut out. On their way down to the farmhouse she wiped the protective goosegrease from her hands and broke the news to him — far more cautiously than she had blurted it out to Frank and Harry. She began by reminding him how their grandfather had exchanged an acre of land for shares in the gas company and had then gone on to become its leading promoter and most dynamic director — and incidentally to lay the foundations of the family's prosperity. Then she pointed out how many Helston businesses — and even a few private houses — had installed their own lighting sets in the past few years, to the extent that the town positively hummed as darkness fell, and the reek of petrol exhausts now vied with coal and wood smoke on a winter's eve.

He saw the point before she needed to make it. "So what Grandpa did with gas, you're going to do with electricity!" He clapped his hands and laughed. "What does Dad think? I bet he'll try to steal the idea from you!"

She put a finger over his lips and said, "For heaven's sake, Godfrey! Don't you dare breathe a *word* to him about this. Nor to anyone else, either. Particularly Cressida!"

"Nor to me?" Cornwallis came into the kitchen.

Jessie realized that his eternal hammering had ceased a minute or two ago; only now, however, did its significance occur to her.

Godfrey stared uncertainly from one to the other.

Cornwallis went on: "Secrets against a man in his own house, eh? The manners of young people these days! Any chance of a cup of tea? I've a poor assistant dying of thirst up there."

Jessie gave her brother a guarded nod. "You can tell him if you like. Harry and Frank are the only other ones who know so far." She thought it would be a good test of reactions outside the family.

Godfrey spilled the beans without finesse. "She wants to form the Helston Electric Light Company," he said. "She's only tinkering with your set for practice, you know."

To her surprise Cornwallis did not laugh; he just looked at her, head cocked on one side, and said, "True?"

She nodded warily and held her breath.

Disappointed Godfrey said, "You don't seem too surprised." Then he turned to Jessie. "You already told him!"

She shook her head and continued to study Cornwallis minutely, alert for any sign of amusement at her presumption.

"What d'you think, then?" Godfrey asked him.

He drew a deep breath and said, "Put me down for a thousand preference shares. When does the offer open formally?"

She wanted to throw her arms around him and hug him half to death — not out of any romantic impulse, of course, but much as she would have hugged Cressida if she had said anything so splendid. Which, naturally, she never would.

Godfrey then revealed that he had not actually taken her idea quite as seriously as he had made it seem; he turned to her and exclaimed, "I say, Sis! It's starting to look quite solid, eh? Any chance of a few shares for me?"

Cornwallis laughed but Jessie held a warning finger toward the pair of them. "You're not to let the slightest hint of this go outside these four walls — d'you understand? Only you and my elder brothers know of it. If the smallest whisper reached Dad, he'd go berserk."

The kettle began to boil. Godfrey rose to make the tea. Jessie started slicing the bread. Cornwallis said, "You realize he's bound to get wind of it before you're even launched, you know. How are you going to get round that?"

"I don't know." She sighed.

"We must put on our thinking caps, then," he said in a tone that showed he meant it — that he wasn't just making a conventional noise. "There must be a way."

When the tea was drawn he put two cups and several jam sandwiches on a short plank — which he then passed to Godfrey, saying, "Take that up to Billy, there's a good chap. Tell him he can go on with the battens when he's had his tea. Oh, and get him to show you where we saw a pair of foxes yesterday."

These final words transformed the lad's reluctance to leave them into eagerness to be gone.

"I don't want to impede the good work," Jessie said as she took a hearty bite of her sandwich.

"It'll keep," he replied. "I don't think your business can, though. You *are* serious?"

She sighed again. "In the ambition, yes. But ..."

"Why?" he asked sharply.

"Because no one else has thought of it — yet — and I have."

He shook his head, implying that wasn't what he meant.

"It's true," she insisted.

"I don't doubt it. But why is *that* your ambition? You must admit it's a most unusual thing for a young lady to want to do."

She gave an awkward shrug. "What's that to you? Why are you so interested all of a sudden, anyway? I thought I was no longer of any *use* to you — except as lighting mechanic, of course!"

He looked stung.

"It's true!" she insisted. "Two months ago you needed me desperately — if you recall? To get all those harpies with unmarried daughters off your back. I haven't heard much of that lately — have I!"

He made an apologetic wave of his hands. "I thought that the reason most mothers stopped leaving their At Home cards might apply in your case, too — I mean, I thought I'd become a brush you'd rather not be tarred with. You should have said. Anyway, if you still wish to be engaged, I'm at your service. Just say the word and we'll pop it in *The Times* tomorrow."

It was her turn to stare at him in amazement.

"Might be just as well," he continued evenly. "If you were promised to me and I didn't seem to mind this Mad March Scheme of yours ..."

She found her voice then: "It's not mad!"

"*I* know that. I'm talking of the way your father will see it — if you'll just let me finish? Thank you. If *I* don't seem to mind your scheme, he'll probably accept it, or tolerate it, anyway. The real question is what Cressida Pym will make of it. He'll be guided by her."

She took her first sip of tea then and said, "You're an extraordinary man, Cornwallis. Either that or all three of my brothers are — they're the only other ones I know well enough to compare you with."

"Extraordinary in what way?" He suspected she was paying him a backhanded compliment.

"Well, Frank — and even Harry, who is the world's *least* businesslike businessman — when I first told them of this ambition, they started to talk about it in straight commercial terms. Neither of them ..."

"So did I," he interrupted. "If you recall? I said put me down for some shares."

"Ha ha! That was when you thought it a joke."

"I didn't! I ..."

"Never mind!" She waved him to silence. "It doesn't matter. The point is that now we *are* talking seriously about it, you put your finger straight on the real nub of my problem — which isn't going to be raising the money or finding a site or ... you know, any of those obvious, commercial things. It's going to be ... well, things like Cressida's response. Among others."

"The human factor."

"Precisely. I'm not saying other men wouldn't see the point. But very few of them would *start* there. That's why I say you're unusual."

He smiled and dipped his head, slightly embarrassed to find her compliment was genuine. "So — do we send in a note to *The Times?*"

She gazed uncertainly at him, biting her lip. An impish smile twitched at the corners of her mouth. "I don't know," she said at length.

"Just now you were complaining that ..."

"I know! But that was when I thought you'd withdrawn the offer." She tensed up the way people do when they expect a firework to explode and tried to cajole him with a smile.

He raked the ceiling with his eyes and said, "Well, I only wish I could say that you are an extraordinary woman, Jessie. I don't know what to say next. I can't go asking you to marry me day after day. Repeated refusal does dent a fellow's *amour propre*, you know. And yet if I fail to ask you, you build up this head of steam and then pour it out on me in a torrent of unbridled abuse and contumely. I can't win, it seems." He concluded with a heavy sigh.

"Oh, diddums!" She laughed. "D'you know why I hesitate?"

He glanced at her sharply, his playfulness gone. Two answers immediately occurred to him, one of them emotionally hazardous. He gave her the other: "Because you're vain enough ... no, I'll rephrase that — because you're *human* enough to want to achieve it as Jessica Kernow, unattached spinster of this parish. You don't want people to say about it afterwards, when *you've* made a success of it, 'Of course, *he* was really behind it all!' Am I right?"

She waved her hands as if resigning from an unequal contest. "You see!" she said, rising to swill her cup and plate at the sink. "You *are* extraordinary. I can't think of any other man who'd appreciate that without prompting. Or even *with* prompting, come to that. What do *you* think Cressida would do?"

He scratched his head and thought the question over. "Now she really *is* an extraordinary woman," he said at last.

"Of a very conventional kind."

"Just so. You're extraordinary for your ambition — and for the strength of will and character to carry it through. I was watching you when Godfrey blurted out your news. I could see at once it wasn't a joke — nor just a piece of idle daydreaming. I have no doubt you'll do it, with or without whatever small assistance I may be able to give you — but we'll come to that later, after we've dealt with the Pym problem. As I was saying, Miss Pym is extraordinary in quite a different way — precisely because she is so *very* conventional." He faltered there and gave her an awkward smile.

At once she realized they had strayed into *that* awkward territory — that penumbral shadow which surrounds the darkness of It. He was talking about Cressida's irregular situation in Barney Kernow's household. True, it was thoroughly conventional in the sense that there must be tens of thousands of widowers and bachelors who lived under the same roof as their female housekeepers — but it was thoroughly unconventional in that few of them would have slept in bedchambers with connecting doors.

Jessie wondered how she could let him know she understood

without embarrassing them both. "Well, I know what you mean, of course," she said quietly.

He misinterpreted it as a signal to continue talking about *that* situation rather than the specific topic of Miss Pym's response to Jessie's ambition. "Has she ever spoken of it to you?" he asked. "I don't wish to pry, of course — except that, yes, dammit! I *do* wish to pry. I cannot for the life of me understand how she balances her ultra-conventional ideas with ... her situation at Wheal Prosper. Can you?"

Jessie, still standing at the sink, turned from him and stared out of the window. The motor in the stables changed its note at that moment, from laboured roar to easy murmur, and she knew it had finished charging the accumulators.

"I'm sorry," he said. "The very last thing I wanted to do was ..."

"No, no!" She cut him short and, reaching out her hand, gave his a squeeze. "I must go and switch off the motor. Come with me."

She kept a hold on his hand and drew him outdoors in her wake. "She hasn't spoken of it to me," she said as they sauntered up the overgrown farmyard. "Except that ... in a way, I suppose, she has. I'd love to talk about it but I don't know where my loyalties lie. If she was just talking generally — which is the way she made it *seem* — then I'm free to tell you. But if she was really speaking personally — about herself and ... the situation at Wheal Prosper, as you tactfully phrase it — then I'm not free at all."

"Oh!" he responded with a sort of jocular confidence. "I feel sure she was talking quite generally!"

"You!" She laughed and punched him playfully as they entered the generator room. She slapped his hand, too, when he reached out for the exhaust-lift handle to stop the motor.

"We are in a bellicose mood today," he remarked when silence fell at last.

The accumulators still bubbled their hydrogen and the heated portions of the engine hummed and pinged as they cooled.

"All right," Jessie said at last. "I'll assume she was talking generally — if she wasn't, she has only herself to blame, right?"

"Absolutely. People should say what they mean."

She wandered down what had once been a feeding passage to the next stable, where the air was sweeter. There she sat on a haybale and, pulling a strand from its side, chewed the stalk as she spoke. "It was the day you first installed that apparatus next door," she said. "When you nearly wrecked it."

He hung his head and grinned.

"That, if you recall, was at a time when the announcement of our engagement was on the cards."

He chuckled. "Sorry. I just used up all my remorse. You should have warned me."

"Anyway, I was dropping a few gentle hints to prepare her for it, and ..."

"I hope she was suitably delighted?"

"Can I tell the story?"

"Sorry."

"Of course she was delighted. But she also started to warn me about ... you know, the dangers of closer intimacy with one's beloved." She shut her eyes and sighed. "How do couples who are truly in love ever talk about this, Cornwallis? It's hard enough with someone who's just a friend, like you."

"I think it gets easier," he replied. "Like running a generator, you know." Then, after the briefest pause he added, "Come to think of it, it's *very* like running a generator — the safe management of a kind of energy that, when used unwisely or inappropriately, can do untold damage. Don't you think so?" He saw her shaking her head and smiling. "What now?"

"How you can pass from flippancy to deadly earnestness! It's very" — she was about to say 'endearing' but changed it to — "good."

"I am serious."

"I know. Anyway, I sort of used what happened here with the generator as an example. I said that whatever I'd learned about electricity up until then was all extremely theoretical — out of books and from talking to my brothers and so on. But it made much more sense when there was something I could look at and touch and ... you know — handle."

He laughed. "I'll bet that frightened her!"

"Yes, of course. Or yes and no. I mean, she warned me about all the dangers of ... well, touching and handling, you know? You're right — it *does* get easier. But anyway, behind all her warnings — this was on our way home, walking across the fields — behind all her warnings I could also sense a great ... I don't know — a sort of excitement. I was walking along holding her arm and, honestly, I never felt such tension in her. She was *saying* all these negative things, you know? *Don't* do this, and *shun* that, and *avoid* the other, and so on. But, in all those ways people can communicate — *other* than by using words — she wasn't saying 'don't' at all!"

"And what did *you* say?"

"I didn't dare say anything — except yes-sir, no-sir, three-bags-full-sir. I kept thinking if only I could find the right words ... it was like a dam or something inside her — a great reservoir of passions and emotions fully charged inside her ... if I could only find the right words, the dam would burst and I'd hear what she really thought about it all."

"She was just giving out the conventional wisdom."

"Yes — and she didn't really believe it. You could tell. Or I could tell, anyway. I know her well enough by now." She threw away the haystalk and turned her large, luminous eyes on him. "I think she *has* to be so conventional because if she weren't, her passions would just tear her to shreds!"

"D'you envy her?" he asked at once, taking her quite aback.

She hedged her reply with a question: "Why d'you ask?"

"D'you think it could never happen to you? Is that why you want to be rather unconventional — because your passions will never threaten you in that way?"

She found she could no longer look at him. "I don't know," she murmured.

"D'you want to find out?"

Still with her eyes closed she shook her head, more in bewilderment than in rejection. "I don't know," she repeated, even less certainly than before.

*A*bout a week after Jessie had revealed her ambitions to Cornwallis she went into Helston with Clarrie, ostensibly to make a few small purchases, actually to meet Frank for luncheon at the Angel; that was some two weeks after he had moved into his own chambers in the town and she was curious to discover how he, as the first Kernow fledgeling to flee the nest, was managing. He, of course, was equally interested in revealing as little as possible; not that he distrusted her in particular, it was just part of his secretive nature. His strategy was one of diversion. They had barely started on the soup when he tossed an austere-looking booklet upon the table at her elbow. "Late birthday present for you," he joked. "Pay particular attention to Section Thirty-One, subsections one and two."

The booklet resembled others she had seen lying around his room, especially during exams in the days of his indenture, so it took a moment for the title — *The Electricity Act, 1899* — to register with her. Then her heart missed a beat and a flush of excitement passed through her. Until this moment her mind had been a whirl of physical images — machinery, furnaces, the power house ... steam on frosty mornings ... people throwing switches in their homes and marvelling at the instant glow and warmth of the miraculous illumination. The muck and magic of electricity, you might say. Frank's casual gift suddenly opened up an entirely new layer of her dreams. Her two-dimensional ambitions suddenly acquired the missing third dimension and, with it, a solidity and volume whose lack she had sensed without being able to put her finger on it quite.

More important than that, even — it showed that Frank believed in her! In his own way he was promoting and encouraging her enterprise. This support meant far more to her than Harry's or Godfrey's. Harry would be amiable enough, and Godfrey young enough, to support any madcap scheme she might have dreamed up. Frank was the cold-water sibling, the one whose instinct was always to say, "This enthusiasm's all very well, but have you considered ..." and out he would trot a chilling list of disadvantages and possible disasters. So the realization that he had written away to the Government Stationery Office to get a copy of this all-important Electricity Act, purely for her benefit, was both touching and encouraging.

She stammered her thanks and tried to remember what he had said about subsection something or other.

He saved her the bother. "It's a typical parliamentary mess," he told her. "The sort of thing you could expect when you let lawyers loose on the modern world, when their only acquaintance with science is through the Greek of Aristotle. Subsection one allows you, the supplier of electricity, to charge the 'ordinary consumer,' as the Act calls him, in one of three ways." He held up three fingers and felled one of them for each clause. "One: by the actual amount of energy supplied. Two: by the quantity of electricity contained in the supply. Three ..."

"But what's the difference?" she asked. "Amount of energy ... quantity of electricity — it's the same, surely?"

He chuckled. "Give a good lawyer enough money and he'll sniff out a difference — have no fear! These lads in parliament aren't fools, you know. Three-quarters of them are lawyers themselves. There's lucrative work here for years to come." He tapped the booklet.

"What was the third method?"

"Ah. That says you can charge by any other method the Board of Trade approves of. It's what we lawyers call the 'face-saver' — to give it the proper technical term. It says, in effect, that if they've made a dog's breakfast of methods one and two, they can dream up some other system and it'll all be perfectly legal."

She gave a dramatic sigh of relief. "Thank heavens for that! So it's all perfectly straightforward?"

"Well ... yes and no." He grinned wickedly. "You see, the *next* subsection, says that even if you do charge a consumer according to some method approved of by the Board of Trade, the consumer can object to it and give you one month's notice in writing."

"And then?"

His grin broadened still further. "And then you have to charge him for the actual amount of energy — or the quantity of electricity — you have supplied!"

She threw up her hands. "Full circle, in fact!"

"*Closed* circle might be a better word for it. You can't teach lawyers anything when it comes to closed circles. Or closed ranks. Are you quite sure, sister dear, that you want to take the plunge into this nasty, dangerous world, full of dirty smelly engines on your right hand and legal pitfalls to your left?"

An ancient vision, warm and tempting, briefly beguiled her — so familiar that she possessed it, or it possessed her, as a perfect whole, entire and simultaneous. Its elements, if she had needed to dissect them out, were: a nursery filled with angelic children, a prosperous and substantial household running like clockwork with a small army of contented and well-trained servants — in short, a warm, female cocoon against that cold, brusque, impersonal world where masculine will and sinew engaged in a never-ending struggle. Was she mad? She who could luxuriate in that warmth and reign supreme in that immaculate little empire ... what drove her now to chance drowning her spirit in that ocean of cool indifference? Especially as, in her case, her body — her person — would live on and endure the pitying smiles of men, the catty smirks of other women. Icarus might have died in his ambitions to reach the sun — but at least they made him a legend; if his sister had similarly tried and failed, she was not even a footnote to his efforts, nor would she ever have become one.

"I *must* be mad," she murmured.

He raised a laconic eyebrow but ventured no remark.

"Don't you think so?" she prompted him.

"It's more a matter of what *you* think," he replied. "As long as you keep that possibility in mind, your sanity's fairly safe, I'd say." He put down his soup spoon and tapped the booklet. "The Board of Trade seems to be permitting the smaller undertakers, which is what you'd be, about a shilling per unit. And, as you'll be selling about forty thousand units *per annum* to start with — at a guess — your gross income will be around two thou'. Have you given much thought yet to the financial side of the enterprise?"

She pulled a hopeless face. "That's the biggest snag so far. I know several places where we could buy the machinery, but ..."

"We?" He raised a hand to his breast in mock alarm, as if he supposed she were including him in her enterprise.

"Well," she admitted hesitantly, "Cornwallis Trelawney has been making noises of financial support — dropping hints that he might be an interested partner."

"Partner?" He seized upon the word. "In every sense?"

She smiled acidly. "Don't *you* start! He'll be a business partner, at least. Anything else is ... pfft!" She waved a hand vaguely.

"A business partner," he echoed. "Well, that would explain why he's been going up and down the town, talking to shopkeepers and hôteliers, asking would they be interested in a central supply of ..."

"What?" Her cry brought the entire dining room to silence. She stared about her in embarrassment and made an apologetic gesture to those at the nearer tables. There were smiles, a little laughter, and then the buzz of conversation was resumed. "He's been doing what?" she asked with quieter vehemence.

"What I said."

"But he'll give the whole game away — the fool! Someone else could step in and pip us to the post."

Frank shook his head. "I'm sorry, Jessie dear, but that's the sort of risk one has to take in business. As Chaucer said: *Women ben full of secrecye.* You're stepping out into a man's world now."

"Oh?" she asked scornfully. "You're trying to tell me there are no secrets in the manly world of business?"

"Of course there are — but they're more about *how* than about *what*. You tell the world *what* you're going to do but not *how* you're going to do it. In your case you should be telling everyone you'll provide the rich man's castle and the poor man's cottage with an unfailing supply of electricity at a price that will make any would-be competitor turn pale and think again. The secret lies in *how* you're going to do it."

She saw his point at once but still a vague objection nagged away at the back of her mind. It did not stay there long. "That may be true of the world of men in general, Frank," she said. "But you're forgetting that *our* world has one particular man in it — a man who changes all those calculations: Father. If he should get wind of this, he'd go out of his mind. He'd go to the edge of ruin to bankrupt me. Just to teach me a lesson."

"Good!" her brother responded evenly. "I was wondering if the point had escaped you."

"Of course it hasn't escaped me!" Her intensity was in danger of silencing the whole room again. He trapped her hand briefly and gave a monitory squeeze. Forcing herself to be calm she continued: "In fact, that's my whole starting point — to put the boot on the other foot: My entire purpose is to escape *him!*"

"And when you meet a locked door ...?" he asked.

Her brother's air of one who has thought the whole thing out, and explored every avenue for miles and miles ahead of her, was beginning to grate — not least because it was possibly true. She wondered at the personality that could see and understand so much without feeling a corresponding desire to *do* something, too. Often in the days of his indenture he had explained some appalling inequality of the law to her — how, for instance, a poor man could be sentenced to a flogging and a year's imprisonment for taking a rabbit worth fourpence off a rich man's land while the rich man could be fined a maximum of two hundred pounds for a City swindle that could make him a profit of thousands. But he had never made these revelations to her in the spirit of a man who intended to right such wrongs one day; his attitude was amused, aloof, ultimately indifferent — very much the attitude he had shown in explaining the Electricity Act to her.

She saw the irony of her situation at once. Experience had taught her that nothing could stir Frank to action when the cause was so abstract; his own pleasure or comfort was a different matter, of course, but, since neither was involved in her ambitions, it would be useless to solicit his effort on her behalf. And yet if, with that idly speculative brilliance of his, he had considered her plans in some detail — purely as an abstract exercise — he would certainly have anticipated problems and traps that might never occur to her until she was actually caught up in their toils.

Therefore, she realized, she must suppress this urge to snap his head off for being so arrogantly superior. The alternative — to plead for his help — was also risky; he would not deny her some modest assistance but he would neither put his heart into it nor accept responsibility for its application. She must find some way of making it conducive to his own pleasure or comfort. His vanity might serve for a while, she supposed.

And thus he reduced her calculations to his own self-serving level. In one way it was a benefit, she realized: At least you knew where you stood with people like him. Self-interest is an almost bottomless well; the well from which flows morality, altruism, love, and all those higher causes, is not. Such a thought had never occurred to her before. She found it rather exciting — as if she suddenly found herself in a room full of treasures, a room whose very existence she had never before suspected.

"Hallo!" He waved a hand before her eyes like a stage hypnotist bringing his victim out of a trance. "Remember me?"

She frowned at him, playing along, and then grinned. "I believe I do. You're that brilliant young lawyer whose touch turns all to gold — who succeeds because he never tangles his own emotions in the causes he defends."

He realized the mockery behind her praise, of course, but, since he had never heard the faintest praise of any kind from her — or not of that particular trait in him — he was, for a moment, flummoxed. "What now?" he asked guardedly.

"Dearest Frank!" She patted his hand encouragingly. "It is but the merest sample of the boundless admiration — even adoration — that will flow from this poor fluttering female heart if you would but vouchsafe me the smallest tithe of your brilliant speculations concerning my ambitions. I cannot believe your ever-fertile mind was satisfied at unravelling Section Thirty-One of the Electricity Supply Act."

It was such a skillful blend of mockery and challenge that he could not help rising to it, even though he saw through her gambit. It was a new Jessie — or new to him. But the revelation that she could be as calculating and manipulative as he himself was intriguing enough to make him do his best. So, while some deep dark chamber of his brain whirred with speculations as to what favours he might require of her in return, he deployed his thoughts and researches into the business of electrical generation and supply as if he were moved by nothing less than the purest brotherly love and selfless desire for her welfare.

He drew out a notebook and opened it at a page on which he had dashed down some figures. These, with some accompanying calculations, showed that the capital charges on 'her' sort of generating station were around thirty pounds sterling per kilowatt of maximum demand. This figure, he claimed was like a golden gateway into the mysteries of costing every customer of her new venture. It would be the one universal figure from which all other calculations started, no matter whether she was working out how much to charge a great iron-foundry (assuming Helston boasted such a thing, which it did not — alas) or a humble labourer's cottage.

That much he would probably have told her anyway, just for the pleasure of leaving her to flounder with all the rest; in the same spirit he might hold out an eight-foot pole to a man struggling in a river, four yards from the bank. But now the mockery in her challenge led him to reveal much more. She watched in fascination as he flipped through several further pages of his notebook, where he had already jotted down the calculations — first for a large factory, then for a club, an hôtel, a shop, and private houses, large, medium, and small. He had omitted nothing — rent, rates, the cost of coal, sinking-fund charges, wages, insurance ... she racked her brains for anything he might have left out. When he had finished, her admiring silence was a kind of praise — as was her comment: "You left out the cost of cheese for the mousetraps, I think."

His figures revealed something she had considered but had not thought very important. A generating station could, he calculated, supply a factory for about a halfpenny a unit; a club or hôtel or large house for about three-halfpence; a shop for fourpence (if it did not light its windows after closing time); and so on, all the way to a charge of around tenpence a unit for a small cottage. She had been vaguely aware that there would be a difference but had no idea it would be so vast — that a cottage would be *twenty times* more expensive to supply than a factory, for instance.

"It concentrates the mind wonderfully, eh?" he remarked as he saw the penny drop. "And have you got room for one more teeny-tiny little thought, I wonder?"

"In this little tiny brain of mine?" she responded. "Try!"

"Time is not on your side. Most of the units you sell will be for lighting. Consumption for lighting is ten times heavier in winter than in summer. If you are not selling electricity by the end of September — that is, if you dawdle along and don't start until this time next year — your first six months will be summer months. They'll bring in next to nothing — two hundred and fifty pounds, say. But if you *can* start in September, your first six months could bring in seventeen hundred and fifty." He laughed. "Jessie! You've turned quite pale!"

She knew it, of course; she could actually feel the blood draining from her cheeks, and the cold pallor it left behind. And yet that was, in every way, a superficial reaction. In her innermost being his warning had filled her with exultation. Until this moment her dreams had clustered round the vaguest focal points — most of them negative.

There was, for instance, her desire *not* simply to follow meekly in the path her father ordained — and *not* to let herself down after the boasts she had made to all three of her brothers at various times. But now Frank had, unwittingly (or perhaps not — one could never tell with him), provided the sharpest possible focus for her, and the oldest one of all: the time and the tide that wait for no man — nor, as she felt she was about to discover, for any woman, either.

Her worried frown gave way to a determined smile. "Thank you, Frank, dear," she said at last. "I hope one day I may be able to help you in some equally important way."

"I think you can do that right now," he responded smoothly.

"Ask and it's yours," she said.

"Tell me what Clarrie really wants in life."

If she'd been given a hundred guesses as to what he might ask, she'd never have come near that one. "Clarrie?" she echoed, still not really associating it with their maidservant.

He smiled faintly but his face remained an impenetrable mask. "Clarrie Williams," he said. "Have you discussed life's ambitions with her ever?"

"*My* ambitions?" she asked in amazement. How could he think such a thing?

He shook his head patiently. "Hers, actually."

"But why d'you want to know?"

"We've finished with *your* business for today," he responded with a smile. "My turn now. Or hers."

"I take your point," she replied frostily. "But if we're talking about *her* ambitions, then it's her business, surely?"

"Ambitions can coincide," he said. "Or at least they can be brought to a point where they converge, however briefly. Don't frown. People will begin to take an interest." He went on smiling though she could see no humour in his eyes now.

She smiled equally coolly. "I can't see why *you're* taking an interest — or where your interests and hers might coincide."

"It's not necessary for you to understand that, Jessie. The fact is, I have briefly skirted the subject with her — one's ambitions in life and that sort of thing. She told me once that she had no great desire to marry and make a home and so forth. But she didn't say what she'd put in its place. It's quite obvious she doesn't want to grow old in service. I just wondered what she really wants out of life — and I thought you might know."

Jessie was more suspicious than ever now. "Why? D'you you wonder about Becky, too? Is this a general or a particular curiosity in you?"

He laughed. "Oh, quite particular, I assure you. Becky's a stock domestic heifer. No spark in her. But Clarrie's something in your line — flint in her soul and iron in her will. There's sparks galore and sparks to spare with both of you."

Jessie had one of those intimations that flit through the mind and then fade to a blur. In that brief moment of clarity she saw something in her brother that was to be infinitely pitied. For all his brilliance and nimbleness of wit, he lacked that flinty soul and iron will he claimed to see in her and Clarrie; there were no sparks of that kind in him. Knowing it, he was doomed, like the Flying Dutchman, to sail forever in search of it elsewhere — to touch that promethean fire in others, or perish for want of it.

But a moment later that insight grew blurred and was replaced by one a good deal less fanciful. She remembered how he had tried — with a quite uncharacteristic clumsiness — to browbeat Clarrie the morning after she and Godfrey had been found tipsy together, after the ball. And she saw that his interest in the girl had a much more obvious cause.

"And you're just dying to help her, of course!" she sneered.

"Only if it'll help me, too," he replied. "I hope no one will ever accuse me of altruism! If you intend going into business, Jessie, you'd best take example from me — in this at least — and learn to distrust all charity, mercy, generosity, unasked-for kindness ... in a word: altruism. Beware of Greeks bearing gifts — or anyone else, for that matter! They're not being honest — as I *am* being honest with you now."

She tried to divert him. "You know Godfrey's hopelessly infatuated with her, I suppose?"

He laughed. "That won't deflect her in the slightest. Any more than another man's infatuation would deflect you. Name some fellow you admire. Trelawney, shall we say?"

"This is growing tedious, Frank."

"Soon be done!" he promised briskly. "Just bear with me. Suppose he dropped in at Wheal Prosper this evening and begged you to call this whole thing off, asked for your hand, promised you anything you wanted — *except* this ambition of yours? What would you tell him?"

"I'd tell him to take a long, cold bath."

"Of course you would. But suppose he said he'd throw himself down some abandoned mineshaft if you refused him?"

"I'd pretend to go along with him until I'd got him seated. Then I'd throw a noose around him and tip buckets of cold water over him until his sanity returned." Suddenly, in the middle of this jocular exaggeration, she realized she was precisely substantiating his point about her single-mindedness. She did not need his smile to alert her to the fact.

But his next question rocked her: "But suppose Trelawney said, 'Very well, then, me proud beauty. Here's the ten thousand pounds you need by way of capital. And I'll throw in two ten-kilowatt generators, free, gratis, and for nothing!'" He broke off and asked conversationally, "Did you know the Trelawneys own factories in and around Leeds? They must have electrical power. Cornwallis or his father would be able to get all you want at a hefty discount."

She shook her head — but her brain cogs were whirring.

Frank continued: "Interesting, what! Anyway, as I was saying — and please don't be shocked at my question. I want you to consider it quite seriously, as something that may very well happen."

"Oh, get on with it!" she exclaimed impatiently.

"Suppose Trelawney said you can have all that — your heart's desire, free on a golden salver — in return for becoming his ..." He paused before saying the word, making it barely audible, "paramour." Swiftly he added, "You know what I mean, I take it?"

She stared at him, knowing she ought to rise from the table and walk away with all the dignity at her command. She consciously ordered her muscles to do just that; but they did not even twitch.

Then she remembered the calculations he had made — all jotted down in that notebook of his, which was now neatly folded and buttoned, and back in his breast pocket. And she knew it would take her weeks to try to remember and recalculate those examples. And then she knew that no matter what insults and crudities he might indulge in, she could not leave him until she had got him to tear out those pages and pass them to her.

And then, finally, she realized that her own unconscious — or unpremeditated — hesitation had in effect answered the question-behind-his-question, which was about the sort of balance she would strike between her notions of honour and her worldly ambitions.

He saw the light of understanding as it dawned in her eyes and smiled warmly at last. "Growing up, eh, sis?" he remarked. "Never mind about my question now. Let me ask you another — more important. Do you think you have the smallest right — never mind duty — to strike that balance on Clarrie's behalf? Don't you think it's a choice she has a right to make for herself? Is she a child or a grown-up? Ask her, if you like."

Jessie shook her head like a woman struggling to awaken from an unpleasant dream. "You want me to tell you what her innermost ambition may be, just so that you can use it to ... to ..." She swallowed heavily and glanced guiltily all around.

"To propose a bargain with her," he said simply. "Yes. A bargain she will be at perfect liberty to consider for as long as she likes — and turn down if she wishes."

"But *what* a bargain, Frank! It's ... it's corrupt."

"It's the way of the world, Jess. I thought you wanted to join it. Believe me, as corruption goes, my little proposal barely scratches the surface — compared with some of the choices you'll face once your dreams start coming true. Go back to the boudoir and the drawing room if you can't face the prospect!" There was no sneer in this last bit of advice; he meant it quite sincerely.

A darkness seemed to settle around her. "You mean I'll end up like the old man," she said glumly.

He nodded as if to imply he wouldn't quite condemn her to that. "You'll certainly end up understanding him better," he promised.

There was quite a silence after that. And then she told him what little she knew about Clarrie's ambition in life — which was little enough and no use to him.

*I*t was a new moon, setting just half an hour behind the sun; Jessie knew as much from her diary, so she opened her window wide (to avoid seeing it for the first time through glass), turned over a coin in her pocket, and made a wish that the final performance of CR, which started in a couple of hours' time, would go as well as the two earlier ones.

A moment later she could have kicked herself for a wasted wish. Of course it would go well! And if it didn't — what then? There had been both dull and brilliant performances by the Helston G&S in the past and the sun had still risen, the moon had still waxed and waned ... and nothing heals faster than an actor's ego, pro or am. She should have wished for success to the Helston Power Company, instead.

But her mood swung again and then she was glad she had not been so foolish — or, rather, that she *had* been so foolish as to wish for something that was, in any case, almost inevitable. The Helston Power Co. needed no support from the realms of superstition and magic;

those fripperies were, indeed, best deployed on trivia, such as two escapist hours spent in a never-never village in Sicily among its improbable peasants.

Later that evening, however, when she was in the Assembly Rooms, making up among all the other ladies in the cast, she paused and gazed in a kind of delayed-action amazement at the creature who was now emerging through the lipstick and cornflour. Santuzza! It *was* Santuzza staring back at her! On the First Night performance, Jessie had been too petrified to recognize her; and last night she had been too fearful that their opening triumph might have been a mere flash in the pan. But now, with the confidence that comes from two good performances, she could put her own terrors — and personality — to rest and confront this poor, lovelorn, star-crossed Santuzza for the very first time.

It was an odd experience after four months of intense rehearsal, which was not just a struggle with the words and notes — the phrasing, the pauses, the rubato, and all those other technical things — but also, she had imagined, a slipping-into the part. Now, however, she realized that that was all she had done — merely slipped into the part, as one might slip into a dress. But tonight was different. Tonight she was discovering the nature of the woman behind the part — the 'real' Santuzza; the notion that such a creature might exist would have been laughable before this night.

Before this night, no shred of reality had clung to this desperate, impassioned girl, the daughter of a wealthy peasant who falls in love with the handsome ne'er-do-well, Turiddu. How *could* she, Jessie had always asked herself scornfully. The man was such an obvious seducer and betrayer that no girl worthy of admiration would look at him twice. And yet ... and yet! Staring now into those eyes that were more Santuzza's than hers, she caught glimpses of that hopeless and overwhelming passion ... felt its power to reach across the division between the actress and her rôle and speak directly to her heart. It was a power that reached across the moral divide, too, for it saw his vanity, his shallowness, and *still* made her wish to abase herself at his feet and be the slave of her love for him — for ever!

These intimations had escaped her in the dusty, echoing emptiness of Liston Court, and among the untenanted stables and byres at Wheal Dream; there the character had become familiar without ever threatening to become real. But now, in the lamplit dark, backstage at the Assembly Rooms, with the audience streaming in and the hushed clatter of preparation going on all around her — that peculiar sort of controlled panic which gives the theatre its buzz for performer and audience alike — she found the reality of Santuzza at last. Indeed, she did more than simply find it, she grasped it, possessed it, heard unsuspected echoes of it deep inside herself. The Jessie who took Cornwallis Trelawney's hand and gave it the usual encouraging squeeze before curtain-up was a defenceless hostage of Santuzza's passion for Turiddu and her despair at ever being able to keep him from his first love, Lola.

She moved through the performance as in a trance — not the dull, leaden daze of the zombie, but the inspirited possession of an emotion that had barely touched her life before. In some curious way it left her critical faculties intact, so that she could hear a new richness in her voice, an unaccustomed vibrancy, which gave each sentiment a depth that neither practice nor coaching could ever have achieved. The others heard it, too, and, in the way that a collective insanity can seize upon a crowd, so a collective vitality seized the entire company and they rode that wild wave of Mediterranean frenzy to the bewilderment and delight of all.

When it came to the great duet of love and betrayal between Turiddu and Santuzza — *Ah! lo vedi ...* — the tension was almost unbearable. Neither Jessie nor Cornwallis sang the words and notes as Verga and Mascagni wrote them — though both the librettist and composer would have sworn they did; they sang of emotions that truly possessed them, and in words and melodies that seemed newborn in the moment they were uttered. And in the duet that followed it, when the betrayed Santuzza is, in her turn, provoked into betraying her deceiver to the dark-souled, unforgiving Alfio, there was a spontaneous cheer from that staid Cornish audience, transformed by the sheer power of the unfolding drama into vengeance-loving Sicilians.

And finally, when Alfio has killed Turiddu, and Santuzza, full of remorse, throws herself into the arms of Lucia — who would have been her mother-in-law if Turiddu had kept his promise of marriage — the tears flowed on both sides of the footlights. They had to give three encores of *Mamma, quel vino è generoso* before the excitement ran its course.

When the curtain fell for the final time and the cast finished hugging one another — to a growing mutual embarrassment as their everyday personalities returned to claim them — and Michael Vestey had finished his rounds, shaking everyone by the hand and blinking back his tears of relief and amazement ... Jessie and Cornwallis were left in the flat, unflattering light of the stage with all the limelights dowsed.

They were still somewhat entranced by what had happened among them all but especially between them.

"Well!" he exclaimed, holding out both hands toward her.

"Well!" she replied, letting hers settle softly in his. There was still a little of the magic of Turiddu in them, to which the remnant of Santuzza could still respond. The silence between them was all it required.

The dream faded until at last it was Jessie Kernow who stared into Cornwallis Trelawney's eyes, and he into hers. There was nothing of the Sicilians' passion in their gaze, yet nor was it quite as it had been before. He was no longer the good chum, the safe pal he had become over these last enjoyable months of growing friendship. There was something extra now. The simple association had not diminished but there was a new intimacy to it, small and insignificant, perhaps, but — as when a tiny piccolo joins its notes to those of an orchestral hundred — still quite noticeable.

"How d'you feel?" he asked at length.

"Ravenous!" She laughed. The spell was broken.

They joined the others in their separate dressing rooms — no 'star' quarters, of course, just one cramped room for the gentlemen and another for the ladies. There each ran a separate gauntlet of congratulations while the lipstick and cornflour, liner and highlight, wigs and peasant dress all came off for the last time. Fifteen minutes later the entire company was reunited for a celebratory dinner at the Angel. There they ran a further gauntlet — indeed, a regular bastinado — of congratulations from the populace.

To Jessie's surprise Godfrey was there, too; he had earlier told them he'd heard all he wanted of Turiddu and Santuzza — enough, anyway, to kill any desire to meet Alfio, Lola, and Lucia as well.

"Well done," he said amiably. "You weren't bad, actually. Any chance of a lift back home later?"

Cornwallis raised an inquiring eyebrow at Jessie, who said, "Whoo! I don't think I'll be able to sleep at all tonight. I was toying with the idea of walking home."

Cornwallis rubbed his hands as if to say that her plan suited his own mood perfectly. He turned to Godfrey with an expansive gesture. "Know how to start her, young 'un?"

The youth stared at him open-jawed. "I'll say!"

"Well, when you get to Wheal Dream don't try to drive her up to the stables. The yard is too wet. But put a tarpaulin over her. Not immediately, mind. Let her cool down first."

Godfrey gave a delighted leap and made for the front door.

"Aren't you staying for supper?" his sister called after him.

"I'll be back in half a jiff!" he shouted over his shoulder. "Just got to see ... someone."

Out in the street he skipped all of three yards down Coinagehall St and then turned abruptly into Angel Passage, hoping no one who knew him had noticed. Twenty yards down the passage he turned into the stable yard and went straight across to the scullery door, where he called out, "Hallo, Tillie!"

The scullery maid turned wearily toward the yard, then, recognizing him, broke into a broad smile. "Hallo, Charley, my ol' lover! Don't 'ee never give up?"

"It's Godfrey. I keep telling you."

She laughed.

"Anyway," he continued, "I was wondering if you'd like a spin in my motor?"

"Gusson!" She laughed again. "*Your* motor, indeed! What's wrong with mine?"

"Honestly!" he assured her. "Come and look!" He jerked his head toward the far end of the yard.

She darted a nervous glance up the corridor and then, wiping her hands in her sack-apron, followed him outside. The moment she saw the Renault, however, she laughed again and said, "Hell, that's Mister Trelawney's that is. Everyone do know that!"

Godfrey nodded patiently. "Did I deny it? But guess who he's lent it to for the evening, eh? Guess whose sister Mister Trelawney is walking home tonight?"

Tillie put her head on one side and stared at him dubiously; hers was not a pretty face yet there was something about her person, or her personality, that he found more and more endearing every time he saw her. He wasn't in love with her, not in the way he loved Clarrie, but he had to admit that his feelings for Tillie were waxing even as those for Clarrie were beginning to wane.

"You do live out Nancegollan," she said.

"And, for some reason, they have taken it into their heads to walk home tonight. Don't look a gift horse in the mouth, Tillie! Wouldn't you like to be the first girl down Five Wells Lane to ride in a motor car? When d'you finish up here?"

"Now," she replied. "Fifteen minutes." She began walking back to the scullery door. "Then I must eat. Then go home and put up me glad rags, I s'pose."

On the threshold she paused so that he almost ran into her. She turned, saw how close he was, and raised a hand to touch his face briefly. "You're a funny one," she murmured. "Where's all this going to lead, eh?"

He was glad he'd told her about the goose-grease — Jessie's trick for keeping your hands nice and ladylike in a working world. He watched her smear a fresh lot of the grease on her hands and plunge them again into the hot, sudsy water.

"Don't you stand there now," she called out without looking at him. "You come back here ten o'clock. I shall be done by then."

Her question — where's all this going to lead — replayed itself in his mind as he strolled back up Angel Passage to join his sister and the other revelers for at least part of their no-doubt gargantuan repast. He knew well enough where it would lead when he boasted of this "conquest" to the chaps at school; but whether it actually would get so far he was far less certain.

He wasn't even sure that he wanted it to — or not just yet, anyway.

*I*t had gone midnight by the time the G&S celebrations finished. The town's gaslighting had lately been converted from the old fishtail burners to the new type with the Welsbach incandescent mantle. As Jessie and Cornwallis set off down the steep hill of Coinagehall Street, she looked up at one of the lamps and said, "It's funny what a difference a month or two can make, eh! Before Christmas I thought these new mantles were the spider's ankles."

"And now you don't?" he asked.

"They're my deadly enemies!" She jutted her jaw pugnaciously.

"But why?"

"Because they've given fifty new years of life to the old gas industry." She laughed. "Father would murder me if he heard me talking like this — if he even knew I was *thinking* like this."

He laughed, too. "I don't see how a simple thing like a gas mantle could do that."

"Oh, but it has. The old fishtails needed a very rich gas, full of expensive chemicals — to make the flame burn bright yellow, you know. But now that it's the hot mantle rather than the flame which gives out the actual light ... well, *anything* will do to heat it. The cheapest, leanest gas you can make. So now the gasworks scrubs the expensive chemicals out of the gas and sells them to industry at a good hefty profit, and then it sells what's left, which is a cheap, lean gas, to households — but *at the same old rate!*" She clutched at his arm. "Listen! I'll murder *you* if you ever let my father know I told you all this."

"I quake in my boots, Jess. Actually, it must be very nice if you have shares in the gasworks — like him."

"But jolly unfair if you're planning to sell electricity — like me. I mean, it's not just that they're making an outrageous profit. The lean gas burns clean — not like the old muck — and it gives this brilliant white light. Why should people give it up for something new and untested? It's not fair! Gas was supposed to be dirty and smelly and dim. Electricity was supposed to be clean and white and odourless. Now it's going to take us an extra fifty years to get rid of gas. And to think I was all in favour of it up until a few weeks ago!" She raised an imaginary rifle to her shoulder and potted the three nearest lamps.

Cornwallis said, "I wonder if Godfrey got home safely?" The moment the words were out he realized how tactless a speculation it was, for they would be walking most of the route he would have taken. "From the police, I mean," he added.

They turned off into Lady Street, where the hill is even steeper; their boots slid a little at each footfall. She took his arm — permanently, this time — to steady herself. "You don't mind?" she asked.

"Delighted," he said.

Sure of her footing, she lifted her skirt a little at the back, so as to avoid doing a bout of unpaid street-sweeping. Somewhere ahead of them, around the bend, they heard the sound of a brawl. When they turned the corner they realized it was coming from inside one of the poorer houses near the junction with Almshouse Hill. A woman and a man were shouting insults at each other, revealing in embarrassing detail precisely how inadequate each was in just about every department of life. Two of their neighbours on the uphill side — a pair of old women in adjacent cottages, were standing in dressing gowns and slippers at their darkened doors, peering out in consternation.

Cornwallis slowed down and asked the first if such arguments were unusual in that house; she tut-tutted and shook her head.

The other ran swiftly up the street to join them, saying, "There'll be bloodshed this time — you'll see." She looked Cornwallis up and down and added, "But they'd harken to a real gentleman the like o' *you*, sir. Couldn't 'e stick a head in the door and tell they to cheese it?"

"Us shan't get no shut-eye else," the other complained.

"What's their name?" Cornwallis asked uncertainly.

"Howard," they chorused. One added, "Billy Howard."

Cornwallis nipped Jessie's arm tighter in his and, murmuring "In for a penny ..." set off for the house of troubles.

The door was open. The house was in darkness but they could tell that the argument was coming from an upstairs room. He stuck his head inside and shouted in his most commanding tones, "You there! Howard! And you, Missus — if you don't both shut up this minute, I'll send for the constable."

Complete silence reigned. Jessie looked toward the women, expecting a sign of approval. But something in their attitude made her give Cornwallis a sharp push in the back, sending him staggering indoors, while she, simultaneously, sprang back and diagonally up the street.

The contents of a chamber pot fell where, a second earlier, they had both been standing. She heard the two old women cackling as she raced up the street; by the time she reached them, however, they had withdrawn inside and bolted the door. She could still hear them laughing hysterically.

When Cornwallis reached her he found her standing inelegantly on one leg, with her skirts hitched up to her knee, scratching a crudely X-shaped mark on the door with the hobnails of her right boot. He offered an arm to steady her and she soon made a better job of it. "What're you going to do?" he asked.

She grinned at him. "I hope that question will worry them for a day or two." She stopped and cocked an ear. Silence reigned within. "Already they don't seem to think it quite so funny."

The domestic battle had started again by the time they passed the Howards' house for the second time. The stench of what might by now be soaking their clothes goaded them to a trot, until they reached St John's at the very bottom of the hill. "What would we have done if that shower had caught us!" she said.

"Gone for a swim in the Cober," he replied evenly.

She giggled at the thought and then said, "We still could."

"Let it warm up for three months more," he commented. Then, in a different tone: "That's all one needs to know about marriage." He jerked his head at the road behind them. "A dog and a cat, yoked on a three-foot chain!"

She thought it over and then said, "D'you think perhaps it's rather different in Sicily?"

"Oh yes. They'd use guns and knives instead of chamber pots."

When she made no response to that he said, "Talking of Sicily, what happened tonight — to you, I mean? You were absolutely inspired."

"Last-night nerves," she said, trying to pass it off.

"Seriously," he insisted.

She was silent so long that he thought she was refusing to answer; he squeezed her hand briefly in the crook of his elbow to jog her into a response.

"I'm thinking," she told him; then immediately went on, "Do you suppose there could be a sort of love that is meant to go on being ... just itself? I mean, a sort of love that could never develop into marriage? Because that's what the opera was about, don't you think? And it's what almost all love poetry is about — and all the great love stories in history, too."

"Yes?" he said after a while. "Go on."

"You *know* what I mean," she replied crossly, thinking he was just being lazy. "Poets say 'My love is like a red, red rose' and 'Shall I compare thee to a summer's day?' They don't say, 'My love is like a living marvel at checking off a laundry list' nor 'Shall I compare thee to a first-class cook?' Yet marriage is much more about laundry lists and cooking than it is about red roses and summer's days."

Her choice of words amused him but he saw a serious point there, too. They paused briefly to recover their breath, leaning on the parapet of the bridge over the Cober. The long walk up Sithney Common Hill lay ahead and the gaslit gloom gave way to stygian darkness just a hundred yards from where they stood.

He said, "Perhaps a marriage based on laundry lists and cooking stands a better chance than one based on red roses and summer days."

The river gurgled beneath their feet. Jessie thought how nice it would be to live near running water. They resumed their homeward walk; from here on, there was nothing but starlight to guide them — and her memory of the road, which she had walked more times than she could remember. "That couple who were arguing back there," she said as they stepped out into the dark beyond the reach of the final streetlamp. "D'you think there was ever a red-rose-in-summer day for people like that?"

"What has prompted all this?" he asked. "Our little opera?"

"When we were singing tonight — about revenge and honour and ... all that passion ..."

"And betrayal."

"Yes, but the betrayal would have been meaningless without the passion first. Anyway, when we were singing tonight I sort of felt I *understood* ... something. I don't know what. Or I can't pin it down now. It's all fading. But didn't you feel it, too?"

"Everyone felt it," he replied. "I mean they felt it in you. It was ..." He gave up searching for the word but she detected a shiver as it passed through him.

She stamped her foot and cried out, "Oh, I can't remember! It's already slipping away — I'm losing it!"

They were now just beyond the new mill house, where the road forked. Ahead ran the old pack-horse trail, which went directly up the steepest part of the hill; the newer turnpike veered off to their right and wound, still fairly steeply, around its flanks, taking an extra quarter of a mile to reach the top. Her annoyance petered out in laughter. "Isn't it funny when you're just a voice in the blackness!" she said.

"And a warm arm." He patted hers.

She slipped free of him then and, hitching up her skirts, ran off laughing — as well as anyone could run up the one-in-five gradient of the ancient road. After a century of neglect, it was more like the bed of a dry stream than any sort of footpath. "Now I'm anything I want to be," she called back to him. "Bet you can't catch me!" And, reaching an unseen hand into the blackness before her, she sped from the blackness behind, while the blackness hemmed her in on every side.

After twenty headlong paces she was breathless. She paused and, controlling her panting as best she could, turned to listen for sounds of his pursuit. On the far side of the valley Helston was laid out like a map — or would have been if there were a moon to see it by; instead, the hateful gaslamps pricked it out like dewdrops on a spider's web. The night was as silent as any she had known. "Aren't you coming?" she called down the track.

Still there was silence.

Had he found some grass at the verge, to deaden his footfall? Had he slipped back down the hill in order to race up the turnpike and meet her at the top? Would he be waiting for her there, ready to mock her slowness?

"Cornwallis?" she cried.

The silence was becoming menacing. "It's not funny!" she snapped.

Down at the gasworks one of the night stokers opened a furnace door. The whole side of her father's office looked as if it had caught fire. So did the side of Cornwallis's face, which was suddenly revealed to her about four feet away.

She let out a shriek of laughter and made a desperate leap at the track above her. His cry of "Gotcha!" was a fraction of a second too late; the tips of his grasping fingers just brushed the back of her arm.

Still shrieking and laughing she raced ahead of him once again. Now that she knew he was definitely chasing her, she jettisoned all caution and pushed her muscles to the limit. He was much the stronger, of course, and could certainly outrun her, both on the flat and on a steep hill like this; but she had the advantage of knowing the old track, while he had to listen to her footfall to know what to expect.

As she fled she let her imagination run free as well. Soon it was not Cornwallis who chased her but a footpad, a murderer, a black panther, an evil spirit. The last was the most terrifying of all because it was driven by causes no human could fathom. The night was suddenly filled with its talons ... drawing closer and ever closer ... lending the strength of terror to her rapidly tiring muscles.

In the end it was the slope itself rather than his pursuit that defeated her. She floundered a little, took an unintended diagonal off the track, and only just felt the overhanging branch in time; if her outstretched hand had been a little higher, it would have caught her smack amidships. She just had time to turn and cry, "Ha! Careful!" when he ran full pelt into her hand, like a runaway train hitting the buffers.

He raised his hands to ward himself off. By chance they found the branch, which he grasped in desperation, one hand each side of her. Their combined weight, added to his impetus, was too much for it; with a crack that rang across the valley, it snapped and deposited them both on the ground, Cornwallis on top of her. They were already winded by their running; the fall took away what little breath was left and for a moment they could do nothing but lie in that embarrassing position, struggling to draw just one good lung-full of air.

She knew she was utterly powerless to move or even to speak; but of his motives she was less certain. He knew he was utterly powerless to move or even to speak; but of her motives he was less certain. The shock of it did nothing to shorten their paralysis.

Her lack of struggle made him wonder if she did not welcome this accident — or its accidental result, at least. If so it would seem churlish to spring back in embarrassed horror and pour out the profuse apologies that were already assembling in his mind.

His stillness made her wonder if some tremendous power had not suddenly overwhelmed all his scruples about love and heedless passion; it would have to be pretty tremendous to do that! But if so, it must have something to do with her. The power must lie somewhere within her — all unsuspected. She began to feel frightened. She would have been more frightened if the feeling of his nearness — the touch of him and the weight of him — had not been so decidedly pleasant.

He, for his part, would have been more eager to find some *un*churlish way of disengaging himself from this embarrassing position if her nearness — the pleasing firmness of her beneath him — had not been so enjoyable.

The whole thing lasted less than five seconds — certainly less than ten. Her paralysis passed and she drew in a mighty gulp of air. He was delivered at almost the same moment; he prepared the words *I'm sorry* in his throat, but when they emerged they had somehow transformed themselves into, "Well, well, well!" — and that was all he could manage before his agonized lungs made him devote all his energy to the simple business of breathing; he panted like a horse ploughing in the heaviest sort of clay.

She was too breathless to respond in any way at all. As he slid to her side the blackness above her was studded with a myriad stars. At first she thought they were a hallucination, because the rolling of her eyes turned them into swirling lines of light; but as she recovered herself she saw their familiar shapes — the Bear, Cassiopeia, Orion ... the Milky Way.

Cassiopeia would be a lovely name for a little girl, she thought as she murmured, "So many stars!"

He was already wondering if there was mud on her back — and what Miss Pym would inevitably think, and say, when she saw it. He rolled on his own back, still panting but no longer desperately ... and then the wonder of the heavens hit him, too. "I never saw so many!" he gasped. "They're like jewels."

She giggled. "I saw quite a different set of stars when you barged into me just now!"

"Oh, I'm sorry about that!" He fumbled for her hand and patted it. "Clumsy me!"

She was on the point of saying it was her fault, adding that it was she who strayed from the path ... when she realized what a coy, arch, embarrassed conversation such a statement might lead them to. "It's nobody's fault," she said. "Are we going to get up?"

He went on looking at the stars; the broken-off branch made a pillow for his neck — the tiny French kind of pillow, like a draught-stopper for a door. "Are you uncomfortable?" he asked. "Get the branch under your neck. I can recommend it."

"It's under the small of my back. I can recommend that, too. It's not cold tonight, is it. I think I could lie here till dawn. What time is it now, I wonder?"

"One. Dawn will be in about three hours."

They lay still and silent awhile, each thinking how extraordinary it was that only moments earlier they had been lying together in the most embarrassing position imaginable — and yet here they were, not the least bit embarrassed, but not talking about it, either. The trouble was, it wasn't one of those topics you could just dip your toe into. True, you could dip your toe into the deepest waters if the bank was low enough and the waters in question were calm. But that was hardly the case here. To test *these* waters you had to jump off the moral or spiritual equivalent of a tall cliff — so tall that you couldn't even see how turbulent the waters were down there. And yet the urge to make that leap was almost overwhelming. Their silence was testimony enough to that.

"Penny for 'em?" he asked, taking the coward's way out.

"Let's see the colour of your money first," she sneered. When he pretended to fiddle in his pocket she added, "No, no! Coin of the realm won't do. It has to be payment in kind."

He laughed gently. "You're a bloated capitalist to your very bones, Jess. But I didn't actually ask to *buy* your thoughts, only to take shares in them, you know."

"Well, my lad," she answered smoothly. "Even for shares there's a premium to be paid. And be warned — they have to be *fully* paid, one fine day."

He chuckled again and laced his fingers behind his head. "I'll tell you what I'm thinking, then, if that'll count as payment in kind? I'm thinking I don't know anyone else — man or woman — I can talk to as easily as you. Don't you feel the same?"

"Perhaps with my brothers?" She tested the idea and then said, "No. I believe you're right. What else are you thinking? I mean, where does that lead?"

"It gives me one good reason why I haven't said too much lately about my earlier plan — to announce a spurious engagement to each other just to keep the world at bay."

"I don't follow ..." she said vaguely — though, of course, she did. And she had the suddenly racing heart to prove it.

"Surely?" he responded. "It means that the attractions of the spurious engagement are beginning to be outweighed by the attractions of a genuine one." He raised himself on one elbow and gazed at the paler darkness that was her face. "There now — it's said and can't be unsaid. I think we'd make rattling good partners for *life*, Jess. But I have no idea what you're feelings might be. Also, I fear that if we went in for a serious engagement, we might lose this, you know, this wonderful ease we now enjoy together. We might degenerate into those couples who can think of nothing but slinking off into secret corners to kiss and cuddle and waste time like that. So I'm torn between suggesting the old, fake arrangement — which I know you're eager for — and this new one, which … well — you tell me."

After a moment's silence she began to laugh.

"I see," he said coldly, exaggerating his wounded pride to a comical degree, to mask how truly hurt he was.

Still laughing she reached out and took his hand. "It's nothing like that," she said. "I'm not laughing at you or your ideas or anything. I'm laughing in despair at *me*."

"Despair?" His hurt turned to surprise.

"Yes. All my life — or certainly since I was ten — whenever I've read those coy proposal scenes in novels where the gentleman pours his heart out and the lady says, 'Oh la, sir! Pray give me time to think it over!' I've always sworn to myself I'd never, never, *never* say that. I might laugh. I might cry. I might throw myself into the gentleman's arms. I might turn and run a thousand miles. But I'd never ask for 'time to think it over'!" She gave a strangulated scream of fury. "Great God in the morning! The poor fellow's already been paying his court to her for years and years in most of those books. What on earth do those simpering ninnies *think* has been on his mind most of that time?"

He cleared his throat and said they probably *would* run a thousand miles if they knew that! Then he instantly regretted it.

But she laughed, wholeheartedly this time, and sidled her body over until it touched his most of the way. "Come on," she said. "I want to know what it's like to waste time. I want to see if it's worth all the fuss people make about it."

*T*he straw bale was a perfect height for Tillie to sit upon; Godfrey's long legs, however, felt gawky and in the way. She leaned her head back, sinking it into the bales piled behind them, and closed her eyes. Her lips parted in a sweetly satisfied smile. Surely, he thought, she didn't want him to kiss her yet again? They had kissed and kissed until his lips felt peeled. He knew what he wanted to do next but was too terrified even to think of it. He ran his eye down over the slender outline of her budding breast and tried even more desperately not to think of it.

"Penny for your thoughts," he said.

"Dunno," she answered without even opening her eyes. "They aren't worth that much."

"Oh," he said.

Should he suggest turning the light off? Would the darkness stir some thoughts worth more than a penny?

There was a hiss from the next-door stable as some part of the Renault cooled down and drew in air.

"It's cooling down," he told her.

"'Es," she replied.

Outside a screech owl called for a mate. He was about to tell her of it but changed his mind and said, "She's caught a vole, I expect."

"Lucky," she said.

"They've got special feathers that let them glide in total silence, you know. And their eyes can sense a warm body in the dark."

She sniggered. "That's handy."

After a pause he tried another tack: "You been working long in the Angel, have you?"

"Dunno," she replied.

"Well you must know a thing like that. A year? Half a year?"

She shrugged. "I s'pose."

"Well, which?"

"A year."

In growing desperation he picked up her hand. She opened her eyes at last. "They were all cracked when I saw you on New Year's Eve. Now they're beautiful."

"That's your old goose-grease, that is." She held her hand at arm's length and surveyed both sides proudly. "Mrs Blackwell, she nearly screamed the roof off when she seen them the way they was."

He corrected her: "When she saw them the way they were."

She smiled at him, half-mischievous, half-wistful. "Teach I to speak proper? Would 'ee do that, Mister?"

"What's my name?"

"Godfrey," she answered, wincing as if she feared a reprisal.

He wanted to stroke her head, the way one strokes a beautiful cat, to soothe it. He wanted to be inside her mind; to know what she was really thinking.

"If I do ..." he began.

"'Es?" she prompted.

He wanted to ask what she'd do in return, but the fear that she'd be able to think of only one answer held him back. Not that he didn't desire that sort of favour — *The* Favour, in the euphemism of the time — but even then he had intimations of some much less tangible prize, something of greater worth, that might arise out of simply knowing her better as a person. "Well ... I mean, *where* could I teach you? We can't always meet like this."

"How?" she asked in a challenging tone — meaning why? — which, in turn, meant why not?

"Well ... your people?" he said vaguely.

"My sister?" she asked.

"The one who divides the work with you at the Angel?"

"No, that's Mary. She'm a twin to I. But the only *people* I got that's worth talking about is Margaret, our oldest sister. She do work up the cop-shop, making tea and scrubbing floors and that."

"You live with her, you mean? She's *in loco* ... that is ..."

"She's the only mother we got. Our real mother's in her box five years or more, when Mary and me was ten."

"How old are you now?"

"Fifteen." She sat up straight and challenged him to say something teasing in response.

"I think you're beautiful," he said, which brought a happy smile back to her lips. His knees began to hurt; he longed to straighten his legs but could not do so without either turning toward her, which would be provocative in his present awkward condition, or away from her, which would be rude. "What about your father?" he added.

"'Tis him as put the mammy in her box. Said she never give 'e nothing but useless daughters." She mimed a hanging and tried to coax a smile out of Godfrey.

He closed his eyes and shook his head in pity. In his mind's eye he had a picture of Helston — very much as it would appear (in daylight, of course) from the old pack-horse trail — where Jessie and Cornwallis were lying down talking at that very moment, did he but know it. Such a picturesque and peaceful-looking little place! "Is your sister Margaret married?" he asked.

Tillie shrugged. "She got a feller."

He lowered his gaze. "'But they're not married, I take it?"

"They will, of course," she assured him.

"Ah."

She saw he knew nothing of the world. "When she's quickened," she explained. "When 'e've bin and gone and fixed a babby in she."

He stared at her in amazement. "They actually wait for ... you mean ... *that's* the order of things."

She laughed scornfully. " 'Twould be a fine thing for 'e to give 'er his ring, and 'er to give 'e no babby! And him with no chance of trying his luck with another maid then! Not legal, anyroad."

"Well!" He shook his head in amazement — that such beliefs and practices could be the commonplace in a town he thought he knew through and through.

To drive the point home she added, " 'Tis bad enough when all the babbies she gives him are girls!" — and she drew an imaginary razor across her throat.

He frowned. "How did we get on to all this? Oh yes! I asked where I could teach you, and wouldn't your parents object! I can see why that made you laugh. Wouldn't your sister object?"

Tillie shook her head. Her eyes were inscrutable as she said, "The sooner we're gone — Mary and me — the happier she'll be."

He rose to his feet and stretched, turning away from her to adjust himself more comfortably. "Let's lie down over there," he suggested, pointing to a darker corner of the barn. "I'll get the blanket off the car and spread it on the hay. It's easier to talk lying down, eh?"

She sniggered again and said lots of things were easier lying down. And when he stretched himself at her side she said, "Shall I take my dress off, or what?"

Panic seized him but it had all happened too quickly for the emotion to take hold and paralyze him. He was amazed to hear his voice saying, quite calmly, "D'you really want to?"

She frowned, as if *that* notion had never occurred to her before. "Don't you?" she countered.

He shook his head and — now that directness was enforced upon him — said, "I did when we set off from Helston, mind. All the way out here I was wondering how best to go about it. But now I'd rather just talk, I think." Something made him add: "And just look at you and, you know, enjoy how beautiful you are!"

"Gusson!" She giggled and blushed and hid half her face under her arm; but he knew that nothing he could have done or said would have pleased her more. Then she peeped out over her arm and said, "Haven't you never done it with no maid afore, then?"

He drew breath to say "Scores o' times!" and assure her she was in veteran hands; but the lie died in his throat and all he did was shake his head. After a pause he asked, "You?"

She shook her head, too, but then she added, "Only fingers." She licked her lips cautiously and added, " 'Tis a lot safer only with fingers, so Mrs Blackwell do say."

"Does she talk about such things with you?" he asked in surprise.

"All the maids," she told him.

He thought of Mrs Blackwell — backbone of the local church, the very pillar of respectability. He could not imagine her advising the maids at the Angel that 'fingers were a lot safer'! Obviously there was a whole female world out there of which he knew nothing — and of which one never spoke.

Except, of course, that he *was* speaking of it now — and in the calmest, most natural manner imaginable.

"I wouldn't mind fingers," she said hopefully.

Before he could stop himself he inserted the fingers of his free hand into the curls above her ear, caressing her tenderly, twining the hair around them as if he would bind them there for the night. "How's that for fingers?" he asked, leaning over and kissing her again.

She stretched out luxuriously, gave a contented little sigh, and murmured, "Much nicer!"

"Much?" He felt very noble and good.

Her lips reached eagerly for his; around the edge of them she squeezed a barely intelligible, "Much!"

An hour and a half later, with dawn breaking over the downs above Porkellis, a footsore Cornwallis left Jessie to boil the kettle while he went up to check on his precious Renault. He was furious when he found the vehicle minus its blanket. But when he looked into the barn next door and discovered the reason, he tiptoed back to the farmhouse, tapped on the window, and beckoned Jessie outside.

"Babes in the wood," he whispered, pointing toward the sleeping pair in the corner.

But she, being made of sterner material, went straight over to her brother and kicked his boots and pinched his cheeks until he showed signs of wakening.

He half sat up, yawned, opened one bleary eye, saw her, and fell back with a groan. Tillie came wide awake, but with less drama; she just lay there, frozen and watchful.

"This is becoming something of a habit with you, brother, dear," Jessie said sharply.

He groaned again.

"It's got to stop," she added.

He opened his eyes then, properly, and sat half-up. "What are *you* doing up so early?" he complained. Then he saw her still in last night's clothes and a broad grin spread across his face. "*You're* a fine one to talk!" he sneered.

"We walked home — remember?" she rejoined.

He looked at the pale sky beyond the open barn door, poised between night and day. "And the snails whizzed past you all the way!" he scoffed.

She licked her lips nervously and glanced at Cornwallis before she said, "For your information, brother dear — I happen to be engaged to this man. It makes a difference, you know."

Godfrey turned to Cornwallis to offer his congratulations. To his amazement he saw that this news came as something of a surprise to his future brother-in-law, too — not an *enormous* surprise, to be sure, but it was not the cut-and-dried matter that Jessie was trying to make it appear.

Cornwallis saw he had given the game away and so tried to make light of it, "I say!" he joked. "Are we?"

She rounded on him, eyes blazing, "Well, thank you for your support, Cornwallis, dear!"

But he just raised a finger to her and said, "You see! You see! What did I say?"

And, to Godfrey's further surprise, his sister calmed down at once and, turning back to him, said, "All the same, little bro, this is quite a different matter."

"All we did was talk," he protested.

She laughed, but with little humour. "Sooner or later people are no longer going to believe that," she warned him. "And sooner rather than later, I think."

"Ask Tillie if you don't believe me."

Jessie smiled thinly. "I think I will," she replied, smiling at the girl. "Tillie? Is that your name? Tillie what?"

"Tillie Lambton, Miss." She sat up awkwardly and ducked her head as a substitute for a curtsey.

Jessie's hands were already wafting the two men away. "You go and make the tea," she said, as if it were a penance they owed her. "Miss Lambton and I will be down shortly."

Much later, when Cornwallis was driving Tillie down to Nancegollan to put her on the milk train to Helston, Godfrey asked his sister, "Well? What did she tell you?"

But all she could do was shake her head in bewilderment and say, "It was like conversing with some member of a tribe on the far side of the globe."

And Godfrey found it best to pretend he had no idea what she was talking about.

When Cornwallis Trelawney and Jessica Kernow announced their engagement, the dovecotes of West Penwith were not greatly fluttered. Disappointed, perhaps, but then … such things are sent to try us. It was obviously a case of love at first sight — which, according to general opinion, was *not* a good thing. There was much tut-tutting over that, and more still when people remembered aloud the scandalous amount of attention Cornwallis had paid to Jessie at the ball. And then to crown it all, Michael Vestey had cast them as lovers in his opera, for the most frivolous of reasons — merely because they had the best voices! It was, in the old Cornish saying, 'like pilchards and cream' — too much. After a season fraught with such emotional provocations, two such healthy, and unattached, youngsters would have been strange characters indeed *not* to have rushed headlong into an engagement. But what lasting benefit could come out of such heedless actions? The omens were not good and already people were looking forward to the day when they could say, 'I told you so!'

Indeed, once the *fact* of the courtship could no longer be gossiped about, its *brevity* became the main talking point among those mothers and daughters who were disappointed of snaring Trelawney for themselves. They could all mention (and many delighted in doing so) couples who had known each other since childhood and whose marriages were, nonetheless, a misery to them. If lifelong friends could not make a go of things, what hope had a marriage based on mere months of acquaintance? Ladies' At Homes and dinner parties all over West Cornwall rang with dire predictions — all issued through smiling lips and greeted with merry eyes. The couple's every public appearance was scrutinized, instant by instant, for hints of ennui, discord, or incompatibility, until at last they were thoroughly wearied by it.

At one party a lady boasted of the number of engagements she had saved from disaster by stepping in with a timely pearl of wisdom at precisely the right moment; she then turned rather obviously to Cornwallis. He merely smiled at her, but later in the evening he found occasion to say, apropos nothing, that, "Some people are so good at helping lame dogs over stiles that they not only build the stile but will actually lame the dog, too, in order to prove it."

Jessie laughed. The lady took offence. Cornwallis apologized if anyone had imagined his purely general observation on English character to have some particular reference. But the couple realized it was time to take the pan off the burner and allow overheated feelings to cool.

"I think you should come to Yorkshire and meet my family," Cornwallis said to Jessie on their way home from that bit of unpleasantness. "I have received so many letters asking when they are to see you — I'm sure they believe our engagement is merely provisional until *they* have sealed it with their approval."

Cressida Pym, who was present when the suggestion was made, pricked her ears up at that; it made her change her plans completely.

The actual business of getting from Penzance to Leeds presented no difficulty. There were five trains a day in each direction — none of them, however, with sleeping cars or dining rooms. The most convenient was the 10.25 in the morning, which, with a single change to a through-carriage at Bristol, arrived at 10.15 the same evening. These timings meant there would be no difficulties about sleeping arrangements for an unmarried girl travelling first class with only a maid for her chaperon (for, of course, Clarrie would accompany her in the second class). And that, in turn, meant there was no need for Miss Pym to join the party. However, when she heard Cornwallis's joke about how his family viewed his engagement — and took it more seriously than he intended — she decided it was her duty to go along, too.

This angered Jessie. Her engagement to Cornwallis was no more than a ruse, so his family was really of no more interest to her than any other group of strangers. She had no qualms about meeting them, nor about making a good impression, since even their outright rejection of her would have no meaning anyway — except in the trivial sense that we all like to be liked. For her the main attraction of a visit to the Trelawneys was their foundry in Hunslett, just south of Leeds. This factory had its own power station, which generated some six hundred thousand units a year; and that was almost exactly the size of station Helston would require to begin with.

Of course, there would be nothing unusual in a visit to such a place by two ladies. They would gasp at the size and power of the steam engines, shriek at the display of electric sparks, and go away none the wiser but with their pretty little heads full of admiration for the wonderful men who kept those titanic forces under control. Such tours were quite regular occurrences. But for Jessie to start asking about the *duty* of their engines and the grade of coal they burned —

including such details as its calorific value, its ratio of fixed-carbon to volatile matter, and its ash content — would not merely raise Cressida's eyebrows, and probably the hair on her scalp as well, it would also alert her to ambitions that Jessie would rather have kept secret until it was too late for anyone to thwart them.

But, since Cressida was not to be shaken out of her decision, Cornwallis persuaded Jessie to turn this potential disaster to her own advantage. "Sooner or later," he pointed out, "your plans will emerge into the open. You may use me as a cloak during the very earliest stages — acquiring the land and ordering the plant and so forth. But, as I say, the day will come when you'll have to step out from behind. Then you'll face the united opposition of your father and Miss Pym — and don't try to pretend it won't be formidable. So why not look upon this visit to Leeds, when she'll be away from his direct influence, as your chance to bring her round to *your* way of thinking? Who was it said 'divide and rule'?"

On the eve of their departure — a Monday evening toward the end of May — Jessie went over to Wheal Dream to 'put the generator to bed for the summer.' Frank, who couldn't knock a nail in straight, went with her to watch and marvel — and (as always with him) to pursue his own interests further, too. However, since there is a limit to the number of times one can gasp with amazement — especially at actions that would seem quite unremarkable if performed by a man — he soon grew bored and drifted down to the farmhouse, where Cornwallis was finishing his packing.

"Hallo, young 'un," Cornwallis greeted him (he was older by thirteen months and two days). "Haven't seen you in an age. What's the girl doing?"

"At this very moment? Squirting oil through holes in the engine and turning it over by hand." He shuddered fastidiously. "Oiling the cylinder walls, she calls it."

"Ah, she must have taken the spark plugs out."

"I suppose she must. D'you want me to sit on that trunk while you snap the lock?" He leaped upon it and added, "Must justify my existence somehow."

Cornwallis snapped the lock and then suggested drawing a glass of beer and going up to watch Jessie justify *her* existence.

Frank accepted the beer but said he'd prefer to sit on the front lawn in the sunshine — a suggestion that his host readily accepted. They sat at a picnic table Cornwallis had knocked together from a few offcuts of the old roof timbers.

Frank took a mighty swig, smacked his lips with relish, and said, "What's the game, then, Trelawney, old chap?"

The other, used by now to his manner, eyed him with amusement and said, "Game?"

"You know what I mean," Frank rejoined. "This engagement lark. What's *really* going on?"

Cornwallis held his glass up to the evening sun and murmured, "We must finish this barrel tonight. The yeast is starting to work again — see?"

"Miss Pym's asking questions," Frank persisted. "She's noticed something fishy, too."

Cornwallis shrugged and gave what he hoped was a winning smile. "When the sun rises on time — as it does every day — I'm sure she has her suspicions about that, too. Would you be a good chap and keep an eye on the place for me? You only need to pop over here a couple of times a week. There are no locks on the doors. Just turf out any tramps you find dossing here."

Frank accepted the commission with a nod. "When's the wedding?" he asked. He did not really expect his friend to answer the question; he just wanted it understood that he knew something was up. He knew of the electricity undertaking, of course, but he suspected an even deeper conspiracy than that.

So he was really quite surprised when Cornwallis gave a backward glance and then asked, in a voice little above a whisper, "Can you keep a secret, young 'un?" He laughed at his own question. "Stupid thing to ask! There's none better. It's been on the tip of my tongue to tell you for some time." He rose to his feet and, lifting his tankard, said, "Care for a stroll along the lane? I'd hate this to be overheard by" — he jerked his head toward the generator room but said — "anybody."

"Intriguing," Frank commented drily as he rose to join him.

"It's an intrigue, anyway," the other agreed. "I don't know if I've done a very clever thing or an incredibly stupid one. I rather need your advice."

He said no more until they reached the lane, where they turned left, toward Nancegollan. "If we go the other way, she won't see us," he explained, "which would be rude." He took another swig of ale and sighed and scratched his head awkwardly. "D'you believe in love-at-first-sight?" he asked suddenly.

Frank let out a whistle of surprise. "Depends on what you mean by 'believe,' rather. Do I believe it has captivated some lovers? Yes — obviously. Do I believe it endures? I have no idea — not having the remotest experience, myself, of love-at-*any*-sight! Why d'you ask — as if I can't guess!"

"Very well — guess, then."

Frank chuckled. "Rather hear it from you — after all, you're the victim of this alleged assault." His eyes narrowed. "Or are you saying Jessie is?"

"You guess very well — for your age. *I'm* the victim in this case, but what I can't decide is ... well, about Jessie. Is she in the same boat?"

"If she isn't, you're going to have fun navigating, man! Suppose we stop talking in riddles and you tell me exactly what's on your mind."

Cornwallis fortified himself with another mouthful; and again he glanced behind them before speaking. "I fell in love with your sister the moment I set eyes on her."

"And had that sort of thing happened often?" Frank asked at once.

"Never! It was the very last thing I expected. I couldn't believe it was actually happening to me." He was lost among his memories for a moment. "To make it even less believable ... now this is going to sound absurd, but it's true. I think I fell in love with Jessie about a second *before* I actually clapped eyes on her."

"Love-*before*-first sight!"

"Just so. It wasn't her voice. I mean, I heard her speaking behind me but it wasn't that. She made some amusing remark — I can't remember what — nothing special but, you know, just lightly amusing. Anyway, I looked round to see who spoke ..." He stopped and turned his back on Frank, who also stopped — and watched him with amusement. "Let's say you're where Jessie was — and here's me turning round. Well, when I reached about here" — he stopped halfway through his swing — "a voice inside me said quite distinctly, 'This is the girl for you'! Now I'm not the sort that goes in for psychic voices and most certainly don't ..."

"Champagne, though. You go in for champagne."

Cornwallis was unamused as he resumed their stroll. "Don't be facetious, Frank. This is serious."

"Sorry," he replied, though he did not look it. "Didn't it frighten you, then — to be stone-cold sober and still hearing voices?"

Cornwallis gritted his teeth and persisted. "Of course it did! That's what I'm coming to. The reason I moved down here to West Penwith is that I was sick to the back teeth with all those Leeds ladies trying to interest me in their daughters."

"Very understandable," Frank said.

"My behaviour? Or theirs?"

"Both. I mean, usually a fellow's getting on for thirty before he's made enough oof and gained a secure-enough place in the world to enable him to marry. Young man like you — just come of age and rich as Croesus — made to order! Very understandable, I'd say."

"All right," Cornwallis responded glumly. "Grant you that. But you'll grant me that it's also very understandable for a fellow to want to get away from it all — to move down here? No?"

The other frowned at him. "Why? Were you suffering the delusion that we have no nubile daughters or ambitious mamas down here?"

Cornwallis sighed. "No — put like that I suppose it makes me seem rather naïve. I just thought there'd be fewer of them and it'd be easier to cope."

"*Sancta simplicitas!*" Frank exclaimed. He drained his glass and set it down at the verge, saying, "Pick it up on the way back."

Cornwallis did likewise. When they resumed their walk he said, "Anyway, my naïveté or otherwise is rather beside the point. The point is the frame of mind I was in. I was dead-set against marriage. It was the very last thing on my mind. Love and marriage were a million miles away when I heard your sister speak behind me. Yet one *second* later — bang! Right between the eyes! I knew — I absolutely *knew* — she was then and always will be the only woman for me."

"Lucky fellow!" Frank waved a hand to dismiss the topic. "You got your answer without all the usual false starts and shillyshallies."

"I wish that were so!" the other sighed. "The fact is, I panicked. Refused to believe it. Tried every way I knew to ridicule this tiresome voice and its ludicrous certainties. I told Jessie all the clever, dismissive things I'd ever thought or read on the subject of love. I even *told* her I'd come to these parts to avoid it."

"And what did she say — as if I couldn't guess! I'll bet she told you how lucky you were to be a man and to have the power to make that sort of decision for yourself."

"Just so. And I'm afraid it led me into a most idiotic gesture — not on the night of the ball but very soon afterwards. When she said she had no interest in getting married — that she wanted to *do* something ... *be* someone — I was absolutely shattered. Desolate! I could see myself losing her in the same moment as I found her." He laughed bitterly. "If she'd thrown herself at my head — like so many other girls ... I mean, I'm not boasting but — you said it yourself — a rich young bachelor is bound to become ..."

"Yes, yes!" Frank cut him short. "If she'd thrown herself at you, you'd probably have been able to reject her in time. Quite swiftly, in fact. But when you're used to that certain glint in their eyes, begging you to choose them, and instead one of them as good as tells you you haven't a hope with her ..." He chortled. "Well, it's apt to get the old blood racing a bit, what?"

Cornwallis laughed, too — not quite so wholeheartedly. "Of course, I thought of all that. I thought, *Here's a clever one!* — even though my heart was bursting with love for her. One *can* go on being quite clear-sighted, you know. Anyway, after we'd met a few times it became obvious to me that she *wasn't* just being extra-cunning. She was quite genuinely not interested in marriage ..."

"But love?" Frank put in.

The other grinned and held up a finger. "I'll come to that. Just let me finish telling you how this situation has come about. When I realized she was quite sincere, I had this awful, bleak ... desolate vision of life without her. I could see I was going to lose her. So I made this ... this *stupid* proposal — that, as soon as we reasonably could, we should announce our engagement. It'd stop all the other matrons from throwing their daughters in my path. It'd stop your father and Miss Pym from nagging her to be ladylike all the time and keep up her accomplishments and all that. And above all it'd give us time. It'd give me time to read and write. It'd give her time to do or be ... you know — whatever she wants."

Frank stopped and stared at him curiously. "Did you know about her ideas to form the power company at that stage?"

He shook his head. "I don't think it was even a gleam in her eye then. In fact, I still have no idea where it came from."

Frank lowered his head. "*Mea culpa!* The suggestion arose quite spontaneously when Harry and I challenged her one evening. The one thing Jessie cannot do is back down from a challenge. How did you take to the idea when she first put it to you?"

Cornwallis shrugged. "She carries that extraordinary air of conviction. Some women do it by being bossy or brash or shouting a lot. She does it so quietly, somehow. It's because there isn't a shred of doubt inside her. You can't shake her. You can't even get a toehold on her sense of conviction. It's like trying to climb a glass mountain. In short, I was just swept up in it. Aren't you?"

Frank ignored his question. "And you still are?"

"I think it's the most exciting thing ever. But that's not what I want to talk about. I mean, it's not a worry to me."

"What *is* then?"

"The fact that I love her now, as much as ever — more than ever. I love her to distraction. I think of her day and night. Her image is before me when ..."

"Yes! All right! I know the sort of thing you mean. Where's the actual difficulty, though?"

"Don't you see? I can't tell her a word of it — because of this ridiculous agreement!"

"But it was your own suggestion."

"I know — you don't need to rub it in. I'm engaged to the most wonderful woman in the world. I love her dearer than life itself. Yet I hardly dare tell her that I'm really quite fond of her company — for fear I'll lose her! How could a sane, level-headed man like me have got himself into such a predicament!"

After a pause Frank said, "The real question is what are you going to do to extricate yourself? Never mind the past."

"Hi!" Jessie's cry came rolling down the lane. "Wait for me!"

They turned around and started to stroll back toward her.

"Has there been no change in her?" Frank asked.

Cornwallis gave an ominous grunt. "Not for the better — from my point of view. Or perhaps it is. That's really what I want to ask you. I'm so caught up in it all, I can't see straight any longer. The fact is, she's starting to talk of love as something quite independent of marriage. Love that could never lead to marriage. Love in its own right."

"Well!" Frank responded cheerfully. "That's a start, surely? A step in the right direction?"

"Is it?" Cornwallis asked gloomily.

Frank's bewilderment deepened. "You obviously don't think so!"

Cornwallis cleared his throat delicately. "I'm thinking of the example she may have in mind. It's jolly difficult to talk about this ... but I'm thinking of Cressida Pym and your father, actually."

"Ah!" At last Frank saw his point.

But alas there was no time left in which to develop it. The evening was too peaceful — and Jessica too close.

Part Two

Porthleven

The New Vision

*F*our days of increasingly sultry weather had built up to a mighty summer storm over the whole North of England. It broke at sunset, as the train left Sheffield on the final thirty miles of Jessie's first journey to that part of the kingdom; it arrived not as a cloudburst but in the most spectacular display of lightning she had ever seen. Huge, lowering cliffs of sulphureous cloud towered over the Pennine Hills, on the horizon to their left, giving them the appearance of active volcanoes. Streaks of a blood-red sunset spanned the skies above and beyond. At the heart of each towering cumulus, it seemed, there sat a crazed electrician, playing with impossible voltages that rose far beyond any sort of control, until at last they spilled over — indeed, exploded — in an almost continuous flashing from cloud to cloud; the display cast a weird, devilish light over a landscape more hellish than she had ever imagined.

She had read, of course, how industry and the coalmines had ruined vast tracts of the North of England; and she had also seen photographs of the ravaged countryside. But nothing of that sort could have prepared her for the reality of the devastation she now saw on every hand. Even in the most lurid photograph an eyesore in the foreground necessarily hides others behind it; also, the lack of colour lends a certain stark dignity to a scene. But when that identical scene is viewed from a moving train, the hidden eyesores ooze into view as one foreground horror succeeds another. Then, too, you see with what a ghastly palette of bilious yellows, acid greens, and aniline violets the industrial   monster paints its landscapes — all of which the camera will chastely render in silver-white or -gray.

And how profligate it is, too, this behemoth — how careless of all it lays its squalid hands upon. Fifty years ago, fields and hedgerows and a clean, pure sky abounded here, from horizon to horizon. No more. Not a trace now remained; all had been obliterated beneath a higgledy-piggledy of brick walls and iron roofs. More chimneys than the eye could comprehend belched smoke and ash of every hue into the darkling sky — some of it so laden with filth it could barely creep over the blackened rim of the stack, from where it then fell in a continuous, ghastly hail of smut and foul vapour.

Nor did the pollution cease with the failure of this or that particular factory; if anything, its pace only quickened. Collapsed roofs and derelict walls loomed over poisoned acres where not even the hardiest and most tolerant of weeds durst grow. Pools of water too acid for life lay like open sores upon a clay too saturated with horrors to absorb any more. Old machines, built with pride and tended lovingly while they could earn their keep, were now piled in forlorn heaps among frayed cables and broken chains, bent rods and twisted girders, all rusting away beneath a decaying hide of hardened grease. It was a world without gratitude or mercy, Jessie thought, where anything that was not immediately useful was condemned to obliteration or heedless ruin.

The thickening blanket of evening did nothing to soften its harshness. For what the setting sun yielded to the grip of night, the almost continuous lightning was swift to illuminate once again. And even in those brief, fitful lulls between flashes, the fires of this man-made inferno were there to murder darkness and peace. From the raised embankment of the railway to a horizon lost in smoke, the night was mocked by the eldritch flames of a hundred blast furnaces, foundry fires, steam boilers, and — ringing the city like a besieging army in the hills — the steam furnaces and gas flares of the collieries on whose labour and produce this hell-on-earth depended.

Jessie and Cressida pressed at the window of their compartment, transfixed and appalled at all they saw. Cornwallis stood behind them, lifting his cloak and spreading it like bat's wings to obscure their reflections in the glass. "It takes you aback when you see it for the first time, eh?" he commented.

Cressida murmured her agreement. Jessie said, "It's beyond anything I ever imagined. But the thing I cannot understand is — how *do* people live amongst it all — when even the weeds refuse to grow?"

"Mind you, the lightning makes it seem even worse than it is," he pointed out.

She saw it was true, though perhaps not in the way he had meant it. The lightning froze little scenes and incidents of poverty and degrada- tion on the eye and held them there until they were obliterated by the next: tattered and barefoot children in the cobbled streets immediately below the embankment, kicking 'footballs' of old rags tied up with string; a man reeling drunk in a circle of onlookers ... laughing? disgusted? indifferent? — impossible to tell; a family with its belongings piled high on a handcart — not scurrying, therefore not doing a moonlight flit ... perhaps the man got a threepenny raise and they were moving proudly up to a 'better' neighbourhood, three streets away; a Salvation Army temperance march with a mocking tail of dancers and dogs; a woman brandishing a laundry dolly chasing a man hell-for-leather toward the palings at the foot of the embankment ... would he clear them in one superhuman leap? He'd have to, to escape that wrath incarnate at his heels. The train swept on and left them out of sight — replacing them with other scenes of meagre pleasure, or pitiable anger, or sheer, incomprehensible persistence in the face of grinding despair.

Even when they had left the city behind, the nightmare pursued them. For the constant lightning revealed a landscape that, though still rural, was undoubtedly being prepared for sacrifice. Collieries dotted the entire way to Barnsley and beyond. And, since the Barnsley field is notoriously 'gassy,' most of them sported flares — tubular stacks from whose barrels rose tall, lazy plumes of orange flame. Tonight they seemed to lick the sky, peeling off baby flames that rose in sinuous flickers, twenty ... thirty feet above their parent, before dying in billows of greasy black, starkly etched against the sheet lightning beyond. Their waste-tips spilled black fingers into the surrounding fields. Their branch railways cut across farms and village greens. The smoke from their furnaces rose a few hundred feet, met some kind of pause, and spread in a pall across the land. On every side the tokens of doom for that ancient rural idyll, where the great orders of monastic Christendom had once farmed and prospered, were only too plain to see.

"How old were you when you first saw all this, Cornwallis?" Jessie asked when her eyes could take no more of the devastation all around.

"About fourteen," he replied. "Of course, the family started migrating here from Cornwall in my grandfather's time, but my own parents only moved here eight or nine years ago."

"And weren't you appalled?" Cressida asked.

He shook his head and smiled apologetically. "I thought it was the most thrilling sight *ever*. All that power! And the wanton ... profligate *waste* of everything. I know it looks pretty infernal now — the dark, satanic mills and so forth — but you wait till you see it on a bright summer's morn with a good breeze to carry the smoke away. The sense of our own might is amazing — puny little creatures though we are! D'you realize — two thousand years ago, which isn't even the ticking of a second in the history of the earth, we were half-naked creatures running around in animal skins and painting ourselves with woad. And now ... all this! I honestly believe there's *nothing* we cannot do if we set our minds to it. In our own lifetime we'll achieve things beyond our wildest dreams."

Cressida returned her gaze to the blighted landscape. "We seem to find it rather hard to tidy up after us, though," she murmured.

"It'll happen," he assured her. "We'll do it when we must. We didn't even think of building decent sewerage systems until nice people like you and me started dying of nasty things like cholera and typhoid fever. We obviously can't go on for ever like that." He waved a hand toward the window.

"Perhaps," Cressida rejoined, "you men need a few women in your great industries. We may not understand much about them but we do at least know the wisdom of not trying to muddle on through your own pollution and filth."

Manfully Cornwallis avoided Jessie's eye as he said, "D'you know, Miss Pym, that's not at all a bad idea!"

*T*he real storm broke as the train rattled over the last five miles to Wellington Station in the centre of Leeds. As they came within sight of their destination, the line ran in a lazy, extended curve, almost a full semicircle from due west to east; again, as in Sheffield, it was raised on embankments or long, low viaducts of arched brick. The landscape — or cityscape — might have been taken from that same city, brick by brick, cobble by cobble, stain by stain; and what Leeds lacked in the way of steelmasters' blast-furnaces, it made up for in copper smelters, foundries, forges, and mills. Each was powered by its own steam engines, every one of which, in turn, had its exclusive furnace. Together they poured out enough smoke and smuts to obliterate the heavens — except on such a night as this, when heaven took revenge on its tormentors and washed it all back again.

The sooty rain fell in long spikes that shattered on the carriage glass and made a pretty kaleidoscope of all those myriad points of light outside. Here and there it formed snaking rivers on the pane, through which Jessie, pressing her nose to the glass, could just capture the occasional vignette, frozen by the lightning, which had now turned from the sheet to the forked variety. In its harsh, vivid illumination she saw people scurrying for shelter, clutching sheets of oilcloth or tarpaulin over their bowed heads ... a patient black cabhorse picked out by naphtha flares from a dance hall, looking like a statue carved in anthracite ... children dancing and splashing in a mid-street lake ... a man nailing an upright piece of board across his threshold — a veteran and victim of many a previous downpour, no doubt. Three nights ago they must have celebrated the Relief of Mafeking here in these mean streets — as in every other town and village in the kingdom. Now not a trace remained of all that jollification.

"Welcome to the North!" Cornwallis exclaimed as the train slowed down on the final curve into the station.

Jessie avoided his eye as she said, apropos almost nothing, "If all those factories had electrical power instead of steam, it would transform this city."

Cressida disagreed. "Instead, you'd have one huge generating station with four great chimneys pouring out smoke," she said. "I've seen it in London."

"It's possible to scrub the smoke, though," Jessie responded.

Cressida eyed her curiously. The picture of taking a scrubbing brush to something as insubstantial as chimney smoke was so absurd that Jessica could not possibly have that in mind; and yet the word had been delivered with such a calm and knowing confidence ... Her mood became thoughtful.

Jessie realized that if Cressida's resistance was to be eroded by a process akin to the Chinese water torture — wearing it away by ten thousand little drops — then each drop would have to be smaller and subtler than the one she had just let fall.

Wellington Station, though not new, had just emerged from one of its periodic spring-cleanings. The soot and grease left behind by hundreds of daily trains and their thousands of passengers had been scraped and scoured and washed away to reveal the mellow York stone, as bright as if it had just left the mason's hands. In those surroundings the train, streaked with grime from its long cross-country journey, and now shedding cataracts of rainwater, too, had the air of a grubby interloper in a rich man's house.

Trelawney père was waiting to greet them on the far side of the ticket barrier. He was a tall man, verging on sixty. His customary demeanour, Cornwallis had told Jessie, was grave, though he was now making an effort to be warm and cheerful. It was a rather determined effort, she suspected, and not one that came quite naturally to him. Cornwallis's puzzled, slightly worried expression seemed to confirm her intuition.

"Not the brightest welcome, ladies, to our fair city!" he remarked as they boarded the carriage. Cornwallis meanwhile saw Clarrie and their luggage aboard the dog cart that would follow them home.

"At least the rain will wash all those wretched, filthy streets clean again," Jessie replied.

"Ah yes! I always think we should enclose the railway in a pergola of roses. Or something floral, anyway. Hunslett and Stourton are quite the poorest quarters of Leeds, you know. They present the most dreadful aspect to visitors from the south."

"Apart," Cornwallis put in as he rejoined them and they set off, "from Cross Green, Rookwood, Burmantofts, Sheepscar, Chapeltown, Burley, Armley ..."

"Yes, yes!" his father interrupted testily.

Again, Cornwallis seemed slightly surprised at his short temper, as if he had expected him to share the jest.

His father, as if realizing that his behaviour was provoking his son's bewilderment, forced a laugh and added, "At least no one can say *this* part of the city is ugly!" He reached forth his hand and turned down the wick on the carriage lamp to make it easier to see out.

They were driving up Quebec Street, past the Mixed Cloth Hall and the White Cloth Hall, twin market buildings whose imposing exteriors testified to the wealth that was generated within. The two visitors peered right and left and were, indeed, impressed at the majestic grandeur of the buildings on every side, especially when, a minute later, they emerged onto Park Lane to be confronted with the lofty columns and classical splendour of the Town Hall, black, black as ebony and brooding against the lightning-torn sky.

"One can hardly believe that such wealth could exist cheek by jowl, a mere mile from the deprivation and wretchedness we saw from the train," Jessie said.

"A timely reminder, perhaps," the old man answered lugubriously.

"Eh, Pater?" His son laughed.

The other turned to him and replied mildly, "You think wealth does not need such reminders — that Old Father Ruin can leave his card at the rich man's door any day of the week?" He turned away and gazed out of the window. "Anyway, I thought our two young visitors might like a glimpse of our city's better face. Thanks to the Midland Railway, they could hardly avoid seeing its worst one!"

The women told him how grateful they were that he had deviated their route to show them these wonders, but again Jessie saw that his behaviour was most puzzling to his son.

Soon they were out at Sheepscar, in that ring of two-up-two-down houses which Cornwallis had listed earlier — street upon street of them, all built back-to-back and without a yard of garden among them. The Trelawneys' home, Allerton Grange, lay near the village of Chapel Allerton, about a mile beyond the city's northern boundary and almost three miles from the station along the road to Harrogate. They made heavy going up the steep hill to Scott Hall; in places there was so much water pouring off the tops that the horses were hock-deep. But once they reached the crest, the macadam was smooth and well drained and they made good progress the rest of the way. The clock over the stables was striking eleven as they drew to a halt on the carriage sweep just before the front door. Mrs Trelawney came out to welcome them as soon as she heard the scrinch of the wheels on the gravel of the drive.

"I felt sure you'd all got washed down to Grimsby," she called out cheerfully. "What a night! Did you ever see the like!" She was a buxom Yorkshire woman in her mid forties, with a bright, observant eye and a ready laugh. While still being hugged by her son she looked over his arm at the two women and said, "Now you must be — let me guess … Miss Pym. And you'd be our Jessie."

Cornwallis broke off and introduced them, confirming her guesses. Cressida was a little taken aback at her familiarity — but not at all displeased at the suggestion that she could easily be confused with a girl of twenty. As they went indoors Mrs Trelawney said she'd had some cold beef put aside for them and if they wanted something hot, she could wake up cook to come down and make an omelette. They all assured her that some cold beef and a few pickles would be more than adequate to their appetites.

As they passed down the hall to the dining room Jessie had the impression of a great many pictures, almost obliterating the oak panelling. She was about to comment on them when she made an even more interesting discovery. "I say — you have the electric lighting!" she exclaimed.

Mrs Trelawney spun round and grinned at her before pointing an accusing finger at her son. "I thought *you'd* be the first to notice that," she chided.

He chuckled and said that electricity was something he left to Jessie — a remark that puzzled his parents until he explained how he had bought an old lighting set and almost blown himself up — until Jessie came along and sorted it all out for him.

His father, whose attention had wandered into some private reverie, came alert at that. "What?" he asked. "Eh?"

"Really, my dear?" Mrs Trelawney stared deep into Jessie's eyes and smiled, hinting that her son was an inveterate leg-puller.

"I do seem to have an odd sort of knack with that particular machine," she replied off-handedly.

"Well, well — d'you say so?" she murmured, still not taking her eye off the girl.

"Have a look at ours tomorrow," her husband said gloomily. "It gives us nothing but trouble. We should never have installed it, I say."

"Jest not, Pater!" Cornwallis warned him. "She'll do it."

"Oh, I hardly think so!" Cressida put in with an awkward laugh and went on to assure the two parents it was just a little conceit between the two youngsters.

"The usual offices are under the stairs, by the way." Cornwallis pointed out the door.

Jessie excused herself and left them to continue.

"Well," Mrs Trelawney said vaguely as she led the other two to the table, "I admire any lass who doesn't feel she must hide her light under a bushel."

Cressida, who already had misgivings about a woman who came to the front door in person to greet her guests, did not feel them much dispelled by these outspoken sentiments. For the moment, however, she considered it wiser to say nothing.

When Jessie returned to the hall she found Mr Trelawney waiting for her. He laid a gentle finger on her arm to detain her a moment. "No ring, I see, Miss Kernow?" he said, glancing at her left hand.

"We're going to buy one while we're up here," she told him. "Cornwallis says there's a jeweller-friend of the family?"

"Ah!" he exclaimed awkwardly. "I see. I see."

She tried to turn his embarrassment into a joke. "Why? Did you think he was trying to fob me off with excuses?"

"No, no!" the other replied. "Jacob Bloom is both a jeweler and a family friend — quite right."

It did nothing to calm his awkwardness, though.

She tried again. "I know! You began to fear I was one of these awful young ladies who think rings are symbols of slavery!"

He laughed then — genuinely — and assured her it was not so. "Though mind you," he added as he led her into the dining room, "any modern young lady who can tame our electricity machine out there is sure to win *my* favour."

Mrs Trelawney could clearly have talked half the night away but she took pity on the travellers' fatigue and showed the two ladies straight to their bedrooms. Cornwallis remained to take a glass of port with his father. He and Jessie had the briefest chance to talk when they met, tooth-powder in hand, on their respective ways to and from the only bathroom.

"What did the Pater ask you?" Cornwallis said.

"He noticed I wasn't wearing a ring yet." She frowned. "It was almost as if he hoped we weren't engaged. *Does* he feel like that?"

Cornwallis glanced toward his parents' bedroom door, behind which they could hear his mother's animated voice — not quite loud enough for her words to be distinguishable. "Something rather odd is going on," he conceded. "You hardly know the Pater, of course, but I can assure you that what you saw tonight was quite unlike him. Whatever it is, it's not good news."

"He told you nothing — when you stayed behind just now?"

He shook his head. "Just vague hints. But that *is* like him — letting the news come out in dribs and drabs. He'll probably say more tomorrow. And then a bit more."

"You know your jeweler friend — Jacob Bloom?" she said.

He nodded.

"When I mentioned that you were hoping to get a nice friendly price from him ... somehow that seemed to embarrass your father."

Cornwallis shrugged. "Curiouser and curiouser!" He grinned. "Well, darling, I suppose I had better give you a kiss and say goodnight."

"*Had* you?" she echoed in surprise.

"Unless you've got some other suggestion up your sleeve?"

"Cornwallis!" She was alarmed. "What's got into you?"

"It's expected of us, you know," he pointed out. "It's what engaged couples usually do."

"Yes, but ..." She glanced nervously all around. "You know that's not ... I mean, in *our* case ..."

"Don't you want to kiss me?" he asked plaintively.

"No!" She gave a brief, angry sigh. "Well, that is ... I don't want us to be distracted by ... or I don't think we should risk ... oh, dammit, Cornwallis — you know full well what I mean!"

For reply he offered his lips to her.

Full of misgiving — not to say embarrassment — she raised hers to him. They touched. Her knees trembled. Her innards felt suddenly hollow. Her breath came in shivers. She broke off abruptly and drew back from him. "*That's* what I mean," she said and, turning on her heel, went directly to her room — or hers and Cressida's — without saying goodnight.

He stood alone on the landing for a moment or two, running the handle of his toothbrush over his lips where she had kissed them.

*T*he sun rose the following morning, just before four o'clock, on a world washed clean beneath a cloudless sky. Shortly before that dawning, shrill, assertive birdsong woke Jessie from a dream in which she was sitting in her carriage, dressed in no more than her underclothes. The wheel had shed its iron tyre outside a huge factory in one of the mean streets she had spied from the train the previous evening. A gang of urchins had run off with it and, though she made repeated appeals to a stream of men going into and out of the factory, they refused to pay her the slightest attention. They did not even notice her immodest attire. Then she was kneeling on the floor, with only her head showing over the carriage window-sill, trying to persuade a policeman to go and retrieve the tyre; but instead of helping her he kept grumbling that an *apparently* respectable woman like her had no business in a street like that. An angry song thrush in the real world woke her before she could reply.

She arose and, with the dream still running through her mind, slipped on her dressing gown to visit the lavatory at the end of the landing. As soon as she was properly awake she realized what she ought to have done. She should simply have got out of the carriage and retrieved the tyre herself — and never mind what anybody thought. It was only a dream, anyway — well, she could say that *now*, of course, but at the time it had seemed all too horribly real. Still, her dream-meekness annoyed her waking self; the fact that she could not go back to bed, return to the dream, and do it all properly simply rubbed salt in the sore.

On her way back to the bedroom she paused by the window at the end of the landing to watch for the moment when the sun broke above the distant skyline. And it was, distant, too, she realized, for Allerton Grange stood almost on the southern rim of the hills to the north of Leeds, between the river valleys — or dales — of the Aire and the Wharfe. Most of the city was out of sight beneath the hillcrest but its southern, industrial, quarter was both visible and unmistakable. Plumes of smoke and steam rose into the unclouded air from a forest of iron stacks and brick chimneys. The view was so clear that she could see one chimney in which the brickwork had been laid with a bulge and a twist to make it resemble a giant length of rope performing the Indian Rope Trick. She wondered which one belonged to the Trelawneys' factory — and would it be too forward of her, and too revealing to Cressida, if she asked to visit it today? Moments later the sun came up and touched the scene with splashes of rose and gold.

Then she understood what Cornwallis had said the previous night — about how different it would look in bright sunshine on a clear day. Civilization was a wonderful thing. Life was challenging and exciting. The terrors at which her dream had hinted were out there, too, but they need not cripple one. Oh, she understood it quite clearly now! That dream had posed her the choice between searching for her proper clothes and sitting in her crippled carriage trying to get men to assist her — or leaving her proper clothes behind and going out half-naked into their world and doing the thing for herself.

Then, of course, it annoyed her more than ever that she could not go back to bed, summon up the dream, and bring it to that most satisfying conclusion. She gazed out at civilization once again and made a silent promise that, if she couldn't manage it in a dream, she'd do it in her waking life, instead. Chuckling to herself at what people might think if they could only listen to the scribble in her mind, she retraced her steps and returned to her bed — if not to dream, then at least to daydream.

The moment she closed her eyes, however, Cressida said in her most governessy voice, "And where, may one ask, have *we* been?"

"We?" Jessie echoed. "Me, myself, and I, d'you mean? Well, how can I put it? We went out to plant a *Lathyrus odoratus*."

"In the garden?"

Jessie sighed and said flatly, "I went to plant a *sweet pea!* For heaven's sake, Cressida, what d'you *imagine* I went out for?"

"That is why ladies have night commodes in their bedrooms — to spare them the necessity of crawling through the house in the small hours and the comment to which such behaviour might give rise if they were observed while doing so."

"Well firstly I didn't crawl and secondly I wasn't observed and thirdly I didn't want to wake you and fourthly I don't like using those things. They give the word *odoratus* quite another meaning."

It suddenly occurred to her what the woman imagined she had been up to. She gave a single despairing laugh.

"Clever but not very funny," Cressida said grumpily. "If you do not understand me — and I think you do understand me very well — then take it on trust. Young ladies of our age do not go creeping about strange houses at night."

Jessie clenched her fists beneath the sheets and counted up to ten.

"What a ridiculous discussion to be having at this hour!" she exclaimed. "There's a breathtaking dawn happening out there. Why don't you get up and watch it. *That's* why I was away so long. I suppose you were counting the minutes?"

"Yes. Fifteen, if you're interested."

Jessie rose on one elbow and, grasping the woman by her shoulder, said in tones of mock horror, "Fifteen minutes? Good heavens, Cressida, I could have suffered a fate worse than death in that time — and you didn't stir foot or finger to rescue me!"

Cressida shook her hand off but refused to turn round and look at her. "I don't know what's got into you," she grumbled. "You are certainly behaving very strangely these days."

Just wait! Jessie thought grimly. "The probable explanation for your inactivity," she went on, "is that you knew jolly well that I wasn't suffering a fate worse than death. In fact, until you started dropping hints like a hundred of bricks just now, the very notion of a fate worse than death had not occurred to me."

Cressida's only response was a sigh that hinted at a snore.

Jessie continued: "But just you keep on dropping these hints and, you never know, I might just be tempted to see if that particular fate really *is* worse than death."

Cressida stopped breathing, too shocked to speak.

Emboldened by her silence, Jessie went further: "Or I could just ask *you*, of course."

Cressida spun round, sat up, and stared at her with such fury that, for a moment, Jessie feared she'd burst a vessel. Then Cressida leaped from the bed, saying, "Oh … *bother!*" The pause before the word and the vehemence behind it showed she would have preferred something much stronger.

She crossed the room and sat on the night-commode for half a minute, staring balefully at Jessie. Then she repeated herself: "Oh — bother-bother-bother!" and, donning her dressing gown, went to 'creep about the house' — at least as far as the lavatory.

She was gone about five minutes. When she returned they were both somewhat calmer. "I can see something in what Cornwallis said last night," she offered by way of an olive branch as she climbed back between their sheets. "About how different it would look on a bright summer morning. It really does."

Jessie, sitting up with a shawl around her shoulders, said, quite calmly now, "Let's talk about Cornwallis, Cressida. And me. And … your suspicions, eh?"

"They weren't suspicions, dear." Cressida patted her hand. "I would never suspect *that* of you. It's just that one must be so careful of one's reputation. People do talk — and memories are long, you know."

"Who's going to talk in *this* house! It's quite obvious that we've arrived among them at a most inconvenient moment."

"Ah!" For a moment Cressida was taken aback. "You're aware of that, too, are you?"

"I'd have to be blind and deaf to miss it. They're all facing some crisis that would put a spot of 'night-crawling,' as you call it, quite out of their minds."

"Did Cornwallis tell you anything about it?"

She shook her head. "He said his father only ever lets things out in little hints. He'll learn more today." She wished she had not started along this side-path.

So, too — apparently — did Cressida. "Well, we must wait for all that to unfold then," she said. "To get back to the main point — it isn't the circumstances of this particular house on this particular visit that matter, dear. It's a *habit*. One must get into the *habit* of protecting one's reputation. It's all that really matters. You can be as pretty as you like, play the piano and sing like an angel, manage a household like a royal steward, blah-blah-blah — but, shorn of your reputation, no man will look at you. No gentleman, anyway."

She was pleased to see that Jessica appeared to be thinking quite seriously over this lesson — until the girl said, "Very well, Cressida — but it does give one the choice, doesn't it."

"Does it?"

"You know very well it does — you, especially. You took that choice when you stayed on after Mama died."

Cressida fought a brave rearguard but she had felt this conversation to be in the offing for some time and realized she could not postpone it for ever. "As housekeeper-companion, dear," she pointed out primly.

"People do talk and memories are long," Jessie quoted back at her. "And I'm sure you know even better than I do what they talk about when the subject of domestic arrangements at Wheal Prosper arises."

Cressida nodded and closed her eyes; for an awful moment Jessie feared she was going to cry. Eventually, however, she sat up, drew a shawl around her shoulders, too, and, inhaling deeply, said, "I should have told you before, perhaps — except ... when *is* the proper time for a conversation like this?"

"Before it has much meaning?" Jessie suggested at once — and to Cressida's surprise for she had not intended it as an actual question.

"Now, whatever you say it'll be muddled up with my life, too."

"But it wouldn't have meant anything then," Cressida objected.

"D'you think geography *meant* anything? 'The principle product of Chile is saltpetre'! I had a picture of a sailor in a funny hat — called Salt Peter! But I *remembered* it. And when I saw a drawer in Wakeham's actually labelled 'saltpetre,' and opened it to have a look — *then* I understood. Teachers should just tell children the *facts* about everything. Life itself will bring the understanding in its own good time." She laughed at her own pomposity. "Here endeth the ninety-tenth lesson! Anyway — you could have told me at fourteen but you didn't, so you're going to tell me now."

To Jessie's amazement Cressida leaned over and kissed her briefly on the ear. "Yes, darling," she replied, "I'm going to tell you now. I love your father ..."

"Oh, well!" Jessie blushed. "I mean ... I didn't intend ..."

"Listen! I fell in love with your father the very moment I saw him."

"How wonderful!" Jessie tried to make amends now.

"It wasn't!" Cressida said firmly. "It was dreadful. Have you no imagination? A young girl, barely out of the schoolroom, employed to teach another, even younger — to nurture in her all her finest, most delicate, most womanly feelings — to teach her the blessings of purity in thought and modesty in action — to awaken in her that veneration for the blessed state of holy matrimony, which is the highest office to which a woman may aspire ..."

"Yes?" Jessie interrupted, hoping to cut the list short; she thought of adding 'blah-blah-blah' but desisted.

"... when all the time I was racked by a passion for my master — that young girl's father — a passion that would give me no peace. Can't you imagine what it was like?"

Jessie shook her head in amazement.

Cressida was, in her turn, astonished at this. "Honestly?" she asked.

Again the girl shook her head.

"You don't feel that ... that *passion* for ... anyone? Not even for Cornwallis?"

Jessie stiffened. "I don't want to."

"Ah!" Cressida gave a hollow laugh. "That's an altogether different thing — *wanting* to. I didn't *want* to feel like that for your father." She seemed at a loss for words then.

"Anyway!" Jessie prompted her.

"Anyway," she echoed bleakly. She continued to stare at Jessie in bewilderment. "Can I ask why you're marrying Cornwallis, then?"

Jessie teetered on the brink of confessing the truth but balked at the last moment. "Because he asked," she replied awkwardly. "Because it's what I've been told I must do, all my life. Heavens, Cressida — you're the one who did most of the telling!"

Cressida felt the blood draining from her face; the dawn light gave the scene a special air of unreality — almost the quality of a dream. "You mean you don't love him?" she asked.

Jessie became even more awkward. She wanted to talk about Cressida and her father and respectability and preserving one's reputation, not all this. "How does one know?" she asked in return.

"Oh, one knows! If you can even ask that question, then you aren't in love and you have no idea what it means. You know if you're in love just as you know whether or not you like chocolate. If I asked, 'Do you like chocolate?' you wouldn't dream of asking me how one *knows* such a thing, would you!" She expelled a sharp sigh and stared at the counterpane. "Here's a pretty pickle! I'm sure he's kissed you? Doesn't that stir any feelings? Don't your innards seem to go all hollow? Your heart beat faster? And an awful … desperate yearning for … something — you know not what — don't you feel that?"

As she listed each symptom she watched her young charge closely — and saw that, indeed, every one of them found its mark; so when Jessie replied, "I don't want any of that … all that side of it … all that hot, dark — I mean, it's too operatic. It's just like the opera — which is where it belongs!" — she was far less worried than she might otherwise have been.

However, she was careful not to show her relief for she knew it would seem patronizing to one in whom those powerful feelings had only just begun to stir. Jessie was right: Life *would* bring understanding in its own good time!

Jessie, for her part, was glad to see that somehow she had found the right form of words to switch off Cressida's inquisition; she had no idea what or how or why but she did nothing to provoke a fresh assault on that tender flank. Instead she went on for a frontal attack of her own: "Why did you let your passions win?" she asked.

"I didn't," Cressida replied. "Not for a long time. There was nothing except my thoughts that the Recording Angel could hold against me. I know what it says in the Bible, about sinful thoughts being as bad as the deeds, but if that were *really* true, then the saints who merely thought of temptations, and then resisted them, might just as well have given way, don't you see? Anyway, I didn't give way — which puts me level with Saint Anthony, at least." She giggled but immediately became serious again. "Until — well — it had to happen sooner or later. Then I'd have married your father ..."

Again she broke off, at a seeming loss what to say next.

"We had this conversation before, remember?" Jessie said. "Backalong in February. Your grandfather's will and all that — and ..."

"I know, dear. I told you of my decision not to marry him — and the reasons for it — but I carefully said nothing about what it actually *meant* to me. Living under the same roof as the man I love ... sharing his life ..."

"And his bed." Jessie spoke the words with a solemn finality, as if to say, *There! Now we both know we can't go back!*

Cressida inhaled deeply and said, "Yes — and his bed." She let out her breath in a sigh. "This is the thing I've been dreading ever since our talk in February — trying to explain it to you. Trying to make you understand why it was the only way out of *my* dilemma, but also why it's something *you* must not even contemplate. That was why I was so worried when you joked about becoming engaged to Cornwallis just to stop us pestering you and to leave him free of the unwelcome attention of other girls' mothers. It would be so easy — human nature being what it is — for an arrangement like that to develop into something not ... well ..."

"An arrangement like yours and Dad's!"

"Quite."

In for a penny, in for a pound, Jessie next asked, "The one thing that puzzles me, though, is ... well, not to go beating about the bush — how do you avoid making babies?"

Cressida gasped as if the words had struck her physically. "Really!" she exclaimed. "There are some things one just doesn't ..."

"Very well," Jessie continued easily. "I take it there are ways?"

After a silence Cressida said, "If you must know, it does not seem to be God's will. Not in our case."

"Ah."

"There are plenty of childless couples," she added defensively. "Well, not plenty, perhaps, but we aren't as rare as hens' teeth, either." After another pause she added, "And if such a thing did happen, we should marry at once — naturally."

"To stop the baby being *natural!*" Jessie chuckled.

"Oh, you can make light of it, Miss!" Cressida responded bitterly. "But you just wait till Love comes along and catches you like that — and shakes you so hard it shreds every scrap of sense and virtue you possess! Just you wait!"

*B*ennett's Lane in Hunslett was uncomfortably reminiscent of Jessie's dream — with the long, gaunt factory wall along most of one side and, halfway down the other, the poky little alleyway along which the ragamuffins had abducted her carriage tyre. Mercifully, the policeman and the stream of surly, uncaring workmen were absent. (And mercifully, too, she was possessed of all her clothes now!)

Trelawney's foundry made parts for mining machinery. Just about every metalworking technique was represented there: pressing, stamping, forging, drawing, rolling, and so forth — which brought the raw metal to workable shape — and then turning, milling, drilling, bending, and so on — to make the finished item. The largest thing they made was a compressor casing weighing two tons; the smallest was an acetylene pilot-light nozzle weighing a tenth of an ounce. There were something like a hundred and thirty machines, few of them duplicates, to perform all these tasks; half of them were driven by belts from an overhead power train that ran throughout every workshop; the remainder each had an electric motor. The power train had one, too, almost as big as the generator that supplied it.

Jessie thought it the most exciting place she had ever visited. The noise was appalling, the pace relentless, the machines uncanny, and the skills of the operatives quite breathtaking. Explanations were impossible except in brief, impossibly generalized remarks between one shop and the next. Everywhere they went they were constantly being asked to step back while one or two porters pushed trolleys and barrows filled with half-completed items between machines and shops.

"There's a lot of moving-things-around," Jessie told Mr Riddoch, the works manager, who was acting as their guide. She spoke for the want of anything more intelligent to say, but he gave her an oddly admiring glance and said, "Aye, there is that!"

Cornwallis noticed his response and said, "Sore point, eh?"

The man nodded. "It's the old problem, sir. Time — our ancient foe. If we could just stop production for a week, we could reorganize the shops and produce twice as much." He smiled at Jessie. "Ye have a guid eye, Miss Kernow, tae see that at once."

Jessie laughed modestly. "I don't know so much about that, Mister Riddoch. When you've been asked to stand back for the twentieth time, the penny does finally drop, even in a head filled with sawdust like mine."

Cressida cleared her throat, warning her not to be so forward. But Jessie's jokingly combative manner seemed to please Riddoch — and to provoke him to make efforts he would not have made for most young lady visitors. Having shown them where the power was consumed, he led them at last to where it was made. "Mister Trelawney tells me you have a special interest in this part of the business, Miss Kernow?" he ventured.

"Ah — of a purely scientific and speculative kind," she replied hastily, turning her head toward him, and away from Cressida, to make a mute plea with her eyes for him not to say too much.

He caught something of her meaning for he leaned forward and said, "Perhaps it's less to your taste, Miss Pym?"

"Oh, it all goes over my head," she assured him with a smile.

"I'll try to keep it simple," he promised, throwing open the door to the generating house and ushering them inside.

After the din in the shops it was surprisingly quiet. They had no difficulty making out his words: "It's a five-hundred kilowatt drum-armature dynamo with a continuous copper winding. Made by Ferranti. And the driver is a three-stage Parsons turbine. At present she's rotating at ... well, guess? How many revolutions per minute d'ye think she's giving us?"

Jessie, who had noted the gauge as they passed the controls, said, "Four thousand, eight hundred?"

He laughed, realizing what she had done, and asked her if she had any questions. She glanced nervously at Cressida, who said, "Go on, dear!" in exactly the same tone, and spirit, as she would have said the words at the zoo, or beside a fairground organ, or at the engine of a funicular railway — or anywhere else where ladies are expected to show a brief but polite interest in the incomprehensible world of science and industry.

Jessie drew breath and plunged in. "Would you say it is easier for an engineer who has worked only with steam engines to pick up a knowledge of electricity as he goes along than it would be for an exclusively electrical engineer pick up a working knowledge of steam as he goes along?"

"Jessie, dear!" Cressida laughed and fanned her face and beamed apologies at Mr Riddoch — who, to her surprise, appeared to be taking the most intense interest in this almost pointless question. It was pointless to Jessica, anyway. Surely he could see that?

"One more question or comment like that, Miss Kernow," he was saying, "and I'll begin to suspect you of pelmanism." He saw she had not heard the word. "Mind-reading," he added. "In thirty minutes' time I'm tae interview two applicants for the position of engineer here." He tapped the iron walkway beneath their feet. "And that is one of the things I shall surely be asking."

"And the answer?"

"Pick the steam engineer every time," he told her — revealing that he knew her purpose in asking the question in the first place. "There's a lot more tae steam than tae electricity still."

"Also," she went on hastily, "do you prefer direct current to alternating current? Obviously with the Ferranti dynamo you've got direct current here, but do you now regret the choice?"

This time Cressida was beside herself with embarrassment. Jessica had obviously mugged up one or two clever things to say from those books she affected to enjoy lately, and she was now just playing to the gallery. "Oh really, Mister Riddoch," she apologized profusely. "Pay no attention to these tiresome ..."

"Och, noo, noo!" He shook his head gravely. "It's another veery pairtinent question. For me, Miss Kernow, it's DC every time — unless you're dealing with kilovolts and long transmission distances."

"As at Niagara," Jessie said.

"Aye. And Deptford ... and that place in Stuttgart. But for a place like this, where the power is produced and consumed within a few hundred yards, there's no point in choosing AC." He licked his lips and added, with a small, sardonic lift of an eyebrow, "Anything up to the size of a small town, I'd say, should definitely be DC. Is that what ye had in mind?"

She asked several further questions of an equally searching nature, until Cressida stopped apologizing and simply stared at her in disbelief. He answered her directly, neither talking up nor talking down to her. That puzzled Cressida even more deeply, for she could not imagine the sort of man who would listen to a detailed question from a lady about something called an 'overload circuit-breaker' and keep a straight face, much less answer her as if she were a fellow engineer.

However, he was surely taking his revenge, she thought, when their time was up and he had to go and interview those two *real* engineers; he turned to Jessica and said, "May I put a question to you, now, Miss Kernow? Would you care tae look over the applications these twa bright young gentlemen have sent me and give me the benefit of your opinion aboot them?"

Cressida quite saw that it would take the girl down a peg or two — to realize how grossly out of her depth she had strayed this afternoon — but all the same there were certain things she could not permit. And one of them was a public humiliation of her Jessica by strangers. "She will not be required to *meet* them?" she asked at once.

Riddoch gave her an odd smile and said, "Just the application papers, ma'am. At this stage."

They went across the yard and into his office. Two rather nervous young men sat waiting in the anteroom. One was a handsome gentleman wearing kid gloves, spats, and carrying a silver-topped cane; the other was in a shiny dark suit that had obviously been his 'Sunday best' since the days when he was six inches shorter. They both scrambled to their feet the moment Riddoch's party entered.

"Shan't keep you more than a moment, gentlemen," he promised as he ushered Cornwallis and the two ladies into his office. In passing he asked his secretary to bring in the applicants' files but the young man told him they were on his desk already.

Jessie glanced through them, wondering what on earth she was going to be able to say after so cursory an inspection; it worried her especially that Riddoch seemed to have some quite definite purpose behind his playful, rather dismissive approach to this business.

Carter Manderlay was obviously the well-dressed young man. He was twenty five, had been to Oundle — a school for the sons of gentlemen — had studied engineering at University College London (only a pass degree, though), and had worked in various engineering capacities for Whitworths in Birmingham, Hadfield Steels in Sheffield, and the Manchester Ship Canal. Three household names. It was a most impressive career, marred only by its brevity.

Frederick Weems had been a welder's apprentice at fourteen; a welder on the Leeds Electric Tramway at sixteen; was now studying at night school for an external degree in Electrical Engineering at London University, and was assistant engineer at the tramway company's generating station. He had probably never been more than fifteen miles from Leeds in his life. Not auspicious.

"Well," she said diffidently, "on paper there's hardly any contest. I'd prefer not to judge on such a shallow acquaintance, though."

"Stay for the interview, then," Cornwallis said suddenly.

Cressida stared at him in amazement. However, as he was her husband-to-be and the future captain of her soul — and the owner of the whole business (or a member of that family, anyway) — she said nothing. In any case, she had already suffered too many shocks.

This time, she was pleased to note, it was Jessie herself who demurred and said, "No ... really ... I couldn't," and so forth. However, she soon spoiled it by changing her tone rather swiftly to, "D'you really suppose I might? What will the young men think?" and so on. "What will you tell them?" she asked.

"Nothing at all," Riddoch said cheerily. "Never tell anybody anything they don't ask about."

"And if one of them *does* ask?"

"Tell them you're taking notes for a *possible* article in a newspaper. In this world, all things are *possible*, surely!"

Cornwallis took Cressida out to wait in the gig; she left with some misgiving but there were one or two things she wanted to ask her young charge's fiancé, so she aquiesced at last. "Don't be forward, now!" was her parting admonition.

Riddoch called young Manderlay in first. Young Manderlay seemed to think it right and proper, too; he had been aw'fly nice to the tonguetied young Weems while they waited — just to make him feel less downcast when he was told he hadn't landed this position.

The interview went well, too. He was a little nervous to start with. He had never before been interviewed with a young lady present. Ladies always brought out the gallànt in him, and how could one give straight, technical answers to dull old engineering questions and be gallànt at the same time? However, when it became clear she wasn't going to say anything, he relaxed and from then on the interview went absolutely swimmingly. He was especially pleased at the number of great engineering names he managed to drop, quite casually and naturally, during the course of his answers.

At last, when he was quite sure he'd impressed them to the skies, he felt confident enough to turn to Jessie and say, gallàntly, "Is the young lady not going to ask any questions?"

Riddoch smiled pleasantly and turned to Jessie, lifting an eyebrow as if to say, 'Well? Are you or aren't you?'

For a moment she panicked; then she was thankful it had fallen to her so suddenly. If she'd had to spend all this time trying to think up an intelligent question that Riddoch had not already asked, she'd have been in a muck sweat by now. On the spur of the moment she said, "Those are most elegant gloves, Mister Manderlay. I do admire them."

He relaxed completely and even smiled at Riddoch, a smile that said, 'Isn't that just like a woman!' He stretched out his hand lovingly and said, "From Geives of Savile Row, don't you know. They make 'em for ladies, too. Mention my name and they'll look after you well."

"Thank you so much," Jessie went on. "Actually, I was wondering if you'd mind slipping them off and showing us your hands?"

The smile froze on his face.

A lethal silence fell.

He tried to laugh. "Well, really! I don't see what my hands have to do with ..." His voice petered out because, of course, he saw precisely what his hands had to to with it. He turned to Riddoch for help.

Riddoch said, "Naturally, if ye'd rather not, Mister Manderlay, I'm sure we'd *understand.*" The stress he laid on the word left the poor young fellow in no doubt as to *what* they'd understand.

A moment later the two naked hands he held out for their inspection trembled with the knowledge that their pristine pinkness was costing their owner this place.

After he had stumped angrily away they sent for Frederick Weems, who knocked and entered diffidently. His first word on seeing them was, "Hands?"

"What about hands?" Riddoch asked, keeping a straight face.

"Yon fancy lad." He jerked a thumb over his shoulder. "He come out there with a face like cat's collop and said to us, 'Show us thy hands!' And when I showed him, he looked all down in't merlygrubs and said I must o' washed them in sike watter."

"Sike watter?" Jessie repeated.

"Canal water," Riddoch interpreted.

"Aye," Weems agreed. "What did he mean by it?"

"Show *us* your hands, then?" Riddoch said.

Weems blushed as he obeyed. "I did me best wi' 'em," he mumbled. "But if I scrub it reet out, they go all cracked. And it's *that* painful, I can't tell ye."

"Never you mind about that, young fellow. Let me tell ye one thing aboot these hands: They're gey clean enough to gain ye *this* position — and that's all that matters, eh? Sit ye doon in yon chair and we'll talk aboot the salary."

For some reason he turned to Jessie, almost as if seeking her confirmation of this extraordinary news.

And Jessie, who had spent the morning (unsuccessfully, as it happened — but she wasn't going to say as much) trying to make the lighting set at Allerton Grange more dependable, peeled off one of her white lace gloves, laid her hand beside his, and said: "Snap!"

*W*hen Cornwallis said his father tended to let important news come out in dribs and drabs, he was not exaggerating; the progress of his revelations was positively glacial. There was no point in trying to hurry him along by anticipation — with remarks like: 'What it boils down to, Pater ... What you're trying to say is ... D'you mean to tell me ...?' and so on. He merely became evasive — with counter-remarks like: 'Let's not anticipate ... I wouldn't go quite so far as to say *that* ... ' and so forth.

By this slow process it emerged that Uncle Raymond Trelawney, the Pater's younger brother, was experiencing a spot of bother in Johannesburg. More than a spot of bother, in fact. Quite a bit of bother. Indeed, a great deal of bother. Candidly, 'bother' was altogether too feeble a word for it. He was in trouble. Quite some trouble. Deep trouble. *Grave* trouble. And, not to put too fine a point on it, the word 'grave' was altogether too apt for what had happened.

By now Jessie and Cressida were into the fourth day of their visit — the last Sunday in May. They had gone a number of pretty walks in Wharfedale; visited York Minster and promenaded around the city's ancient walls; and visited the Dropping Well at Knaresborough, where Cressida had bought a baby's shoe petrified in its lime-rich water. Excursions to Fountains Abbey, Haworth parsonage, and Harrogate Spa were pending. And Jessie had at last managed to get the Grange's lighting set going properly.

After morning service, just as they took their places for lunch, Mr Trelawney made a final, clean breast of the family's difficulties. By then he knew something of his son's plans to invest in a generating station in Cornwall. He also knew that his future daughter-in-law was in some way connected with the project, though Cornwallis had spared him the details. Also that Miss Pym knew nothing of it as yet and that his son would be obliged if he was allowed to break the news to her in his own good time. So the Pater had to choose his words with particular care.

Uncle Raymond, it seemed, had made a number of rash investments out there on the Rand. A gold mine had proved worthless. A hundred-per-cent-sure-fire-guaranteed diamond pipe was yielding stones of a most inferior quality. His race horse had won an important handicap — and died of a heart attack ten yards beyond the finishing line. As a result of these setbacks he had, even more rashly, borrowed money from the only people willing to lend it to him — who were also the sort of people who demanded interest at the rate of two hundred per cent a year and did not take kindly to the smallest default on repayment. In fact, he concluded grimly, if it had not been for the existence of the Imperial Cable Company, Uncle Raymond would in all probability be dead by now.

"And the threat to kill him," Cornwallis remarked, "makes certain sure that the family will rally round to help, of course!"

His father nodde. "We should be monsters to do otherwise. Ladies! I regret more than I can ever express that you should have to listen to this sordid tale, which redounds to the shame of us all. But, as you, Jessica, will one day be a member of our family — and you, Miss Pym, stand somewhat *in loco parentis,* — I thought it only fair that you should hear of it at first hand."

They thanked him for this courtesy. Jessie ventured to ask how much it might affect her plans — hoping he understood what she meant and would be guarded in his reply.

"For a while last week, my dear," he replied, "I believed we should all end up in Carey Street. Fortunately, Imperial Cables exist not merely to enable men to reveal to their brothers the extent of their debts. They also permit negotiations with the sharks who did the lending. In short, we have reached an accommodation with the Eezee-Lend Company of Johannesburg that will save Raymond's life without entirely ruining ours. It will, however, mean that the family will have to draw in its horns for a number of years to come."

Cornwallis put it even more succinctly. "No more allowance for me!" he told her.

Cressida blanched. "Does that mean your marriage is ... well, also to be postponed for a number of years?" she asked.

He nodded but his expression was uncertain. "That would be for Jessie to decide," he said, turning to her. "You must obviously consider yourself freed from any promises you have given me."

"Let's talk about it after luncheon," she suggested. The promises she wished to discuss could not, of course, be raised with Cressida there. She told the Trelawneys she was so sorry this blow had befallen them but was sure she and Cornwallis could scrape along somehow.

The rest of the meal passed in a rather subdued atmosphere; even the ebullient Mrs Trelawney was, understandably, somewhat crushed.

Cressida had taken the suggestion that 'they' should talk the matter over after lunch to include herself, so she was surprised when Jessie said, "D'you mind awfully, Cressida, if Cornwallis and I discuss this alone?" She smiled engagingly and added, "If he is not to become captain of my soul as swiftly as we expected, then the sooner *I* adopt that rôle, the better. Don't you agree?"

Cressida could think of no good argument to the contrary but she still felt miffed at her exclusion.

Anna Trelawney found her standing sulkily at the drawing-room window, watching the two young ones pacing the terrace outside. "Ah!" she said, forcing more brightness into her tone than she had managed at lunchtime, "there you are! I was hoping to find you free. I think that you and I should put our heads together and make up our minds about certain things ... no matter what those two out there may decide. Don't you?"

They took their parasols, for it was a warm, sunny day with little breeze, and went for a walk over the tops, across Brandon Moss. Cressida began by repeating Jessie's condolences on their misfortune and saying how heartily she wished to be joined in them. "I could not help noticing how deeply the news has affected you, Mrs Trelawney," she concluded. "I'm only amazed that you managed to be so cheerful in welcoming us here last Tuesday — for you surely knew about it then, too?"

The woman laughed. "Bless you, Miss Pym, but it's not the money, you know. We can live on cat-collop and chimpings if we must. And I often think that the style of life supposedly enjoyed by people who live in houses like *that*" — she jerked an almost contemptuous thumb toward the Grange — "is a very mixed sort of blessing." She collapsed her parasol as they passed into the shade of some trees; then she levelled it at a picturesque little cabin bordering the Harrogate road. "D'you see yon cottage?" she asked. "My dressmaker lives there — Mrs Taylor, funnily enough. Widowed these ten years. Her husband, old Dan Taylor was run down by the Earl of Harewood's coach one morning in September. He was trying to rescue a hedgehog from under its wheels. You know the stupid way they curl up when danger's about. He was as soft as a sucking duck, as they say round here."

She paused and turned to Cressida with a puzzled frown. "Why did I start telling you this. Oh yes! Widow Taylor, living in yon cottage with her daughter Selina, sewing dresses, milking her two goats, tending their bees and hens, fattening a pig for Christmas, and looking out on a cottage garden with more flowers than we've got at the Grange ... d'you know, many's the time I've come away from there, going back home to the usual round of *my* life — a dispute to settle between cook and the housekeeper, or to discipline a maid who's been keeping too much company, or a deputation from the parish council to placate, or a board meeting of the home for waifs and strays, or a guest list for the garden party to be cut back to *only* a hundred and twenty ... you know the sort of thing, I'm sure. Anyroad, I compare her life with mine and I wonder — am I a fool or what? I could be living just like Widow Taylor if I wanted. I wouldn't even need to take in sewing! I could put my money in the funds, take a charming little cottage like that — only not on the highway — keep bees and goats and hens and a pig ..." Her voice trailed off into a laugh, to show how inexpressibly happy she'd be. "So why do we go on living at the Grange and putting up with all its aggravations?"

Cressida wanted to say, 'Duty?' but it seemed much too elementary a point to make. Surely Anna Trelawney did not need that sort of reminder? Then, to her surprise, the emotional force of the argument slipped under the guard-rail of her own sense of duty. She had a sudden picture of Wheal Dream, the twin of Wheal Prosper except for the addition of the classical façade — and somehow that was significant. She had a picture of Jessie living in the old farmhouse with Cornwallis, no longer enjoying his allowance but having to live by his own labour. Their life would be something like the rural idyll Anna Trelawney had just described. Contrasted with it was her own life in that identical-but-gentrified house, the equivalent of Mrs Trelawney's life at Atherton Grange. And the pang of jealousy that pierced her was proof enough that she understood very well what her hostess was driving at. "In an ideal world, you're right, of course," she said wistfully.

"What's the opposite of an ideal world, I wonder," Mrs Trelawney said. Then, with a laugh to dissociate herself from the Shrieking Sisterhood, she said, "A man's world?"

Cressida laughed, too, to show she understood that the woman didn't *really* mean it but that, like her, she, Cressida, did see a little nugget of truth in the gibe.

"We sit on charitable committees," Mrs Trelawney said, "and give big garden parties and employ a small army of servants because we're in business and we expect the custom and support of others in business — who do the same thing with their lives and expect the same of us. Round and round and round we go! We all keep each other afloat in a sea of mutual expectations." She sniffed. "At least, I hope it *is* a sea and not a bath, because baths have plugholes and there's a lot of folk around with fingers that'd itch to pull the plug out. We'd go round and round *then*, all right! Perhaps that's why they call it revolution!"

Cressida, who wanted more than anything to talk about Jessica's changed prospects, was nonetheless seduced by these much more general remarks, which seemed to have particular bearing on her own life. She felt revealed to herself in ways she had never before experienced. Truths that had hovered somewhere near the edge of her understanding — *very* near, she now felt — were being dragged those last few inches into its light. Half-formed notions that had lain higgledy-piggledy in her mind, like uncooperative bits of a large jigsaw puzzle, were now dropping easily into place. She had been taught, and, in her turn, had tried to teach Jessica, the notions of a woman's duty — but quite blindly, as if they were self-evident truths. 'Water is wet' was a self-evident truth; one might speculate as to *why* it is wet but it would be pointless to question *that* it is so. And all the questioning and speculating in the world wouldn't alter the fact of the matter. Until now her notions of a woman's duty had been like that, too.

But now she could see they were being eroded — and had been eroded for some time — by numerous contradictory little rivulets of thought, feelings ... events. First there was the fact that she was now thirty (admitting to twenty-nine but inescapably thirty). Her birthday had brought the first intimations that she was not, after all, going to live for ever, and that her ambiguous status at Wheal Prosper would grow more and more awkward as that protective wall of Kernow youngsters took wing and left. When Jessica went, her exposure would be severe. Indeed, it would probably become quite unendurable. Why had she never faced these uncomfortable facts before?

And why did talk of a rural idyll prompt them all of a sudden?

"My, you're in quite a brown study!" Anna Trelawney remarked.

"Oh, I'm sorry!" Cressida said. "Your picture of a little cottage up some wooded valley stirred such contradictory thoughts in me."

"Ah well!" Mrs Trelawney gave a resigned sort of sigh. "It's still possible for you, isn't it! Mrs Taylor's a widow. You're a spinster. Two ends of the same plank."

Was she fishing? Cressida wondered. Had Cornwallis told her about the domestic arrangements at Wheal Prosper? A man might say something quite unwittingly that a woman's nimble mind would see through at once, hitting upon the truth that had escaped him. Well, that same nimbleness could be put to work in her favour, too. She could explain her predicament without openly confessing to anything. Mrs Trelawney was surely woman-of-the-world enough to read between the lines. And so Cressida explained about her grandfather's restrictive will and the constraints it put upon her marrying.

"I usually tell people it all goes to a dogs' and cats' home," she concluded. "But that's just to stop further inquiry — and to make my predicament slightly more pathetic. But I'll tell you the truth in confidence, Mrs Trelawney. The fact is — if I marry, the forty thousand pounds that's held in trust goes to my brothers, or their heirs, or *their* heirs — and so on in perpetuity — even if I live to be a hundred and marry then!"

The word 'perpetuity' struck a chord in Mrs Trelawney. "You say you've told no one this?" she asked. "None of the Kernows?"

"Not even their father," Cressida admitted.

"Nor Frank? He's the lawyer, isn't he?"

"Certainly not to Frank!"

"Why d'you say it in that tone? Is he what they call the town crier?"

"No!" Cressida laughed. "The very opposite. He's a charming young man, but ... well, to be honest, part of his charm is that he makes no secret of the fact that ... how can I put it? Frank's interests come top of any list. He's quite unscrupulous but he also disarms all criticism by telling you how utterly unscrupulous he is, and giving you a winning smile into the bargain."

Anna Trelawney clapped her hands with delight. "Oh, I do *love* dealing with men like that. No humbug. You know where you stand with them — *if*, that is, you believe them."

"Oh, you'd believe Frank, I promise you."

"Really? I should so like to meet him. I feel a visit to Wheal Dream is in the offing."

Cressida laughed and told her it was out of the question. It would be some months yet before it even reached dream-cottage standards. "But you must stay at Wheal Prosper, of course," she added — thinking that if the woman did not read between the lines *now*, she soon would. Then she added, "Why should one not believe men who admit to being unscrupulous like that?".

"Oh ... I've met only a handful in my life, but they've all turned out to have a soft, sentimental streak. I think they pretend to be unscrupulous — and, indeed, often act in unscrupulous ways, too — in less important matters where the damage is slight — but they pretend, you see, in order to mask that softness within them. Anyway, I was going to suggest that you mention this will of your grandfather's to young Frank. You may be able to apply to the Court of Probate for its conditions to be set aside, you know. It's a well known legal principle that English law abhors perpetuities when it comes to inheritance. Charities, yes — inheritance, no."

The prospect so excited Cressida that for a moment she could think of no reply. To fill the silence, Mrs Trelawney said, "I happen to know a little about it because a cousin of mine has successfully broken an in-perpetuity trust quite recently. Of course, his case may differ from yours. I should hate to raise your hopes without proper warrant."

"It has just occurred to me," Cressida said slowly, "that it's entirely possible that Frank already knows all about it. I can't believe he *hasn't* looked up my grandfather's will. He's probably got a copy in his office right now. And I'm sure this point about perpetuities has occurred to him, too."

"And yet he's said nothing?"

"He'll be saving it up for a moment when it's useful. Useful to *him*, of course."

"Well, well, well! The more I hear about him, the more interesting he becomes."

They reached the end of the lane beside the woods and put up their parasols again. Here at the crest of the hill they could look up the valley to Eccup reservoir, at its head. Today those usually dark waters sparkled invitingly in the bright sunlight. Anna Trelawney drew her companion's attention to the line of an old Roman road to York. At the end of her sweep her finger accidentally pointed to a young woman coming toward them. "Oh dear," she said to Cressida under her breath, "I hope she doesn't think I was pointing at her!"

She was about seventeen, Cressida judged as the girl came nearer — tall, willowy, fair-skinned, and with ash-blonde hair. She walked with such grace that the two women were content to watch her, as one might watch a dancer between set pieces. When she drew close enough she bobbed a curtsey and said, "Good afternoon, Mrs Trelawney," in a strong Yorkshire accent — stronger than Mrs Trelawney's. Even in the few days she had been here Cressida realized that accent was no guide to class in Yorkshire; but the fact that the girl was unchaperoned almost certainly meant she was of humble origin.

"Good afternoon, Selina," Anna replied. "Out picking wild flowers?"

She held forth a posy of flowers like little white buttons and said, "Milkmaids' pearls, ma'am. One of the goats is kidding and it seem to ease her travail."

"Good lass!" Anna said. "Tell your mother I shall call with a little work for her on Tuesday."

"She can call to the Grange, ma'am. So can I, come to that."

"And deprive me of the chance to enjoy your perfect little garden, you cruel girl? Never!"

The girl gave a strangely satisfied smile, curtsied again, and went her way.

"Talk of the devil!" Anna said as they climbed the stile into the field and started along the path by which the girl had approached them.

"That's Mrs Taylor's daughter, I take it?" Cressida asked.

"The same." Anna turned and eyed her companion speculatively. "What did you make of her?" she asked.

"She has great poise," Cressida offered. "And a rather sensitive face, I thought. There's an Elizabethan miniature I've seen, just like her — but of a man. The Earl of … I don't know. Darnley and Leicester are the only Elizabethan earls I can think of."

Anna chuckled. "You're closer than you realize, my dear — though it couldn't have been the Earl of Harewood. The barony was only created just over a hundred years ago and the earldom's even younger." She put on a mock-snobbish air and added, "Utter parvenoos, don't you know!" and laughed. Then, more seriously, she added, "But she's one of them. She's a Lascelles. The Harewood girls are a *lively* lot — if you follow? Spirited and independent. And every now and then there's a little *accident*." She turned and stared after the diminishing figure of the girl. "And there, but for the grace of God — or the grace of the marriage sacrament, to be precise — goes the Honourable Selina Lascelles, believe it or not!"

"Does she *know*?" Cressida asked, fascinated at this revelation.

"They call them 'fitzies' around here," Anna went on. "I used to think it had something to do with fits of madness or fits of unbridled passion. But its the old heraldic *fitz*, meaning bastard offspring of the king. The children used to call her Fitzielena at school, so I'm sure she knows. Actually, you've only got to look at her bearing to see that she knows very well."

Cressida watched Selina pass out of sight behind the hedgerow. "Poor child," she murmured. "What'll she do?"

Anna paused before she replied. "As a matter of fact," she said, "it was Selina put those ideas into my head. I was standing in her garden one afternoon last summer — an afternoon like this it was. I call it *her* garden because she's the one who's made it the picture it is. And we were standing there when a governess cart from Harewood House went by with four or five young nabobs in it — children her age — all looking so uncomfortable in their Eton collars and heavy dresses. And cross! They were all arguing. They looked like boiled puddings. And I was watching her, Selina, to see if she gave away any feelings. I mean, any one of them could have been brother or sister to her for all we knew! There were certainly cousins there. And ... you saw that little smile she gave just now? Well, that's the smile she had on her face then as she watched them drive by."

"And did you discuss it with her?" Cressida asked, wondering if the smile alone had been enough to set Mrs Trelawney thinking the way she did.

"In a roundabout way, yes. I said I wondered what they were quarelling about, and she said caged birds always fight. And then, on my way home, I suddenly thought — caged bird! Which of us was the caged bird, Selina or me? We think we need money because it buys us freedom — yet all we do is go out and buy a better cage! Forgive me, Miss Pym. Such thoughts are obviously on my mind at this particular moment. But that's no reason to burden you with them, too. You clearly have no such cause for worry."

"Oh!" Cressida exclaimed. "I wouldn't say that."

Anna looked at her in surprise but all she said was, "Ah. Forgive me again. I wouldn't have said that, except that you had already told me the size of your trust fund. Forty thousand, even in the dullest funds, would earn enough to keep a house and carriage and six servants."

"I really have no need of it," Cressida said. "I give some to various charities and keep the rest on deposit. Jessica's father pays me a generous honorarium, you see, sufficient for all my reasonable wants."

"And of course" — Anna smiled mischievously — "you have no unreasonable ones, I'm sure."

"I'm beginning to think I must be a very dull person," Cressida said unhappily.

"Oh, come!" Anna took her arm and gave it a reassuring squeeze. "That's the very last thing I'd say about you — truly! You don't really think it, do you?"

"Compared with Jessica, yes."

They had reached the line of the old Roman road, though she had to take Anna's word for it; only the portion that had been adopted by the turnpike commission, a quarter of a mile away, showed where it had run almost two thousand years earlier. They stared at it awhile in silence. Anna usually said a little piece about the legions marching to the next fort, whose earthworks were visible to the south of Eccup reservoir, but she didn't want to break Miss Pym's line of thought at that interesting moment. They turned about and retraced their steps.

"I agree that Jessie is a fascinating young person," she said, taking Cressida's arm once again. "But I hardly think you'd suffer in any comparison, you know. Why d'you believe you do?"

"Oh ... my wants are so simple and hers are not. My views on life are so straightforward ..."

"And hers are not?" Anna prompted.

"She's still trying to arrive at them. She doesn't take things on trust. Tell her a candle flame burns and the first thing she does is stick her hand in it. Then she'll agree you were right."

"Tell me something about her brothers — her other brothers, I mean, apart from Frank. Cornwallis has spoken about them, of course, but men are never very informative about one another, are they. He says Harry is 'a good fellow' ... vague things like that."

"Harry *is* a good fellow — also very artistic. His father despises him for it."

"But you don't?" To her surprise Anna saw that her question left Cressida slightly flustered — so slightly that she might not have noticed it if she had not actually been observing her.

"He is what he is," Cressida said. "He can't help it. Mister Kernow has very traditional views on what is proper to eldest sons — and poor Harry simply cannot live up to them."

"And has he views on what is proper for daughters?" Anna guessed. "Do stop me if I trespass, only I *should* like to know all that it is proper to know about my son's future in-laws."

"Of course," Cressida assured her. "Please don't mistake my silence for disapproval. You have every right to ask such things. If I have difficulty in answering, it's because the whole family is outwardly so conventional and inwardly not at all. Harry conforms to his father's wishes not out of cowardice but to make life easier. In fact, he doesn't conform at all. For instance, Mister Kernow gives him some of the firm's accounts to study and so he takes them straight to Jessica, who looks at them and tells him three clever points to make about them. Then he spends the rest of the time doing little sketches in them."

"It sounds as if Harry should be sent off to art school and Jessie should be taken into the business!"

Cressida nodded unhappily. "Mister Kernow would never agree to it, but you're quite right. It should be Kernow and Daughter, not 'and Son.' I did once mention it, half in jest."

"And?"

"He nearly went up in smoke. In fact ..." she continued warily, "I'm not at all sure ..." She hesitated and the hair bristled on her neck, for this was another of those ideas that had been lying around just beneath the level of her consciousness for some time past, and it was only coming to the surface as she spoke of it.

"Yes?" Anna prompted her.

"Well, I'm not at all sure she isn't planning something. Some business venture with Cornwallis. Something to do with electricity. She makes a joke of it — pretends it's some eccentric new whim of hers — the way adolescents go in for intellectual rebellion, you know. She's done a lot of that in her time, too, but this is different. She thinks I don't know her, but I do. And I know this is different. She's persisting with this one — and taking it much too far to be a joke."

"She certainly persisted with our lighting set until she mastered the problem. No one told *us* not to put linseed oil on those bits. They just said keep them oiled — and that was the only oil we had in the house." The full implication of Cressida's words struck her then. "When you say she's planning something, d'you mean she and Cornwallis?"

Cressida shrugged awkwardly. "This idea has only just struck me, Mrs Trelawney. But ... yes. I suppose he'd have to be let into the secret — if, indeed, secret it is. Perhaps that's what they were discussing so earnestly on the terrace after lunch."

"Dear me! If her father went up in smoke at the thought of her joining the family business, what's he going to do if your thoughts prove well founded?"

Cressida shuddered. "Quite!" she said.

*fter Evensong the day cooled down enough to allow a game of croquet to be played with proper vigour. Jessie, an aggressive player at any time, was in a particularly assertive mood that evening. When she dispatched Cornwallis to the shrubbery for the third time, he finished the round and said he'd sit the next one out. Half way through that next round his mother retired, too, leaving only her husband, Jessie, and Cressida in play.

"Now!" Jessie said gleefully, rubbing her hands with delight, "we can get down to some really murderous strokes!"

Anna found her son standing to one side of the terrace, staring out over the fruit cage, more or less with his back to the croquet lawn. "Your beloved is in a somewhat overpowering mood tonight," she commented as she joined him. "Having second thoughts?"

He laughed, but with little humour. "Not at all, Mater."

"Don't call me that. You're not at school now. Mother or Mum will do. She's not a secret suffragist, is she?"

"Jessie?" He shook his head. "She's too single-minded for that."

"Oh?" his mother exclaimed in surprise. "I thought *those* women were *all* highly single-minded."

"Yes, but not about themselves. They say give *us* the vote, not *me*. Jessie's really only interested in her own advancement. Lord!" He raised his hands as if to pluck back his words. "Hark at me! I don't mean she's a monster of selfishness. It's just that she's just grown up among three brothers whose father encourages them night and day to think about their own careers and advancement."

"Whereas he encourages her to think about being a young lady — and she doesn't believe that's good enough?"

He turned and stared at her quite a while, as if he expected to provoke her into smiling and confessing she was being deliberately provocative. When she merely stared back he said, "I've never heard you talk like that before ... Mumsie."

"Oh heavens! Anything but that — even Mater!"

"All right, Mother. I always thought you were among those who feel that all is for the best in the best of all possible worlds. I didn't think you'd approve of Jessie at all."

"Why did you bring her here, then? To provoke a final break-up between us?"

This was so uncomfortably near the truth that he avoided a direct answer. "I mean I feared you'd openly *disapprove* of her. Yet you seem quite neutral."

"She has shaken some of my convictions," Anna admitted. "But then, after what Uncle Raymond has done to our family, the foundations were already pretty shaky. Something like that does prepare one to *listen*, at least, to new ideas. And say what you like about Jessie, she certainly bristles with new ideas! You do realize that marriage with her is never going to be a smooth ride along a broad highway?"

He returned his gaze to the garden and tried to think of reasons for ending this conversation, though the impulse to tell her everything was strong — and growing.

"You *are* going to marry her, I suppose?" she added. "This Uncle-Raymond business hasn't changed any of that?"

"I'm not sure," he said awkwardly.

"Isn't that what you and she were talking about while Miss Pym and I went our walk?"

"No!" He put his hands to his head and gave a helpless laugh. "If you want to know, we talked about raising the finance to build an electrical station in Helston!"

"Goodness me!" Anna could think of nothing more intelligent to say. After a pause she added, "Well, I suppose it helps pass the time — that sort of conversation — until your wedding day."

He laughed then and put an arm round her shoulder. "Oh dear — there's no one quite like you for surprises, Mother! I can see I'll have to tell you everything or you'll just go on and on and on until you've mined it all, anyway." He glanced nervously at the croquet players and then, hastily — for fear the game would break up before he'd done — told her all: how he and Jessie had entered into this pact to keep the whole matchmaking world at bay; how her real ambition was to emulate her grandfather's success in bringing gas supplies to Helston; and what Barney Kernow's response would be if he ever got wind of it. "The thing that really hurts her," he concluded, "is that her father would be like a dog with two tails if one of his sons had the same ambition."

"That's a matter for him," she said. "If he has determined views about the place of men and women in society, he'd be wrong to set them aside just to indulge her. However, I'm more concerned about this ridiculous agreement to become engaged. It was a very dangerous deception to embark upon."

"You don't need to tell me!" he replied. "That's what I was about to add. You see — it hasn't exactly gone as we planned. The truth is, I think I've fallen in love with her. No, I don't think it, I know it. And I'm pretty sure she's fallen in love with me, too."

"Well then!" His mother laughed and became jovial again. "The problem's solved! All's well that ends well."

He did not share her gaiety. "I wish that were so. Jessie's resisting it like billy-oh. Her ambitions are very strong. Overwhelming, even. And she sees love and marriage as their worst enemies. *Her* worst enemies. You remember how saints and monks in the olden days used to scourge themselves and go in for starvation and so on whenever they felt the odd temptation coming over them? Well, she does something like that — mentally, I mean, or spiritually, perhaps — whenever she feels part of her succumbing to the temptation to confess her love and set a date for a genuine marriage. You probably find it hard to believe — that all those passions are seething away inside her — and I'm sure she'd deny it. Her father has trained her to remain very calm and placid on the surface — very stiff-upper-lip — but ..."

"Not Miss Pym? I mean, isn't she more likely to be the one who carried out the training?"

"Her father did it through Miss Pym. She's merely been his agent in that. Actually — to change the subject slightly — I think Miss Pym herself is undergoing a few changes of heart and mind just recently ..." He broke off. The whole business was getting too complicated to explain in a few brief words.

Anna said, "I think I'd like some orange squash, dear — with just a dash of gin, perhaps. You know how much I like."

He returned a few minutes later with two tall glasses, clinking with ice. "I made up a jug for them when they've finished," he said.

She swirled the glass to make the ice ring. "Such a merry sound! I'm glad we bought the refrigerator *before* Uncle Raymond struck. It was a fearful extravagance, I must confess." She took a sip and added, "And so clever of Jessie to get the electricity going again! I can quite see what you mean by persistence."

"And that's when she's on holiday!"

Anna chuckled. "Tell me about the rest of the family. What is Miss Pym's function in the household now that her young charge will soon be married — as far as they know, I mean. Or does she suspect you're not entirely serious?"

He stared at her sharply. "Did she say anything this afternoon?"

"Lots! But nothing as to that. She admits that Jessie is not the most conventional young lady — well, she could hardly pretend otherwise. She's gone from governess to housekeeper, I gather?"

Cornwallis cleared his throat awkwardly. "Well, if it weren't for certain legal ... er, impediments, she'd probably have been Jessie's stepmother for the past ten years. She's been ... how can one put it delicately? *Understudying* the part all that time?" He saw a knowing smile play briefly about his mother's lips and added in surprise, "Did she actually tell you about it this afternoon?"

"Not in so many words." She turned and squeezed her son's forearm. "What a fascinating family, Cornwallis! You are so clever to have found them. Miss Pym *is* an extremely conventional young lady — the very pattern Mister Kernow wished for his daughter to copy. One can see why *he* employed her. But why did *she* take the position? That's the mystery. She has an income of between one and two thousand, you know — enough to keep a good household and carriage. And travel every winter. And yet she *chooses* a semi-menial post in an obscure house at the back of beyond ... she *chooses* to live in sin — let's not mince words — with a man almost old enough to be her father. And she just puts all her income back into the funds! D'you know that in another ten years or so she will have accumulated a greater capital than the endowment she might lose by marriage. Don't you think she's a most *interesting* person?"

Cornwallis drew breath and let it out with bellowed cheeks. "You certainly seem to have had an interesting conversation with her — I'll say that!"

"She told me about the will, anyway. And I advised her to ask Frank about breaking perpetuities in wills."

"He's the lawyer of the family — I suppose she told you?"

"*You* did, dear — in your first letter home, last January. *I* don't forget these details. Anyway, her reply was the most startling thing of all. She said Frank probably had a copy of her grandfather's will all ready to spring upon her, together with advice on how to break the perpetuity. Now until I mentioned it, she hadn't even heard of breaking perpetuities. Yet the very next moment she's calmly accepting that Frank knows all about it and is just waiting for an advantageous moment to break the news — advantageous to Frank, of course! I tell you, it's getting harder and harder for me *not* to jump aboard the very next train for Penzance! Tell me about Frank."

"He's a good fellow," Cornwallis said at once.

Anna closed her eyes and counted silently to ten. "And?" she said. "But? However? Nevertheless?"

Cornwallis laughed and held up a hand to stop this flow of heavy prompts. "All right! He's clever, witty, secretive … ambitious …"

"Which of that family isn't!"

"Oh — Harry isn't. Harry would love to be a lighthouse keeper — or just go away and live in a remote cottage somewhere and paint and write poetry and … well, be another Dante Gabriel Rossetti. Or a William Morris. Or" — he cleared his throat again — "a bit of an Oscar Wilde, perhaps. If you follow."

His mother caught his inference and said, "Oh? Like *that* is he?"

"I think so. I may be quite wrong — so don't spread it round."

"You'll be quite safe?" She pretended to be alarmed but there was an amused twinkle in her eye.

"Mother!" He was caught between surprise and embarrassment.

"Well, dear — you know what men are!" she added, as if speaking to a daughter.

He shook his head and stared into his half-empty glass. "I thought that was the one thing I'd never be able to tell you."

"And yet you did it very nicely, dear. Now tell me about Frank — nothing like that there, I suppose."

"God no!"

His vehemence alerted her at once — as the writhing twig of a water-dowser tells him where to dig most profitably. "You sound very positive?" she said.

He put his glass in the hole designed for it in the arm of his chair. "Well!" He waved both hands in a gesture of helplessness. "Here's another thing I thought I'd never tell you. You know the maid who came up here with us — Clarrie?"

"A nice girl. Servants like that are getting few and far between."

"Yes, well, Frank has his eye on her."

"Goodness, how unusual! A young male of ... what? Twenty? Twenty-one? And a good-looking female of nineteen? Twenty? What can his interest possibly be?"

"Spare the sarcasm, Mother. It's actually rather serious."

"It always is, dear. If I mentioned the names of Barbara Hollingsworth ... Sally Maxton ... Mary Crawford ...?"

"Yes, yes!" He no longer blushed at the names.

"Pretty young maidservants all," she added.

"Yes but all I did was turn scarlet when they spoke to me — and dream about marrying them and taking them out of a life of drudgery."

"And Frank? This is like squeezing milk from a dry cow, dear."

"Let's say he wants to take Clarrie out of a life of drudgery but *without* any question of marriage."

His mother appeared to lose interest, as if she had expected something much more complicated. "That's entirely up to her, surely? She's old enough to weigh up the pros and cons of such a proposition. I've hardly exchanged more than half a dozen words with her but my guess is that she's the sort of girl who'll turn it down flat."

"And it's Frank's guess, too," Cornwallis went on. "So he asked me to find out what she really ... Oh God!" He broke off, closed his eyes, and shook his head.

"What, dear?" Anna sat up and stared at her son.

"I can't believe I agreed to go through with it! You'd have to know Frank to understand. You see, he made a direct approach to her once, back in January, and Jessie interrupted him and sent him off with a flea in his ear."

"You've discussed this with Jessie?"

"Good heavens, no! Frank told me. Anyway, he wants to know more about Clarrie — he wants to prepare his ground better before he makes another approach."

"He wants to know what Clarrie really wants out of life — and he's asked you to find out!"

Cornwallis collapsed with a sigh of relief. "Exactly. And I foolishly agreed. As I say, you'd have to know Frank to understand how he can make the most outrageous things seem quite normal."

"My dear!" Anna said wearily. "What is normal? Frank is a young man still making his way in the world. He wants to marry well one day, so he'll have to be much better established in his profession than he is now. Clarrie is a young servant girl with — Frank hopes — ambitions much larger than her prospects. She has certain assets that might assist her to close the distance between the two. The arrangement is *very* normal — certainly very commonplace."

He stared at her uncertainly. "You almost sound as if you approve?"

"If the arrangement is quiet and discreet, and the girl is not cajoled or coerced in any way — and is helped to achieve goals that were otherwise quite beyond her reach … well, it's very hard to *dis*approve, surely? Such arrangements are certainly as old as civilization. They've probably done more than all the philosophers and political reformers to keep society mobile and dynamic and all those other catchwords."

"But … morally?" Cornwallis objected.

"Listen, dear — all the sermonizing in the world is never going to *prevent* young men and women from coming to such understandings. We would never say so openly, of course, but among ourselves we must surely agree that if a thing is inevitable, it were better done well than badly. By which I mean: to the greatest mutual benefit of all concerned. However, I think you're right when you call yourself foolish for agreeing to broker the thing on Frank's behalf. Clarrie is, after all, your fiancée's maid. It could lead to all sorts of misunderstandings. Perhaps you should leave it to me?"

His jaw dropped. "You?"

She smiled and tilted her head in affectionate accusation. "Why else did you unburden yourself to me, eh?"

"Well certainly not so that you … I mean, I unburdened my *woes*, not, I hope, my responsibilities."

"Well, you have quite enough responsibilities in other directions, my dear. Take my advice and leave this commission with me."

Cornwallis shook his head as if he thought he were dreaming. "I don't know what Frank will say."

"You may leave that young man to me, too."

Cornwallis burst out laughing. "What? Are you going to summon him up here?"

"No, dear. I think I shall accompany you back to Cornwall next week. Miss Pym kindly invited me this afternoon. She may have offered uxorial comforts to Mister Kernow senior; but the Messrs Kernow junior — or one of them — does seem to be in need of someone who can play a proper maternal rôle."

"Proper!" he exclaimed ironically. Then a new thought struck him and he eyed her suspiciously. "Tell me — if *I* had come to you with such a suggestion a couple of years ago, when I was Frank's age: See what Sally Maxton would like in return for becoming my fancy woman? Would you have *brokered* it for me?"

Anna did not hesitate. "But you didn't, dear. And you wouldn't have, either. You're much too romantic even to contemplate such a down-to-earth arrangement. You just dreamed of an impossible union."

"But if I had?" He pressed her.

"You would have been a different son. I'd have brought you up differently." She waved a hand airily. "It becomes an impossible question to answer."

"Which is very convenient!" he sneered.

"Bringing up children is not the simple matter it used to be. In my grandmother's time they simply consulted *The Whole Duty of Man* and pressed the right levers. We have progressed greatly since then. They had reach-me-down children. Ours are bespoke!"

He saw that no matter how he approached the subject she would dart away into flippancy, like a wily, unfishable trout in home waters. "What are these other responsibilities I have quite enough of, then?" he asked.

"If you really do love Jessica ..." she began.

"Yes?"

"And if you really do wish her to succeed in these extraordinary ambitions of hers ...?"

"I think they've become *our* ambitions by now, actually."

"Good! Then I should have thought your main responsibility is absolutely clear."

"To raise the money!" he said glumly. "Fat chance of that now!"

"No, dear." Her tone was patient, a little weary. "It is to discover about Miss Pym what Frank wished you to discover about Clarrie — what she *really* wants out of life. And then to use the knowledge to get her on your side." Almost as an afterthought she added: "Fortunately, that's where the money is, too — especially if Frank can do something about that perpetuity." She smiled as people smile when they place the last piece into a jigsaw puzzle. "How neatly it all fits!"

*I*t was artfully done, and really very simple. Anna knew that if the day promised fine, Clarrie liked to hang the previous day's laundry out to air before folding it away in the press. (She would not call it an *'airing* cupboard' for it usually did no such thing, especially not in Cornwall.) The first Wednesday in June — the day before the visitors returned to Cornwall — promised fine. So Anna waited until there were only a couple more petticoats to hang, then she took two flower baskets, left one just inside the back door, and set out for the fields.

Half way across the yard she cried out, "Oh! You *did* give me a start — I didn't see you." Peering closely at the girl, she added, "Clarrie, isn't it? You are up bright and early."

Clarrie bobbed a curtsey and said it was a lovely day.

"I'm on my way to gather some wild flowers," Anna went on. "They make such a refreshing change every now and then, don't you think?" An idea occurred to her. "Would you care to join me, Clarrie? I can promise you, there are few better ways to start the day."

Clarrie's eyes gleamed at the prospect, for gathering flowers — even wild flowers — was really lady's work, only occasionally delegated to housekeepers and very upper maids. But she glanced nervously at the clock over the stables.

"Oh, don't worry about *them!*" Anna said almost contemptuously. "I'll make it all right there."

So now there was an *us* and a *them* in the air.

"I believe I saw a basket just inside the back door," Anna went on. "You won't need a bonnet as early as this." And she took her own off to prove it.

Bare-headed democracy was rampant as they strode out to the fields together. "Pick any sorrel leaves you come across, too," Anna said as they began their gathering. "Not the young and tender ones, nor the old, shriveled ones — the in-betweenies. We press the juice and use it to dress salads, you know."

For the next ten minutes they stooped low over the meadow sward, chatting about this and that but nothing in particular, while Clarrie luxuriated in the fantasy of being a lady of leisure. Her shy, monosyllabic replies, liberally larded with 'ma'ams' and 'missizes,' expanded bit by bit into whole sentences; and careful statements of fact became tinged with opinions she was surprised to hear herself voicing at all. Why, for instance, should a grand lady like Mrs Trelawney be interested to hear that she, Clarrie, thought that some art-silk colours were too gaudy? But she was — indeed, she herself was of the same opinion and gave several examples, not all of which Clarrie agreed with. She thought that the deep mauve, for one, was quite heavenly because it brought out the colour in her own eyes so well. And then, to her absolute horror, she heard herself saying so, just like as if Mrs Trelawney was another maidservant working alongside of her!

Before she could die of mortification, however, she felt the woman grasp her gently by the shoulder and turn her face into full view. "Ye-es," she said slowly, peering deep into Clarrie's eyes, "I can see that that colour would suit you perfectly."

Another of those sudden thoughts struck her and she said, "Which is actually very fortunate, because my sister in India sent me a beautiful art-silk shawl for Christmas. They can pick them up out there *very cheaply* you know!"

So now Clarrie was on the inside when it came to Mrs T.'s opinion of her sister's 'generosity'!

"And," Anna went on, "I've never been able to wear it because there's so much of that particular mauve in it — which doesn't suit me at all. But *you* shall have it! No, I insist! I'd have given it away to Betty, my own maid, except that Lydia would have seen it next time she came home to the old country. And anyway it wouldn't suit Betty half as well as it will you. I'll bring it down to Cornwall with me and you shall have it there."

This conclusion produced the required effect on Clarrie — confusion, delight, gratitude ... and surprise to hear that Mrs Trelawney was coming down to Cornwall, too. "*You* ma'am?" she asked. "You coming back with us, are you?"

"It would be rather uncivil not to, don't you think? After all, Miss Pym made the effort to visit us."

If any other grand lady had said such a thing, Clarrie would have felt snubbed — as if the underlying meaning was 'you wouldn't understand such niceties, of course'! But somehow Mrs Trelawney made it sound ... well, almost like a mother might tell a daughter. Or a teacher a pupil, anyway. Like as if she was *grooming* her to understand such things. The girl's sense of confusion did not diminish but her warmth toward this lovely lady was certainly augmented.

"I understand, however," Anna went on, "that my son's house is not fit to receive visitors?"

Clarrie laughed and said that was a fact and no mistake.

"So Miss Pym has kindly invited me to stay at Wheal Prosper. I must say, I'm looking forward to it immensely. But I must also confess — and I don't mind confessing it to *you*, Clarrie, because I know you won't breathe a word to another living soul — I am just a teeny bit terrified about the whole thing, too."

Clarrie just stared at her, jaw agape. *"You,* ma'am?" she asked in a near-whisper. "Gusson!"

"Oh but I am, I assure you. They are such an *interesting* family. *So* unusual. I don't believe I have *ever* met another young lady like Miss Jessie. You probably don't see it, of course, because you've grown up with it, more or less. You've become used to her. But, believe me, she is a remarkable young lady, your mistress. You are lucky — knowing all about them. I'm so afraid I'll put a foot wrong. In my ignorance."

Clarrie turned away and gazed across the fields. A train went chugging up the Leeds and Wetherby line to the east of them, about half a mile away. She followed it with her eyes — unhappy, uncertain eyes. Of course she wanted to offer all the help she could to Mrs T. But it seemed like such cheek, somehow.

Anna let the girl's consternation grow to the point where it became clear she was not yet ready to offer help and advice, then she said, "What a lovely morning! And how kind this low, slanting sun is to the skin. Let's just sit here a few minutes and recover from our heavy, *heavy* labours!"

It broke the spell. Clarrie laughed and obeyed with delight — and relief, to be sure. Then, somehow, it became the easiest thing in the world to say, "I s'pose they are some remarkable family, come to think of it. I mean, their grandfather was 'prenticed to *my* old grandad in Nancegollan forge. They was equal with we in those days. Then 'e got a forge of his own down Saint John's in Helston, and he had the good fortune to own the land where the gasworks wanted to build. So that's when their family started to rise."

"Yes, so Miss Jessie told me," Anna said. She did not want the girl to feel she was blabbing all the family secrets. "But you know, Clarrie, I think it's more than simply having the luck to be sitting on the right bit of land at the right time. That would bring in the money — true. But a lot of people get a sudden windfall of money and then, a year or two later, where are they? Like Samson in Gaza — they're back at the wheel with slaves! No, it needs something rather more than just a windfall of money." She tapped her brow. "It needs that little worm of ambition to be eating away up here. We don't all have it. I don't, I'm afraid. I'm one of life's natural passengers. But your Miss Jessie does. Nothing's going to stop her."

Clarrie didn't know how to respond to this; she made vague murmurs of assent and kept her thoughts to herself. She glanced shyly across at Mrs T., only to meet her kindly eyes. Suddenly she felt plumbed to her very depths.

"I've embarrassed you!" Anna said and smiled a teasing smile as the girl protested she'd done no such thing. "Perhaps *you* have that worm of ambition ganwing away inside you, too!" she chided. "And why not! You're a bright, intelligent young woman — quick-witted and observant — it would be amazing if you wanted to remain a lady's maid all your days."

The fact that Clarrie was really only an acting-temporary-lady's maid encouraged a rush of honest protest within her. But when it came out, instead of denying she was as yet anything so exalted as a *proper* lady's maid, she heard herself admitting, bold as brass, that she did, indeed, have ambitions beyond even that — she wanted to own and run the village store one day.

Mrs Trelawney stared at her in amazement, a delighted smile spreading across her face. "How *very* extraordinary, Clarrie!" she exclaimed. "D'you know — there are only two women in this district whose lives I truly envy. One is the widow who lives in that cottage you can just see over there — with the tall hollyhocks and the thick stone slabs on the roof. The other is Mrs Thorn who runs our village post office and general store, here in Chapel Allerton."

"Does she own it?" Clarrie asked at once.

"Ah — that's important, is it? I don't know. But I do know that she as good as owns the lives of half the village. She's at the centre of everything. Nothing happens but she knows of it first. She's doctor, lawyer, banker, confessor, and comforter — all rolled into one. Is that what you'd enjoy about it, too?"

There was a sudden sharp lump in Clarrie's throat. It was such a perfect picture of all she wanted most in life. She could have sucked on a pencil for a year and not come up with better. And now all she could do was nod, and smile, and blink, and hope Mrs T. wouldn't notice how tonguetied she was all of a sudden.

"Well, this won't do at all!" Anna said briskly, rising to her feet and dusting the pollen and hay off her dress.

Clarrie took over the office and then let the amazing lady do the same for her. And Anna, while she dusted away, said idly, "You must keep a sharp eye out for that windfall, Clarrie. It may be fool's gold or it may be the real thing. You must be quick to judge it for what it really is and then seize it if it's the right thing."

Clarrie had once suffered a religious conversion; it hadn't lasted more than an hour because the preacher, seeing her exalted passions, had tried to take advantage of them — and her. But she recalled the feeling even after she lost the calling. And she had an intimation of it now, too. She had daydreamed many hours of her life away with thoughts of 'her' village shop — too many hours, she often thought. But this was the first moment when the idea seemed to move out of the realm of pure daydream and took on some of the colour of reality. It was because Mrs Trelawney had filled in some of that vague, intermediate ground, which until now had been littered with impossible obstacles. She had cleared some of that litter aside and, in its place, put the beginnings of a *process* there. True, it was vaguely called 'windfall' at the moment, but, as Mrs T. had also said, she was a bright, intelligent young woman; she was certainly bright enough to know that a 'windfall' could take an almost infinite number of forms.

On that same day, the day before their return to Cornwall (*not* with Anna Trelawney, who had decided to put her visit off for three weeks), Jessie had one of those trivial experiences that can, nonetheless, change the entire course of a person's life. Cornwallis's father, a cautious man, did not doubt that she had done something quite miraculous with the lighting set out in the stables; but he did suspect it might be something unorthodox — and therefore unrepeatable once she had gone. So he arranged for John Riddoch to call at Atherton Grange and cast a professional eye over her handiwork. He came at mid-morning.

He inspected everything that could be inspected without stripping the machine to its last nut and bolt, and he asked Jessie herself what faults she had found and what adjustments she had made. Her answers were so satisfactory that he was good enough to say he could not have done better himself.

Jessie went with him to the stable yard, where his pony and trap were waiting. "May I ask a rather forward question, Mister Riddoch?" she said. "I mean, why *didn't* you 'do better yourself'?"

"I surely would have if I'd been asked, lassie," he replied amiably.

"Ah. In that case, why didn't they ask you?

"Pride. I advised against buying yon contraption. They'll be able to connect to the municipal supply before the year's out, and buy their electricity at a tenth of the cost. But rich people must have their own water wells, their own carriages on the railway, their own boxes at the opera — and now, it seems, their own lighting sets, too." He sucked a tooth and shook his head at such reckless folly.

Then, just as he took his seat and was about to set off, he leaned over and said, "May I proffer a wee bit of advice, Mistress Kernow?"

"I'd be more than grateful, Mister Riddoch."

"Ye have a natural bent for all things mechanical and electrical. It'll be a sair temptation to ye to prove it aye and again tae a doubting world. My advice is the same as any minister's: Resist temptation! Do not be so eager to acquire skills that will only hamper you on your way up. I could write whole textbooks on electricity and steam. Mister Trelawney wouldn't know an ignition plug from an oil can. But he has the new carriage and pair and I have the twenty-year-old pony and trap. Ponder that!"

And he smiled and clucked his pony to be off. At the gate he raised his hat and called out, "Guid day tae ye, Mistress Jessica — and guid luck attend ye!"

*I*t was the June garden party of the G&S in Helston — where the bickering usually began about what piece to perform for Christmas, and, more bitter still, who should perform it. Once again Michael Vestey used his friendship with the absent Troys to borrow Liston Court, or at least its grounds, for the grand occasion. People were sorry — but then again perhaps not *quite* so sorry as might have been expected — when both Jessie and Cornwallis pleaded the pressure of other business and asked not to be considered for anything more demanding than a place in the chorus in December. Cornwallis especially had, in the last production, sung his part to an almost professional standard quite out of keeping with the traditions of the G&S. Their retirement to the chorus would at least allow the society to get back to normal.

Besides, everyone knew what 'pressures of business' meant — which was not what it usually meant on a gentleman's lips. Usually it referred to the demands of an estate or a profession; but in Trelawney's case it really meant *business*, the distasteful commercial stuff.

They had all heard that some calamitous financial nemesis had befallen the Trelawneys. The scientists of the day were sparing no effort to discover the speed of light, which was just within the measuring power of the most modern apparatus; but most ordinary people would have been far more interested in measuring the speed of gossip, which was several orders of magnitude faster. Jessie and Cornwallis had become aware of that fact the moment they stepped off the mainline train at Gwinear Road, to change onto the branch for Nancegollan and Helston. The nudges and heads-together confidences that passed among those on the opposite platform — friends and neighbours who had alighted *from* the branch-line train ten minutes earlier — were evidence enough. By the time of the garden party, some ten days later, they hardly noticed such attentions.

People said it only showed that one could not escape kismet. Some of the rich old families had stayed in Cornwall and sunk into poverty as the price of tin collapsed. The Trelawneys had tried to escape by getting out of tin and founding new fortunes in other industries in the North. Indeed, they had succeeded there, but ... kismet! Cheap tin from the empire or a family black sheep — the *mechanism* of ruin was immaterial; if your card was marked, the Fates would always find a way to trump you.

They shook their heads sadly as they said these things. And no one could deny there was compassion in their tone. And yet ...

And yet, discomfort is all quite relative. The most discomforted person present that bright Saturday afternoon was neither Cornwallis nor Jessie but her younger brother, Godfrey.

There is a brief, magical age in the life of a respectable young girl, set uncertainly between her sixteenth and seventeenth birthdays, when she is permitted a freedom she will not experience again until she announces her engagement. Within her she feels the first stirrings of mature womanhood and, with it, an interest in young men that would have embarrassed her only twelve months earlier. Generally, though, her guardians do not consider her adventurous (or devious) enough to carry her curiosity to dangerous lengths.

Hence the relative freedom they permit her.

Also there is the fact that the corresponding process among young men of that age is not in any way reciprocal. Their newly awakened interest in young women *does* embarrass them — whereas twelve months ago it would merely have amused. They may *dream* endlessly of girls but the girls they dream of are dream-girls; the real flesh-and-blood creatures are alarming beyond words.

And it was one of those flesh-and-blood girls who, on that particular Saturday, was responsible for Godfrey's misery. Her name was Monica Trebilcock, youngest daughter of Trebilcock, the Helston jeweler who had recently opened branches in Penzance and Camborne. She had turned sixteen in March. She had a broad, rather flat face that people said would be pretty *one* day; her eyes were already extremely fetching; her hair was chestnut brown and her skin was very pale, almost imperceptibly freckled. She had been a fat child and there was still a certain pudginess about her; but people also said that would all disappear one day. Godfrey's friends, when they sniggered about her among themselves (not especially about her, mind, just when her turn came around), said her puppy fat wasn't disappearing, it was just rearranging itself in some very interesting places.

They thought he was a lucky dog that she had asked him to squire her to the garden party; he thought so, too, until the terrifying afternoon came. Of course, she hadn't asked him directly. She had spoken to her parents; they had spoken to Miss Pym; and she had suggested it to Godfrey. So the afternoon began with the pretence that the grown-ups had foisted this arrangement upon them — which made it impossible, certainly for two inexperienced people of that age, to talk about the thing they had most in common, which was her desire to be squired by him and his delight to be so chosen.

So they talked instead about how lucky they were with the weather. And how good Jessie had been in 'Cav rust.' And would Michael Vestey forget to thank Miss Waters again this year for arranging all the catering? And how lucky they were with the weather ...

And strawberries were plentiful this year. That was the weather, too, of course.

And then Monica started telling a long and — to her — fascinating story about the birds in their garden and her cat, Woofah. It petered out at some point — or no point — but it was clear she adored Woofah. He was called Woofah because baby Monica had been unable to say loofah, which is what she thought he looked like. Godfrey imagined himself soaping Monica's back in the bath and scrubbing it with a loofah, so it was a minute or so before he realized the story had ended. Then he couldn't think of anything to say, except that cats should be allowed to kill birds because it was part of the natural order. To which Monica said, "Oh." Later she added that it was interesting. And although it was quite a while later, he knew she was still talking about birds and cats because, unfortunately, they hadn't found anything else to talk about in between.

And so their afternoon wore on in all its ghastly, clammy embarrassment. The more predictable and conventional their conversation became, the more his spirit rebelled and the more outrageous were the suggestions it whispered in the unswept corners of his mind. He imagined himself taking away her strawberries and cream ... she'd draw breath to protest and then, catching sight of the sardonic, masterful little smile twitching at the corners of his lips, would fall into a demure but trusting silence ... he'd take her in his arms, bending her ever so slightly backward and to one side, which was what all the strong, silent heroes did to the wild, impetuous heroines in *Peg o' My Heart*, which Tillie read like a religious duty every week ... and crush his lips to hers. So far he'd only crushed his lips to Clarrie's (who was having nothing to do with him nowadays) and Tillie's, whose sister Margaret had forbidden her to see him any more because 'no good would come of it, only babbies.'

He wondered if Monica might not actually *want* him to take away her strawberries and cream with a sardonic little smile ... et cetera. She must want *something* — other than this endless misery-go-round of inane chatter, surely? Why couldn't girls just step up to a chap and *say* what they want?

"My sister Jessie says ..." he began before he realized he was speaking his thoughts aloud. He stopped in confusion.

"Eh?" she asked inelegantly — but there was the first gleam of genuine interest in her eyes.

"Oh," he said awkwardly. "Nothing, really. I don't know what made me think of it suddenly. We were talking about succeeding and failing at things, you know. And Jessie said that men are taught how to fail and women aren't. I'm sorry! It has nothing to do with what you were saying. Er ... what were you saying, actually?"

"Nothing," she replied glumly.

She thought over Jessie's words and said — again with more animation than he'd noticed in her all afternoon, "Your sister's quite right, though, Godfrey. All those competitive sports you boys have. We girls have them, too, of course, but you have ten times more. And all that business about cheering the man who comes last as loudly as the winner — playing the game is more important than winning, and so on. You get so many chances to practise losing gracefully and picking yourselves up and starting again. We don't. Shall we go and sit on that bench over there — under the tree?" She nodded toward the back wall of Liston Court, beyond the tea tent in whose lee they were then standing.

His heart fell, for the tree was the one that shaded the cabbage patch behind the house where Tillie lived. Still, he could hardly explain that to Monica! "Splendid," he said. "Shall we try for some more ice cream on the way?"

With their bowls refilled they made their way to the bench by the back wall.

"There's another difference I've just thought of," Monica remarked as they seated themselves. "Going on from what your sister said. You boys get taught that success comes from hard work."

"And aren't you girls?" he asked in surprise.

"Oh, we may be *taught* it," she said dismissively, "but who are all the successful girls at school? The ones who work hard and win the prizes? Not a bit. It's the glamorous girls who are the real successes."

"The beauties?"

"Not necessarily. Good looks help, of course, but it's personality as well. Anyway, it doesn't matter *what* it is — the point I'm making is that it's not something you can work hard to get. You're born with it or you aren't. We may not be taught that, not in so many words, but it's what we all learn at school nonetheless." She laughed, a trifle bitterly. "Your sister thinks we aren't taught how to fail gracefully. I think we learn that failure and success are *both* outside our control." She became aware that she was talking a trifle heatedly — something a well-brought-up girl should never do. "I'm sorry," she said and tried to recruit a smile from him. "Hark at me!"

"I am," he said admiringly. "Gosh!"

She blushed — greatly to her own annoyance. "I really don't like these ghastly affairs very much," she said, setting down her ice, which was only half consumed, and waving at the garden party in general. "I'd much rather be ... I don't know. Almost anywhere else. What would you rather be doing?"

There was a snigger somewhere, from out of thin air. The leaves overhead quivered against the cloudless blue. Godfrey looked up — straight into the eyes of Tillie Lambton, sitting not six feet above him, stuffing her knuckles into her mouth. When she saw she was observed, she broke her silence and said, "Hallo, Charley!"

In a panic he grasped Monica by the elbow and said, "Let's go and find my sister and ... er, tell her your thoughts."

Tillie laughed as they scurried off.

"What a hoyden!" Monica said.

Halfway across the lawn between the wall and the tent he said, "Our dishes! She'll pinch them."

He dashed back and, gathering up the bowls, hissed at Tillie, "How dare you! Get down out of there!"

"Usual time this evening?" she replied.

He walked away without a word — mainly because he could not say no. She waited until he had rejoined the fat doll-girl before she called out, "Charley!"

The couple turned. She had hitched her skirts well above her knees and was dangling a slim, shapely leg, bare of any stocking, into the shadows, more or less where they had been seated. Both of them, for different reasons, stared at it in horrified fascination until, a moment or two later, it was withdrawn again.

"Why did she call you Charley?" Monica asked when they had recovered from the shock.

"It's their name for every man — girls of that sort."

Monica, who had only recently become aware of the existence of girls 'of that sort' and who still had only the vaguest idea of their purpose, did not dare risk any response to this. They strolled in silence — and it was an easy silence now — until they arrived at the main gate to the property.

"Oh — you never told me what you'd rather be doing than this," she said.

"Swimming," he replied at once. "Just think — to be diving into a deep rock pool now, somewhere west of Porthleven! Down among the kelp. Have you ever swum through strands of kelp?"

"Mmmm!" she responded.

The gates were wide open but they stood just inside and stared out as if they were not only closed but chained as well. They were thinking how wonderful it would be to slip away, get Monica's bathing costume, and one of her brothers' swimming trunks, and take the bus to Porthleven, walk out along the cliffs, then down to the rocks, and slip into the cool, briny water, and ... and ... and let the rest of the world think and do what it liked. Neither of them said as much, though, for they both knew it was so utterly, unthinkably impossible.

*I*t was convenient having Frank's chambers in Helston, for a sister could call upon her brother with no stricter chaperonage than a maid — and even a maid was needed only for the journey there and back. And if the brother happened to be out or the hour proved inconvenient, the sister could not be faulted for employing the time usefully in a healthy country walk. To the casual observer it might have seemed unfortunate that Jessie so often chose to call upon Frank at moments when he could not see her; and it might, to some hyper-curious busybodies, have seemed strange that several of her healthy country walks were in the direction of the sewage farm, where the Cober left the town and meandered through a short stretch of marshland before opening out into the Loe Pool. True, other rambles were in more salubrious directions — up the Cober valley, for instance, toward Gwealhellis; and on a few occasions she and Clarrie took a stroll around Gwealfolds, beyond the railway station at the top of the town.

It would have taken a hyper-hyper-curious — and intelligent — observer to see that the one link between these three very different walks was *water*, for the tiny Helston River, which ran in open granite drains down each side of Wendron and Coinagehall streets, from the top of the town to the bottom, had its source near Gwealfolds.

Clarrie, being no more than ordinarily curious and intelligent, did not make the connection until the third or fourth of these supposedly frustrating visits to brother Frank. They had gone some way up the Cober valley from St John's, beyond the old mill, which was now used once a year by the Pallas home farm for sprouting seed potatoes. They paused at the gate to a field just beyond the mill and Clarrie's eyes darted forth and back between her mistress and the landscape, hoping to discover what had brought them to a halt here rather than anywhere else up this rather ordinary lane.

There was no vixen playing with her cubs, no bronzed young farm lad hoeing the turnips, indeed nothing that would have made Clarrie herself stop if she were out here walking on her own. But Miss Jessie's eyes quartered the field like a goshawk's; her lips moved as if she were committing figures to memory; and when she stepped back from the gate she stamped her heel into the metal of the road like Rumpelstiltskin in the story.

At last Jessie saw the girl's eye on her, inquisitive and slightly worried. "You must think I'm off my hinges," she said.

"No, Miss!" Clarrie said unconvincingly.

Jessie decided it would be more prudent to let the girl into at least part of her secret. Even an uncomprehending report of her activities — 'Guess what Miss Jessie done today!' — would alert somebody somewhere down the gossip line. "I'm looking for a site," she said. "To build on."

Clarrie remembered the marsh beyond the sewage farm and the bleak, exposed fields at the top of the hill; her puzzlement was plain. "Won't you be stopping along of Mister Trelawney up Wheal Dream, Miss, once you've tied the knot?"

"It's not for a house, but a place of business."

"Ah?" The puzzlement remained though its focus shifted. What sort of business site would *she* be choosing rather than Mister Trelawney? Jessie did not need to be a mind-reader to know that was the new direction of Clarrie's thinking.

She explained further: "If *he* were to be observed wandering around like this — in places where only fanatics like Godfrey would walk for pleasure — people would soon put two and two together and prices would leap."

"Ah!" No more questions remained. A lady standing at a gate gazing intently into a field might very well be involved in 'business'; but it would be woman's business — the search for flowers to press in her herbarium, for instance. If anyone were to say, 'That lady looks to me as if she's calculating how many cubic yards need to be removed to make a level factory site here,' it would be a sure-fire laugh. You had to admire Miss Jessie. She thought of everything. Clarrie began to understand why that nice Mrs Trelawney had said nothing would stop her. She said, "It's Mrs Trelawney's visit next week, isn't it, Miss? It'll be nice seeing her again, having her stop at Wheal Prosper."

Jessie agreed but asked, "What made you think of her suddenly?"

The girl shrugged. "Dunno. I've thought of her a lot — knowing she's coming to stop, and that."

Jessie returned to the gate and resumed her inspection of the field. "She obviously made a great impression on you, Clarrie. What did you talk about on your wild-flower expedition together that morning?"

"Dunno, Miss. Nothing much. Scribble really." Hesitantly she added, "I think the ... you know — family misfortunes and all that caper were on her mind a bit."

Jessie looked at her in surprise. "She spoke about that?"

"Not in so many words. She said ..."

Jessie interrupted. "But you do know about their present troubles?"

Clarrie smiled, a little tolerantly. "You do know what the servants' hall is like, Miss — in any house that size."

"I suppose so."

"I haven't said nothing since we come back, and nor shall I, neither."

"I'm relieved to hear it — and, of course, I'd be grateful ... Mister Trelawney and I would both be grateful, if you'd continue to be discreet. But I interrupted you. You were saying she didn't refer directly to their misfortune but ...?"

"Yes. She spoke about, you know, the sort of things she *really* wanted out of life."

It stirred Jessie's memory. "Ah! Did she mention her seamstress — Widow Taylor — with the beautiful daughter?"

"In the cottage with the hollyhocks? Yes. Also a Mrs Thorn, who do run the village post office and general store — lucky woman!"

The fervour with which Clarrie spoke those last two words impressed Jessie. "Is that your opinion or hers?" she asked.

Clarrie bit her lip, realizing how close her own enthusiasm had brought her to revealing those dreams that might expose her to ridicule. "Bit o' both really, Miss," she replied. "I mean, the way she described it and all, you could see how a life like that — I mean, having your own little businesss and being at the centre of things — would be very good."

It was a side to Clarrie that Jessie had never seen before. The amazing Mrs Trelawney had obviously discovered more about the girl in one brief walk than she, Jessie, had managed in all these years. Familiarity breeds blindness, she thought, not contempt.

She remembered vaguely that a couple of months ago Frank had asked her to find out what Clarrie really wanted in life. She had not pursued the matter, mainly because she knew what Frank was after and she wanted no part in such a scandalous business — also because Frank himself seemed to have gone cool on the idea; anyway, he hadn't pestered her to follow up her vague sort of half-promise to get him the information.

But now it occurred to her that all Frank's reasons for wanting to know about Clarrie also applied to her — not his particular *purpose*, of course, but his reasoning. Conspiracies would spawn and multiply around this electrical project before it was secure enough to come out of hiding — not merely conspiracies at Wheal Prosper but against almost every man she'd eventually have to deal with. In such an atmosphere a lady's maid who thought more of her job and character reference than of furthering her mistress's plans was a liability; but one who had powerful ambitions of her own and who saw a way to achieve them by helping her mistress achieve hers could be turned into an incalculable asset.

She also recalled another part of that conversation with her brother — which provided a further and much deeper-seated reason for having done nothing about it since — her fear that she would turn out like her father if she started misusing people in this way. Frank had just laughed, of course, and welcomed her to 'the real world.' Now she realized that the dilemma was still there; she had done nothing to resolve it by simply ignoring it. Every time she came close to taking some positive step to further her own ambitions, it seemed she must exploit those of someone else, to induce them to help her.

Even her 'betrothal of convenience' with Cornwallis could be seen in that light. He had put a proposition to her; she had thought it over and seen how well it suited her own ambitions; she had agreed. If she had followed up Frank's request and discovered the information he said he needed, he would now put a proposition to Clarrie; she would think it over and see how well (or ill) it suited her own ambitions; and she would agree (or not). Where was the difference? The fact that carnal relations were part of it? But why should that sin be more scarlet than the bluffs, conspiracies, deceptions — in a word: the lies — in which she, Jessie, would inevitably be entangled?

Wriggle as she might, she was caught on the hook of a moral dilemma. "Oh, it's so easy for men!" she exclaimed aloud — and much to Clarrie's surprise. The maid wondered why her brief description of Mrs Thorn's idyllic life had provoked so long a silence in her young mistress; but how it had led to such an outburst as *that* she could not conceive. Anyway, hadn't she just said it would be easier for her to scout out the ground like this than it would be for *him*?

Jessie laughed. "I'm sorry, Clarrie, that doesn't make any sense, does it. Let's start drifting back into the town. We *are* going to have lunch with Frank."

"You mean you arranged for him not to be home ... of course!" Clarrie chuckled at the cunning of it all.

"What I mean when I said it's so easy for men is that they're *expected* to fight rough. They go into business. They wangle clever deals. They do other people in the eye. Not actually cheating, you understand, just showing no mercy and taking advantage of every little weakness they spot in the other fellow. And nobody calls it disgraceful or tells them they ought to be ashamed of it. Frank warned me about this and I've tried not to think of it ever since. Let a woman try any one of those commercial tricks and the world will be down on her like a hundred of bricks. Exploit another man's financial weakness? Disgraceful! Use a little secret information to beat him to some lucrative deal? What a brazen hussy! But let a man do those things and they'd all want to put him up for the club." She stopped and stared at Clarrie. "Am I mad to be wanting to join in that most uneven battle, Clarrie? Shouldn't I be going out and picking wild flowers like Mrs Trelawney?"

The maid dimly perceived the drift of her mistress's thoughts. "That's where 'tis easy to be a woman, Miss. Gathering flowers and staying clear of all that."

Jessie nodded in sad agreement. "Stay on the pedestal! They put us up on these pedestals because — they *say* — they need our inspiration. They need someone in their world who is above the sordid commercial fray. They see weakness and they exploit it, even if it means ruining a fellow man. They know it's wrong. They feel guilty. But Woman on her pedestal is like a beacon in all that murkiness. Her purity of soul, her superior moral spirit points them toward redemption. It's so easy for us to retain that superior moral spirit, though, because *they* spare us the necessity to claw and gouge and elbow our way in the sordid world of commerce! Again — am I mad to turn my back on that temptingly sheltered existence?"

They resumed their stroll. "I'm not quite sure I do see, Miss ..." Clarrie said hesitantly.

"The long and the short of it is, Clarrie, that I'm planning to supply this town with electricity, from a central power station, just as my grandfather helped supply it with gas."

It took a moment or two for this astonishing announcement to sink in; when it did, the girl clapped her hands in delight and said, "With that contraption you got working in Mister Trelawney's stables, Miss?" She glanced back up the lane. "Going to build a shed for 'n up there, are 'ee?"

Jessie smiled. "Oh, if it were only so simple! But you're right in a way. It will be a machine something like that — only several hundred times more powerful. Not several hundred times bigger, mind. Just more powerful. I'll give you an idea. You know those steam traction engines we have down in Saint John's? It'll be as powerful as half a dozen of them all connected up together."

Clarrie whistled, at a loss for words. Jessie could have thrown her arms around the girl and hugged her. She hadn't burst out laughing!

To her it seemed a perfectly natural ambition for anyone to have — and perfectly reasonable for her, Jessie, to be the one to carry it through. For that alone, Jessie would have financed whatever ambition the maid might have — once her own was taken care of, to be sure.

"So," Jessie concluded, "you can appreciate why I'm looking for a site with plenty of water!"

"And a good road for the coal lorries!" Clarrie laughed. "That's why you stamped so hard on the lane back there! Well, you do know *this* road's all right, don't 'ee, Miss."

"Do I? Why?"

"'Cos it do go all the way up the valley to that old, abandoned quarry, up Lowertown. My father used to work there. He said your grandfather got all the stone for his place down Saint John's from there. So if Harvey Goldsworthy's carts full of stone did come down that lane for fifty years or more, 'e i'nt going to crumble under a few tons of coal, is 'e!"

Jessie could take the suspense no longer. "You don't seem at all surprised, Clarrie — to hear that this is what I want to do. You don't think I'm mad?"

Clarrie stared at her blankly. "How?" she asked, genuinely puzzled at the question.

"Or just building castles in Spain?"

"Gusson, Miss — you build castles in Spain? Never — I shan't live to see that day!"

"Very well, then." Jessie rubbed her hands to suggest a more businesslike atmosphere. "Down to brass tacks. Can I count on your support? You don't have to say yes or no now. In fact, I'd prefer you to think it over and come back with a considered response. I shall be taking the plunge into that devious, murky world where men are praised for sharp dealing but woman are reviled as interloping hussies. There will be conspiracies and secrets. People will try to get information from you about my dealings. My father will be chief among them once he gets wind of what's afoot. He'll use charm, bluster, threats — everything short of actual physical force — and his powers are considerable ..."

"And Miss Pym, Miss?"

Jessie pursed her lips and nodded grimly. "Somehow — don't ask me how — but by hook or by crook I have to get Miss Pym round to my side. If you get any ideas on the subject, I'd be most grateful to hear of them. I have to advance this project to the point where it's quite clear that I'm serious — that I'm not simply daydreaming. Obviously that's a point where it's still not public knowledge. In other words, I must take care of all the legal and financial preliminaries — and *then* try to recruit her to my side. If she and my father unite against me, I don't think I'll stand a chance. So there you are! Those are my thoughts on Miss Pym."

"You do make it sound very easy, Miss."

"There's one more thing," Jessie added. "I ought to tell you what's in it for you. If you take the risky course and throw your lot in with me, it's only fair you should stand to gain, too. Now do I understand from the light I saw shining in your eyes a while back that you'd rather like to stop being a lady's maid and start running a village post office and general store, instead?"

Clarrie, who had been about to protest that, of course, she'd do it all out of liking for Jessie and wouldn't expect a penny for herself, was unable to get out a single syllable to that effect. The single syllable she *did* manage to get out was: "Yes!" — a breathless, astonished, ecstatic, "Yes!"

Jessie had toyed with the idea of putting *all* her cards on the table, by telling Clarrie that Frank might make a similar proposition to her, though for quite different reasons. That would show the girl she was hiding nothing. Now, however, it had all turned out so satisfactorily that there would never be the slightest need to placate Frank with this little tidbit of information. Therefore he would never make the offer. Therefore the matter need never arise.

It was a good beginning, she felt — to manage to preserve her superior womanly virtue *and* further her own commercial interests in one and the same action.

*I*t was a bachelor's luncheon — cold beef, pickles, salad, cheese, and bread in slices to rival granite doorsteps. Frank whipped the muslin fly-cloth off the table with an awkward sort of pride, suggesting that he wanted his sister to know he had managed it all by himself but did not want her to comment upon the fact. "You'll have to start getting used to bread and cheese and kisses yourself now, I hear," he said.

"Oh, not you, too," she replied wearily. "Surely *you* understand, even if the populace in general can't, that when people as rich as the Trelawneys fall on hard times, they can still travel first class and afford a house and twelve servants. It's not like Jones the grocer lying drunk in the gutter and muttering, 'That used to be my shop'!"

"I stand corrected," her brother replied. "Or, rather, I sit." As he slipped into his chair he called, "Are you all right, Clarrie? Got everything you want out there?"

From the next room, in the long, narrow ex-corridor that served as his kitchen, the maid called back to tell them that she was very comfy, thanks. They could hardly hear her through the closed door, which was reassuring.

"Anyway," Jessie went on, "I think it'll be bread-and-cheese lunches *at best* from now on for me. Time will be scarcer than money. This is good beef, Frank."

"I got it sent down from Oliver's, that new butcher up Meneage Street. Have you picked a site at last, then?"

"I think so."

"Let me guess! Not the top of the town. Not upstream from Saint John's. But out past the sewage farm — right?"

She stared at him in surprise. "How did you know that? Until this morning I was practically set on the field upstream of the old mill. Clarrie and I were out there looking at it just now. I only decided against it on the way back."

He eyed her speculatively and lowered his voice. "That girl must have some idea what you're up to by now. What have you told her — that you're looking out for birds' eggs for Godfrey?"

She gave a single contemptuous laugh. "Godfrey would just hoot to hear you ask that! So would Clarrie if I tried to fob her off with it. You'd starve on all the birds' eggs left in the whole of Cornwall by this time. Anyway, I asked you how you knew?"

He smiled confidently, glad to be back on his sort of territory. "I never for one moment imagined you'd go anywhere else."

"Because it'll be the cheapest land?"

"No. The land will only be a small fraction of your outlay, wherever you build. I knew you'd pick the sewage-farm site because it's the only one in view of Kernow and Son!"

She wanted to deny it but her scalp tingled at its truth. She closed her eyes and shook her head. "D'you really think I'm like that?" she asked. "So petty?"

He was not daunted. "No," he said. "If either of the other sites showed some *overwhelming* advantage, you'd forgo that pleasure. But, since neither does, you see no reason to deny yourself." He became animated suddenly. "Think of it, Jess! Every day — every single time he looked out of his window or went out into the yard — he'd see *your* chimneys pouring out smoke, a furlong down the valley! He wouldn't stand for it. He'd set cypresses all down the eastern fence. And he'd have to brick up that office window on the south wall and open a new one looking out this way. When I moved here he said at least he wouldn't be able to see my digs from down there. What a cruel choice!" He rubbed his hands gleefully.

But his attitude puzzled her. "Why are you so bitter, Frank? Harry's bitterness is quite understandable — and I certainly understand my own! But the old man has always treated you rather cautiously, as if he doesn't know quite what to do in your case. So why all this?" She imitated his gleeful gestures.

Frank glanced at the door to the kitchen and lowered his voice once again. "Can't mumble for ever. Can't explain it properly with ... you know — that one out there." He tilted his head in Clarrie's direction. "The fact is, I can't stand the risks he takes."

"Financial?"

"No. You know what I mean. Sailing a few points fine of the law. One day he'll be caught red-handed and drag us all down. But let's talk about it some other time. Poor old Harry's out of his depth before he even begins. It's you and me, Jess — we'll have to save the Kernow name one day. And the family fortune. Talking of which — d'you think you could do *me* a favour?"

She wondered if he'd actually forgotten the last favour he'd asked of her. Was he about to repeat it? The notion that a brother might actually *forget* asking his sister to abet him in something so scurrilous gave her fresh insight, if such were needed, into his character — or, at least, that side of it; for Frank had so many sides that no single opinion of him was possible. "In return for what?" she asked. "A plate of beef and cheese?"

He chuckled, not deceived by this deliberate red herring. "No — for securing the sewage-farm site for you. And for next to nothing. Take it as in your bag already. No — this favour concerns Cressida Pym."

She could not conceal her surprise. For a giddy moment she confused his designs on Clarrie Williams with ... whatever he wanted of Cressida, and she almost blurted out that, in that case, the stakes would be a great deal higher. Then she realized he could not possibly mean anything so disgraceful, so she merely said, "Go on."

"I don't know if you know anything about her own private financial affairs? Do you and she talk about such things? Or does the Surface Angel think it too utterly unladylike?"

His use of the old nickname made Jessie realize how out of touch her brother had become with the more recent developments at Wheal Prosper, especially in relations between her and Cressida Pym. "I shall give away none of her confidences," she warned him. "I shall merely say that I am aware of her grandfather's will ..."

"And of the sums involved?"

"Yes, that, too. And I know that Cornwallis's mother had a talk with her about it because some cousin of hers — or some relation, anyway — was recently involved in a successful action to break a similar deed of trust."

"Ah!" He spoke the single word as if she had just relieved him of all his doubts. "I was going to approach her about that. I've only lately had sight of a copy of the will in question."

Jessie thought what a splendid phrase 'had sight of' was. He could have looked at the will daily for the past five years and still truthfully claim he had 'only lately had sight of it' — especially in Cornwall, where to say, 'I've only now seen him coming down the street,' does not imply the first sighting of one's life. 'Had sight of' — she stored it away for future use.

Frank was meanwhile saying, "She's the one who misled me — misled us all. She said the capital goes to a cats-and-dogs' home on her marriage or death."

"And you're going to tell her she can break the deed of trust and inherit the money outright?" she asked.

He was taken aback by the suggestion in her tone that this would be a most reckless act on his part. "Why not? You don't think she'll be happy to hear it?"

Jessie shrugged. "I have no idea, but I think it's something you should consider very carefully first."

"Don't you *want* her to marry the old fellow? Surely it's in all our interests to see that situation regularized? Especially if he comes a cropper in business. People won't be nearly so tolerant about it then! It's all very easy to turn a blind eye while Barney Kernow's a useful man, ever-ready with a handy donation to a good cause. Don't tell me you haven't thought over these things, too."

She finished and placed the knife and fork together. He pressed her to take more but she declined. He repeated that she must surely have thought about such things.

"I think more of Cressida herself," she told him. "We've grown a lot closer since you left ..."

"No connection, of course!" he joked.

"Except in the vague sense that when one fledgeling leaves the nest, the older birds begin to realize the time is drawing on for the others, too. Anyway, I think the existence of that provision in the will gave Cressida an odd kind of *permission* to ..." She, too, lowered her voice — even though they were already speaking too quietly for their words to travel through the solid pitch-pine door — "to live in sin with the old man. She actually *enjoys* it."

"Most people do," he pointed out. "Or there'd never be new feet for old babys' boots. Talking of which ..."

"Not *that!*" she said wearily. "I mean she enjoys the intrigue, the illicitness of it, the secret knowledge that she's a Scarlet Woman though all the while living as a respectable housekeeper-companion, running an immaculate household and bringing up a perfect lady like me — ha ha! Really, she's very like our father. He doesn't need to sail close to the law at all — not for the money it brings in, anyway. He could double his income if he only managed the legitimate parts of the business effectively ..."

"As someone not a million miles from here would!"

"Will — one day — you'll see! And you may wipe that smirk off you face! Anyway, I was saying, he doesn't need his risky little side-ventures and shady deals. He doesn't do it for gain. He does it for the thrill of *not* being found out. And so does Cressida. If you come along and set her free to marry the old man tomorrow ... well, I don't know what she'd do. She'd suddenly realize how drab life is."

"Forty thousand pounds covers an awful lot of drab!" He was disappointed that his revelation of the sum did not surprise her, for he had not quite believed her earlier claim to know all the figures. "You knew already," he said.

"I told you! She explained it all to me — months ago. I warned you that things had changed since you left home."

"They certainly have! So — you believe I should say nothing to her? And after all my hard work, too!"

"I didn't say that. I said ponder it very carefully. Anyway — wait and see if she comes to you. She might — now that Cornwallis's mother has put a flame to the fuse."

Frank considered her words and then, somewhat surprisingly, nodded in agreement. "If she doesn't come to me, it means you're probably right — she just wants everything to go on as it is." A new thought took precedence: "I wonder what she does with the income? Even in the most conservative funds it'd bring in a thou' a year. More likely two. D'you think the old fellow gets his hands on it?"

Jessie, who did not wish her brother either to learn the truth or to know that *she* knew it, said vaguely, "What do you think!"

He dropped the subject for the moment though she was sure he wouldn't just let it lie. "Talking of favours," he said, "you still owe me one from previously — remember?"

She smiled feebly and without humour. "I thought you'd forgotten. I hoped you had. I want no part in any such ... arrangement."

"Oh well — why didn't you say so?" His smile was bland and forgiving. "I'd never have embarrassed you by asking if I'd known. I'll ask her myself, now." And before she could stop him — before she even *believed* him — he raised his voice and called out, "Clarrie!"

"No!" Jessie squeezed his arm until he winced. "You dare!"

Clarrie stood in the doorway. "Yes?" she asked. Since the incident in January she had not dignified him with a title.

"Oh, nothing," he replied. "Only we've finished with our plates."

When she cleared his things away he did not move to one side to make it easy for her but continued to sit four-square. She almost unbalanced in reaching for things while leaning sideways so as to prevent her bosom from touching his provocatively placed arm. Jessie had to reach across the table and move things to a more convenient location for her.

"You!" she spat angrily when the maid had gone.

"What's she paid at Wheal Prosper?" he asked nonchalantly. "Twelve quid a year plus board, livery, and beer? I'd pay her eighty-five — to look after *all* my requirements."

Jessie looked at the kitchen door and realized with horror that Clarrie had not closed it fully. Had she heard? She picked up the empty water jug, which the girl had overlooked, and carried it out to the kitchen.

The moment Clarrie saw her mistress in the doorway she busied herself with the washing up — wrapping her pinny round the kettle handle and lifting it with some exaggeration of effort off the gas. With cultivated unconcern she said, " 'E's only now boiled, Miss Jessica. I could brew a cup of tee for 'ee."

Jessie declined the offer and was careful to close the door before she returned to the table; all the girl's composure could not disguise the fact that she had heard Frank's words — which thus amounted to an offer. When Jessie had first pushed wide the door, she had found Clarrie standing at the table, her knuckles white, her jaw agape.

"She heard you," she said angrily.

"Good," he replied, not in the least bit ruffled.

Cornwallis took Jessie to meet his mother off the main-line express at Gwinear Road, which was nothing but a railway station way out in the middle of nowhere. The 'Road' in its name must have referred to the railroad, for the public highway was no more than a narrow, winding country lane with Praze-an-Beeble at one end and nothing you could put a name to at the other. The branch-line train, being timed to meet an earlier up-train, got them there at two o'clock, with half an hour to spare before Anna's down-train arrived; she had refused her son's offer to meet her with the Renault.

"Where are you going?" Cornwallis asked as Jessie set off with some apparent purpose down the platform.

"Exercise," she replied. "I can't sit still for half an hour."

"You can't sit still for half a minute," he complained as he jogged to catch up with her.

"You can sit down if you like," she pointed out. "You don't have to yap at my heels all the time."

"The way you snap my head off these days!" he remarked, trying to keep his tone light and jocular. "Anyone would suppose we're engaged." He looked at her, willing her to face him — which she stubbornly refused to do. His heart turned over in his breast and not for the first time he wished he had never made that idiotic suggestion, or that Jessie had never accepted it.

"All I did was point out ..." she began

"What's the matter?" he interrupted her. "Ever since we returned from Yorkshire you've ..."

"It has nothing to do with Yorkshire," she snapped.

"I'm not saying it has. At least you don't deny *it* exists — this snappish mood."

After five more paces, all in silence, they came to the top of the slope at the end of the platform. NO PASSENGERS BEYOND THIS POINT, read the notice. BY ORDER OF THE DIRECTORS OF THE GREAT WESTERN RAILWAY.

"Passenger," Jessie murmured absently, her eyes reading and re-reading the notice.

He ached so much to hold her that he had to force himself to look away. He knew he was behaving stupidly. What he ought to do was turn on his heel, walk back up the platform, and sit and read the newspaper, paying her no attention whatever. What he ought to do was take her in his arms and kiss her. What he ought to do was lay down the law a little — 'either you marry me as soon as we can get the banns called or *I'll* call the whole thing off!' What he ought to do was anything other than yap at her heels all the time.

"We can't go on like this," he said.

She pointed at the notice and replied, "Clearly not."

"You know what I mean. The arrangement we made — it's not working, is it."

"Oh?" she asked pugnaciously. "Are the good ladies of West Penwith beating a path to your door again? I'm certainly not being pestered to trap a man by Cressida and my father."

"That must be why you're so happy!" He picked up a pebble and shied it at a bird, sitting on the fence beside the track. "Missed by a mile," he said with satisfaction. "I shan't even bother to point out that you know very well I don't mean *that* aspect of it isn't working. I mean between *us*. It's making us ... it's doing us no good." He glanced sidelong at her and added, "And I'm sure you know why, Jessie."

She persisted in her refusal to look at him. "And I'm sure I don't," she said.

"It's not working because it was an idiotic thing to do from the very outset. D'you know what I think happened?"

"No, but I'm sure you'll tell me." She turned about and began sauntering away up the platform — veering to her right to have a word with the driver of the branch-line train.

"Stay here," he said; it was a curious blend of command and plea. The ambiguity made her pause so long that to ignore him and resume her departure would have seemed too deliberately provocative, as if she were to challenge him openly to make her stay; by staying she made it a favour.

"We have to talk this over, Jess," he went on in a conciliatory tone. "We never seem to get the chance nowadays. We've still got the best part of half an hour to fill, so we might as well use it. Otherwise ..." He broke off, not having considered any alternative.

She seized on his hesitation: "Otherwise what?"

Driven to it, he said, "Otherwise I think we'd both be relieved to call the whole thing off."

"A fine conclusion to reach — with your mother due at any moment!" She wished she felt as confident inside as her ebullient words made her seem. She knew he wanted to talk of things that were always hovering at the rim of her mind and which she kept pushing away, refusing to consider.

"It's not 'any moment,' it's a godsent twenty-five minutes away — even assuming the train's on time."

She looked up the line and down the line, avoiding his eyes in passing. No help was in sight.

After a pause he continued. "I believe that neither of us has any real experience of love ..."

"That didn't stop you sounding terribly knowledgeable on the subject at the Centennial Ball!" she said huffily.

"Which merely proves that chickens always come home to roost. But I'm not the only one who hatched a few of that homing breed! If you'll let me just say what's on my mind? I think I fell in love with you the moment I saw you." He was avoiding her gaze as he spoke the words — to such an extent that he was facing away from her; so he did not notice her stiffen at the word and dart him a pleading glance. He went on doggedly: "However, since falling in love and all that love implies — I mean marriage, family, domesticity, et cetera — was the very last thing on my mind at that time, I believe I panicked and thought only of ways to ... I can't call it 'to get out of' the situation since I wasn't aware of getting *into* it. Ways of deflecting it, I suppose. Neutralizing it. That's what all my lofty talk was, that night. Something to neutralize those feelings."

He vanished into a brief reverie, then, turning to her, he touched her elbow gingerly and added, "But it was *fun*, wasn't it, Jess! We had real fun that night."

For the first time that day — and for many previous days, too — she smiled at him, a wan, hesitant smile, but a smile nonetheless. "Yes," she admitted.

He became serious again. "I know it's dangerous to speak *for* you, but, on the understanding that I'm merely putting forward a theory here, will you let me say it without any explosions and expostulations from you? You can tell me what utter balderdash and poppycock it is after. All right?"

She gave a guarded nod and watched him suspiciously.

Relieved, he went on: "I think we had so much fun, not just that night but all through Cav Rust and doing up Wheal Dream and all that — we enjoyed it all because we could develop our mutual feelings for each other without being threatened by them. The odd thing is, you see — I haven't changed. I *still* don't want to get married!"

She stared at him in amazement.

"Yes!" he insisted. "I *don't* want family ... domesticity ... playing the paterfamilias and so on. I want to stay free. And yet I love you to utter distraction. I think about you night and day. I'm hollow with longing for you." His voice began to shiver. His dry tongue licked his dry lips, leaving tiny flecks of foam at the corners of his mouth. "Just to see you is to want to hold you and ... oh, God! There are a few seconds of panic and confusion when I wake up each morning. I know who I am. I know where I am. And I know there's a huge, stupendous ... *something* filling the sky, stretching itself over the whole world, filling everything. I can feel it there. And I know that I know what it is but I can't remember. And then I do remember. It's you! You *exist!* You're *there!* The world contains you. The very air I breathe is different because you live and breathe in it, too." He gripped her elbow now and gave a helpless laugh. "And yet I have not changed! I *don't* want to marry you ... set up home ... drive out in the dog cart on Sundays ... you know what I mean."

He had spent enough of his emotions by now to become aware that she was trembling, too. And now, too, she seemed no longer willing to look at him.

"My theory is that it's the same with you," he said in a more collected voice. "I think you've found yourself stretched on the same impossible rack, between loving me and not wanting to marry me. Am I right? Now's your chance to tell me I'm talking tripe."

She drew her arm out of his grip, but not petulantly; in fact, a certain reluctance accompanied her withdrawal. "It's not that I *don't* want to marry you," she said. "It's that I want other things more. I want to *do* something, make something, be something first. These feelings of love just get in the way. I have this picture of Mother Nature standing there, rattling her shackles and telling me not to get ideas above my station. That's what those romantic feelings inside me are — shackles waiting to slip round my ankles."

"Love!" he said morosely.

She took it as a question. "What else!" she replied in the same dour tone. "The trouble is that trying to fight it probably takes up more time than giving way to it would. I'm caught both ways! I get distracted as much by thoughts of *not* giving way to it as I probably would if I did. Give way, I mean."

He looked all about them and gave a single, ironic laugh. "What an idiotic conversation to have on a crowded platform!" he said.

"Crowded?" she echoed. "Six people — four of them huddling out of the sun in the waiting room?"

"The way I feel at this moment," he replied, "you, me, and one more is a crowd."

She smiled at him again, sympathetically this time. "Perhaps it's just as well, then. Because I still haven't quite decided — between giving way and not giving way, you know."

"Well, we know where *not* giving way leads! It leads to snapping and almost permanent grumpiness — which I, frankly, cannot take much more of."

"But what's the alternative? If we admit we have these feelings about each other and ..."

He laughed in surprise. "We've just done that, surely?"

"*Just!*" She emphasized his word. "We can admit it, turn our backs on each other, and walk away ..."

"Oh yes!" he said ironically. "Like two people fighting a duel!" He shook his head. "We couldn't do it, love. You think Mother Nature's still waving her shackles in the air? If so it's her reserve set. She's already put the main ones on us, one end round your ankle, the other round mine. I said just now — we know where trying to fight it leads. We can't get away from each other and the shackle hurts! What we don't know yet is what'll happen if we *don't* fight it."

"If we get married, you mean?" she asked glumly. "Let's go and sit on that bench." She led the way to a spindly contraption of wrought iron and oak between the uprights of the Gwinear Road sign. Both were in need of paint.

"No," he replied, taking her arm. "If we just stop denying it. Accept it, instead. Accept that we were already in love when we made our counterfeit engagement — that we were simply trying to find a way of indulging that love without admitting it, even to ourselves. Which, of course — as anyone with half our intelligence would have been able to tell us — has been a disaster. It's given us the worst of every possible world — because you can live a lie and pretend it's the truth but you can't live the truth and pretend it's a lie!"

Jessie had heard too many clever words and neatly turned phrases from him to be so easily persuaded. "But how can we keep the other things we value, then?" she asked. "You say you still don't want marriage and all that. And I still want to *do* things before I get burdened down by ... you know, domesticity and all that. How do we keep those things if we do as you suggest?"

He closed his thumb and long finger like a steel band around her wrist. "You're a terrier!" he said.

"But I'm right."

"Terriers usually are. The answer is, I don't know. We may simply be exchanging one sort of folly for another. But at least we know the folly we've tried doesn't work. If you come to a fork in the road and the left branch has a sign saying *Dead End*, you haven't much choice, have you!"

She sighed but said nothing.

"Have you?" he insisted.

"What if the other branch leads into a dark, mysterious jungle and there's a sign saying *Here be tygers?*"

He shook his head. "I'm afraid you've lost me, love. What might these tigers be?"

Again she was silent. He began to feel uneasy.

At length she said, "I must tell you something about Frank. But if I do, you must promise me faithfully — absolutely ... cross your heart and hope to die — you'll never breathe a word of it back to him? Promise me now?"

"Cross my heart and hope to die." His tone was jocular but his unease was growing.

"I don't think it's right to call him a cold fish because in many ways he's been very warm and brotherly to me. But there is something very ... I mean, there's a cool, calculating streak in his character. You know what I mean, I'm sure."

"Yes. Also ... oh God!" He closed his eyes and shook his head. "I think I know what's coming next. If so, I'd do anything to spare you having to tell me. It's taking a great risk, I know — yet knowing Frank as I do somehow lessens it. Suppose I just say the name of a certain pretty, young maidservant ...?"

She stared at him aghast.

"No?" he asked, now tortured with embarrassment.

"Yes," she breathed. "But how did you ...? D'you mean he asked you, too?"

He nodded. "Not to ... to actually ... not ..." He gazed miserably past her, up the line. Why was his mother's train not fifteen minutes early today?

To his amazement, Jessie laughed. "The young devil!" she exclaimed. "Let's get this clear now. Frank asked you to find out what Clarrie Williams's deepest-held ambition might be — is that right?"

"Yes." He gulped. "But not to — you know — carry the conversation any further."

"All right!" She gave a huge sigh of relief. "Let's stop mincing all round the subject, eh? Cards on the table! I'll even let you be dummy and play your hand for you. Frank wants Clarrie as his mistress. Being the sort of man he is — with that mile-wide calculating streak running all through him — he's probably worked it out that the *usual* bachelor's answer to the *usual* bachelor's problem will cost ..."

"I say," he protested. "Less of your *usual*, please! It doesn't apply all round, let me tell you."

She leaned across and kissed him on the cheek. "Well it applies to Frank, I'm sure." She waited a moment and then added, "At least you don't quarrel with *that!* I think that Frank has calculated it would be cheaper to ..." Her voice trailed off when she saw him shaking his head. "You *do* quarrel with it?" she asked.

"I think Frank is in love with Clarrie — but, being Frank, he cannot possibly admit it, not even to himself. Especially not to himself."

The possibility, which had never once crossed her mind, left her feeling quite stunned.

Cornwallis chuckled. "In a way, it's a Frank-style version of the dilemma that faced *us* until a few minutes ago."

"It still does," she reminded him swiftly. "But I must say it never occurred to me that ... I mean, Frank — in love! I never suspected. It'd be like suspecting Bob Fitzsimmons of doing embroidery! Yet who knows — perhaps he did!"

Bob Fitzsimmons was the Helston-born heavyweight boxing champion; he had lost his world title only the previous year.

After a moment's further thought, she added, "I'm almost tempted to tell him, now. Unless *you* did? Or didn't you find out?" She grinned. "How *would* you find out — except by asking her directly? Now that's a conversation I'd love to have overheard!"

"You treat it very lightly," he said, slightly miffed at her tone.

"Well, you're the one who agreed to it."

He gave a rueful nod. "I know. I can't think what possessed me."

"Frank did. He can do that to people."

"But not to his sister, apparently! You speak as if you know but won't tell."

She nodded. "What about you? *Did* you ask her?"

He shook his head. "I got cold feet — then confessed it all to my mother. She winkled it out of Clarrie, of course. Took her out in the fields to pick flowers ... talked about this and that ..."

"Ah!" Jessie clapped her hands with delight as that stubbornly resistant bit of life's jigsaw puzzle fell into place at last. "*That's* what they were doing! Well, well, well! Your mother is a woman who'll repay some study, Cornwallis."

"Anyway," he said, "how did we get from *our* problem to Frank's? I don't think *I* mentioned him first, did I?"

"Ah." She knew she had brought the subject up but she had to run a brief audit back through their conversation to remember why. When she arrived at the reason she hesitated. The fact that Frank might actually be in love with Clarrie made a subtle change to the argument she had been going to put to him — which was difficult enough in any case. She said, "It's just that when Frank first put the bargain to me — namely, that he'd swap legal information concerning my scheme to build the power station in return for personal information concerning his plans toward Clarrie, I thought how lucky I am to be a woman and not have to bother about such things. But ..." She closed her eyes and hugged herself tight against his arm. "The more I began to suspect we might be genuinely falling in love, my darling ..." She swallowed heavily and whispered, "Oh Lord!"

"It's all right, love. I understand. You needn't ..."

"No! I've got to say it now! There've been too many half-spoken things between us. Besides, *not* to say it implies a measure of shame. And I'm not ashamed, Cornwallis. I'm not!"

"I believe you," he said, to calm her agitation.

"The reason I've been out-of-sorts with you lately is, one, because my genuine feelings about us were based on a fraud — I mean, our counterfeit engagement — and, two, because the closer we drew together, you and I, the more agitated I became by the passions that I was so superior about in poor Frank's case." She breathed heavily two or three times and said, "There!"

"There!" he echoed her and let out a deep breath he had not really been aware of holding in.

"You despise me now," she said flatly. "Now that you know the awful truth about me."

He slipped an arm around her and pulled her head down upon his shoulder. "I despise you so much I'd marry you this very second if only we had a vicar to make it right."

She swallowed audibly but said nothing.

"We have to make it right, Jess," he said.

*A*nna wandered through the half-restored farmhouse at Wheal Dream, trying not to feel proud of what her son had achieved — for, indeed, the genteel part of her was quite appalled at how well he had carried out the restoration. At length, after running her gloved finger daintily along the underside of a banister rail that Cornwallis had cut into the existing staircase, vainly seeking a splinter or some roughness she might comment upon, she said, "It was clearly a waste of time and money to give you that expensive education, my boy. We should have apprenticed you to Higgs and Copely at twelve!" — naming one of the biggest building firms in Leeds.

"Oh, I'd never survive as a tradesman," he replied modestly; he ran his fingers where she had made her test, just to see if she'd missed anything. "I go much too slowly. Twopence an hour is all I'd get. The best of them can get a shilling, you know."

He winked surreptitiously at Jessie to show her he knew his mother was trying to provoke him and that he was not going to rise to it.

"It's a scandal," Anna murmured, almost automatically. Then, "At least you aren't losing sight of life's fundamentals, though. The question of income is a matter of sudden and painful importance, now. You won't be able to carry on with *this* work until the coffers are replenished from some other source, eh?"

Cornwallis and Jessie exchanged glances. Jessie murmured something about going out to have a look at the lighting set and left them at the foot of the stairs.

"Come and have a look at the roof," Cornwallis said. "That's my greatest achievement so far."

"Did I say something out of place?" Anna asked as she followed him up.

"No," he assured her. "Well, not really."

"What does that mean?"

"It's a bit of a sore point, actually. You're right when you say I've obviously got to turn my hand to something now. And the most obvious thing — it seemed to me — but that's because I'm a man and tend to think logically, it seems ..."

"Get on with it!"

He stood at the top of the stair, biting the quick of one fingernail, suddenly lost in thought.

"The most obvious thing, it seemed to you ...?" his mother prompted. Then, when he continued to stare blankly into space, she lost her patience and added, "... was to throw in your lot with Jessie in this power-company scheme of hers, I suppose."

The suggestion galvanized him at last. He broke into a broad smile and said, "There! You see it, too! It *is* the most obvious and logical thing, isn't it!"

His mother sniffed and took half a cautious step backward. "I doubt if the bonny lass herself saw it quite in that light."

"Oh." His face fell. "You're right, actually. She roasted me alive. We're only just back on speaking terms."

She frowned. "When did this happen? You were like a pair of cooing doves at the station yesterday."

"This morning," he replied glumly. "Before breakfast — when I'm never at my best."

"She *is* an early bird!"

He nodded. "She used not to be. But since this notion has taken hold ..."

"Still, if you're already back on speaking terms, it can't have been a real quarrel. Just a warning shot across your bows, I expect."

He led her along the passage, to the trap-door into the roof space. "How did you know she'd object? Did you talk about it on one of your walks in Allerton? You seem to have discussed almost everything with everybody up there."

Anna smiled primly. "Only doing my duty, dear. How did I know? Any woman would know. Jessie's set herself an impossible task in my opinion. She'll succeed, of course, because *she* doesn't realize it's impossible, which is always the secret to success. But she does realize how difficult it's going to be — especially to get the important men, the men who sign contracts and bills of exchange, to take her seriously. If there's even a whiff that you're in it with her — never mind if you go around wearing a sandwich-board saying 'I merely sharpen the quills,' they'll wink at one another and pat the sides of their noses knowingly and say, '*He's* the real brains behind it all, of course!' It isn't logical of them, I know, but then" — she smiled wickedly — "men aren't really logical at all, are they!"

"Well ..." he said awkwardly, and pointed invitingly at the ladder that vanished through the trapdoor up into the dark, "it wasn't *intuition* that put up this roof, I can tell you."

She gazed uncertainly at the dark rectangle that swallowed the top of the ladder. "There wouldn't be any bats up there, I suppose?"

"As a matter of fact," he replied, "there are. They arrived last week. Summer quarters, Godfrey says."

Anna warded off his invitation with her hand. "I'll take your word for it, dear — both about the bats and the mathematical logic that led to your attic triumph. At least you now understand why your very kind offer to sharpen the power company's quills was not at all kindly received?"

He sighed and, because his bedroom was not in a mother-worthy state, started to lead her back downstairs. "Not entirely. She was perfectly ready to use my capital — when we thought I had a bit."

"What's the view from the front window like up here?" she asked.

"Oh," he replied vaguely, "not bad. The panes are filthy, though. You won't see a thing."

But it was too late. She had already opened the door and was picking her way — like a soldier avoiding tripwires — over mounds of day-old, week-old, month-old clothing toward windows that were, though not entirely clean, certainly the cleanest objects in sight. "I misheard you, dear," she said, looking at his things. "I could have sworn you said the *panes* were filthy! Jessie was ready to accept your capital, of course, because she knows that the men who understand money are, in turn, well aware how little it contributes to any successful enterprise. In fact, that's the whole point of capital, isn't it? The capitalist lends it to the real workers of the world so that he can go away and swig and guzzle and sleep and have fun while the money works *for* him! So of course she'll accept your capital — yours or anyone's else."

He threw up his hands, yielding the point to her — and with it every other point she had made, too, for they were all one logical whole. He led the way back to the kitchen.

"And, talking of capital," Anna went on as they descended the stair, "has anyone approached Miss Pym yet?"

He crossed the kitchen, put the kettle on the stove, and lit the wick.

She glanced at the cups in the sink and said, "If you were thinking of making tea for me, dear, I'll wait until we get back to Wheal Prosper, thank you. *Has* anyone?"

He went and stood in the back doorway, leaning against the jamb and gazing at Jessie, who was not looking at the lighting set but sitting in the Renault chatting with Clarrie and pretending to drive through what was obviously a large and admiring audience — the inaugural day of the Helston Power Company, no doubt. "It's all rather difficult," he told her

"Most things worth achieving are," she said.

"You remember Uncle Raymond boasting about going out to shoot gazelle with only one bullet up the spout and none in his pocket? It's a bit like that — only worse. We'll only get one shot at Cressida Pym. If it doesn't find its mark, she won't simply run away, leaving us the hope of a second pot at her another day. She'll run to Barney Kernow — and then the sky will fall in!"

Anna was silent awhile before she said, "It seems that you need someone to sound her out for you — tactfully, of course."

He turned and smiled at her. "Of course," he agreed.

But she remained thoughtful; after a further pause she said, "One hates people who come between man and wife — and even those who come between men and women who are, how can one put it? — one station down the line from that terminus. But it would be awfully *useful* if there were a brief period of cooling-off between Cressida Pym and Jessie's father."

*J*essie sat twiddling the wheel of the Renault, making 'Vroom-vroom!' noises with her lips, and causing a slightly embarrassed Clarrie to laugh. "And look!" she cried, "isn't that Alderman Gilbert? And Mayor Bowden? And Lord Saint-Levan? And Viscount Saint-Alban? And the Duke of Cornwall, too, if my eyes don't deceive me! My goodness — simply everyone's here for our grand inauguration!"

"Oh, Miss Kernow!" Clarrie exclaimed, caught between awkwardness and excitement. "D'you think such things will ever be?"

"As night follows day," Jessie replied confidently. Then she added the more sober afterthought: "Though whether you or I will be part of them is quite another matter."

She let go of the steering wheel and sat demurely with her hands in her lap. "I have to come up with the money for the land quite soon," she said glumly. "Frank got a very good price but he couldn't get it for nothing. Down past the sewage farm, you know?"

" 'Es, Miss, so you said. I still think out past the old mill was a handsome place."

"But too expensive, Clarrie. Talking of my brother … you remember a little set-to I interrupted between him and you once — the morning after the Centennial Ball?"

The girl said, "'Es," warily and licked her lips.

"He never tried to follow that up, I suppose? You can tell me. I shouldn't be angry — except, possibly, with him."

"Well ..." She scratched the dome behind her ear. "Not in so many words, he hasn't."

Jessie stared at her closely. "You mean he's left notes lying around for you to read ... or what?"

"Lor' no — nothing like that! Only ... you know the way a body can *look* at a body?"

"Can't take his eyes off you? That sort of look?"

Clarrie shook her head. "There's more of a question in it than that, if you do know what I mean?"

"Not entirely, Clarrie. What sort of question?"

"Dunno, Miss. A sort of hope, maybe."

Jessie laughed drily. "A hopeful sort of question — or a questionable sort of hope? There's a difference, you know!"

Clarrie joined her laughter. "I do, Miss. That's one thing I do know *very* well!"

She said no more. Yet Jessie gained the impression that she wished to. However, the last thing Jessie wanted was for her to remember this conversation as a question-and-answer session devoted to the single topic of Frank; if the girl wanted to say more, she'd find her own way to do so. Jessie said, "And talking of that Centennial Ball — I don't suppose Godfrey has tried to follow it up?"

"Ha!" The maid was surprisingly bitter all of a sudden. "Not since he took up with that orpheling skivvy — that Williams maid."

"Who?" Jessie asked, pretending to be surprised, for she had told no one about finding Godfrey and Tillie asleep at Wheal Dream that Sunday morning at the end of May.

But she saw in Clarrie's hesitation that the maid knew all about it. "Oh!" She hit her own forehead. "Tillie, you mean! That was just a bit of bravado, surely? She happened to be leaving the Angel just as Godfrey arrived to drive the car home." She peered at Clarrie once again, to see how much she really knew. "Are you saying it was more than that?"

The shutters fell. "Dunno, Miss. There's some as seems to think so."

Jessie knew better than to try for more at once; when a limpet clams itself tight to a rock, it's best for the shell-picker to walk on and pick other shells for a while. "Anyway," she said, "he hasn't bothered you again, I trust?"

"I can look after myself, Miss. But thanks for your cognizance."

Cognizance! Jessie thought. From what homily had Clarrie plucked the word? "I'm sure you can. You must get plenty of practice. And it must be very trying to work in a house with three young sons all looking for a bit of adventure."

"Not Master Harry!" Clarrie exclaimed without thinking. "He's ..."

"Yes?" Jessie prompted.

"He's always been the perfect gent to us, Becky and me."

"Anyway, you can take on any of them in a fair fight — *and* send them home with a flea in their ears. That's all I wanted to know. I don't mean to pry."

"Oh I wasn't going to suggest ... I mean I never even thought ..."

"Enough said." Jessie cut across her embarrassed protestations. "Only if either of them does become a nuisance and you think I might help, you wouldn't hesitate to say, would you."

"No, Miss, 'course I shouldn't." After a pause she added thoughtfully. "What you said is right, though — 'tis difficult in a house like that. All the same, we'm only human — and 'tis flattery to a girl if a feller like Master Frank do show a bit of interest. Can't deny it."

Jessie smiled. "Of course, he's well aware of that. He knows full well that you'd feel flattered."

Clarrie grinned pugnaciously. "And I'm well aware as *he's* aware. So that's the top and tail of it. That's where it do stop. As old Billy Chigwidden used to say — you can keep any horseshoe you do find on the road, and good luck to 'ee. There's no man may force you to pay for 'n."

"So all's well that ends well," Jessie concluded. Then, apropos nothing, murmured, "All's fair in love and war."

"Had you some particular reason for inquiring, Miss?" Clarrie asked hesitantly.

She clearly did not wish to let the subject drop just yet, Jessie was pleased to notice. "Only a rather vague one, Clarrie," she said. "I've noticed that when men get given a rebuff in that particular region of their conceit, some of them are apt to take it too much to heart and become obsessive about it."

"And you think that's gone and happened with Master Godfrey?"

Looking into the girl's eyes Jessie saw she did not mean Godfrey at all; she just didn't want to be the one to say Frank's name first. "I never thought it of *him*," she replied. "Young men of sixteen are solid gutta percha in my experience!"

"Ah!" The maid's eyes gleamed with sudden interest. "Master Frank, then? How?"

Jessie decided to take the plunge — or at least to dip something more than a toe in the water. "He was talking with me about ambition, that day last week — a week ago today, in fact — when we had luncheon with him, remember? *My* ambitions mostly, of course, and the need to conceal them from my father. And he said it must be awful to have ambitions and yet be compelled to keep them secret from the entire world. And I couldn't think what he meant. And he hunted round for an example and then he said, as if he'd only just thought of it — 'Take Clarrie out there in the kitchen. She might have some ambition every bit as grand as yours, but she'd never dare tell anyone because they'd only laugh and tell her she was getting ideas above her station. It must be awful for her.' And I ..."

"You said '*as if* he'd only just thought of it'?" Clarrie reminded her.

"Well, I was just coming to that. You see, I thought it was eerie — because we'd only just been talking about it, hadn't we — remember? And you often get that feeling with Frank, that he can overhear conversations a mile off. Anyway, I said 'as if' because I don't believe he had only just thought of it. I felt it was his whole purpose in starting that conversation at all. So of course, I didn't know *what* to do."

"How did 'ee answer 'n, then?" Clarrie asked.

"By implying that, even if you did have large daydreams, I knew nothing about them. I just said, 'Go on — I don't expect she's bothered by any such thing!' or something like that. And then he said, 'Let's call her in and ask her, in that case. See which of us is right.' D'you remember he called you in?"

Clarrie laughed. "And you said, 'Don't you dare!'"

"You heard me, did you!" Jessie pulled a face, wondering how much else she had heard, too.

"Only that bit," Clarrie responded swiftly.

Jessie still wondered. "Anyway, that's when he just smiled and asked you to clear the dishes. But I'm sure he really wanted to know about your real ambitions in life. Should I have told him, I wonder?"

She threw out the question casually enough but the maid was not deceived. In an equally casual tone she said there'd be no harm in it, because Frank would only do what he predicted others would — namely, laugh.

Jessie took a further step toward total immersion. "What if he didn't?" she asked. "What if he made you a serious offer — which, knowing my brother, would be a full-fledged legal contract, I'm sure — that he would provide the capital for your dream if, in return, you would ... well, need I go on?"

"A serious offer?" Clarrie said slowly.

"Very serious — for a girl in your position, I'd say."

"Well, *I'd* say any serious offer like that, 'specially from a serious young gentleman with the power to carry it out should ought to be tooken seriously, Miss."

She must have thought that was the end of the matter between them, for she half rose and prepared to descend. Jessie's peremptory, "But ...!" halted her and the words that followed it brought her swiftly back to her seat.

"But," Jessie said, "suppose that Frank is deluding himself? He wouldn't be the first young man to do so. Suppose he is actually in love with you, Clarrie. No, don't laugh — it's no more laughable than your ambition to own the village store is ... if you'll just think about it a mo. If you are going to give it serious consideration, that's one of the serious possibilities you'll have to consider."

Clarrie, now as pale as china, said, "Do *you* think he is, Miss Jessie?"

Her mistress shrugged. "The thought would never have crossed my mind. I can't believe that dear Frank would ever allow himself to fall in love with any woman below the rank of Honourable. But we can't always exercise that control. If you'll promise me never to tell anyone — especially not Frank — I'll admit it was Mister Trelawney who put the idea into ..."

"Old Man Trelawney?" Clarrie asked in amazement. "Up Leeds?"

"No! *My* Mister Trelawney — Cornwallis. He and Frank must have had some discussion on the subject of love because he thinks it's quite possible — he's not certain, mind, but he thinks it quite possible that Frank is in love with you — and isn't able to admit it to himself. So he dresses it up in this rather ..." She was about to say 'sordid' but thought she'd better not, in case Clarrie took up the proposition. "This *interesting* offer," she concluded. After a pause she added, "I say, Clarrie — woman to woman — *do* you find it interesting?"

The maid's tongue ran rapidly round her lips. "Like I said — if 'tis a serious notion, then I s'll consider 'n seriously. You may tell Master Frank so from me."

"Good heavens!" Jessie put her hand to her breast in alarm, almost all of it genuine. "I'm not his messenger in this! Please don't think that of me!"

Clarrie merely smiled. "Well then," she replied, "woman to woman — you can be mine, instead, can't 'ee!"

Jessie raised both hands in surrender.

"Another thing you'd better tell 'n, Miss," Clarrie added.

"Yes?"

"Tell 'n I don't love 'n and never shall. So he'd better put all such notions out of his head. *If* they'm there at all."

For a moment Jessie's only response was a baffled laugh. Then she said, "I don't understand you, Clarrie. Surely to be Mrs Frank Kernow, wife of the man who will one day be Alderman Kernow, or Mayor Kernow, or even Mister Frank Kernow, MP — is a cut above owning a little village shop?"

The girl's eyes blazed with sudden fire. "No, Miss! Begging your pardon, Miss. I'd be a fool to deny what you just said — 'tis true, of course. But the shop would be *mine*, see! There's no man will ever cut hisself a piece of *that* cake — especially after what I may have to do to get it!"

Clarrie had no idea why her mistress suddenly laughed, and threw an impulsive arm around her shoulders, and gave her a rash kiss vaguely near her ear, and laughed again and said, "Bless you, Clarrie, if you haven't shown me the answer to everything!"

*H*elston had markets on Wednesdays and Saturdays, with early closing on Fridays, in between. That last Friday in June — the first of Anna Trelawney's visit — was therefore a slack day at Kernow's Farm Machinery depot and had seemed to be an ideal occasion for Barney to show her around the place. Not that there was a great deal to show, but Anna, who belonged to that generation of gentlefolk who were trained to be both perfect hosts and ideal guests, could always find at least one complimentary thing to say about any topic in the calendar. In her case she often liked to put it in the form of a question, because it threw the onus upon the other party.

"Why?" she asked, fixing Barney with her large, intense eyes, "does *agricultural* machinery always seem *so* much more interesting than machinery of any other kind. Railway engines frankly leave me cold — as, indeed, they do their own carriages all too often. And I shrink in horror from the great whirring, clanking, stamping monsters at our factories in Leeds. But good old ploughs and" — she waved a hand vaguely at the array of machinery — "*things* ... they're so ... what's the word? Not 'chummy' but you know what I mean. Friendly. Why is that, Mister Kernow?"

Barney had never quite appreciated his stock in that light; he had seen too much of it rust, peel, bend, fracture, and resist the blacksmith's weld to put it in any category one might label 'friendly.' He took a deep breath in case inspiration struck, and when it did not, he said, "I don't know about that, I'm sure."

As they passed the main office building she caught sight of Harry inside. He had folded some piece of paper into the form of a dart and was cruising it across the room. She glanced swiftly at the young man's father but saw he had not noticed. "D'you believe in reincarnation?" she asked out of the blue. "I think the church is coming round to it, don't you? I'm sure we all go through many lives. Traveling down on the train I saw heaps of places that seemed familiar to me. Even little fields, you know. I'm sure I've been a ploughman or something in the past. I feel such an affinity for these ... these ... what d'you call them?"

"Harves," Barney told her. "Up in England they do call them 'harrows,' but we belong to say 'harves,' see?" He saw her inhaling for some fresh outburst and so added, "There's your spring-tine harve. That's best in a dry, loose tilth for checking young weeds. And your fixed-tine harve — that's mostly for burying broadcast seed. And your chain harve. That'll just level out every little bump when the others have broken the tilth down fine."

Anna stared at him with undisguised admiration. "You describe it so vividly, Mister Kernow. Every word you say only adds to my conviction that I have somehow engaged in all these bucolic pastimes with, er, *tilth* and things in some previous existence. You are obviously a man passionately devoted to the soil or you could not have built up such a thriving business here. Is that the famous gasworks?"

Barney, who had been looking around anxiously for Jessie or Cornwallis to come and rescue him, had to turn his back on his own property and stare at the large, cylindrical gasholder next door. "Yes," he said. "I don't know about famous, though."

"Jessie was telling us — it was one of the sources of your family's prosperity, I believe."

Barney admitted that his father had played a part in founding the local gas company.

"I think families have cycles, too," she went on. "Rather like reincarnation, you know, where one may be a duchess in one life and a ploughboy in the next. Your family, for instance, may have been merchant princes in the early days of Helston. I understand this land on which we are now standing was then a harbour open to the sea?"

At that point Barney began to realize that his daughter's future mother-in-law was not the featherbrain she affected to be. He had dealt with many a self-proclaimed blockhead in his time, some of whom had almost got the better of him by their deception. There was no outward change in his demeanour but he no longer listened with only half an ear.

He told her she was correct and went on to point out the ancient boundaries of the port of Helston, now a mere marshy waste on the southern side of the Penzance road.

"And then perhaps," she continued, "you Kernows suffered a decline while the great tin fortunes were made — only to be followed by a rise once more as tin itself declined and other industries like gas and farming rose to prominence. Cycles! All goes in cycles, you see. Where are my son and your daughter?"

"I was wondering the same myself, ma'am," Barney replied with some fervour.

"And what will the next cycle be, mmm?" she said casually, as if to fill the time until the youngsters appeared. When he did no more than smile at her fancy she added, still in the same inconsequential tone, "Which local family will reincarnate from ploughboy to duke even as families like ours fall from duke to mere earl?" And when he still did not respond, she added, "Or duchess to countess, of course."

"There they are!" he exclaimed, like a castaway sighting a sail.

He hardly needed draw attention to their arrival; the Renault motor was advertising it splendidly, though they were all of a furlong away, still; and half a furlong behind them, Miss Pym was having difficulty managing the horse between the shafts of her gig.

Anna decided either that the idea of electricity generation had not crossed his mind yet — which she could scarcely believe — or that it was in the forefront of his thoughts these days, which was why he'd say absolutely nothing about it. Either way, however, she was pretty certain that not a whiff of Jessie's interest had reached him so far. For a man who clearly needed many friends in the community, especially for their eyes and ears, it did not bode well. Her banter about families rising and falling might not, after all, be such utter nonsense as she had supposed.

Cornwallis pulled to a halt inside the gate; he obviously wasn't going to risk his tyres over the yard, which had too many old bits of metal scattered about for his liking. A flustered Cressida Pym pulled to a halt beside the Renault and immediately engaged them in rather animated conversation.

Anna saw that she had a little time yet in which to pursue her inquiries — not as much as she'd like, but she was used to being denied that luxury. It simply meant that her approach would have to be slightly more direct. "Now *there's* a woman I truly admire," she said. "Dear Miss Pym."

"She worked wonders on my brood," Barney replied, taking an eager step toward the rescue party. "Made a proper lady of my Jessica. Better, though I shouldn't ought to say it, than what her own mother, God rest her, would have done."

She fell in at his side but dragged the pace to a saunter. "She *is* a lady," Anna agreed. "Through and through. I felt it the moment we met. And, of course, her sacrifice only confirms it."

"Yes," he replied absently, being more keen to reach the new arrivals than to prolong his conversation with this edjack woman. Then he stopped in his tracks, having just registered her actual words. "Sacrifice?" he echoed.

"Her inheritance — she told me all about it."

"Ah ..." He resumed their stroll but at an even slower pace than hers now. It did not disturb him that Cressida had mentioned the matter; indeed, she had made sure her story was known *and understood* from the Lizard to Land's End. All the same, he wondered in what circumstances the tale had come out between the two ladies in Yorkshire — and why Cressida had said nothing about it after her return. And in any case, what sacrifice was there in accepting a thousand-odd a year for doing nothing?

Anna was saying: "I told her of a relation of mine who was trapped in a similarly restrictive will last year and who managed to have its provisions overturned in the Court of Probate. I wish they still called it *Chancery,* don't you? So much more appropriate. 'Probate' sounds like nasty probing investigations of a kind few of us emerge from with any character left. 'Chancery' is so apt. Inheritances and so on — it's all terribly *chancy,* isn't it."

"Had it overturned?" he asked fretfully, barely able to remain civil to her now. How could a woman drop a bombshell like that and then prate on about probings and chanciness and stuff? His old father, God rest him, had a special phrase for women like her: "She do want a good fist between the eyes," he used to say. Barney imagined dotting her one, right on the bridge of her nose, and felt better for it.

"Yes. It was way over my head, of course," Anna told him. "Something to do with the law in England. It doesn't like per-pe-tui-ties, whatever they are." She spoke the word slowly and with stress so that he would not forget it. "Your son Frank could tell you, I expect. I'm surprised he's never mentioned it to Miss Pym — but then he has the advantage of knowing her so well. When I mentioned it to her — the possibility of turning her trust into an outright inheritance, lock, stock, and barrel — she simply was not interested! Her grandfather must have known what was best for her. He had devised a will for her protection as a helpless, defenceless woman in a hurly-burly world of scheming adventurers. A true lady is always guided in such worldly matters by the menfolk around her ..."

"She said that?" Barney asked in surprise.

"Not in so many words. She didn't need to, though. It is her entire attitude as a lady that speaks for her. It shines out of her as a beacon to more cynical and worldly creatures — among whom, I'm ashamed to say, I number myself. I felt both chastened and uplifted by her splendid sacrifice — as I feel sure you do, dear Mister Kernow." She smiled sweetly and added, "Now that you know about it."

*I*t was a fair-sized garden party but not really big — only a hundred and twenty or so people. Wheal Prosper's lawns were not large enough for anything grander. And even to accommodate that number they had to remove part of the iron fence and put a large tea tent up in the field beyond, with its flaps open where the fence had been. Another tent, open-sided, stood a little way off and housed the Helston Silver Band, who played selections from Gilbert and Sullivan — and, on this occasion, of *Cavalleria rusticana*, too. A pretty touch, people said.

In a way it was an engagement party, though not officially described as such. It was, in any case, the first chance most people had had to congratulate the happy couple. By way of a bonus, it was also their chance to meet Anna Trelawney. But for Anna herself, of course, it was none of these things. It was her chance, at last, to meet Frank.

'At last' was the phrase to decsribe it, too, for the entire affair slipped by and she had still not exchanged more than a dozen words with him. Mostly those words had been, "Ah, Frank — I may call you that *en famille*, I trust? — I'm so glad to meet you at last ..." or, "Well, Frank, here we are again!" ... at which point Cressida or Jessie or Cornwallis had collared her, saying, "You can talk to Frank any old time" as they bore her off to be introduced to someone she absolutely had to meet.

And so it was, indeed, 'at last' — when the gigs and carriages had gone and the servants were mopping up the debris — that people stopped collaring her and she could go in search of Frank. The first Kernow she came across, however, was Godfrey, who was sauntering across the lawn, whistling. He appeared to be looking for something in the grass.

"Lost something, young man?" she asked.

He looked up, startled, then gave a slightly embarrassed laugh. "No, Mrs Trelawney. I'm looking for earthworms."

"Ah," she said, "of course you are. How silly of me!"

"I was just wondering if the thunder of so many feet would fetch them up — the way rain does, you know."

"And does it?"

"Not noticeably, I must say."

"That's why you're so cheerful, I expect. You seem a lot more cheerful now than you appeared this morning, anyway."

"Ah, yes ..." He blushed at the tips of his ears and looked away. Something to do with a girl, then, she thought.

"I've ... er ..." He gave up trying to improvise a reason. Some instinct warned him it was dangerous to improvise anything around Cornwallis's rather formidable mother. Instead he adapted the truth. "A friend of mine and I were going swimming today. I forgot about this garden party when I made the arrangement, you see. But the friend — that is, *he* has managed to swap his duties around and will now be free on Tuesday, instead."

"He?" She queried the word delicately. "You enjoy swimming with a male companion best, do you?" She patted him on the arm and added confidentially, "So did I when I was a girl." Her eyes twinkled and his smile gave him away. "Don't worry." She lowered her voice still further. "Your secret is safe with me. I only hope this glorious weather holds for you. I don't suppose you've seen your brother Frank, have you? Too intent upon your worms!"

Godfrey said he thought he'd seen his elder brother heading toward the summer house; he added that he had been carrying a book. He resumed his search for the elusive nematodes while Anna went round Wheal Prosper to where the summer house stood, open to the lawn but sheltered to its north by a small grove of ash-leaved maples.

The summer house was in the form of an octagon with four windows and three solid flaps in its walls — the eighth wall contained the door, of course. The flaps could be let down to make tables or sideboards for picnics — and had, in fact, been used in that way throughout the garden party that afternoon. In front of the door was a wooden verandah large enough to accommodate three rattan chairs, tables for drinks, copies of *Punch*, fly whisks, and so on. A pagoda-like roof crowned the octagon and was, in turn, crowned with a small, elegantly turned steeple, about two feet high. The whole ornate structure was mounted on a circular iron rail on a brick plinth so that it could be turned, in winter, to follow the sun and, in summer, to avoid it.

At that particular moment, with evening hastening on, Frank had turned it to capture the fading heat and light in the west; it was thus facing Anna for most of her walk across the grass.

Frank, sitting in one of the verandah chairs and deeply engrossed in his book, must have assumed she was one of the maids, for one of the flap-sideboards had still not been cleared. He did not glance up until her shadow fell across his lap; then, recognizing her, he scrambled to his feet and fussed her into one of the other cane chairs, apologizing for his neglect.

She remarked that it must be an interesting book, for she saw he had arranged it so that the title would not be visible. He said, "Not really," but did not elaborate or show it to her. She did not press the point but merely noted it was a new book, anyway, not some old legal tome. "Godfrey said I might find you here," she remarked. "He is trying to pacify the earthworms and assure them it's safe to come up again now. He really has a heart of gold. You must all be so proud of him."

"He wants to be a naturalist when he leaves school." Frank seated himself again and asked, "Shall I ring for one of the maids to bring you a glass of lemonade or something, Mrs Trelawney?"

She thanked him but said she thought it would be a good week before she could look a lemonade in the face again. However, she could face a small dry sherry without flinching.

He rang a handbell on the table at his side. While they waited for a maid to come, he asked if she approved of all the work her son was doing at Wheal Dream.

"Ah, well," she replied, "between you and me, Frank, I don't. I don't really think it right for young gentlemen to do tradesmen's work. But if they are quite set on it, then I think they ought to do it badly, so as not to discourage the genuine tradesmen, you see. I mean, how would you like it if some bricklayer or engine driver wrote you a letter that made it clear he knew the law a good sight better than you do? I'm sure most of them *do* these days, thanks to their trade unions, but they don't go rubbing your nose in it, do they! I hope you haven't been encouraging my son?"

Frank chuckled. Anna Trelawney was a refreshing change from the strait-laced and rather humourless Miss Pym. "On the subject of approval and disapproval," he said, "I hope, when you consider my sister, that you lean toward the positive?"

"I lean toward *anything* at this time of day," she replied. "Particularly dry sherry."

He rang the bell again, this time more sharply, and was rewarded with an equally impatient: "Coming! Coming! Can't 'ee wait?" from Clarrie, who, having been picking up paper on the other side of the maple grove, approached them from the north. When she came in sight of them and saw Anna sitting there, too, she put her hand to her mouth and cried out, "Oh my gidge! I'm sorry, ma'am!"

"Not at all, Clarrie," Anna called back jovially. "It was a very natural response and our impatience does us no credit. But how odd — we were just on the point of talking about you — and here you are!" She turned to Frank, who had sat up sharply at her last remark.

Then he remembered why he had rung the bell and he asked the girl to bring out the sherry decanter and some glasses. "Tell anyone you meet that the sherry's out here," he added as she left.

Anna noticed that his eye lingered on her departing back and that it held a certain wistful light. She said nothing to break the spell.

"*Were* we just about to discuss her?" Frank asked evenly when Clarrie was well out of earshot.

Anna sighed. "I really ought to guard my tongue more. I was simply going to remark that I hadn't seen her for an hour or so and that I hoped she had not succumbed to the heat. Wasn't it unbearable! I took a great liking to her during your sister's visit to Allerton. She's a cut above the ordinary servant — as I'm sure you know."

"She's been with us since she was fourteen," he said neutrally.

"When you would have been what?" She looked him up and down. "Fifteen? Sixteen?"

He nodded and kept his gaze level upon her.

"You practically grew up together, then. She's the last of the good wine, I believe. There won't be another generation of servants like her. Indeed, there may not be another generation of servants at all. One can feel it in the air. And you may be quite certain *Clarrie's* children won't go into service when they grow up."

Frank breathed in deeply and still felt the need for more air. He simply had to stop her prattling on and on. He couldn't quite put his finger on it but everything she said seemed to hint at secret knowledge — facts that she possessed, things he would just love to know, things he *ought* to know, things he ought to be begging her to tell him. Yet she said nothing substantive at all. It was all hints. By chance they both started speaking together:

"When she was in Allerton ..." She stopped.

"I don't suppose anyone ..." He stopped.

They laughed and did a polite verbal two-step, each begging the other to go on. Frank proved the more easily persuaded, though. "I was going to say," he told her, "we had a small earth-tremor here last week. It just rattled the cups a bit. But it made me think — suppose it had been a real earthquake like the one in Lisbon in fourteen-something, was it? Anyway, a truly big one. I thought I'd be lying in my own cellar, buried under Lord knows how many tons of rubble, probably dying."

"Goodness, how morbid!" She rubbed her hands with glee. "And what would you be thinking as life ebbed away?"

"The waste," he replied simply. "The way we live from day to day, mostly engaged in quite meaningless rituals — not realizing that something like that could ... *pfft!*"

"*Pfft?*" She copied him precisely, but gave the sound an interrogatory twist at the end.

It made him laugh. "I mean it would show up the entire charade as meaningless. And when you said just now about the servant class itself vanishing, well, that's going to be a kind of earthquake, too, don't you think? And yet here we are, blithely going through rituals that will be revealed to us as equally meaningless, once it has struck — once they have vanished."

Ater a pause she said, "Your thoughts about the earthquake did not actually lead you to reform your life, though? You have not shed any of these 'meaningless charades'?"

He shrugged complacently. "Of course not, Mrs Trelawney. It's no good just one person swimming against the tide. He'd merely get called a crank or a rebel. One must wait for the tide itself to turn."

"Ah, you are a pragmatist, Frank," she said approvingly. "I wish you'd speak to my own dear Cornwallis. There are disturbing streaks of idealism in that boy. I don't know where he gets them from, I'm sure. Certainly not from his father, nor from me. I take it that when you rise in your profession to the point where you may set up an establishment of your own, you will embellish it with every servant that money can buy?"

He gave a confident nod. "Until the sad day when *your* earthquake strikes us, Mrs Trelawney."

He was delighted with the way he had managed to push the conversation away from all present realities — into the remote future, and into fantasies about that future.

So it made his disappointment that much more bitter when, in one simple question, she managed to undo all his good work. "But," she said, "I understand that you already have a modest establishment of your own in Helston? Do you have a correspondingly modest roll-call of servants — or just *one* servant, perhaps? Do you already practise what you preach?"

What made it worse was that, all during this speech — almost as if Anna Trelawney had timed it so — Clarrie had been approaching them across the lawn, bearing a salver on which clinked the decanter and half a dozen glasses. When she arrived they both saw she was pretty agitated. Her hands trembled as she set down the salver and she made no attempt to serve them. She gulped heavily and blurted out "I hope as I do give satisfaction, ma'am."

Anna looked at her in surprise. "Well there's the man to ask *that* question," she said, waving a hand toward Frank but not taking her eye off the girl for a moment.

Frank jerked upright, stung. "Me?" he cried in alarm.

"Well, it's hardly *my* place to reassure the girl," Anna explained amiably. Then she turned to the maid and added, "Though, if reassurance from me is what you seek, Clarrie, then reassurance you shall have. If Mister Trelawney were to command me that I may employ just one single servant from now on, then I should move heaven and earth for that servant to be you. There now!"

Clarrie realized she had strayed into something far above her head. When Mrs Trelawney had said they were about to discuss her, it hadn't been true — or it hadn't been the sort of discussion that might lead to dismissal, which was all that concerned her. So she relaxed and smiled broadly at Frank.

But her smile only unnerved him further. He took it to be saying, in effect, 'There! That's what Mrs Trelawney thinks of me — now see if you can do better!' He rearranged his cravat to no purpose and said, "I endorse every word of that, Clarrie."

Anna saw that total confusion of purpose now reigned between the young master and the one he would make his young mistress. She decided it was time to rescue the girl. "There, Clarrie," she said. "Now you know just how valuable you are to one and all. If you were thinking of doing a bit more tidying up, there are some dirty dishes on that window-flap there."

Clarrie would have skipped all the way to the house if the dirty dishes had permitted it.

Frank, seeing how swiftly Mrs Trelawney had taken command of the situation, realized her hand had never been very far from the tiller all along. The realization that she had been so much in control of her own behaviour helped him strengthen his grip on his, too. He decided to take the risk of puncturing her cool, cultivated exterior. "Did Cornwallis speak to you about that girl when he was home with you last month?" he asked.

She, too — for her own reasons — decided it was time to speak plainly. "You should never have asked such a favour of Cornwallis," she said in a tone more kindly than critical. "Suppose your sister had overheard him quizzing the girl on what she'd want in return for that particular favour! It could have been disastrous."

He nodded glumly. "I only thought about that after he left. It was too late then, of course. I'm sorry."

"No harm done, fortunately."

"You aren't shocked?"

She chuckled. "Dear young man! In three years' time I shall be half a century old — without giving my age away, now, as my Irish nanny used to say, God rest her. I was also brought up in India, where even the most sheltered young girl could hardly help noticing that young bachelors who did *not* make certain, ah, *recreational arrangements* turned into very strange men indeed. And almost uniformly repellent. So of course I am not shocked. D'you want to know what Clarrie's great ambition is? I think it would be well within your gift."

He gawped at her. "But how do *you* know?"

"I asked her, of course."

He laughed feebly and then became alarmed again. "You didn't mention … I mean, you didn't say I'd asked Cornwallis about …?"

She stared at him pityingly, not even deigning to reply.

He apologized for not thinking very straight.

"Yes," she said, "I've been noticing that. It's almost as if your actual *emotions* are involved."

Frank appeared not to hear her. "When she comes back to clear the rest of those dishes," he said pensively, "would you mind awfully pretending you need to go indoors and get a shawl or something?"

"I will if we've concluded our other business by then," she agreed.

"Other business?"

"You know — your sister's ambitions, your father's likely views of the matter, Miss Pym's inheritance …"

*W*hat Frank didn't know was that Tillie had taken an earlier bus to Porthleven. In fact, he had known nothing about Tillie at all until Clarrie Williams, in turning down the offer he had put before her in the summer-house that evening, had passed some sneering comment about the Kernow brothers and their fascination for girls beneath their own station in life. All Frank saw from his office window in Coinagehall Street on that sweltering-hot Tuesday afternoon was his brother Godfrey hanging around Zacky Wearne's bus, patting the horses, trying desperately to look nonchalant — and slipping on board at the last minute. Frank tried to carry on with his work, which was a rather tedious conveyance, but the thought — indeed, the certainty — that his young brother was up to something nagged away and eventually got the better of him. Godfrey would be seventeen in a few weeks; when youths of that age get up to something, Frank reasoned, there was usually a bit of skirt in it somewhere.

Fascinated by the possibilities he saddled up his own horse and set out in pursuit, catching sight of Zacky's bus at the top of Penrose Hill, where it stopped to let off someone for Sunset Farm. He hung back just beyond the bend on the hill until Zacky set off again. Then, in that same circumspect manner, he followed the bus all the way down the hill to the fishing village of Porthleven.

It is hard to imagine what the harbour and surrounding landscape must have looked like before there was any human settlement; certainly no other inlet is quite like it along the whole twenty-mile shoreline of Mount's Bay. The cove itself is more than a quarter of a mile deep and has the shape of a crescent, with its bulge toward the east; tens of thousands of man-hours and hundreds of twenty-ton blocks of granite have transformed it into an outer, middle, and inner harbour. Steep, almost cliff-like hills beetle over it on the western, or Breage, side while gentler, more rounded hills rise on the eastern, or Sithney side. The inlet continues a couple of miles inland in the form of a river valley, which runs more or less due north between these hills and — as one might guess — between the villages of Breage and Sithney, too, which thus lend their names to the two sides of Porthleven.

But, Frank wondered as he rounded the sharp bend between the inner harbour and the coal yard, which of those two sides was now lending cover to young Godfrey — and, perhaps, some little paramour, too? Zacky's coach was standing there by the small bus shelter built into the coal-yard wall, but of his younger brother there was no immediate sign. If he had vanished into the maze of little alleys on the Sithney side, there would be scant chance of tracing him. Frank turned his hopeful gaze to the steeper Breage side. There the upper terrace of houses appeared to stand upon the roofs of the lower terrace of chandlers' warehouses and sail lofts, which fringed the side of the harbour. In fact, though it was invisible from where Frank stood, a metaled road ran uphill between the two, with a buttress wall on its seaward side. And it was in a gap between the stones atop this wall that Frank caught his first fleeting glimpse of Godfrey, or someone very like him. His eye wandered along the wall to the next such gap, four or five yards up the hill — and sure enough, a few seconds later Godfrey's blond head passed swiftly across it. Alone. So there was to be no romantic assignation.

Somewhat disappointed, Frank slipped sixpence to the ostler in the coal yard, to look after his horse, and then raced along the Breage-side quay, to catch up with Godfrey; from the end of the quay a narrow lane led steeply up to join the gentler-sloping road the young fellow had taken. He arrived, panting, at the junction just in time to see Godfrey, a hundred yards ahead, climbing a gate that led into a clifftop field.

That took care of the first puzzle: Why was his brother walking out of Porthleven on a road that led nowhere — or, rather that meandered several miles across country to Breage and Ashton, two villages that would be much more conveniently reached by bus along the main road? The answer was, he wasn't doing that at all; he was going swimming. But that created a new puzzle: Where were his towel and trunks? As mystified as ever, he waited for the lad to vanish into the field and then set off once again in pursuit.

Keeping his distance, he followed the youngster a good half-mile, past Methleigh Beacon and on to Bullion Cliffs. Every now and then he had to crouch down among the sea-pinks and tufty clifftop grasses, for Godfrey kept looking round rather guiltily. Frank scurried to a low wall beyond the beacon and raised his head above it, only to discover he had lost sight of his quarry. But now he was not worried, for he knew precisely where his brother had gone — down a steep path, which in places was more like a series of steps or handholds, to a flat, rocky foreshore where there were sheer-sided pools large enough and deep enough for diving and swimming.

The young monkey! Frank thought. Sneaking off without a word to anyone for a swim in one of the Kernow family's favourite watering holes! And walking right past his dear elder bro's office, too, on a sweltering day like this. Since there clearly wasn't a young filly in it after all, he might have called by with the invite to join him. Frank looked all about, annoyed that he had not thought for himself to bring his swimming trunks and towel; after all, Godfrey had boarded the *Porthleven* bus, and there was precious little else to do in that village. Though the afternoon was hot, Tuesday is Tuesday and the world must work; so, as far as he could tell, he and his brother had the place to themselves — indeed, the entire bay below Bullion Cliffs was otherwise deserted. So who needed a costume, anyway? And come to that, with this sun and the countless little gullies between the rocks, who needed a towel, either?

Throwing stealth to the winds he raced across the field to the point where the path led down to the rocks. What he saw there, however, stopped him in his tracks, dried the cry of *Godfrey!* in his throat, and made him throw himself back among the grassy tussocks before he might be seen. Then it was no longer 'the little monkey!' but rather 'the young devil!' For there *was* a bit of skirt in it after all; and at that very moment the skirt (but not its owner) was spread out on the rocks below, together with some female underwear, all carefully pinned down by half a dozen large pebbles.

He drew right back from the cliff's edge and sidled along to a point where the rock fell perpendicular from the grassy rim; there he could intrude his head among the tussocks and observe with little risk of being observed in return. Bullion Cliffs were quite low — little more than thirty feet at that point — so the prospects for an eavesdropper were good. For a Peeping Tom they were even better.

The owner of the skirt was swimming alone in the pool; she looked a year or two younger than Godfrey — as far as one could tell when only her head was showing above water. Its rippling surface turned the rest of her nakedness into hithering-thithering streaks of pale ochre; but her movements and yells of encouragement were those of a mere kiddie. Her long, loose hair floated out in a pale-brown aura around her.

A skivvy? Frank wondered. He remembered Clarrie's contemptuous description of … what was her name? Tallulah? Tara? Something that began with a T. Tillie! From one of the hovels in Five Wells Lane. Was that fair young water-nymph down there a mere skivvy? Nakedness was a great leveler!

Frank had to tear his eyes away to search for Godfrey, who was not where he, Frank, would have chosen to stand and disrobe in such circumastances — right on the edge of the pool, getting (and giving) a far better eyeful than was possible from this distance.

He found his brother crouching down in a gully between two high rocks; from there no sort of eyeful at all was available in either direction. He undressed like the coyest maiden in a doctor's consulting room, using the rocks in place of the modesty screen. So, Frank surmised, he and the kiddie were not on terms of any intimacy. Or not yet. He rubbed his hands, and settled himself into a more comfortable position to watch for developments in that direction. And he made a silent promise to the nymph that, if the youngest Kernow was too shy to make any advances, an elder one stood ready to fill the breach. He still smarted from Clarrie's refusal — and he was still trying to suppress an impulse to applaud her for turning him down and to court her with redoubled zeal. A little bit of fluff like this Tillie creature would soothe him wonderfully.

Godfrey finished undressing, put his boots on top of his clothes to pin them down, and then crept along the gully to the point where it entered the pool; it allowed him to slide into the water, all out of sight of his fair companion. Frank, becoming Godfrey in imagination, drew a deep breath, swam to the bottom of the pool, and picked his way among the weed and boulders to a point where he could flip on his back and gaze up, all unsuspected, at his fair companion. Godfrey, Lord love him, splashed and trudgened his way across the pool, snorting like a grampus; when he came to within six feet of the girl, he paused uncertainly and trod water. What a simp! He couldn't manage even an accidental touch from that distance. For a minute or two their heads faced each other and they chatted in voices too quiet for actual words to carry up the cliff. Then she paddled backwards, away from him, to the side of the pool, where a submerged rock gave her a foothold at last.

Frank, who knew every inch of that pool blindfold, watched with especial interest, for that rock was only three feet below the water, which, if she stood right up, would cover her only to her hips. Now he would see who was leading whom in these ancient rituals of courtship. She stood up all right, but with her back to Godfrey. However, since that meant she was sideways-on to Frank, he did not grumble. She caught up her long, dripping hair between both hands and swept it back over her shoulders, flinging her elbows high in the air. The gesture showed that her bosom was hardly developed as yet; indeed,

Frank wondered why she bothered to hide it. Jessie had swum bareskin here with her brothers for some time after reaching that puny stage.

He began to lose interest, both as a potential purchaser of the girl's favours and as a mere voyeur. He realized that, what with his brother's coyness and the girl's immaturity, nothing of an incandescent nature was going to take place here today. Then the girl performed a trick that changed his mind completely. She crouched down, facing the shore — and facing Frank, too, though she did not realize it. Then, with a cry of "Watch me!" she did a backward somersault into the water. She did a complete turn, then another, then another. Frank watched goggle-eyed as her head, breasts, belly, delta, thighs, ankles, and wriggling feet followed each other in a cascade of water that only part-obscured their charms. Godfrey, watching the same artless display from only feet away, quickly managed to drift to a point between her and the cliff, where the view was unrivalled.

When she ran out of breath she dog-paddled, gasping, to the rock and rose again to a crouching position. With her head just breaking the water she laughed with exhilaration. This time she arranged her hair like the mermaids in all the *un*-saucy pictures and then stood up, facing Godfrey with confidence. "Bet you can't do turns like that!" she challenged him loud enough for Frank to hear.

Her accent was broad — *ca-a-ant* and *tha-a-a'*. Skivvy or no, she was not of that class whose daughters' honour a gentleman is brought up to protect, even when the girls themselves might wish it otherwise.

It was roasting among the grass and out of the breeze; yet he durst not take off his dark-blue jacket for fear his white shirt would give him away. He tried panting like a dog but it only made him giddy.

Godfrey was panting, too, trying to build up enough oxygen in his blood to outdo the girl's acrobatics; however, he did not risk those revealing backward somersaults but confined himself to a series of coy forward ones, instead — taking care to tuck the family jewels away safely before he began. Did she mind? Especially after her own exhibitionist generosity. If so, she said nothing of it.

He did six loops, two more than she had managed. Frank hoped she might try again but instead she stood on the rock and said something in which he heard no more than the one word, "kelp." She also pointed to the sea inlet beside the pool, so he assumed she was talking about a dense growth of that particular weed at its seaward end; now, at low tide, dark bands of it mottled the surface, turning lazily this way and that with the pluck and push of the light swell. It deadened the ripples and gave the sea an unreal, oily calm.

She held out a hand to Godfrey. He shook his head and laughed. She shrugged, turned her back to him, and took one huge underwater stride that brought her to the edge of the pool. There, with the grace and agility of an acrobat, she sprang out of the water and landed on the rock. Without looking back she started to pick her way delicately over the fissured surface to the sea; the rocks were mottled with patches the colour of faded raw umber, marking colonies of tiny limpets, each a sharp torment to dainty feet. The natural grace of her movements — her swaying hips and girlish elbows — made Frank sweat more even than the heat had induced him to.

Watching her go, Godfrey had second thoughts and, swimming to the side of the pool, clambered awkwardly out and ran to her side. He lifted his feet high and yelled *ouch! ouch! ouch!* at every step.

The girl stopped and held out a hand to him. The gesture was so childlike and innocent — and Godfrey's acceptance of it so unabashed — that Frank felt *almost* ashamed of his earlier suspicions. The scene had a charm that his own prurient thoughts had sullied. These were two children at play; his desire for the girl was an intrusion here.

The desire did not go away, however; it was simply tinged with a guilt that had been absent earlier.

He watched them dive into the sea and swim with a gentle sidestroke toward the kelp bed, laughing and chatting all the way. When they reached it, she did a fishlike flip and vanished beneath the surface; Godfrey followed. Frank could mark their progress among the weed by the sudden twitching and bobbing of the parts that floated at the top. Though not a single glimmer of either swimmer was visible, he found the jiggling and quivering of the kelp even more erotic than the candid display the girl had given earlier. It was all in the mind, of course — and once again he was in young Godfrey's mind. He saw the lithe figure of the girl as she wriggled like an eel among the fronds of the seaweed ... how the weed wrapped its long, flat fingers round her childish breast, her womanly waist, her strong, slender thighs ... how she closed her eyes and stretched luxuriously to accept its sensuous embrace ... and he scorned his brother for a fool.

The girl might be still half a child but she was obviously ready for it, asking for it, pleading for it. What was Godfrey thinking of — playing games of juvenile innocence with her? He had a good mind to go down there and show the young idiot what the kiddie wanted.

After a while the kelp ceased to twitch, the bubbles no longer popped among the surface flotsam; but still the couple had not come up for air. Were they trapped? Had she got tangled among the thick, gristly stalks and was he, even now, tearing at them desperately with his nails and teeth to free her?

Frank waited a few moments longer, until he was sure they must by now be desperate for air, and then, rising to his feet, half-fell half-slipped down the path to where they had left their clothes. He ran around the inner edge of the pool and started up the long shelf of rock that divided it from the inlet and the sea proper. Shod in good leather, he had no fear of the sharp little molluscs. He had hardly gone six strides, however, when he heard the girl shriek and Godfrey laugh; then the girl laughed and Godfrey shrieked. The spreading ripples showed that they must have surfaced immediately beyond the rocks at the end of the shelf, which were tall enough to shield them, even from Frank's clifftop vantage.

Now he was in a quandary. There was little chance he could make it back to his hiding place without at least one of them spotting him. Therefore, he told himself, make a virtue of necessity. Virtue or necessity — Frank always knew how to make one out of the other.

"Godfrey?" he called out in a sort of reproachful surprise. "Is that you, old chap?"

Silence fell beyond the concealing rocks. Then Godfrey himself poked an astounded — and guilty — face over the parapet. "Oh ... hallo," he said wanly, and then scrambled out rather hastily.

"Cramp?" Frank asked sympathetically.

"No!" He laughed. Then, developing a limp, and bending almost double, he said, "Well, yes, actually — a bit. What are *you* doing here?"

"Same as you, I imagine," Frank replied evenly — folding his jacket neatly on the rocks and starting to take off his tie.

"Oh. Ah. See here, Frank ... er ..."

"You look crippled." Frank opened his shirt. "Anything wrong?"

"No. Of course not. Why should there be?" After a pause he added, "Actually, the sea's bloody cold. But I can recommend the pool. Much warmer. Much."

Frank laughed. "You're bloody lucky to be able to get a bone on you if the sea's *that* cold, young 'un! Damned if I could do it at my advanced age!"

"Ah, well ..." Godfrey mumbled miserably. He stood up straight again, because he no longer suffered from that condition, anyway. "You know how it is — a fellow gets to daydreaming certain things. We're not responsible for our dreams, as Saint Augustine said."

Frank had by now stripped off his shirt and trousers. He sat cross-legged to remove his shoes and socks. "Did you bring that set of lady's clothes with you?" he asked amiably. "Perhaps you come down here to put them on in secret!"

"Oh, hell!" Godfrey exclaimed. Then, turning to face the sea, he called out, "All right, Tillie, you can come out of there. He saw us."

"Saw her clothing," Frank corrected him, to make it clear he had only that minute arrived.

"Ah!" Godfrey's tone was relieved.

"Tillie who? I'm not sure we know a Tillie anybody." Frank placed his shoes, like Godfrey's boots, on his clothes. "Never mind," he said. "Any friend of yours is a friend of mine, I'm sure. Don't worry — I'll introduce myself."

Tillie was standing on an underwater rock, staring fearfully over the edge of the shelf with just her eyes showing. Unashamed, Frank stood up, took a pair of nonchalant strides to the edge of the rock, and dived straight into the water.

The sea off Cornwall, coming as it does straight out of the deep Atlantic, rarely climbs higher than, nor sinks much beneath, the low forties. The best time for a swim is during a howling blizzard in midwinter. Then, once your naked flesh has grown used to the effects of a howling blizzard, it actually feels almost warm. Frank now suffered the opposite illusion — that he had jumped from tropical bliss into a bath of liquid nitrogen. It was the sort of shock and pain that the body happily forgets between times; but the moment that unbelievable iciness closed around him, needling his eyes, drilling his armpits, clutching his scrotum, he remembered it in all its ghastliness — remembered all those earlier plunges on just such days as this, when he wondered if such cold could actually stop the heart and bring all life's other processes to a stark and sudden halt. And then, as his head broke the surface again and his lungs reached for air, he remembered how it always ended, too — which was his only hope and wish in the midst of that icy torment.

It soon came — a paradoxical moment when stinging cold became scalding hot, when salt turned sweet, and the sun lost its power to quicken and warm the skin. Time, too, played its tricks for you suddenly discovered that, though you had suffered the cold for at least one of eternity's long ages, you were now — a mere five seconds after diving in — able to shout, "Ho! Isn't that marvellous!"

And, on this occasion, he was able to go further — to swim a few powerful and impressive strokes around to the end of the shelf and say, "Hallo, Miss Tillie. I'm Godfrey's brother Frank. No doubt he's told you *all* about me!"

*C*larrie made several visits to the laundry yard that evening, though she could ill afford the time, for they were busy with a rather special dinner. Anna Trelawney had jokingly called it the 'fatted calf' dinner — the first meal Frank had taken with his family since leaving for his own chambers in Helston. In some obscure way, which no one quite understood, Anna had brought it about. She had not directly mediated between the mildly estranged son and father — who had been unable to face each other without a hundred-strong garden party gathered about them; nor had she suggested it to Cressida; yet her very presence had somehow impelled the housekeeper to arrange the get-together and had simultaneously induced Barney Kernow to raise no objection. In any case, Frank's star was rising with his father in the same measure as Harry's was sinking.

The one who had most cause to object was the one who had no say in the matter at all — Clarrie, for she was paid to keep her opinions to herself. All the same, it was young Godfrey's behaviour that disturbed her most on that particular evening — which was why she kept going out to the laundry yard. From there she gained the best view of the summer house. Godfrey had taken a book out there earlier but it still lay unopened on the table and he still paced up and down, occasionally giving the verandah rail a ritual thumping with his clenched fist.

Clarrie had no idea what might be upsetting him, but her intuition told her that his anger, in some obscure way, touched her; or perhaps it was just that he chose to fret in that particular place, where she herself had undergone a rather painful scene with Frank the previous Saturday evening. The three long days since then had done nothing to relieve her pain, either.

It had been a curious encounter right from the start. Thanks to all the to-ing and fro-ing that had taken place in advance, she'd started out with a pretty good idea of the sort of offer Frank was going to make. She thought she knew just how he'd make it, too. He'd be a suave man of the world who'd speak his piece crisply and without embarrassment; he wouldn't embarrass her, anyway. He'd make it a straightforward business proposition. And he'd carry it off with such aplomb that she'd feel no qualms about accepting — or refusing. On the whole, she thought she'd probably accept. The only discussion would be about how they could dress it up to protect her reputation.

And, indeed, it had started out like that. She had almost come to the point of agreeing — after a few ceremonial protestations of the 'what d'you take me for' variety. But then some disquieting change had come over him. A kind of desperation had broken through his debonair smoothness; his eyes had *begged* her to agree. Then she had realized that he was moved by something more than a man's elementary need for a woman — *any* woman, almost; he needed *her!* His eyes were mutely begging *her* to agree because she was the only one he wanted.

And in that moment Clarrie had discovered that, though she could easily have accepted his embraces as long as she represented 'any woman' for him, she was not ready to be *the* woman that he plainly desired. And so, in a panic, she had turned him down — more than turned him down — she had said things she now bitterly regretted. In that panic she had thought his particular need for her-and-no-one-else was repellent; now, in calmer mood, she saw it had merely terrified her. She would still reject his offer if the impossible were to happen and he repeated it, but at least she would talk it over with him next time. But, of course, there never would be a next time, not after the things she'd said; and that now gave her pain.

And pain, in turn, had sharpened her sensibilities to fleeting hints and nuances of emotions in others, which might otherwise have passed her by. Godfrey's tantrums on that evening of the fatted calf, for instance, might well have passed her by — not unnoticed but dismissed as the sort of behaviour to which growing youths and maidens were all too prone. Now, however, she sensed the hand of Frank in it somewhere. Frank did not take kindly to rebuff. He might smile and say it was all water off a goose's quills and there were plenty more fish in the sea, but underneath he'd be seething. And he'd take it out on the next vulnerable thing that crossed his path.

Godfrey had never looked more vulnerable to her than he did in the summer house that evening.

At last her chance to approach him came. Miss Pym had noticed Godfrey 'skulking over there,' as she called it. She sent Clarrie to fetch him in to dress for dinner.

Since time was short, shock tactics were the only ones available to her. "What's that Frank been and gone and done now?" she called out when she was still some way off.

He started and stared at her wildly. "Who says he's done anything?" he asked crossly.

"Your fizzog, for one. Black as a thundercloud. You used to look like that when he took your lead soldiers off of you. What's he gone

and tooken off of you now?" She already had more than an inkling —
remembering her sneers about poor Godfrey and that Tillie Lambton
who skivvied at the Angel. But she wasn't willing to risk everything
on mere suspicion. "Miss Pym says you're to come in and dress," she
added, to make him realize that time was short and if he wanted to
pour out his woes into a sympathetic ear, he'd better be quick about it.

"What's it to you, anyway?" he asked belligerently.

"Nothing," she admitted, and then added a provocative, "Maybe."

"It couldn't *possibly* be your business," he replied, over-stressing the
word so much that it removed all conviction from the statement. He
gazed at her hopefully.

"You only think like that because you don't know what Frank said
to me here, in this very summer house, last Saturday. And you don't
know as how I sent him off with a flea in his ear. But you *do* know as
how your brother can't abide a check in his plans like that! And you *do*
know as how he'd lash out, the first chance he got, at the first bit o'
game as crossed his path. So that's what I think he's been and gone
and done with you."

She had spun these thoughts out, mainly to give him time to lift his
eyes from the trough of his own misery and see its subtle connections
to things he knew nothing of. She stopped when she saw him staring
at her, mouth slightly open, a new light dawning in his eyes. "You?"
he asked incredulously. "And Frank!"

"So what's he been and gone and done, then? Come-us on! You're
supposed to be dressing in your monkey suit." She turned and started
back toward the house, but slowly. "Did he play gooseberry with you
and that Lambton maid?"

"Worse." Godfrey fell in glumly at her side.

"Oh, my gidge!"

He became animated. "Anyway, how do you know about *her*?"

To the tune of 'Away in a Manger' she sang: "And that dear little
Tillie, Asleep in the hay!"

"That's blasphemous! How dare you!" Though shocked, he also
had a struggle not to laugh. Later he felt embarrassed that his 'night in
the hay' with Tillie had been discussed in such ribald terms in the
servants' hall — but that was much later.

"Speak plain," she commanded. "Worse than gooseberry, you said.
How worse?"

Because her tone hinted she could do something about it, Godfrey
told her. "He says Tillie is just begging to be taken advantage of, and if
I don't see it — or won't — he'll step in and give her what she wants."

"And what did you say?"

"I said I'd kill him if he did. The trouble is, he means it and he knows I don't."

She chuckled. "The only reason you *don't* mean it is you know a better way than killing anyone."

"What?"

"You just did it — you told *me!* And I'm the one who knows just how to put a spanner in his works — don't 'ee fret! Go up and dress now, or Miss Pym will be killing *me!*"

Ten minutes later, when Frank rode into the stable yard, she was ready for him by the back door. He saw to his horse and then walked toward her with the intention written plain on his face of sweeping on by without a word.

"The answer's Yes," she said quietly when he came within earshot of a murmur.

It stopped him dead and, because it was the very last thing he expected to hear her say (for, after all, his experience of women was very limited, as his recent behaviour had shown), he had no flippant answer to give.

"Yes — we'll talk it over, nice and easy," she added, swiftly qualifying her Yes. "And we'll try and teach you how to say such things as you said to me *without* putting a poor maid in such a panic as she starts saying all sorts of things she doesn't mean. And you're late, too. They're waiting on 'ee inside." And she turned and left him making goldfish movements of his lower lip.

He continued thus for a moment while it dawned on him that, in a few brief words, Clarrie had transformed the entire evening as he had projected it on the way here. Indeed, she had probably transformed his life — but the notion was too large and formless to grasp at that moment. The one fact he did grasp was that he had to make amends with Godfrey at once.

He raced up the back stair, praying his younger brother was no better at timekeeping this year than he had been for the previous sixteen. They met at the threshold to Godfrey's door. Frank said, "I brush aside your glacial smile, dear bro, and the handshake you were not going to offer. Instead I offer you one of my own — and with it the profoundest apology for my behaviour this afternoon. It was quite unspeakable and will, I assure you, never be repeated."

Godfrey, who had not only never seen Frank in this attitude but had never imagined him capable of getting within ten miles of it, could only stand there and stare.

"Ah!" Frank went on. "You're wondering about" — he lowered his voice — "the fair water-nymph herself. She is still *v. intacta,* as we discreetly put it when we send out copying to the lady typewriters. Vee, *vee* intact, I should imagine. But what I think will delight you even more is that, during all the time we were alone together in that cave, she could talk of nothing and no one but you and how lucky I am to be your brother. I hope you're about to help me echo the sentiment? My arm's getting tired."

If one is going to give a fulsome apology, he believed, the emphasis should be more on the *ful* than the *some.*

"God, Frank, you're a white man!" Godfrey grasped his brother's hand and shook it vigorously until Frank winced and extricated it.

Arm in arm they went downstairs. Jessie saw them descending the last flight and cried out, "Just like the good old times!"

But it was not just like old times — quite apart from the fact that neither brother could recall a single occasion on which they had walked downstairs arm in arm. The 'good old times' had gone for ever. They departed when Godfrey, scourged by the stirring giant of manhood, had kissed and toasted the new century in with Clarrie. They departed when Frank had left home, which gave Harry the idea (as yet only half formed) of following him. They departed when Jessie, in a moment of bravado, picked on by her brothers, had made a boast she durst not now revoke. And they vanished beyond trace in that moment when she and Cornwallis finally dared admit, not merely that they loved each other, but that they had no idea what to do about it. For if the absolute opposite of the good old times is the blank, uncertain future, it was the absolute opposite of the good old times that faced them all that evening.

arney Kernow functioned best when his feelings were cold. People often said he had a kind of sixth sense. If you were speaking one set of thoughts but thinking another, he could hear the ones you were thinking; if you held back secret plans while putting forward a bogus but very convincing alternative, he could always sniff them out. But when his feelings grew heated — as tended to happen where his own family was concerned — half his ability deserted him. He retained the faculty of knowing that all was not as it was being made to seem, that people were holding things back. But his uncanny knack of filling out the blank portions in the picture deserted him.

He went to his bed that night in the certain knowledge that every one of his children — and Miss Pym, too, in all likelihood — was witholding something important from him. He had seen it in their eyes — or, rather, in the way they averted their gaze after the briefest meeting with his. He had seen it in the way they had caught one another's attention from time to time and had shared certain secret understandings with a smile. Even that damned Anna Trelawney had joined in the game; she unnerved him. He would not go so far as to say she actually frightened him, but she went some way toward it.

When the house fell quiet and Miss Pym slipped into his bed he just grunted and refused to turn and kiss her goodnight.

"I'll go back to my own room, if you prefer," she said, miffed at his coolness but relieved that the Demon slumbered tonight.

"What was Frank talking to 'ee about?" he asked gruffly.

"Who?" she asked in surprise. "I hardly exchanged a dozen words with Frank this evening — and they were all in your presence, anyway."

"Last Saturday, I mean," he said.

"Last Saturday?" She was perplexed and not a little alarmed at this unexpected line of questioning. "Why bring that up now?"

"You don't deny it, then."

"I haven't got that far, yet — I'm still wondering why you bring it up *now* — at gone eleven, three nights later?"

"Never mind all that, woman. I'll bring up any subject as strikes my fancy. Any time. A month later. A year later, if I want. The main thing is I do expect an answer, no matter when."

She turned her back on him and yanked at the sheet, the only covering they could tolerate in such warm weather. "Good night!" she said emphatically. "We can discuss that — and anything else that disturbs you — at a more reasonable hour."

"No," he barked. "Now!"

"It's waited three days," she pointed out stubbornly.

He had a way of breathing that murdered sleep. It was neither loud nor aggressive; indeed, if anything, it was the opposite — soft and menacing. She endured it for two minutes, until he began to grind his teeth, too, and then, flinging herself on her back, snapped, "Very well, then — since you'll not sleep nor let me sleep until you've unburdened yourself — out with it! What about last Saturday night? We only spoke for a few minutes ..."

"You walked him and his horse down to Nancegollan."

"A few minutes, as I said. He spoke far longer with Anna Trelawney in the summer house. Are you going to interrogate her, too?"

"Not her!" he replied with conviction. "Frank, mebbe. But he's not here and you are."

"More's the pity!" she murmured.

"How?" he asked sharply. When she made no reply he said bitterly, "Now we're getting to it!"

"Getting to what? I hope you realize you're the only person here who has the faintest idea what all this is about — the only person in the whole world, probably."

"You say 'tis a pity you're here at all ..." he began.

"I say it's a pity to be here when you're in *this* frame of mind, Kernow. As you well know — there are times when it's the greatest pleasure to be here — when you're in quite a different frame of mind."

"So you say — *now!*" he exclaimed darkly.

She sighed. "*Now* is the only time one can ever say anything, if you work it out. Whenever I speak, it's *now* — at the moment of speaking."

"Bloody women!" he exclaimed bitterly. "You'll twist anything."

"I'll not stay here and listen to foul language!" she told him furiously as she raised herself to depart.

But he reached out a hand and gripped her wrist — hard enough to bruise her slightly, as she discovered next day. "You'll stay here and listen," he growled. "You pick a fight with me only because you want to go back to your own ..."

"*I* pick a fight with *you?*" She almost screamed in her frustration.

"Keep your bloody voice down, dam'ee!" he said fiercely.

"All I want is to go quietly to sleep."

"And turn over in your mind what Frank told you last Saturday!" he accused.

"You keep hinting at this, but I tell you ..."

" 'Tis no hint! I do know very well what he told 'ee."

"If you know, then why d'you ask? And why d'you wait until midnight to put these idiotic questions?"

"Talk, talk, talk!" he said angrily. "Butter wouldn't melt in your mouth. But I do know that Frank told you about them old per-pet-ui-ties and how to go about breaking them and all that."

He wished he could remember all those other fine things Mrs Trelawney had said — about true ladies knowing that gentlemen only ever did things for their benefit. Only she'd put it much more refined. He couldn't bring himself to like the woman but he had to be thankful to her for that little bit of information.

He spent so long trying to remember her words that he suddenly woke up to the fact that Miss Pym had made no response at all to his allegation. He was sure that Frank had been talking to her about her grandfather's will and the perpetual trust fund. "What harm did I ever do to him — my own son?" he whined.

It was on the tip of Cressida's tongue to point out that, though he had done Frank, indeed his entire family, no harm as yet — more by luck than good judgement — his buccaneering approach to business might yet harm them all. But, as she at once realized, it was probably the one topic that could never be discussed between them. Her only recourse then was to address his accusation directly.

But what could she say? She had intended to unveil her intentions to him as a kind of birthday treat on his fifty-fifth, next month — namely to get Frank to apply to the Court of Probate and seek to have the trust set aside; then, with her finances secured, she would be free to marry him. She had wanted to find out all about it from Frank in the meantime. If she breathed a word of it now, it would spoil the surprise; and in any case, talk of wedding bells did not exactly chime with his present disposition.

"It is a matter I prefer to keep to myself for the time being," she said.

"So the plot's not yet hatched!" he replied.

"What plot? You seem to have conspiracies on the brain tonight."

"Oh! 'Tin't just tonight ..."

"Who's in this alleged plot, then? And what are we supposed ..."

"Everyone, woman! Jessie and that Cornwallis — they're up to no good, somehow. Harry's off over Saint Ives if he gets half a chance. And that Frank ... well, he's the biggest disappointment of the lot." He stopped for breath, panting as if he had sprinted a hundred yards.

"Don't leave me out!" she sneered. "I notice you haven't said what any of them are actually *doing* in this so-called plot."

"I don't *know*, woman!" he said fiercely. "If I did I should put a stop to it. I don't even know what *you're* planning — though I note you don't deny you are planning something. 'It's a matter I prefer to keep to myself.' If that's not a plot, then what is?"

"A surprise? A pleasant surprise? A happy surprise? You've never heard of them, have you!"

He just lay there, breathing heavily; clearly he had not considered such a possibility. Also he saw he had been led far from his main purpose in picking this quarrel. "Some people could talk their way out of the Tower of London," he grumbled.

"You mean me, I suppose?"

"If the cap fits … Anyway, the only thing I wanted to tell 'ee was to forbid 'ee to meddle with that there old will of your grandfather's. That's all."

"*Forbid*, Kernow?" she asked angrily.

"He knew a thing or two, your old grandad. He knew a lady isn't meant to have capital like that. He knew it should be held in trust by those who have the natural adequacy to manage large sums."

"Men, you mean."

"'Course I do mean men! A woman hasn't got the brain nor the capacity for …"

"Men like Cornwallis's Uncle Raymond, for instance? Or your own son Harry? How can you be so blind with that boy?"

"Boy? He's twenty-four. He's a man. I only wish he'd start acting like one — that's all."

"It is not all. He'll *never* act like a man — not the sort of man *you'd* wish him to be. You know very well why he shoots off to Saint Ives at the drop of a hat. That artist, Peter Fisher, he's the cause …"

"Don't talk to me about Peter Fisher! Bloody artists — they do want a good fist between the eyes, the lot of them!"

"All right." Cressida suddenly felt herself becoming quite calm — which was a novel sensation for her. She knew this was an important moment in her life and usually such knowledge made her nervous and her voice sound all flustered. "Let's *not* talk about Harry and artists. Let's talk about Jessica, instead."

"That's another one who do …"

"… who do want a good fist between the eyes. I know, Kernow, dear. But that's not talking about her, is it. Doesn't it strike you that she has all those qualities in which Harry has so bitterly disappointed you? Whereas Harry has all those qualities in which Jessica …"

He exploded. "Jessie has all those qualities a *good* governess would have disciplined out of her."

Cressida could not understand it. Normally such an accusation, with its monstrous unfairness, would have brought on floods of tears, a flight to her own bed, and hours of quiet sobbing into the pillow before she fell into merciful sleep. And tomorrow, for the sake of peace and harmony in the house, *she'd* be the one to apologize. But somehow she had found a way out of that self-perpetuating cycle of guilt and tears, apology and subjection. She sat there feeling quite calm, telling herself how calm she was, being amazed to find herself so calm … and saying nothing.

He tried again: "I said Jessie has all those qualities …"

"I heard what you said," she told him. "Every stupid word."

He gasped. After a shocked silence he said, "What did you say?"

She wondered if he'd go so far as to strike her — give her the proverbial fist between the eyes. To her surprise, only part of her was afraid; the rest exulted that she could stir him to such passion. All the same, she did not risk going further. "If you went into one of your workshops," she said, "and saw a man trying to knock a nail into a piece of wood by holding the wood in his hand and banging the nail down on a hammer held fast in a vice, what would you say to him?"

He saw where the argument led, of course, and wanted no part of it. "Never mind all that ole rigmarole," he said. "The point is ..."

"But I *do* mind all that, Kernow. Because that's exactly what you've been attempting to do with Harry — and what you've expected me to do with Jessica."

"What I've *paid* you to do with Jessica," he corrected her.

"I shall treat that remark with the contempt it deserves. I know you're only trying to make me angry — to lead me away from my point. But you shall not do it, sir! I shall continue to press this point until you either concede it or answer me with *good* reasons, rather than your usual bullying bluster."

"Hah!" He sat up at last and shook both fists at the ceiling. "What's got into 'ee, woman? I never seen 'ee like this afore."

"No," she said quietly — now that she had discovered how much her quietness unnerved him — "I don't think I have, either."

"It's that ... that ... *Trelawney* woman." He spoke her name as if it were a foul epithet. "She's behind all this somewhere. I'm sure of it."

"Harry was the way Harry is from birth, I think. And Jessica, Jessica. It's only because you believe the human spirit is like blacksmith's iron — to be beaten into any shape you wish — that both of them trouble you now."

He gave a single amazed, angry laugh. "What's the alternative, then? You speak as if we could have gone down some other road than what we did."

"The alternative is to bow to the inevitable. Give Harry an allowance to go and paint in Saint Ives. And put Jessica in the office ..."

"What?" he asked incredulously.

"Or, if you can't stomach the idea of working with her every minute of the day, open a branch in Penzance — or Redruth, or Truro — and put her in charge of it."

"Have you gone out of your mind, woman? Kernow and Daughter? What sort of business name is that when a man's got three sons. I should be the laughing stock of Cornwall. I'd sooner take Frank back out of the law than ..."

"Take Frank *back?*" she echoed derisively. "Back, did you say?"

He did not try to dispute the point, nor to say he'd wait for Godfrey to come along. "Well, there'll never be no Kernow and Daughter — not while I live and breathe."

She settled herself again to sleep, feeling a strange confidence that these emotional turmoils would not interfere with her slumber now. "Live and enjoy it while you may, then," she said. "Good night."

"Here! We haven't done yet, Pym, you and me."

"I quite agree there, Kernow. But anything else we may have to say will keep until tomorrow, I'm sure. Don't you think we've already said quite enough for one night?"

He half settled himself again. "As long as you do understand," he said grumpily.

"I understand very well — never better, I think."

"Good. About leaving your grandfather's will untouched, I mean. 'Tisn't your fault you're only a woman. That's the way things are."

She yawned. "I said — I understand you very well."

She fell asleep in moments. His breathing, quiet and menacing, did nothing to disturb her, though it, and the grinding of his teeth, continued for some while.

*B*arney gave up the unequal struggle with sleep at around five the following morning. He rose, shaved, carved a breakfast slice of cold pie in the larder, saddled his horse himself, and went into Helston to see Frank. If he couldn't sleep, he decided, he might as well put his time to good use. And the good use that was uppermost in his mind that morning was the purchase of some land on which he and one or two cronies hoped to build 'an important new amenity' to serve Helston.

Frank, a reluctant riser at first, came wide awake the moment he heard his father's intentions. "And which piece of land are you hoping to buy?" he asked.

It was, of course, the most obvious acre in the entire district, where the nearby 'amenities' would rule out house building and the marshy ground conspired with the shade of the valley bottom to reduce its value to a farmer — namely the plot of land beside the sewage farm.

Frank shook his head. "You'll have to think again, Father," he said. "I happen to know that bit of land is no longer available."

"How?" Barney laughed incredulously. "What do 'ee mean — 'not available'? Every acre in England is available if the price is right."

"Well ..." The young man conceded the point with a judicious tilt of the head. "I daresay you could get it for five hundred."

Barney nearly choked. "Five? Why not five thousand while you're at it? If you ask ..."

"Oh, you could certainly get it for five *thousand*."

"Fifty would be daylight robbery." His eyes narrowed. "Anyway, how do you know so much about it?"

"I'm not at liberty to say, I'm afraid."

"What d'you mean — 'not at liberty to say'?" Barney took a step back from his son as the implication dawned on him. "You mean *you* acted for the purchaser? Who is it? I've got something we could use against most people in Helston."

Frank repeated the formula.

Barney grew angry. He maintained that professional standards were all very well in their place, which was to regulate professional business. Impersonal business. But they had to yield to higher principles when *family* was involved.

Frank was tempted to tell him that he'd hit the nail squarely on the head there — but he wouldn't have been Frank if he'd succumbed to the temptation. Instead he yawned, smiled apologetically, yawned again, and asked his father if he'd like a bite of breakfast.

Barney kept up the assault on his son's professional virtue until he began to believe the unbelievable — that his own flesh and blood would put the law and professional codes above the demands of the Kernow family. He turned on his heel, leaving Frank in mid-yawn, and remounted for home. It was already the most unpleasant morning of his life and it was not yet two hours old.

Meanwhile Cressida had awakened early, too, and, finding herself alone in the bed, had risen and gone for a walk. She did not exactly intend it so, but nor did she resist it when she found her feet taking her in the direction of Wheal Dream. She knew she had to talk things over with *someone*. And she could hardly tell the youngsters the details of her quarrel with their father. And in any case she was determined not to leave her money lying idly in the funds any longer — which was another thing she needed to get off her chest and seek *someone's* advice about. And the best 'someone' — in both instances — was either Cornwallis or his mother.

Cressida's reason for preferring Cornwallis, at that particular hour, was something she did not wish to probe too closely. She could find any number of shallow explanations — for instance, that a conversation with Anna Trelawney would have to take place at Wheal Prosper, with all the risk of being overheard. But deep inside her she knew that in talking with Cornwallis she would, by proxy, be talking with Jessica. And it was Jessica, above all, whom she wished to consult most. She shied from it because a lifetime spent in deference to the wishes of 'her master' is not something to be lightly shrugged off. So, although she knew why she was going to talk with Cornwallis instead of his mother, she tucked the knowledge away and refused to consider it just yet.

Instead she let her mind run back over last night's extraordinary argument. And what was particularly extraordinary to her was the strength of her own anger, the force behind her own impulse to argue. If Kernow had not started out so belligerently — if he had begun a calm discussion about the disparity of talent between men and women when it came to managing large funds of money — it would all have gone so differently. If he had praised her grandfather's wisdom in relieving her of the burdens of managing such a large trust while permitting her to enjoy the fruits of the management of other, wiser heads, she would almost certainly have agreed with him. Indeed, quite a large part of her *still* felt that way. She was most definitely *not* looking forward to a long, frustrating battle to set the conditions of the will aside, still less to taking over the management of the trust and having to make all those frightening decisions for herself. It would take very little in the way of apology and reasonable talk from Kernow to bring her back to that way of thinking.

But he had goaded some other part of her to rebellion and now she could not simply ...

"Yoo-hoo! Tally-ho! Cressida!" Jessica's cry came from some way behind her.

Fate, she thought as she turned and waited.

Jessica was panting by the time she arrived. "Oh, will this weather ever break?" she gasped. "Not yet seven and already too warm for comfort. Shall we all go for a swim today — down at Bullion Cliffs? I simply couldn't sleep last night, could you?"

Cressida jokingly used her bonnet to fan the girl's glowing face. "I was going over to see if Cornwallis was up yet," she said. "I, too, had thought of suggesting a sea bathe." Well, it wasn't necessarily a fib. She might very well have made the suggestion to him — who knows?

"I wasn't going over to see him," Jessie said defensively. "I saw you slipping out of the house for a walk and decided to join you."

Cressida laughed and took her arm. "Why so defensive, dear? There'd be nothing *wrong* in going to see him at this hour, dear. You are, after all, engaged."

"Yes, but we're in love now as well — which makes it all much more complicated. We enjoyed each other's company far better when we were merely engaged. But, anyway, I don't want to talk about all that side of things now."

"All right." Cressida could feel the tension in the girl's arm. "Let's talk about something else — anything you want. You decide."

Jessie took a deep breath and said, "Were you and Father discussing me last night? I only ask because it sounded rather heated and I'd hate to be the cause ... you know ..."

It is fate, Cressida thought. Slowly, calmly, she said, "Your father and I had a very serious dispute last night, dear — the most serious we've ever had, I think."

"About me?" Jessie held her breath.

They breasted the ridge, where Wheal Dream came into view at last. "Escape!" Cressida murmured. The word came to her from nowhere. "Yes, it was about you — and Harry — and Frank ... everything. My inheritance, too."

The tension in Jessica's arm at these last few words was electric. "Money!" Cressida exclaimed with all the easy scorn of one who has plenty. "The troubles it brings!"

Jessie still held her tongue.

Cressida felt forced to continue. As they stepped out down the by now well worn path between the two 'Wheals,' she said, "I had the temerity to suggest to your father that Harry was never going to be the sort of son that was implied in the title Kernow and Son."

Jessica drew breath to speak but no words followed.

Cressida went on, "I had the even greater temerity to suggest it should be Kernow and Daughter."

Jessica gripped her arm so fiercely she had to wriggle free with a laughing protest. That was when she discovered Kernow had bruised her slightly by his grip the previous evening; and that was when the last shreds of her discretion fell from her. "He said never while he lived and breathed. He said women haven't a big enough brain to manage a business."

"To manage *his* business?" Jessie burst out scornfully. "It doesn't take *brain* to manage his business. All it needs is ..."

"I know, darling. You don't have to convince *me* any more. He practically commanded me — no! He *did* command me to make no attempt to set aside the restrictions governing my inheritance. There!" She shivered with a fury she had somehow been spared last night — otherwise she would certainly not have slept so soundly.

Jessie licked her lips and said, "And ...?" She thought if this tension persisted much longer she'd scream.

"And ..." Cressida hesitated only because she could not think of anything grand enough, and reckless enough, to say by way of defiance. When her imagination failed her — or those long years of submission proved too influential for her to overcome all at once — she said, rather meekly, "Well, I intend to instruct Frank to brief counsel to take my case to the Court of Probate, of course."

Something in Jessie whispered, *Now or never*. She said, "It's a beautiful sunny morning, Cressida. Let's just sit here a bit and relish it awhile. And let Cornwallis enjoy his beauty sleep ten minutes longer, eh? That's all it'll take."

*W*hen one has a shoulder to the wheel, helping a horse pull a cart over a hilltop, there comes a moment, usually just before gaining the crest, when one becomes convinced one will never manage to roll it those last few feet; seconds later one is running hell for leather to get back in the driving seat and pull hard on the brake. So it was when Jessie put her shoulder to the wheel in order to roll Cressida those last few feet over the crest of the hill that had marked her sole horizon for the previous thirty years. Once she saw the countryside beyond, there was no holding her back.

Cressida, for her part, had always thought Frank the silver-tongued one of the family; but when she heard Jessica out on the subject of Electricity, Liberator of Humankind (and Enricher of its Providers), Frank wasn't even in the halfpenny place. By the time they arrived at Wheal Dream, where Cornwallis was frying himself breakfast, a whole army of lawyers could not have parted them.

Cornwallis needed only a glance at Jessie's face to learn that great things were afoot. In fact, a glance is all he got before she flung her arms around him and smothered his face with kisses. One kind of hungry man inside him continued trying to flip an egg in the pan before it could spoil, while another, equally hungry, responded with a warmth he had not felt between them for weeks — not since that miserable hour (he could admit it now) in which they finally acknowledged they were in love.

Cressida looked on, beaming, yet slightly embarrassed to discover that she was not at all embarrassed by the intimacy of their embrace.

"What's all this?" he asked out of the only free corner of his mouth. One wild eye, peering over her straining arm, noted happily that the egg-flipping had been successful.

She broke contact at last and said, "The proprietor and the chairwoman of the Helston Power Company, taking pity on your reduced mode of living, and fearing an even greater decline in it should you attempt to take up farming in earnest, would like to offer you the position of clerk to the company at a salary of one hundred and twenty pounds a year plus bonuses and a seat on the board."

"Jessica!" Ancient instincts stirred Cressida to cry out. Then she put her hand to her lips and laughed. Then the laughter died and was replaced by a worried frown. "Did you just invent all that?"

"Did it sound at all spur-of-the-moment?"

"No. That's why I ask."

"Well, you're right. It's something I've been dying to say to Cornwallis for ... I don't know how long." She turned to him and put a warning finger near his nose. "Now it's *my* company, you understand? Well — mine and Cressida's. You're not to try ..." Her voice trailed off when she saw him shaking his head. "It is!" she insisted.

He broke three more eggs into the pan while he answered her. "I have no doubt of that, darling. I'm shaking my head because I am rejecting your kind offer."

"What?"

"I know you're making it with the best of intentions but I think it would spell d-i-s-a-s-t-e-r."

"But you must accept, Cornwallis. What'll you do instead?"

"Look after your house and family, of course. You *will* need a house of your own now, you realize? You won't be able to stay at Wheal Prosper once your father finds out about this." He looked at Cressida. "Neither will you. I assume it'll be your capital? That's what all this is about?"

Cressida nodded, unable to find words.

Jessie, too, was stunned; so much so that she could only repeat herself: "But you *must* accept. We're counting on you. We can't manage without you."

She kept waiting for him to burst out laughing and say he was only joking — poking fun at her as the breadwinner by saying she needed a loyal little husband in an apron at home. But he didn't laugh at all. He said, "What can I do that you can't?"

"Well!" She spoke in the annoyed tones of someone being forced to state the obvious. "For a start, who's going round all the shops and inns and houses in Helston to talk subscribers into signing up?"

"You can do that."

She looked at Cressida for support against this exasperating man; but Cressida was still dazzled by the view from the ridge she thought she'd never scale. She merely nodded in support of Cornwallis.

"Tskoh!" Jessie clenched her fists and pulled a punch on his shoulder. "You're just trying to give me enough rope to hang myself. I don't think you ever wanted me to do any of this. You only encouraged me because you thought it would never be more than a daydream."

He just shook his head and said, "Not true."

Cressida watched him in secret amazement. Where had he learned how to manage Jessica so perfectly? It was an art she herself had not mastered in all her years at Wheal Prosper.

"How *can* I go round drumming up trade?" she asked angrily.

"On foot?" he suggested.

"Aargh!" This time she did hit him. Cressida only just managed not to cry out a reprimand. "You know jolly well — people just won't take me seriously," Jessie added.

"They never will unless you give them the chance. If you try to skulk in the background like some *éminence grise*, leaving lesser minions" — he patted his breastbone here — "to represent the public face of your company, you might just as well not bother. You can give me any lowly title you like — but if I go about the town drumming up trade, no one will ever believe you're the genius behind it all."

The argument itself pleased her, of course, but not its obvious conclusion. "And if *I* go about Helston drumming up trade, as you put it, people still won't believe it's my idea. They'll think it's my father's."

To Jessie's surprise, Cressida intervened at these words. She touched Jessie on the arm and said, "They'd not think it for long, dear, but it might just be *long enough!* And when they realized they were wrong ..." She bit her lip and shivered with happiness. "Just think of your father's face!"

Part Three

Fore St
Saint Ives

The New Woman

*I*n all human affairs good moral reasons give way to better practical ones. And so it was that Cornwallis's admirable intention to play *absolutely* no part in Jessie's business crumbled under the weight of practical circumstance — and of two circumstances in particular. First, there was no local banker who could be trusted to keep secret the fact that Cressida Pym was the source of the new company's capital. Secondly, there was no local engineer of sufficient skill and experience to advise the company on all technical matters — at least, those who might qualify were already working for rival companies or would derive a greater part of their income from one or other of Barney Kernow's enterprises or through one of his many cronies.

When it came to engineers, Jessie naturally thought of John Riddoch. To any other company the fact that he lived twelve hours away by train would have been a crucial disadvantage; to Jessie and the fledgeling Helston Power Co. it was his principal attraction. Then it occurred to her that she might kill two birds with the one stone — make him a director *and* channel Cressida's funds through him so that he appeared to be the source of the capital. People would assume that he represented a group of anonymous Yorkshire businessmen with a typically Yorkishire eye for a good thing.

The four of them — Jessie, Cressida, Cornwallis, and his mother — discussed the notion from every angle, testing it for flaws and finding none serious enough to make them abandon it. And that was how Cornwallis had to nudge his principles aside and take the more active part he had earlier rejected; if he accompanied his mother back to Leeds, especially at a time of crisis in the family fortunes, it would rouse no suspicions, not even in the most distrusting mind in Cornwall — that of Barney Kernow.

And so, the following Tuesday, the tenth of July, Cornwallis returned to Leeds with his mother, armed with Letters of Credit for ten thousand pounds from Cressida's bank in London. Jessie accompanied them as far as Gwinear Road. Anna, equivocal to the last, bade her farewell, wished her the very best of luck, and gaily added that she was sure the whole venture would end in ruin but that — 'in the long nothingness of life' — it wouldn't matter a scrap; the important thing was to have tried. "People who *try* are the salt of the earth," she said. "They are the good wine. Success is a vinegar fly. It turns them sour."

"Goodness!" As always, Jessie did not know how seriously to take her future mother-in-law. "Perhaps I should reject the very idea of success at the outset?"

Anna nodded eagerly but added, "It won't make a bit of difference, though. Life has this terrible habit of giving us what we reject, whether we want it or not. You and Cornwallis rejected the very idea of love — and where did it get you, eh!"

The question rang on in Jessie's mind after they had parted. The weeks of dreaming and planning and staring at that huge, unscaleable brick wall of masculine disbelief and prejudice were over. The die was now cast, the game afoot, and all that sort of thing; it left her feeling like a swimmer who, having dithered in the shallows of a swift-flowing river for weeks, has finally taken the plunge into the main-stream, only to realize that her most powerful strokes are feeble when pitted against the random buffeting of the turbulent waters all about. The notion that she was in control of affairs — that *any* human being has the slightest control over her destiny — seemed laughable.

"Did you hear Mrs Trelawney's farewell message?" she asked Clarrie as they boarded the Ladies Only carriage on the branch-line train for Helston, which, they were pleased to discover, they had to themselves. The train set off almost at once.

"I couldn't hardly help it, Miss," the girl replied apologetically.

"Oh, I'm sure she intended you to hear it, as well. Especially her remark about Life giving us all the things we reject, too, whether we want them or not — that was for your ears as much as for mine."

"It fair made my hair stand on end," Clarrie admitted.

Jessie detected a more-than-conventional emphasis on the phrase. "Oh?" she asked.

Clarrie swallowed heavily and said, "I was wondering, Miss, how to go about handing in my notice, as I've never done such a thing in my life afore nor never thought to do it, neither."

After a pause Jessie said, "Frank?"

The maid nodded unhappily.

This revelation stirred Jessie's own feelings to a fine confusion — hardly less than Clarrie's own at that moment. As the thought of a genuine engagement to Cornwallis had taken hold in her mind, and with it the thought of a genuine marriage, she had naturally thought of that moment when she would surrender herself to him. The thought uppermost in her mind, then, had been about how utterly inappropriate the word 'surrender' was, with its overtones of submission, resignation, yielding, and so forth. She had not cared to discover a more appropriate word, though — until now, when Clarrie's choice forced her to retrace her train of thought. Intuition told her that, in Clarrie's mind, there would be no simple 'surrender' either; she would resign herself to nothing, submit to nothing, yield nothing. It would be something altogether richer and more complex.

"Now you're maggoty, Miss," Clarrie said — meaning annoyed.

Jessie laughed. "*Mis-mazed* would be better Cornish for it, Clarrie. What changed your mind — if I may pry?"

"Dunno, Miss." She shrugged uncomfortably. "Dunno as I did change my mind. I've been all of a dalver for weeks now."

"All I know is that Frank had a face like a month of wet Sundays last week — so I assumed you'd given him a pretty firm No."

"Well ... there's No, and then again there's No."

"Heaven knows why a woman 'Noes'!"

Clarrie nodded. "And why she 'Yesses' in the end."

"If you really don't know why you're saying Yes now, I don't think you should try and delve too deeply to find out. People go mad when they look inside themselves too much — because there's nowhere to hide, I suppose. As long as you *feel* it's right, you should just do it and let clever people torment themselves with wondering why."

"Oh, I know *why*," Clarrie said robustly. "I just aren't proud of it, that's all."

Jessie smiled broadly, forgiving her in advance and encouraging her to tell all.

"As soon as Master Godfrey told I as Frank was cutting in — that's when I got all maggoty and swore that kitey little skivvy shouldn't have 'n."

Jessie clicked her fingers a couple of times before the name came back to her. "Not Tillie ... Tillie Lambton!" she exclaimed. "You mean that's still going on?"

Clarrie nodded. "Till Frank cut in. 'Course, to a giglet like Tillie he'd be some bobby-dazzler. Anyway ..." She drew breath and squared herself. "About giving in my notice, Miss?"

"Don't," Jessie told her.

Clarrie stared at her in amazement. "But I can't just walk out ... I mean, can I?"

"We *both* may have to."

Understanding dawned. And just in case it didn't, Jessie added, "It just so happens there's an empty set of chambers above Frank's in Cross Street. I've already asked him to take them for me — to use as offices, if nothing else."

The joy in Clarrie's eyes showed that she saw the beauty of the arrangement. In the eyes of the world Jessie would be thrown out by her father; naturally, she'd take lodgings in the same house as her brother; and, naturally, her lady's maid would accompany her there; any link between maid and brother would be quite incidental. And any open suspicion would reflect more on the one who voiced it than on the victim of such evil gossip. Now if only the stairs didn't creak!

As the train entered the cutting before Nancegollan, Clarrie prepared to alight; but Jessie pushed her back into her seat and said, "We'll go on to Helston. Strike while the iron is hot — or, rather, before my courage fails!"

She wanted to ask Clarrie if she'd really thought about what her arrangement with Frank would entail ... had she really faced the full awfulness (or otherwise) of that moment when one of them climbed into the other's bed? If awful, would she be able to go through with it? If otherwise, would she become a genuinely 'ruin'd maid,' with that as merely the first downward step in a long path of degradation into misery? It wasn't that she wished to place these thoughts in Clarrie's mind. Quite the reverse, she wanted the girl to have meditated on the whole business already, through and through, every way to Christmas; she wanted to share the result of all that careful cogitation, not to provoke its onset. However, she lacked the courage to say a word about it — just then, anyway. Instead, she passed the eight extra minutes of their journey in outlining her strategy to Clarrie — "by way of *Clarrie-fication*," she joked, tapping her own forehead.

Clarrie groaned dutifully — something she would have felt too diffident to do in all the years she had known her young mistress. It was, she realized, the start of a subtly different relationship between them — something to do with the fact that she herself would soon be a mistress, too.

M any a good business venture is floated on the back of a good meal — or so Frank assured his sister and Clarrie as he joined them for luncheon at the Angel. The two women had arrived earlier so that Jessie's request for a private room — where she could naturally dine with her maid — would not seem odd. Jessie noticed that he was not in the least abashed to find Clarrie there, sitting at her own small table near the window; in fact, he picked up half her cutlery and carried it to the main table, telling her to bring the rest and join them. Not for the first time in her life she envied her brother his aplomb, his ability to carry off outrageous actions without ruffling a hair. If Clarrie was secretly in love with him — or fell under his spell as a result of the arrangement she was about to accept — she would not blame the girl one jot.

One of the hôtel maids took their order — she *was* surprised to see her old classmate Clarrie Williams sitting there among the quality, bold as brass; and she did little to hide it, too.

After she left, Jessie ran once again through the outline of her immediate plan with her brother. The only uncertain bit was how much discount to offer. Frank said that as she was intending to offer it to only one subscriber — and only for the first year — she could afford to make it flamboyantly generous.

Clarrie sat and listened eagerly; she told herself she'd be managing a little business of her own, too, one day. Of course, it'd be nothing like so grand as the Helston Power Co., but all the same there might be one or two little tricks she could apply. For instance, what Frank said about being stupidly generous in one very limited direction was appealing. In her village shop, she could apply that same principle by selling sugar or flour, or something everybody *had* to buy each week, at a ridiculously low price — even at a farthing or two's loss. It would get everybody talking about her shop and bring them flocking to see if it was true ... and she could make good every lost penny with an extra farthing here and an extra farthing there on other things where they might not notice. So she listened very carefully to every word the two Kernows said.

The moment Walter Blackwell came on his traditional 'mine-host' tour of the tables, Jessie put her plan into action. She told the Angel's proprietor that she was out canvassing for subscribers.

He, thinking she meant subscribers to some worthy little magazine, got up by ladies and of strictly local interest, began marshaling all the usual excuses for not subscribing to anything of that kind. So he was a little taken aback when she said something about "seventeen pounds" — a sum that would keep him in newspapers and periodicals for the best part of a decade. "Eh?" he asked. Then, remembering his manners: "I beg your pardon, Miss Kernow?"

"Seventeen pounds a year," she replied.

"A year?" His voice quavered. What *was* she talking about?

"One hot plate," she explained. "A toast-maker — I presume? A heated press for the valet? And, of course, lighting and bells in every room. And the sign over the entrance. Each little device seems small enough but they soon mount up."

"I'm sorry, Miss Kernow?" He shook his head as if to clear it and continued to stare at her blankly. Magazine subs had faded from his mind but nothing had replaced them yet.

"Those are your present electrical appliances — except for the toast-maker, which I assume you might wish to add."

He smiled as he jumped to the next conclusion. "Are you atempting to sell me a toasting-machine? Because I should warn you that seventeen pounds is ..."

"I'm sure I can get you a toasting-machine, Mister Blackwell, if you fail through the regular suppliers. But that is not what I'm selling. What I *am* selling is the electricity — the *juice,* as we call it — to make the toasting-machine go. And your hot plate. And all your lights ..."

He held up a gentle, kindly hand to silence her. "But, my dear young lady, as I'm sure you are aware — I have an electrical set already. And a very good one, too."

She nodded calmly. "A two-horsepower Norris with almost two-thousand ampère-hours of battery. I know. And I would advise you to retain it as a reserve until you feel confident of the public supply. Then you could return that coach house to *profitable* use."

"Public supply?" He frowned but the penny was beginning to drop: the Kernows ... the gas works ... electricity ... "Ah — *public* supply. I see! I see! The kind of public supply that has the name Barney Kernow all over it, eh!"

He addressed the quip to Frank, who replied, "You could be half right there, Mister Blackwell."

The man misinterpreted Jessie's angry glance to mean he had scored a bullseye with his guess. "So," he said to her, "is there any good reason why I should not continue to make and use my own electricity, as and when I need it, Miss Kernow?"

"Would one good reason convince you, Mister Blackwell?"

He said it would have to be a *good* one.

"I'll give you two, then," she told him. "Each unit of electricity you make with your own set will cost you over sixpence. Whereas ..."

He shook his head and interrupted her. "Forgive me for being technical, Miss Kernow, but I do understand these things a little. It's a two-horsepower engine — which is equivalent to one and a half kilowatts. Correct me if I'm wrong?"

"It's actually one thousand, four hundred, and eighty watts," she said with an impish grin. "But let's not quibble."

His smile thinned perceptibly. "And it ran last week for four hours on one measured gallon of petroleum spirit. Which — sparing your pretty little head the mathematics — works out at six kilowatt-hours for fourpence — or two-thirds of a penny per unit." He smiled triumphantly. "Your father should realize that if ..."

She interrupted him: "May I ask who assisted you to arrive at these conclusions, Mister Blackwell?"

He produced what he thought was the *coup-de-grâce*: "Mister George Blaney, a Member of the Insititute of Mechanical and Electrical Engineers, Miss Kernow."

"Little Geo Blaney! He maintains the machine for you, I believe? He's hardly likely to let you in on all the ifs and ands and buts on a subject like that, is he!"

"Well, I'd like to know what he left out!" Blackwell challenged her.

"Then what did he allow for heat losses via the exhaust?" Jessie said at once. And while the man floundered she went on: "And friction? Did he mention that for every three units of electricity you put *into* a wet cell like yours, you only get one unit back out — when it's bran new? Did he make any allowance for the fact that when a cell is fully charged the charging relay trips out but *your* motor, lacking an automatic cut-out, continues to idle — and to burn petrol? The fact is, Mister Blackwell, that a two-horsepower motor has only one horse-power available for electricity generation and that only a third of that electricity ever gets back out of the wet cells. So, though I never bothered my pretty little head with much mathematics, even I can see you must multiply your basic costs by six to get nearer the true figure. What's more, I'll bet you the price of this meal that I could prove to you that your electricity is costing you at least seven pence a unit — once you take in the capital and maintenance costs of your machinery, depreciation on the cells, and maintenance payments to Mister George Blaney, who, as a Member of the Insititute of Mechanical and Electrical Engineers, does not sell himself cheap! Now, *I* could supply that same juice to you for twopence! And you'd never have to cross the yard in the pouring rain again!"

Blackwell licked his lips nervously and looked to Frank for support of some vague kind.

Frank winked at him and kicked out a chair. "Sit down, Mister Blackwell," he said.

The hôtelier obeyed as if in a trance — looking from one to the other. But he had enough of his wits about him to say, "You mentioned *two* good reasons?"

"Yes," Jessie said crisply. "The second is much easier to explain — even though it, too, involves a little mathematics that are far above my pretty little head."

"I'm sorry I said that," he murmured.

"Not half as sorry as you will be if you say it again," she assured him. "I think you'll be using just over two thousand units a year — hence my estimate of around seventeen pounds as your annual bill — *at my rate!* (At *your* present rate it's more like sixty pounds, but let that pass.) I'll supply you with twenty free units for each shopkeeper, tradesman, or household you manage to recruit as a customer."

"For *ever?*" he asked at once.

She laughed and shook her head. "For the first year."

He laughed and shook his head. "For the first ten years."

She pretended to consider the offer; at length, and with great reluctance, she conceded: "Five."

"Eight?"

She shook her head. "This is excellent tongue. Is it from Oliver's?"

"Seven?" he tried.

"Five. That's already four more than I was prepared to offer when I came in here, Mister Blackwell. If you don't like the terms, I'm sure I'll find others who'll leap at them."

"Very well," he said, trying to sound dejected. "Twenty free units per year for the next five years for each new customer." He held out his hand and she shook it solemnly. "How will you know a new customer was talked into it by me? What if I talk them into it but they drop by your office and sign on there?"

"I'll give you a sheaf of application forms. You can tell them you're saving them the trouble. I'll get the printer to use a different paper for yours — a different watermark, anyway."

He chuckled. "One can't teach your father any new trick under the sun," he said admiringly.

He thought he understood what had happened now. There must have been some slightly heated family discussion at Wheal Prosper, during which old man Kernow must have flung down a challenge to his daughter to prove her point by going out and recruiting new customers for his next venture — the Helston Power Co., of which he, Blackwell, had already heard one or two rumours. And Miss Jessica hadn't been able to refuse. However, she'd soon cooled down and realized how impossible it would be for her, as a woman. But, being a Kernow, too, she had used her cunning and enlisted him, Walter Blackwell, to do the dirty work for her. He just hoped old Barney himself would agree to honour his daughter's promises. He'd have a word with the old boy about that — but not before he'd recruited enough new subscribers to show he was worth his commission.

As he rose to go he said, "If you came in here determined to give me the free units for only one year, Miss Kernow, may I ask what made you agree to five?"

She smiled. "Your face, Mister Blackwell."

He preened himself in a jocular fashion. "Well, I know I'm no oil painting, but ..."

"No," she went on. "Your face turned quite pale when I started pointing out the true cost of your present generating equipment. D'you remember our old gardener, Moses Kenwyn — I'm sure you remember him!"

"The man who preached on the Demon Drink outside my bar until he died last summer? Indeed, I remember him!"

"He had that same pale look in his face, I remember, when old Doc Montagu told him if he touched another drop of liquor, he'd die. In your case, I went up to five years because I'm quite sure you'll be an even more effective preacher in the cause of the Helston Power Company than old Moses ever was in the cause of temperance."

He chuckled and shook his head, not really understanding why her words made him feel so encouraged — indeed, inspired. "You'll teach your father a thing or two yet, Miss Kernow," he said ruefully.

"Such is my earnest hope, Mister Blackwell," she assured him, making her tone deliberately pompous so as to mask the deeper emotions that attended the sentiment.

As soon as he had gone, Frank chuckled and said to her, "You meant to offer him five years all along."

She nodded. "I calculate he'll give away one year's worth in free ale and porter. Maybe even free dinners to the bigger customers. That'll be his money, not ours, all spent on bringing in customers to us. I was only afraid he'd ask for shares!"

"And that business about the watermarked paper. Did you think that out in advance, too?"

She shook her head. "That came to me on the spur of the moment."

He stared at her quite a while before he said, "D'you know, Jess, I haven't really believed in all this until now."

She felt absurdly pleased at the compliment; there was a prickling behind her eyelids which, if she wasn't careful, would develop into tears. "And now you do?" she asked.

He grinned. "Just try and stop *me* asking for shares!"

Jessie excused herself to pay a call of nature. He felt a moment of panic when he realized he was alone in the room with Clarrie. "Well!" He smiled awkwardly.

"Miss Jessie says you've taken extra rooms where you live," she said, like one making conversation.

His eyes narrowed. "And so?"

"She says when the master finds out about all this, she'll be out on her ear."

"Ah!" Light began to dawn on him.

"I should come with her, of course."

"Good," he said, wishing his heart didn't hammer so hard. It would be a straightforward business transaction, he reminded himself for the hundredth time; why did he get so hot under the collar at moments like this?

And why didn't she say what she was really thinking?

She was very beautiful, he thought. He couldn't understand why some people considered her rather plain. She was exactly the sort of 'fluff' people had in mind when they spoke of 'a bit of' it.

"We've probably got less than two weeks before the old man goes off like Mont Pelé," he said. "Maybe only one."

She reached out and touched his hand — a touch as electric as anything they had discussed that day. "Maybe less — if some little dickey-bird was to go tweet-tweet!"

*A*bout a week after Jessie recruited Blackwell to her scheme her father brought a few business acquaintances up to the Angel for luncheon. Chief among them was Jim Kenney, the main shareholder in the Penzance Electricity Company; James Gordon and Giles Curnow were local businessmen — as was Michael Vestey when he was not producing musical comedies and operettas for the Helston G&S. They had spent a productive morning poring over the map of the town, looking for a site for their project to furnish it with electrical power, which was, naturally, a closely guarded secret still. They were annoyed that their previous choice — that worthless bit of marshland down by the sewage farm — had been taken by A. N. Other. They were even more annoyed that Barney Kernow had not been able to discover his identity or purpose. But, apart from that petty irritation, they were in good humour for they had chosen an alternative site that was almost as good, up the Cober valley, just beyond the old mill house. It would cost more but building there would be easier.

They dined in a private room so that they could continue to discuss their business. Walter Blackwell served them personally. Not for the first time he was amazed at wily old Kernow's self-control. The old boy had obviously got his clerk, or his son Frank's clerk, to make a fair copy from *Kelly's Directory* of every commercial premises in town, and all the larger private houses, too. The five businessmen spent almost the entire luncheon going down the list, discussing each name:

"Gilbert — will he come in d'ye think?"

"He will if Bowden does."

"Bowden will. I heard him talking about it to Wallis quite recently."

"What about Wearne?"

And so forth. Every name was on the identical list that Frank had sent up to the Angel after that meeting with his sister the previous week. And every day since then he, Blackwell, had given the young lawyer the names of those he'd seen that day who were interested in being supplied from the Helston Power Co. Those of Gilbert, Bowden, Wearne, and Wallis were all among them — all enthusiastic. And so were many of the others the five diners had so far discussed. Bowden and Wallis had even signed up — on his own specially watermarked paper. It was unthinkable that Frank would not have conveyed this excellent news to his father. It was even more unthinkable that the old man would let a day go by without at least glancing at the list of new recruits. Therefore it was doubly unthinkable that he knew nothing about it. Yet not by the smallest hesitation or stutter did he show it. As name followed name — many of them already signed up — his pretence of ignorance as to their intentions was flawless. If Michael Vestey ever went in for amateur dramatics, he had his star performer right there beside him.

Blackwell had always known that old Kernow was an astute man of affairs but he'd never seen him in action at such close quarters, nor from such a privileged position as the possessor of inside information. Every now and then, when no one else was looking, he gave Barney a surreptitious wink of encouragement — to show the old fellow how reliable he was, not saying a word, not even clearing his throat.

Barney dismissed the first wink as a nervous tic; the second he thought a little odd; the third made him uneasy; by the fourth he was positively alarmed. Blackwell obviously knew something and was trying to communicate the fact. At last he excused himself and left the room to search out the landlord and discover what was behind all this winking business.

He found him in the yard, attending to a delivery of ale. As soon as Blackwell saw him he left the drayman and came anxiously toward him, saying, "Why, Mister Kernow — is anything amiss? I hope you don't think I'm neglecting you, only we were a barrel short after ..."

"I want to know what all this winking business is about," Barney said. "Or is there something the matter with your eye?"

Blackwell broke into a broad smile and dug him daringly in the ribs.

"Well?" Barney prompted when the man seemed to think that a sly chuckle was all the reply required of him.

"Gilbert!" Blackwell said. "And Bowden! And Wallis! Very good! Very good, indeed, Mister Kernow. You almost had *me* believing you."

Barney's face darkened. "Believing me?" he echoed in confusion.

"Yes. But you may rely on me, Mister." He cut his throat with a finger. "Not a word! These lips are sealed."

"For God's sake, boy — speak plain, can't 'ee?"

"Well, well, well!" the landlord shook his head in admiration. Then he spun on his heel and started back toward the dray.

"Blackwell!" Barney snapped. "Have you gone and tooken leave of your senses?"

The man turned round and held up both hands as if to ward off an attack. "Of course not," he replied. "I'll tell you how 'insane' I am, if you like." And he came back to Barney's side, leaned his head toward him in a conspiratorial pose, and murmured. "I've got a dozen new subscribers to your electric company just this lunch time — there now! If I get only half as many tomorrow, that'll make the century. I tell you — it's gathering like a snowball, man! Surely Frank has told you? Another ten days like this and we'll have the whole town signed up."

Barney just stood there and stared at him. He was experiencing one of those hallucinatory moments where your eyes rove over the scene and, although your mind can identify walls, windows, cobbles, people ... even individuals with names ... individuals who speak words whose individual meanings are quite familiar to you, you can take nothing in. Individual elements, full of meaning, somehow add up to a whole that is utterly void.

Until that moment Blackwell had dismissed Barney Kernow's odd behaviour as an obsessive but, in his case, unnecessary extension of the need for secrecy. Now he began to worry. Obviously Frank and his sister had said nothing to their father about their cleverness in recruiting him to do the legwork for them. The old man clearly thought his clever youngsters were doing it all themselves. And they were clever, too — he realized that now — giving him paper with a different watermark but no other distinguishing sign. Their father would never see the difference, and even if he did, he'd not think it had the slightest significance.

"Listen," he said apologetically, "don't be too hard on them. They mean no harm, I'm sure. I thought they'd surely tell you, that's all."

Barney was still having trouble understanding the man. "Them?" he asked.

Was the old fellow having a stroke? Blackwell felt a new twinge of alarm. He'd read in *The Spectator* recently how doctors had discovered that people could have petty strokes without being aware of it; they'd just think it was a momentary loss of concentration or dizziness. It was funny how, no sooner did you read a thing like that than it started happening right, left, and centre, all about you, though you never saw it once before in all your life. "Your boy Frank," he said in a kindly tone. "And Miss Jessica. Obviously they haven't told you that they've involved *me* in signing up people to your electricity scheme ..."

Barney almost did have a stroke at that. There was a huge thump somewhere at the base of his skull — which might have been the beat of his heart as it caught up on one of the longest pauses it had ever made, or it might have been the sound of about a ton of pennies dropping. Frank and Jessie! Of course! Frank refusing to tell him about who bought the sewage-farm site ... and Jessie being as nice as pie lately and as tractable as a copybook daughter could possibly be!

What a fool he'd been — a blind, trusting, old fool.

But no more of that. Forewarned is forearmed. He'd show them now. His heart was going double tides now and his blood was racing; he was an old warhorse with the shrill of trumpets in his ear again. He hadn't felt so alive, so strong, so fighting fit in years. Oh, wouldn't he just show them now!

Blackwell was relieved to see the old boy grinning again. "I felt sure they'd tell you," he said apologetically. "Don't be too hard on them, will you, old boy. It was a clever thing they did — getting me to sound out the likely customers for your scheme — don't you see? It put you at two removes from me. And, since half of Helston drinks at my bar, and the other half dines at my tables ... who better? They're a credit to you, Mister Kernow."

"They are," Barney said proudly — and now he truly would have deserved the leading rôle if Vestey ever went in for amateur dramatics. "And you're quite right, they didn't tell me."

Blackwell chuckled, with relief as much as anything. "You mean Frank's been showing you the lists daily as if it was all his work?"

"He has — the artful young devil!"

The landlord wanted to say that the lad was a chip off the old block but didn't quite dare. Instead he said, "Well, I'm sure I don't begrudge him the triumph. After all, I'll wager it was he who had the good sense to turn to me."

"I'm sure I don't begrudge him, either," Barney said jovially. "So listen! We'll say nothing about it, eh?" He laid a finger to his nose. "Not a word to either of them about any of this. Not a syllable. Not even a *wink*, eh!"

"Mum's the word!" Blackwell winked.

$\mathcal{B}$arney returned to the luncheon party to say that, thanks to something Blackwell had let slip, he now had a good idea as to the name of the mystery purchaser of the sewage-farm site. (That, of course, was to stop the other four gentlemen from pursuing their own independent inquiries, which would now be highly embarrassing to him.) He added that he might be able to name at least one name by the time of their next meeting. (And the one name he hoped to announce was, of course, his own, as successor in title to the land — though he would not be adding that it was as the result of a victory in a battle-royal with his two younger children.)

He declined the offer of a lift back to his office, saying, quite truthfully, that he needed a breath of fresh air. All the way down Coinagehall Street he smiled and waved and greeted friends and cronies, though inwardly fuming at the perfidy of his children. How could they do such a thing? How dared they think they could steal a march on an astute old bird like himself? (That they so nearly had managed it was a thought to gnaw at the vitals and make any lunch hard to digest.) Above all, where was their money coming from?

Paradoxically, that most puzzling question of all brought him the first small ray of hope. If the Trelawneys weren't so strapped for cash, he'd have suspected the hand of Cornwallis in all this. He was a likeable enough youngster and would no doubt make a good husband to a difficult woman like his Jessie; but Barney distrusted all Cornish people who had risen above their station — who 'went all high-quarter,' as he put it. The Trelawneys had two counts against them —

they not only spoke with lah-di-dah English accents, they had deserted their native land and 'gone to live amongst furriners,' taking their money with them. So, if they had had a lot of that money still loose about them, they'd have been his first suspects.

The fact that they were on the ropes themselves at the moment excluded that possibility; it left him with two others to consider, one of which contained that ray of hope: Either Frank and Jessie had acquired capital backing from somewhere, or they had not. If they had, then it was from outside Cornwall, for he could not conceive of their raising ten thousand pounds — the least that the project would require — without word of it reaching him. He had too much dirt on too many people for them to take such a risk. Since the Trelawneys were ruled out, the next likely source would be some group of Yorkshire business-men, friends of Cornwallis's who had talked the matter over with him during his visit there back in June. And, to add weight to this possibility, where was the young man at that very moment? Why, back there again! Making a progress report? In that case, Jessie and Frank were merely his agents down here — not the prime movers at all. And they had done the sensible thing by getting Blackwell to do their scouting for them. What were they offering him, quid-pro-quo? A shilling a signature? A pound? They were mere babes in business. Whatever they'd offered, he'd still manage to wean Walter Blackwell away from them — probably without Blackwell himself even noticing the shift. After all, he already thought he *was* working for Barney Kernow at arm's length! Oh yes — things were beginning to look considerably less gloomy by the time he arrived at the bottom of the street.

As he set off down the steps to the market place he considered the second possibility — that they had no capital behind them at all. In that case, they were either hoping to gather enough evidence to enable them to raise it in the market or they were conducting their survey in the hope of surprising and delighting their dear old dad! How could they know that he and his friends were already working along those same lines? It was his birthday in less than a month — his fifty-fifth; not a particularly significant one in any man's life, to be sure, but all the same, a neatly conducted survey of the potential business an electricity generator might expect would make an unusual — and unusually welcoming — present on any day of the year. He was sure he hadn't told Frank *why* he was interested in that bit of marshy land when he woke him up that morning a couple of weeks ago; but perhaps the young fellow had put two and two together — or perhaps they had got wind of the idea from some other direction.

All the same, since none of these explanations was, on the face of it, particularly convincing, his wisest course was, for the moment, to do nothing irrevocable and to work like a beaver to find out precisely what they *were* up to. It would be going too far to say that his anger had evaporated by the time he arrived back at his office; but he had managed to fit it all into some kind of container and to put it into storage against the day when he might need it in earnest.

As he stepped inside, Harry snapped a book shut and stuffed it hastily into a drawer of his desk.

Barney sighed. "Get it out again, son," he said wearily. "Let's see how you've been wasting your lunch hour."

"Half hour," the young man said as he opened the drawer and drew forth a large book bound in red morocco.

"The firm's ledger?" Barney was mystified — even more so when he reopened the drawer and found it empty. So the lad must have been studying the ledger.

He flipped through the pages, looking for unauthorized sketches. One page had every zero turned into owls' eyes but that was ancient — he'd ticked Harry off about that weeks ago. Another had a very fine spider's web drawn all across it with a mapping pen; but that was also old hat — and had also been covered by a severe reprimand.

There was no new artistic transgression — and the figures were up to date, even.

"How did you go and snap it shut like that, boy? And stow it away with such a guilty look?" Barney asked.

Harry shrugged. "Dunno."

"Force o' habit!" His father sounded even more disgusted at this possibility. "Listen, now! D'you know what your sister and your brother Frank may be up to in the way of devilment and truckle?"

Harry, who was hatching a plan or two of his own, was interested in this possibility; he was not much of a tactician, but then it doesn't take much to appreciate the value of covering fire. "No," he said. "What?"

"I'm asking of 'ee, not telling. You haven't heard nothing?"

He shook his head, disappointed. "No. Jessie's so moony about Cornwallis lately, I shouldn't think she's had time to get up to much. But Frank ..." He hesitated.

"Yes?" His father leaped at the possibility. "Frank? What about 'n? What's he gone and done?"

"Nothing, really. He's been teasing Godfrey over some ... calf-love or something. I don't know. Godfrey was pretty fed up about it."

Barney gave up trying to get any sense out of the boy — as he still thought of Harry, despite his twenty-four years. "Calf-love," he echoed. "Nothing more serious than that?"

Harry shrugged again. "I don't know. It always seems serious enough to the people involved."

"Who's the maid?"

"A skivvy up the Angel, I hear. I think it's the same girl Godfrey took for a spin in Cornwallis's motor in April."

"The *same?*" his father asked. "Then it begins to look serious. What's her name?"

"Totty? Tallulah? Something beginning with T, anyway. She's a Lambton — from that troublesome family down Five Wells Lane."

Barney stared moodily out of the window. "Bringing up a family!" he said. "If there's a more thankless task, I'd be glad to know of it. 'Tis like patching a sea wall. You stop one breach and another do open up alongside of 'n. Still, if 'twas serious, Miss Pym would have told me, so I suppose it can't be too bad."

After work that day Harry called at Frank's to warn him that, whatever he and Jessie were up to, their father was onto it. But Frank was out playing tennis and Harry didn't feel like missing a train just to be sure he got the warning. Later that evening he took the chance to get Jessie on her own, as she walked over to check on Wheal Dream, and he gave her the news instead.

Far from being grateful, Jessie was furiious with him for not asking the old man for more details: What sort of devilment and truckle? How much had he heard? Who had told him? How long had he been brooding on it?

"You *are* up to something, then!" Harry concluded.

Jessie bit her lip and looked all about them, almost as if she expected to find their father lurking behind the hedges. "I didn't tell you because, in fact, there's nothing substantial yet to tell anyone about — though I hope there will be soon. Also, there's nothing to beat *genuine* innocence. If I do tell you now, promise on your absolute honour you won't breathe a word about it? Not to *anyone* — because it's bound to get back to him."

"I promise," Harry replied. "Actually, it might be as well to let one another know what we're up to — for all sorts of reasons."

Jessie caught a particular tone in his voice, not quite despairing but certainly bitter and frustrated. "What are *you* up to, then?" she asked.

He sighed and, picking up a broken piece of withy, slashed ineffectually at the hedge several times. He stirred up a pair of bumble bees and they had to run a short stretch, stopping when they were out of breath. "I can't take this office-boy life much longer, Jess," he said.

"Well!" She took his arm and hugged it sympathetically. "I'm surprised you've stuck it so long. Yet what else is there for you?"

"That's the thing," he replied. "You remember Mother took out some small annuities for us before she died? It's only fifty quid, I know, but I'm thinking of trying to live on it."

"Where?" Jessie asked in surprise. "And how long could you survive on that little money?"

"In Saint Ives. There's room for me in Peter Fisher's loft, which he gets for a florin a week. So if I chip in it'll only be a shilling each. And he reckons that, if we're careful, we can get by on a quid a week each, including money for paints and canvases ..."

"And booze?"

He shook his head. "None of that, I'm afraid. We shall be the Cornish branch of the *Société des Buveurs d'Eau*. You know — *La Vie Bohème*, and all that."

"You can have *my* fifty," Jessie said at once.

This time he took her arm. "You're an absolute brick, Jessie. One could almost predict you'd say that. Generous to a fault — but I wouldn't dream of it."

"Oh, it's got very little to do with generosity, I'm afraid, Harry. There'd be a condition attached to it."

"Ah."

"Yes. You could have my fifty quid — or whatever it comes to — actually, I think it's more like sixty — anyway, whatever it is, you can have mine, too, if you let *me* choose the moment when you do a bolt. I promise it won't be long. Certainly within the next six weeks."

He agreed then, like a shot, without even wishing to know her reasons. But she told him, nonetheless — all their hopes and dreams about the Helston Power Co.

Then, without reaching Wheal Dream, they turned about and hurried home, for it occurred to both of them that the next person their father would quiz — having drawn a blank with Harry — would be Cressida Pym.

*A*bout a week after his departure to Leeds, Cornwallis returned, bringing both banker's drafts and John Riddoch with him. Riddoch, in his turn, brought the plans for the power house at the Hunslett factory, which, he said, would do admirably for the Helston installation, too, and with very little modification. He thought that three smaller generators, driven from one turbine, would give them more flexibility than the single big Ferranti Jessie had seen.

The first sod of the foundation was dug at noon on the third Saturday in July — and not before time, Walter Blackwell told Frank; between them they had signed up all the town's visionaries and optimists and had come up against the brick wall of doubting Thomases who wanted to see some sort of building going up before they put their names to anything so nebulous.

For Barney, too, the laying of the foundations marked an important turning point. It was one thing to know that a building of some undefined character would one day be built on that particular plot of land; but when brick began to pile upon brick, and he stood at his office window and saw the scaffolding poking up above the low scrub surrounding that area ... the whole enterprise took on an entirely different character. For one thing, he could no longer sustain the hope that his middle son and daughter were preparing a birthday surprise for him.

But the alternative — that they were actually managing the whole thing by themsleves — was hardly more credible. Time and again he was on the point of demanding to know of either Jessie or Frank what their game was; but he hated asking a question to which he did not already know the answer. Even "What's the time?" fell more comfortably from his lips if he could check whether or not his respondent was lying. And that habit was so deep in the grain of his character that opportunity after opportunity slipped by without a word spoken.

In any case, Jessie — the one he saw most — was behaving in an utterly exemplary fashion these days. He never came across her without some piece of needlework in her hands ... or she'd be practising at the piano or dashing off a charming little water colour. Heaven knows what she got up to while he was away at the office, mind, but when he was at home — and no matter at what hour he arrived, early or late — there she was, being the dutiful daughter and practising her lady's accomplishments and generally being the sort of girl he'd been bribing and punishing and begging her to be for as long as he could remember.

There were other forces to restrain him, too — deeper within him ... things he did not particularly wish to confront. A man gets used to having his own way with his children; he bends their will to his and moulds them as he wishes them to be. He knows they are pliable but he forgets that their pliability goes in both directions — what bends easily one way can just as easily bend itself back again. Or perhaps he doesn't forget it so much as suppress the knowledge, which then lies somewhere deep inside him, nudging the underside of his self-congratulation, discomfiting it without ever breaking its surface. Some such unease now ruled Barney Kernow; he might not have been able to put it into words but he knew, dimly, somewhere within, that his next quarrel with his children might very well be his last. The pliable, bending days were over. Therefore, the longer he held his peace, the better he preserved the old illusions.

On the first day of August, when the walls of the new power house were half up and the nearer houses were already being prepared for connection, he had a very trying morning. A Wednesday, it was. Half a dozen people stopped him in the street to tell him they'd signed up as subscribers to 'his' new company — the Helston Power Co. And he'd been forced to slap them on the back and tell them they'd not regret it. His silent reassurance to himself — that one day soon it *would* be his company, too, was losing its power to comfort him. His foul mood was made no better when he returned to the office only to discover that Harry had gone on some errand without leaving word.

He went back up the town to ask Frank if he'd seen his brother but the clerk said Frank had gone to see a client in Penzance. Barney knew the man was lying but there was nothing he could do about it. The incident was yet another reminder that his once-absolute control of his world was weakening all the time. Powerless and angry, then, he returned home to Wheal Prosper, where he was rarely seen at lunchtime.

He stormed into the house, slamming doors and leaving a trail of clay and gravel as he went through room after room shouting, "Harry? Where are 'ee? Come out, you good-for-nothing jannack!"

Cressida did her best to pacify him, and eventually succeeded. His mood did not improve but at least he stopped shouting and storming through the place.

Jessie had a terrible foreboding that her brother had jumped the gun and gone to St Ives without waiting for her say-so. Her father ate a hearty luncheon, just as he would if he knew he was to be hanged within the hour; nothing, he claimed, would keep him from his food. Every minute of it was a torment to Jessie, who now wanted to get to St Ives and back before her father returned for the next fixed point in his diurnal calendar — dinner.

"I wonder where Harry can be?" Cressida asked when the man in their life had gone back to town.

Jessie revealed her fears. Fifteen minutes later they were in the gig and passing through Nancegollan on the road to Leedstown and, ultimately, St Ives — a journey of about ninety minutes if one did not strain the pony. Jessie packed a suitcase of Harry's shirts, underwear, sponge-bag, and other similar necessities — on the offchance her guess was correct. She had no idea where Peter Fisher's loft might be, but St Ives was small and one could walk the entire artist's colony in about ten minutes.

"Did he give you any idea that this was on his mind?" Cressida asked as they left Nancegollan behind them.

"A couple of weeks ago, but not lately," Jessie told her. "Certainly not this morning. He promised he'd wait. He's going to live on ... d'you remember Mama's annuity?"

"But that'd be less than a hundred pounds," Cressida said in surprise.

"He says he'll join the Society of Water Drinkers — *La Vie Bohème*, you know, and all that. I said I'd give him my annuity, too, if only he'd wait. I thought it would make a good flanking attack when the old man found out about us and exploded. Why *hasn't* he!"

Barney's failure to go off the deep end had been almost their sole topic of conversation for days past.

"I felt sure he'd found out this morning," Cressida said. "When he went storming through the house like that."

"I know. Me, too. I was so glad.'"

"Glad?"

"Yes. I thought, *at last!* He must have found out by now. He must have known about it for days — if not weeks. The building's half up and yet he hasn't said a word. D'you think he's trying to drive us mad?" She laughed but not very humorously.

"We've been round and round all that," Cressida replied. "I'm more worried about Harry. Does he have any idea what living on bread and cheese is like?"

Jessie looked at her in surprise. "You speak as if you do."

Cressida drew breath to speak but thought better of it.

"Surely you never have?" Jessie pressed her.

"Well ..." the other began, and then was silent again.

"But when?" Jessie asked. "I mean, you were only ... what? Eighteen when you came to Wheal Prosper? You can't have. Unless ..." She laughed at a sudden thought. "Unless coming to us was the equivalent of living on bread and cheese for you!"

"No, it wasn't that," Cressida said mildly. There was a nostalgic edge to her voice as she went on. "I knew a young man ... you see ..."

"Ah!" Jessie said encouragingly. "Was he penniless and terribly romantic? I do hope so!"

Her eagerness forced Cressida to laugh and to drop her sad tone. "Yes," she said more crisply. "I suppose it was just a lot of silly, empty-headed romancing. But oh he was so ... I don't know ... I wanted to ... I'd have done anything to be with him. Perhaps if I'd known how easy it was to overturn my grandfather's trust ... who knows?"

"What was his name? Was he handsome? Had you been sweethearts since childhood? You're not giving away anything, Cressida."

"It was all a long, long time ago, dear. His name was Stewart. Stewart Drysdale. He was twenty-three and I was seventeen and he went off to Paris to be a painter and live in poverty and I thought my heart would break."

Jessie emitted an excited sigh.

"But it didn't." Cressida was brisk again. "And yet the idea of a simple life like that has never quite lost its ... you know? No servants — think of never having to lower your voice or guard your tongue or look over your shoulder again! Wouldn't it be bliss?"

Jessie took up the theme: "And being able to get rid of all those ornaments whose only purpose is to give them something to clean when all their other work is done."

"To clean — and to smash slowly, one by one," Cressida agreed fervently. "And all the other freedoms that go with that simple sort of life. I know I'm just being selfish, really. It's do-as-you-please. It's pleasing oneself. But then *who* do we please now! No one."

For a while they contemplated this happy daydream. Then Cressida said, "Perhaps Harry couldn't wait. Who knows why people suddenly ... crack like that — and make such a huge leap?"

Sobriety returned to Jessie. "It's messed up my plans, though," she said. "Perhaps my father's right. There's a lot to be said for sticking to a world where the biggest tragedy is the milk going sour, or a leak in the roof. I've been reared for the choppy waters of a little duckpond, at worst, and I'm setting out on an ocean noted for its storms!"

Cressida felt the mild sting of reproof in this last remark — for she had done much of that rearing. "Go on with you!" she chided. "You

were born for those storms — and your rearing did no harm to your capacity to withstand them. If your father could only apply to his own family the acumen that has made him so successful out there ..." She waved her hand vaguely across the landscape of West Penwith and left the rest of her thought unspoken.

It emboldened Jessie to ask, "D'you think you'll stay with him for ever, Cressida?"

The older woman gave such a jolt that the pony halted. She shook it forward again and said, in a flustered tone, "What ever made you ask such a question, dear?"

"Oh ... just the way things seem to be moving. Frank's gone. Harry's gone now. In a matter of weeks — if not days — he'll either throw me out or I'll run away ..."

"But I'm no longer *in loco parentis* to any of you — not even to Godfrey, really. I just make sure his shirts are ironed and his socks get darned. But he's a law unto himself."

Jessie said nothing. She had intended her question to refer to Cressida's more intimate relationship with her father but did not know how to rephrase it delicately along those lines.

Cressida was aware of it, though — and, like Jessie did not know how to put her feelings into words. "I owe your father a great deal," she said vaguely.

"Of course!" Jessie overdid the enthusiasm. To counter it she added, "But there's gratitude on both sides, surely."

"Ye-es." Cressida's tone was guarded. When she found that the sentiment did not bite her she added in a more positive manner, "Yes. Of course there is."

"I mean," Jessie went on, "it wouldn't be as if you're deeply in his debt — emotionally or any other way."

"No."

"So — my question shouldn't startle you, really. If you did part company, it wouldn't be ... well, treachery or anything like that."

"It'd be a wrench — an upheaval."

"Yes, well, so is moving house. So is getting married, which is a move in the opposite direction. Tell me to mind my own business if you like, but" — she breathed deeply and said it: "Do you actually *love* my father?"

One of the reins fell from Cressida's fingers. She retrieved it hastily and made great play of sorting them out again — all to give herself time to respond with something other than a cry of surprise.

"Eh?" Jessie prompted.

"I heard the question, dear."

"I know it's none of my business — and yet in some ways it is. I wouldn't ask at all if you hadn't put up our capital — which would be an odd sort of action if you *did* love him."

Cressida had recovered sufficiently to give a feeble laugh to that. "Love!" she said. "It's not at all the way the poets like to paint it. There is an exasperated sort of love that might very easily induce a woman to do a thing like that — against the interests of the man she loves. Because, you see, in my case, I don't really believe it *is* against his interests. I think if he could only have his eyes opened to what a wonderful daughter he's managed to produce — *despite* his attempts to crib, cabin, and confine you — well, he'd be an even bigger character than he is. So, you see, it's quite possible to do such a thing purely out of love."

"And is that why you've done it?"

Cressida gave a dour laugh and said, "No." But she did not elaborate.

"Talking of being *confined*," Jessie said, "what about that?"

Cressida, still thinking of the word in terms of detention or locking away, said, slightly mystified, "What about it? Wheal Prosper would make a very inadequate gaol!"

"No!" Jessie was exasperated at having to do all the work. "When I finally found the courage to admit I really do love Cornwallis, I began thinking about babies — imagining a baby in my arms ... holding it up over my head at arm's length and letting it drool on me — you know, the way one does? In fact, I've had to stop myself thinking about it altogether. When I feel that mood coming on I just shut it right ..."

"But why?"

"Because it's so tantalizing ... so alluring."

"No, I mean why don't you want to be tantalized and allured?"

"Oh! Because I want to *do* something first — make something of my life. We don't *have* to produce our brood before we're twenty-five, surely? I know Jane Matthews says she wants the lot over and done with before she's thirty so she can have the rest of her life to herself. I can see some point in that, but still, it's not the only way, is it. But actually I was asking you — having now passed thirty and *not* having got it all over and done with ... well, how *you* feel about it? Or don't you want children at all? I don't think I could go through with this power-company business if I thought it meant I'd *never* have any children. But that's just ..."

"Is there going to be a break in this monologue, Jessica? I keep breathing in and having to let it out again."

"Sorry! Sorry!" Jessie laughed and squeezed her arm. "It's pure embarrassment, really, because I know it's a most improper question to ask, only, as I said ..."

"No no! Don't go off again. I know what you said very well. And — given the unusual circumstances in which we've lately plunged ourselves — it's not at all an improper question. If you'd asked me as recently as six months ago, I'd probably have said no, I don't want to have babies. It would have been tinged with regret but mainly of a sentimental kind. But now — lately — I don't know why ..." She vanished into some kind of reverie.

"You've changed your mind?"

"It has changed almost without my realizing it. Perhaps it's your engagement that's brought it on me. In a way you've taken the place of any baby I might have had. And Godfrey — who was only six when I came to Wheal Prosper, after all. But with you going off to get married ... perhaps reality has overtaken me at last. Or maybe there's some sort of telepathy between us — and I'm getting a stray whiff of your suppressed longings."

Jessie nodded sympathetically, thought the matter over in silence awhile, and then said, "I don't suppose you've discussed it with my father at all? Would you marry him? Would he permit you to have a baby now — at your age?"

"Hold fast!" Cressida protested. "I've not got one foot in the grave yet, you know!"

"No, I meant at *his* age, really. Would he permit it?"

Cressida cleared her throat delicately and said, "In fact, dear, permission doesn't really come into it."

"Ah." Jessie had only the vaguest notion of what she meant.

"I mean, I don't think it would be possible at all — no matter how desperately we might wish for it to be."

Jessie, understanding the *fact* of the matter now but nothing of its cause or causes, felt she nonethless had to say something; so she said, "But how dreadful! How utterly awful!" And she squeezed her friend's arm again.

Cressida interpreted these deliberately vague expressions as some kind of sympathy for her — for a deficiency in *her*. She felt obliged to explain: "It's not my fault, I'm sure. In fact, ..."

"Oh please!" Jessie blushed furiously. "I didn't mean to pry into ..."

"No no! We'll clear this matter up if nothing else. D'you remember once I smacked you and sent you to bed for stealing chocolate fudge off a tray in ..."

"On the top shelf in the pantry! I'll never forget that! I've had an instaiable craving for fudge ever since — forbidden fruit, you see."

Cressida laughed at that. "Little do you know!" she said. "Actually, it wasn't fudge at all. It was … it was a … well, it was a mixture of cocoa butter and quinine, and if a woman puts a lozenge of it inside her — where the man's … D'you know all about that sort of thing?"

Jessie, pink as a lobster, closed her eyes and nodded. "Yes."

"I see," Cressida said heavily. "Well, that saves a half-hour detour!" More briskly she added, "If a woman puts one of those lozenges inside her, *there,* the quinine has some harmful effect on the man's seed. It kills it."

Jessie laughed immoderately. "Killing does indeed come under the heading of 'harmful effect,' I'd say!"

"Anyway," Cressida ploughed on, "I made up three successive batches of those lozenges using pure tapwater under the impression that the bottle still contained quinine. It was labelled *tapwater,* you see, so that Clarrie and Becky wouldn't see it and get funny ideas. And Becky took it out on a walk with her one very hot day. First she tipped the contents out, thinking the water smelled a trifle bitter, then she refilled it at the tap, drank it on her walk, and refilled it when she came back! So, for the best part of a year, I slept with your father without any protection against 'love's predicament,' as they call it! And no baby resulted from it. Not even a false alarm. Since when we haven't bothered. And that was three years ago. Just before last Christmas I asked Doctor Watts was I barren or your father sterile, and he said neither, probably. Your father could very well sire babies on another woman just as I could have them with another man." She heaved a deep sigh and added, "So now you know!"

By now Jessie's mind was in a turmoil. She remembered the tray of 'fudge' very well. It had had been divided into seven rows and seven columns — forty-nine lozenges in all. So if three trays had lasted 'the best part of a year,' that meant they had used three lozenges a week. Three times a week! From whispers with other girls and with the help of her own intuition she had guessed that It happened about once a month between married couples. Three times a week! There was obviously something about It that had so far eluded her and her friends — in all their blasé ignorance.

"Have I shocked you?" Cressida asked at length.

"Not in any sense of being embarrassed." Jessie was surprised at how calm she sounded — and, in fact, was.

"In what other sense, then?"

"After all — it is a very *natural* sort of thing."

"Very!"

"Did I understand you correctly, though? Do you — or did you — use *three* lozenges a week?"

"Ah!" Cressida laughed a little more loudly than was quite warranted. "I'd forgotten your penchant for mathematics!"

"Well, it does stretch to knowing that seven sevens make forty-nine. And thrice forty-nine is about a hundred and fifty!"

"Yes, dear! Three lozenges a week."

"Gosh!"

After a silence, Cressida said, "It is one of the greatest pleasures available here on earth below, you know."

"For girls as well?"

"Why d'you think society goes to such painful lengths to keep the knowledge from you?"

"Who kept it from you, then? Or who *didn't* keep it from you?"

"Ah, well!" Cressida's voice signaled a happy memory coming up. "I had a wonderful but not very discreet aunt. Aunt Isolde, God rest her. Shortly after I began visiting your father's bed — and discovering for myself what enormous fun it can be — and feeling dreadfully guilty about it at the same time — I confessed all to Aunt Isolde. She laughed her head off and told me not to be such a goose. When she first got married — and she lived in the most respectable part of Plymouth, let me say, overlooking the Hoe, and at the height of the Victorian period ... before any of this Yellow Book decadence and so on ..."

"Yes! Anyway?" Jessie interrupted eagerly.

"Well ..." Cressida looked carefully all about them and, although they were still a hundred yards short of the cottage that marked the start of Leedstown, lowered her voice. "She told me that when she first got married she was one of five or six young 'gels' — she always said 'gels' — who'd been school chums and all got married within weeks of one another and all still lived in Plymouth. And they used to meet every week to play whist or something in the afternoon but actually all they did was talk about the wonderful things they got up to in bed with their husbands!"

They had to talk of neutral matters as they passed through the village — pausing to greet one or two acquaintances, as well. As they left the place behind them, making across the moor to Fraddam, Cressida said, "I'm not at all sure it's wise to be telling you all this — except that, well, it would have saved me a great deal of heartache and troubled conscience if I'd had that little talk with Aunt Isolde a few months earlier."

They drove on in silence awhile. Jessie wanted to ask how many drops of quinine went into each lozenge and did one add gelatine to make the cocoa butter set? But she lacked the final ounce of courage.

Then Cressida said, "We've strayed a long way from your original question, I'm afraid — about whether or not I'll be with your father for ever. And the answer is, I just don't know. Which, I suppose — being ruthlessly honest — is like saying, 'No — I'll leave him one day.' But we'll just have to cross that bridge when we come to it."

*P*eter Fisher's loft proved so easy to find that at first the two visitors did not believe they really had found it — that is, they could not believe the place was any sort of human habitation at all. It was on Porthmeor Back Road, a winding street of tumbledown fishermen's cottages and picturesque sail lofts, overlooking Porthmeor beach and bisected by Norway Square. Most of the streets were perilously narrow, even for a small gig like theirs. The mean but grandly named Norway Square they did not even attempt to enter, but went round the end of the huddled row and parked the gig at the top of the beach. They left the pony his well-earned nosebag of oats and went back to the loft they had been assured was Fisher's.

The door was open. There was no one at home — though 'home' was not a word that sprang readily to mind there. It had been a netmaker's workshop until recently. The small, north-facing rooflight by which he had worked had been enlarged and now filled the entire centre half of the roof with glass. Jessie was more taken aback by the spartan simplicity of the place than was her companion; Cressida stood in the doorway, closed her eyes, and inhaled deeply through her nose, relishing the clean, sweet fragrance of turpentine and the subtler aroma of linseed oil.

A rug and a few threadbare cushions occupied the centre of the loft. Beyond it stood an easel, supporting a canvas measuring about three foot by two, facing away from them. Behind it, against the farther wall, stood a table laden with paint tubes, jars containing various liquids, broken pitchers filled with brushes, and pots of powdered pigment. A palette with five paint-laden brushes stuck through the thumbhole lay on the ground between the tripod feet of the easel. Just inside the door, down by the jamb, stood a mug half full of tea — or it could have been coffee — with a dead fly floating in it. There was a bottle of wine and two cleanish glasses on the windowsill — and a stack of paintings, face-to-the-wall beside it. And that completed the domestic arrangements.

"Does he sleep on this blanket, with these cushions?" Cressida asked, taking a hesitant step into the studio.

Jessie, more boldly, crossed the bare-board floor, carefully skirting the blanket, and looked at the canvas. "Here's your answer," she said.

Cressida joined her and they stared in silence at a painting of the blanket and cushions — plus the addition of a nude young woman. She was in her mid-twenties, of the Celtic type with long, raven-black hair and intensely blue eyes. She was depicted lying on her back, one knee raised, holding her right arm at almost full stretch above her, with her hand bent over and one of its fingers outstretched to make a perch for a little yellow canary.

Looking all about, Cressida realized that what she had, from a distance, taken to be a blob of yellow paint on the table was, in fact, a stuffed canary with wire sticking out beneath its feet. She picked it up, wrapped the wire round her own finger, which she then held in the same pose as the model, only immediately in front of the canvas. "Extraordinary," she said. "The life he's managed to put back into that bundle of feathers."

In fact, there was life in every inch of the painting. Jessie suspected that a lot of it was easy trickery — all facile technique with little passion behind it; but there was no doubting that Peter Fisher could do almost anything he wanted with paint on a canvas. The blanket was wool, and looked like it, just as the cushions were undoubtedly satin, and the floorboards, pine.

And the flesh was flesh! You could see the bone beneath the hips, the softness of her belly and breasts, the tension in her upraised arm compared with the utter relaxation in the other, and the merriment in her face at the cheeky, shall-I-flit? gleam in the bird's beady little eye. Also, neither woman had ever before seen a nude with all her body hair — and depicted in such a matter-of-fact manner, too.

"Why not?" Cressida said.

And Jessie knew what she was talking about. "Absolutely," she replied. "What d'you think the picture is called?"

"Did it say on the back?"

"No. Let's guess. I'll bet it's quite pedestrian, like *Nude with canary*. Or something teasing like *Sunday morning*."

"I'd call it *Freedom* or something like that," Cressida said. *"Liberty on the wing."*

"Liberty on the wing!" cried a man's voice from outside the door. They heard his footfall on the stair and exchanged a panicstricken glance. Cressida looked about her as if for somewhere to hide, but Jessie put a hand to her arm and murmured, "Too late." She raised her voice and called out, "Harry?"

There was a shadow, or a darkening in the light that reached up the staircase and fell on the jamb of the open door. It hesitated and the same male voice said, "Ah."

"Is that Mister Fisher?" Jessie asked.

He stood in the doorway then, head on the slant, eyes half-closed — the way painters look at the world. "Miss Kernow and Miss Pym," he guessed, making it a statement rather than a question.

He was, they judged, in his mid-thirties, with a shock of angry ginger hair, slightly receding at the temples; it continued in a well-groomed fashion down his cheeks and round his lips and chin where it formed a vandyke beard. If he'd been wearing a beret instead of being altogether hatless, he'd have been the very picture of 'an artist' as conventionally depicted in jokes in *Punch*. Every other item of clothing was there — the flowing smock, the fisherman's trousers, the bare feet in leather sandals. "What d'you think of it?" he asked. "Should make a few quid, what?"

The two women turned back to the painting; Cressida began to apologize for their intrusion but he waved her words aside. "Don't be deceived. Don't mistake it for art. It's just a bit of sentimental lechery to bring in the moo-lah. Otherwise we could not possibly afford all this luxury. If you want art, it's stacked against the wall there."

He spoke airily enough but they could tell he wanted them to look at it — or them — some two dozen canvases of a very different character. As they scanned through them, Jessie recalled Ruskin's famous jibe against Whistler: 'He has thrown a pot of paint in the public's face.' To her it had always seemed a grossly exaggerated opinion of Whistler's serene and gentle landscapes, but these violent pictures seemed ready-made for the accusation. If he hadn't been there she'd have continued in her title-bestowing mood with suggestions like, *St Ives after the earthquake ... The great paint-factory disaster ... Guess what I've been eating, Doctor!* ... and so forth. "Very ... powerful," she said at length.

Fisher was disappointed. He'd hoped she'd say they were 'very nice,' which would have launched him on an angry diatribe against all bourgeois philistines.

"I assume my brother *is* around here somewhere, Mister Fisher?" she asked.

"Oh, Peter, please," he replied.

"That's for me to decide," she told him. Actually, one of his 'real art' paintings would look quite well in the office she was planning for the power station; it had a very busy surface and was full of hints of machinery and factory chimneys and things.

He was not put out by her reprimand; her attention to the painting interested him far more. "You like it?" he asked.

"I know a place where it would earn its keep," she said.

"Really?" Cressida had not yet taken her eyes off Fisher.

"We'll see." Jessie turned reluctantly from the painting.

"Thirty pounds," Fisher said.

"We'll see," she repeated.

"Twenty."

She laughed. "Why, Mister Fisher — it'll soon be cheap enough to do a straight swap for Harry. Are you going to keep him, by the way?"

"I heard that!" Harry cried from the foot of the stairs. "My sister," he explained to whoever was with him. Then he raised his voice again and called out "Didn't take you long to work it out!" By then he was standing in the doorway.

His companion was the model for the painting — except that her eyes were brown, not blue, her complexion was slightly spotty, and her figure not nearly so voluptuous. "Allow me to present Miss Iris Pawl," Harry said, and went on to complete the introductions all round — even, jocularly, to Fisher himself. Miss Iris Pawl looked at his painting of her, then at him, and said, "Hah!"

"I suppose the old man has missed me," Harry said to Jessie.

"I don't think 'missed' is quite the word," she replied. "But he has certainly noticed your absence."

"He even thought you might be hiding in one of the rooms at home," Cressida put in.

"You couldn't just have waited a few days longer, could you!" Jessie said bitterly.

"I'd have gone mad, little face — honestly."

She nodded gloomily but conceded the point. "It's certainly a contrast," she said, looking all about her. "D'you just sleep on the floor or what?"

"Downstairs," he replied. "D'you want to come and see?" He glanced at Fisher and Miss Pawl before turning back to her and adding, "There are two rooms. And a sort of kitchen."

So, Jessie thought, that answered one unvoiced — indeed, unvoiceable — question about Miss Pawl's sleeping arrangements. "I brought your suitcase with some clothes and things," she went on. "They're in the gig."

Cressida returned to the stacks of real art, by the walls.

"Oh, you are an angel," Harry told her.

"You really could have thought of it for yourself. You could have come home on your way here and thrown a few things into a suitcase — and in passing you'd have been able to let me know you couldn't stick to our agreement any longer."

"Was that your gig up on the beach?" Miss Pawl asked. And, on being told it was, she left the room in three long strides, saying to Harry, "I'll go and fetch your case, then."

To Jessie's amazement he simply let her go. "Harry!" she cried.

"She enjoys it," he assured her.

Fisher went over to join Cressida. He took her forearm casually in his hand, almost as if he were unaware of doing it, and started to explain their 'inner meaning.'

"Whether she enjoys it or not, you shouldn't let her carry your things around," Jessie said.

"But she really does enjoy it, Miss Kernow," Fisher interrupted. "She's that self-sacrificing kind, you know."

"No, Mister Fisher, I do *not* know," she replied tartly.

He pretended to take it as a direct statement of fact. "Oh, well in that case I'll give you an example," he said affably. "I fell down dead drunk one night — bitterly cold night — hit my head and could not be roused. She took off her coat and wrapped me up in it, all nice and warm, and she stayed by my side until dawn. Absolutely *blue* with cold. Very nearly died, in fact. But swore she'd do the same again. She's an absolute brick. Some women are like that."

"And some men know how to use them!" Jessie retorted. She was amazed that Cressida had not joined in the protests — indeed, she seemed rather cross with Jessie for having interrupted her *tête-à-tête* with the painter.

"Absolutely!" Fisher agreed avidly. "If there's one thing I hate, it's to see kind-heartedness going to waste."

"Talking of which," Harry put in. "Do I still get your share of the annuity. I'm rather counting on it, actually."

Jessie was aware that, with Cressida refusing to support her, she was beginning to sound isolated and shrewish. "Let's go down and look at your room," she said. "Are you coming, Cressida?"

"I think I'll stay up here, dear," she replied. "It looked dreadfully cramped down there."

Harry led the way.

"You can be as irresponsible as you like with the old man," his sister said as she followed him down. "But when you play fast and loose with *my* plans I get very peevish. I'm not at all inclined to give you any money. Why should I?"

"Life will be very hard for me without it."

"Life *is* very hard, Harry. Is this your room? There quite literally isn't room to swing a cat. You'll have to sleep diagonally."

He sniffed. "Actually, this is Peter's room. I was hoping to impress you with mine by showing you his first."

"They *both* sleep in here?" Jessie asked in amazement.

This time he cleared his throat awkwardly. "No. Actually, little face, Iris is with me."

"But I thought he said ..."

"Yes, she *was* with him, but now she's with me. She told me yesterday — that's why I ran away in such a hurry. In case she changed her mind back again." He shrugged as if he owed her an apology for Iris Pawl's shifting allegiance.

"And Fisher doesn't mind?"

"I think he's rather glad. He told me he's looking for someone new."

"I give up," she said. "It's like living in a sand dune. Nothing permanent. I don't understand you."

"Come and see." He crossed the dingy little passage and opened the other door.

"No thank you!" She strode past him and stomped back upstairs.

"Shall I?" he called after her.

"Shall you what?"

"Get the money you promised me?"

"Yes!" she shouted in exasperation. "Come on, Cressida — this is just too depressing for words."

Cressida did not even look at her — she simply waved her to silence with a dismissive flap of her hand and went on hanging on Fisher's every word.

"If my father gets home before us," Jessie warned her, "I shall leave you to do the explaining."

That fetched her away smartly enough! But there was still a marked reluctance in her manner as she took her leave of Fisher. And, to Jessie's amazement, her first question on getting back into the gig was, "I wonder if Miss Pawl and he are *very* attached?"

*C*ressida was noticeably silent on the way home. Jessie thought she must be wondering how the old man would take his eldest son's desertion, coming so hard on the heels of his next two children's perfidy. She tried to steer the conversation toward other topics — though nothing else really interested them when set beside this amazing change in Harry. It still seemed a bit dreamlike to Jessie. Not only had her brother shown little interest in girls up until now, he had also been one of the world's drifters, always taking the line of least resistance. She did not know much about men who loved other men — just what had been passed around in sniggers and whispers after the Oscar Wilde trials — but she had often wondered if Harry wasn't one of *them*. Well, he had answered her unspoken questions in a rather spectacular way, now! And yet he was so calm about it — 'As a matter of fact, Iris is with me now' — just like that!

There was an unresolved conflict between her idea of 'normal' and the everyday normality of life all around; but the more she thought about it — and she did little else on that long drive home — the more she realized that she had, in fact, lived with it for as long as she could remember. The utter normality of Cressida's relationship with her father could hardly contrast more sharply with the ideals they had both taught her. But the conflict was merely a matter of words. It existed on paper, or in theory … *anywhere*, in fact, but in her heart, her true feelings. She could tell herself, 'They are living in sin,' and for a few brief seconds she could sustain the sense of shock; but then it all faded away and the utterly boring normality of their life reclaimed her; and the frightful statement became a mere string of empty words. And that realization, in turn, led her to the greatest discovery of all on that eventful day.

Until then she had always assumed that the Ten Commandments, and all other high moral pronouncements, had a kind of cast-iron quality. She knew, of course, that they were broken in countless ways every day — always had been and always would be. But they retained their permanence, somehow; whereas the transgressions had a furtive and fleeting character. Now she began to see that the truth was precisely the opposite: Transgression was the absolute, the permanent, the universal thing; the high morality, however, was kept in storage — like a best porcelain dinner service, brought out and used only on special and rather artificial occasions.

The moment this comparison entered her mind something deep inside her came welling up to meet it with a great shout of happy recognition. 'Yes, of course!' it cried. 'That's how life has always been — and what a blind idiot I was not to see it until this moment!' In fact, she laughed aloud, so that Cressida asked her to share the joke.

But the thought was, as yet, too nebulous, too ill-formed for her to risk putting it into words. She merely said, "Who would have thought it of Harry, eh!"

"Well," Cressida replied, "I wonder if he'll be quite so starry eyed about life in an unheated loft, facing north, straight onto the Atlantic, in January!"

"I'd imagine Iris Pawl might be even less enthusiastic then. Even in summer ..."

"Yes?" Cressida said when she hesitated to continue.

"Well, I was going to say — fancy taking off all your clothes like that and letting a man stare at you for hours every day — even a man you love. I couldn't do it, I'm sure."

"Not for Cornwallis?"

"But he's not an artist."

"That's ducking the question," Cressida said, but she did not press the point. Instead she asked, "Do you think about death often? Or mortality, rather — your own mortality?"

Jessie, a little taken aback, said, "Well, in church, I suppose," but not very convincingly. So she added, "No. Hardly ever, to be honest. Why — do you?"

"Lately, yes. You cross that mental line labeled 'thirty' and you suddenly realize that half your life could be gone."

"Oh, come! You're hardly facing into a decline!"

"No," Cressida murmured. "I'm not. That's the point."

She spoke these words so much to herself that Jessie felt it unwarranted to pursue the matter.

They dined alone that evening, for Godfrey was camping out on Tregathennan Hill and Barney had sent to say he'd be eating at the Angel. Later, Jessie went over to Wheal Dream to tell Cornwallis of the day's startling development.

But he had already heard of it; in fact, he had news for her. He'd met Frank in Helston that afternoon, who had told him that the old man had called on him with the information that he had 'allowed Harry a six-month ticket-of-leave to get this artist nonsense out of his system'!

"He really is a most amazing man," Cornwallis concluded. "You can see why people go in awe of him."

"Awe?" The word amazed Jessie.

"Yes. I was thinking about it on the way home. You remember those two men who fought a duel in Paris a few years back — with billiard balls and both of them blindfolded. People laughed because they thought it rather whimsical. But just think of the terror of it! Imagine yourself blindfolded like that, in a room completely devoid of cover. You hear the swish of clothing as your opponent throws a ball. Or perhaps he's only pretending — so that you'll duck and make a noise and then he can really let you have it. But even if he has thrown a ball at you — what's best to do? If you duck, you might easily move your head into the path of the ball. It's the total unknowability and unpredictability of the situation, you see? And those are the very words that most fittingly describe old Barney Kernow — total unknowability and unpredictability. See what I mean?"

Jessie shivered, for she saw all too clearly what he meant.

"How did Cressida Pym take to Saint Ives?" he asked.

She was happy to turn from the subject of her father. "In a way that was the most extraordinary part of all. I thought she'd be bristling with disapproval and almost telling Harry not to be such a naughty little boy and to say goodbye to his new friends and come home this minute. But not at all." She put her arms about Cornwallis and hugged him. "What's happening to the world, darling?" she asked.

He kissed her and she felt a passion in him that was new — or was it that she'd been incapable of recognizing it before? When his lips parted with hers he said, "Let's go for a walk." And for the first time since they had acknowledged their love she realized it was because he feared what might happen if they stayed indoors. She also realized that she, by contrast, did *not* fear it. And that, too, was for the first time — at least consciously. But whether it was truly the first she could not say, for now she knew that the heart and soul can have thoughts of their own, too — thoughts that do not always surface into consciousness. And her lack of fear of him was surprising in only one way — namely that it did not surprise her one bit.

She pinched his sleeve and held him, trying to show she didn't mind the thing he feared, but it was too feeble a gesture, too remote from the matter, to have that impact. A moment later they were strolling down his front path, making for the lane.

The evening was heading for a golden sunset over Trigonning Hill, but the air was close and almost breezeless, heavy with the promise of drenching thunderstorms. At the gate they turned right toward Releath, away from Nancegollan and the main road — and Wheal Prosper.

"I think I can imagine what must be going through Cressida's mind these days," Cornwallis said as he slipped an arm around her waist and pulled hers about his.

They fell into step — inner legs, outer legs — so that their hips remained in firm contact. It was not, of course, the first time they had walked like that. But Jessie now had a picture of her limbs and his swinging in perfect unison. She could almost see them there, naked under her skirts and his trousers. She supposed it was in some obscure way connected with seeing Fisher's painting of Iris Pawl — how he had depicted her as a *real* woman, not as some shaven, half-marbled classical beauty. Whatever the cause, it filled her with a desire she could now recognize. "What's Cressida thinking, then?" she asked.

"How old was she when she came to you? Twenty? And Harry was fourteen? And Godfrey only six? You were all children, and your mother had been dead six years. So she took over that rôle ..."

"In more ways than one!" Jessie interrupted.

"Yes, well, that's my point, in a way. She sort of slipped into a ready-made situation. But it wasn't of her making and really it wasn't part of her. And now it's all dissolved about her, you see? None of you needs mothering any more, not even Godfrey. And she's no longer got the excuse of her grandfather's will to keep her from marrying your father and putting *that* side of things on a proper moral foundation."

"Excuse?" Jessie echoed. "D'you mean she's now thinking of marrying him?"

"No! The very opposite. I don't think she ever wanted to marry him. Except that she might have wanted to in the *very* beginning — when she was rather an innocent young girl and he was ... well, he's a very impressive and magnetic sort of man. I'm sure it was love drove her to his bed in the beginning ..."

"What else could it have been?"

"What it is now," he replied. "I get the feeling she hasn't been in love with your father for some time. Or she's become more mature in herself and the sort of love she felt for him hasn't. Matured, I mean. Anyway — no matter what's changing or not changing between her and him — everything else most certainly is changing around her. No more being a mother to you children. No more need to choose between marriage and inheritance — she can have both."

"*That's* why the old man tried to argue her out of going to Chancery!" Jessie exclaimed. "He knows in his heart of hearts that she no longer loves him! And she wouldn't choose to marry him if she were free to marry at all. He doesn't want her to have that freedom!"

"Did she tell you that?" Cornwallis asked. "About his wanting to leave the will as it is?"

"She sort of hinted at it. Anyway, I think you're right about her. She said something very strange today. She asked me if I ever thought about mortality ... and life slipping away, and so on."

He chuckled. "And do you?"

"No. I just laughed — like you. And I told her she was hardly facing a long decline. And she said, yes, that was the point. I wanted to ask her what she meant, but there was something so ... I don't know ... *final* about it — about the way she said it. I felt that if I asked her to explain, she'd be giving me some final revelation about herself."

"And you — a woman — *resisted* the temptation to ask?"

She took her hand briefly from his waist to punch him in the back. Then, serious again, she said, "We've all been so caught up in our own changes and preoccupations we haven't noticed that the biggest change of all is happening with Cressida."

"I have," he said.

"Oh, you're so marvellous you notice everything!"

"I try."

"Oh!" She laughed and shook him. "You can be so maddening!"

He held her tighter until she was still again. Then he said, "I think that today's events are going to provoke quite a ... I mean, they've been a sort of spiritual earthquake to Cressida. A lot of old bricks and mortar will have come tumbling down. Talking of which ..." He patted his pocket. "Yes. I have a letter for you from Frank."

She pricked up her ears. "Did he say it was important?"

"No. I think it's just his daily building report. But it's important in that the bricklayers have reached the wall plate — whatever that is."

She laughed. Of course he knew what the wall plate was! She'd first heard the word from him when he was rebuilding the roof at Wheal Dream. It was just his way of stressing how utterly uninterfering he was being with *her* project. Frank could very easily tell him how the building was progressing and he could tell her; but he insisted on this business of sealed letters, of whose contents he pretended to have only the vaguest knowledge. In fact, she was getting rather tired of it — but then, she realized, that was precisely his intention. He wanted her to admit she had been too dog-in-the-mangerish; he wanted to play a bigger part in the day-to-day organization of the Helston Power Co.; and it was very inconvenient for her to have to pretend to be the dutiful, needleworking, water-colouring, piano-practising daughter and manage the whole thing at two arms-lengths ... And yet, somehow, she could not bring herself to say those easy little words: 'Sorry, darling, I was wrong'! Not when she had made such a thing of it.

Instead — and slightly to her own surprise — she said, "Yes, well Harry may have started a fashion. I don't think there's any point in waiting for the old man to explode and chuck me out. If he can go around telling the world he's given Harry a ticket-of-leave, he's capable of anything."

"He always was."

"So I think I'll be moving out, too. I'll have to talk it over with Cressida first, of course."

"You'll move into Cross Street with Frank?"

"In the chambers above Frank's, yes."

He said nothing; she could feel a tension in his arm.

"Why?" she asked.

"There is an alternative. You could marry me."

He held his breath for her reply. She became aware of it before she realized she was doing the same. "Don't tempt me!" she said.

"Tempt you!" He laughed at the incongruity of the word.

"Well, it would be so easy, Cornwallis. If women really were angels — if I were the angel I've been brought up to imitate — I'd accept like a shot. It would be so kind to everyone. The old man wouldn't lose any face. And he'd pass off the Helston Power Company as *your* brainchild — and he'd positively shower it with his blessings, and there'd be no struggle. The town would end up talking about *his* contribution to progress. I've climbed this mountain with him on my back every inch of the way. I'm not going to let him leap off at the last minute and plant *his* standard at the summit."

"Good!" he said.

"That sounded very enthusiastic!"

"No, I really mean it. I think it would be quite wrong for you to marry me just to make it easier to leave home ..."

"Well, I do love you, too!" she protested.

He laughed at the irony of their unique situation. "Yes! But even *that* would be a bad reason for getting married just at this moment. In the world's eyes you'd never be anything more than Trelawney's wife. And it's *not* enough for just you-and-me to know better, is it."

"Oh, Cornwallis!" She stopped and hugged herself tight against him, putting her arms around his neck and pulling his face down to kiss her. He shivered as their smiles met. He touched her lightly parted lips with the tip of his tongue. Greedily she opened her mouth to his, and eagerly his tongue entered in. Without thought she formed her own tongue into a tube around his. She had never done such a thing before but he recognized the symbolism at once — and the implied invitation — and shivered more violently yet.

It gave her a feeling of power over him — even though their embrace had the same effect on her; she, too, was all a-shiver and filled with a longing for him that was no longer vague and sentimentalized. And, as she was her father's daughter in her stubbornness, her ambition, her cunning, so, too, in this: She could not be offered a glimpse of power over another without desiring to use it.

"And that's another reason to get married," he said, in a fluttering voice, quite unlike his own, when they finally parted to draw breath.

She kissed him again, lightly, on the nose. "Come on," she said, grasping his hand and pulling him back the way they had walked.

"What?" he asked, thinking it might be the most idiotic question that ever fell from his lips.

"I just said," she replied. "I can't go on pretending to be a saint."

A person can plan to take some terrifying step in life — and plan it again, and yet again, until it has no power left except the power to bore. And so it was with Jessie when she took the awesome step of leaving the *protection* of her father and setting up her own modest establishment in Helston. She had planned it in so many imagined circumstances — casually, after breakfast, hastily, in the teeth of some crisis, clandestinely, in the wee, small hours — that no matter when or how it came, she felt it would all be old hat and boring. But when the day actually dawned — the day after Harry's defection from the same family fold — she learned that the commonest and least appreciated fault in all human planning is not that the plan itself goes wrong but that, by making the planner bored, it fails to prepare her for the emotions the event itself will unleash.

She was suddenly terrified at the enormity of what she was doing — not, mind you, that anyone watching her would have guessed it. She and Clarrie calmly took down all her dresses, folded them neatly, with tissue paper in between — like any lady of leisure setting out on a long sea-cruise; but with every unflustered gesture a flustered voice within her said, 'You can't really be doing this. You'll never be allowed to succeed. You'll only be humiliated. There is still time to reconsider ...' and so on.

Every tiny action acquired a strange sort of crystal clarity. Her terror split her into two people. One was a creature under compulsion, an automaton who had set this scheme in motion and could not now deviate an inch from the chosen path; she it was who folded each dress with such care and answered Clarrie's excited comments with the most reassuring words. The other was an observer, oddly calm toward the mere facts of what she saw but aghast at their implication.

'You'll never be allowed home,' it told her. 'Except in utter shame.'

The calm hands went on smoothing out the cottons, the muslins, the velvets; the calm voice went on, doggedly trying to damp down Clarrie's excitement.

'If it all goes wrong — if the venture fails and your father and his cronies have to rescue it — Cressida will lose money and you'll be a laughing stock until the day you die.'

The automaton held up a pair of stockings and said, "Worth one more darn before we pass them on, I think?"

'You've seen your father wipe out his opponents before. You've seen them come begging at the kitchen door for him to leave them to lick their wounds in peace. What makes you think he won't do the same to you?'

Cressida came breezing into the room, saying, "What? Not ready yet? You'll miss the eleven-seventeen!"

"Tell me to stop, Cressida," Jessie begged. "Command me to hang all these dresses back where they belong and put this silly nonsense out of my head!"

Cressida merely laughed. "But your dresses don't belong here any more, do they, dear! We decided all that last night — or early this morning, rather." She yawned to prove it.

Her eager encouragement of this rebellion was the most puzzling feature of all. Jessie began to see how perceptive Cornwallis had been about her. The ancient need to keep up a respectable façade to mask her 'life of sin' and to lead the Kernow youngsters into the paths of respectability had vanished. Now the *real* Cressida Pym was emerging from under that cloak — not the girl who had entered this house a decade ago but a mature woman who had successfully pursued a dual life during all that time and who had been granted an unrivalled chance to observe the world, warts and all.

Cressida joined in the packing so as to speed it along. "Don't worry if you forget the odd thing," she said. "It's not as if you're going to live on the far side of the moon." She paused and stared into Jessie's eyes. "You're not really getting cold feet, are you?"

Jessie shrugged. "I don't know. When Cornwallis is all for it, and you're all for it, and Frank's all for it ..."

"And me," Clarrie put in.

Jessie laughed. "Yes, well, when *everybody's* for it, I begin to feel there must be a catch in it somewhere."

Cressida laid two blouses in the suitcase and said, "If you fill that any more, you'll crush them. The trouble with you is that you actually *need* opposition. You're just like your father."

"Thank you so much," Jessie replied sarcastically. "One *good* reason for going is that I shall be spared comparisons like that!"

"You think so?" Cressida asked in surprise. "Soon the whole of Helston will be saying, 'She's a real chip off the old block'!"

Jessie closed the door on the now empty wardrobe and banged her forehead against it several times, murmuring, "No! No!"

Cressida took her arm and brought her back to the bed, where the suitcase stood. "Come on, dear, or you really will miss that train. We'll have to take one of these down ourselves. Clarrie, can you take the gladstone bag? Shaw can come up for the trunk."

"Clothes for occasions I shall have no time for now!" Jessie commented grimly as she and Cressida manhandled the suitcase.

"Oh — what about the letter for your father?" Cressida said suddenly. "Don't forget to leave that with me."

Jessie shook her head.

"Not written it yet?" Cressida was horrified. "You little coward! Leaving me to tell him, I suppose!" She actually looked and sounded as if she'd relish the office.

"No," Jessie said as they waddled along the passage toward the back door, where Shaw was waiting with the gig. "I'm going to see him this afternoon — beard the lion in his den. I thought a letter would be cowardice. Besides, if you write things down, there's a record. If they're only spoken, it's his memory against mine."

Cressida laughed again. "By heavens, Jessica, you *are* his daughter."

Jessie did not deign to reply.

The gig was so laden by the time Shaw had brought down the trunk that Cressida decided not to accompany them to the station. Instead, she stood at the top of the drive, waving them out of sight, forcing Jessie to turn and wave back at her every so often. "Honestly!" she said to Clarrie, "you'd think I was going to India for ever and ever!"

India! Clarrie remembered the beautiful Indian silk Mrs Trelawney had given her. She'd wear it when she went down to Frank's bedroom tonight — and nothing else.

Soon they were on the train for the brief journey into Helston. Jessie had decided to go that way because it would bring her in at the top of the town and the cab from there down to Cross Street would not even come within sight of Kernow's Farm Machinery — though her father's office would be visible from her window up on the second floor.

As soon as they were in the railway carriage Clarrie said, "I wonder if Miss Pym will replace me at Wheal Prosper? She hasn't said anything."

Only a few months ago, Jessie reflected, she'd have said 'replace I' and 'she haven't said nothing' — even though, as an avid reader of good books, she knew the difference between her dialect and proper English perfectly well. Her accent, too, with its heavy West Country burr on the r-sounds, had also veered more toward the standard. It was curious how her confirmation as lady's maid, and the prospect of being sole housekeeper in a small way, had changed her. Or perhaps the other prospect — her clandestine arrangement with Frank and the ultimate prize of the village shop — had been even more instrumental. Jessie herself had had certain qualms about all that, until last night with Cornwallis. That had changed *her* outlook as much as this move to Helston had changed Clarrie's. Had it not been for that, she might have funked this flit today.

"Penny for your thoughts, Miss?" Clarrie prompted when Jessie did not respond to her question. "D'you think Miss Pym will replace me?"

"I honestly don't know," Jessie replied. "Six months ago, I'd have said Yes, because Miss Pym made all her decisions by the form of the thing — by what *looked* right — rather than by asking what was actually necessary. But she's changed — well, we all have, I think."

Clarrie bit her lip uncertainly and Jessie realized she wanted to talk about herself in that context but didn't quite dare. "You have, too," she told the girl. "Don't you think so?"

"Dunno." She shrugged and reverted briefly to an older self. "It's funny how little things can lead on to big ones you'd never guess were there. I think all this started for me when Godfrey kissed me that night — when we saw the new century in together."

"How?" Jessie was intrigued. "Surely nothing of that sort ever happened again?"

"No, but I think Frank had got so used to seeing me about the house that he never looked at me at all. What Godfrey did made him look at me with new eyes, and ... well, now there's this."

"*This!*" Jessie smiled. "Talk about understatement! May I ask a rather personal question? Don't answer if you don't want to — but do you have any ... I mean, what are your real feelings about Frank?"

"I *like* him," Clarrie answered firmly. "I always did. I know he's got his odd side, and you never know what his true feelings are − or, if you do, you still can't tell how strong they might be. But I always liked him. I couldn't do ... well, what I've agreed if I didn't. Why?"

"It wouldn't be just a little bit stronger than mere liking, would it?"

The maid tilted her head awkwardly to one side. "There wouldn't be much point in that, would there!"

"I don't know. Would there?" Jessie was really trying to discover whether the possibility of a deeper liaison with Frank had crossed her mind; her unsurprised response confirmed that it had.

But all Clarrie said was, "Like I said, you can never tell with him."

Jessie did not press the point further; instead she took up a new one. "You say that he only started looking at you with new eyes after the incident with Godfrey? You mean it was some kind of brotherly jealousy started him off?"

"Well, that'd be only natural, wouldn't it? I'm much more of an age for him than I am for Godfrey − don't you think?"

Jessie chuckled. "That's certainly true. But I was thinking of something else. D'you remember a few weeks ago, when you told me you'd had another think about Frank's offer to you? And I asked you why? And you said because he'd started taking an interest in that scullerymaid at the Angel ... whatsername? Tillie. Remember that?"

"Yes?" Clarrie shifted uneasily. "Why?"

"It just shows you're not all that different from Frank in a way. You both have firm ambitions. And you're both stirred to action when you see others preparing to walk off with a prize you think should be yours. That's putting it rather unkindly, I know. But you do see what I mean, I hope?"

Clarrie did her best to hide her smile but could not, at last, deny it.

When the cab drew up in Cross Street, Frank was there to greet them. He had a bunch of flowers in his hand but he appeared to have forgotten them − just as he appeared to have forgotten his arrangement with Clarrie, for he hardly gave her a glance. A moment later, however, when Ted Rose, the cab driver, had deposited their luggage inside the little gate, the reason became clear.

"Why didn't you let old Rose take them upstairs?" Jessie asked.

Frank nodded toward the house. "I've got the old man in there," he replied glumly. "He wants to take me out to lunch. He's still pretending he has no idea who's behind the Helston Power Company. He talks about 'this group of Englishmen' − meaning Riddoch and his Yorkshire pals, of course ..."

"I'm sure old Riddoch would just love to hear himself called *English!*" Jessie put in.

"Quite. But he wants me to get in touch with this 'group' and find out how much they'll sell out for."

"Oh ... God!" Jessie stamped her foot and turned to grip the top rail of the little gate in her frustration. "Now it's one of his games!"

"He knows it's us, of course. But I don't think he suspects ..." He lowered his voice and said, "Cressida. He thinks Cornwallis is the one who raised the spondulicks."

"Which is what we hoped he would. At least *some* of our plans aren't ganging aft agley! Is this a good thing or a bad thing, Frank? If he's asking you to find the price the company would want for selling out to him ... doesn't that put him in the weaker position?"

Frank smiled thinly. "He's never more dangerous than when he's in the weaker position."

"Oh yes he is," Jessie said stoutly. "He's an absolute killer in the stronger position."

"All right! He's dangerous in every position. We've always known that." He noticed Clarrie suddenly and beamed at her. "Look at you!" he said. "I'll bet you never talk about *your* old man like this!"

Clarrie just shook her head slowly. They both saw her heartbeat shivering the flesh at the base of her neck. To Jessie's surprise, Frank touched the maid gently on the arm and said, "Clarrie — you can pull out of the arrangement at any time. Don't feel it's all become irrevocable just because my sister felt she had to leave Wheal Prosper."

The contrast between his earlier behaviour and this — first ignoring her, now being so solicitous — was so great that it brought tears to the maid's eyes, though she did not go so far as to shed them.

Uncharitably perhaps, Jessie wondered how deliberate Frank's action had been. "What's the old man doing at this moment?" she asked, hoping to bring him back to the main issue.

"Going through some accounts he asked Harry to do — books he can't leave around the office! I get the feeling that he's pleading with us to play up to this fiction — that the Helston Power Company is an anonymous group of businessmen from up in England. 'Let's all pretend that,' he's saying. 'We all know who it really is but to save my amour propre, let's pretend otherwise. You sell out. I'll pay up. No questions asked.' What d'you think?"

"What do I think? You know b. well what I think!"

"Oh my gidge!" Clarrie put a hand to her mouth to hear her mistress's profanity.

"Are you getting cold feet?" she asked her brother, still angry.

He shrugged. "I'm just the company's solicitor. I act on instructions."

"Hah!" she cried scornfully. "You just don't want any recriminations if it all comes unstuck and he wins. I'm obviously talking to the wrong man." And she stalked off toward the entrance to the house, a dozen yards or so farther up the path. "If you want instructions — help Clarrie get those cases upstairs!"

"Are you going to talk to him?"

"What d'you think!"

No one would have sneered that Frank's chambers were 'typical bachelor quarters.' Not only was everything in place, everything was in *its* place, and every surface gleamed. Of course, he had a very good cleaning lady who came in for a couple of hours every day, but, Jessie felt sure, she would often complain there was almost nothing to do. Frank could live in a room without disturbing or ruffling a thing. There was a joke in the family that if you wanted a shirt pressed, let Frank wear it for a day or two.

She found her father in the sitting room. He must have thought she was Frank because he did not snap his account book shut until he heard the swish of her skirts. When he saw it was her, his face darkened. "You!" he said gruffly.

"Me," she said, sitting in a window seat where he would have either to turn his chair or sit at an awkward angle to see her properly. "We should talk, Father." She wanted to say more but did not trust her voice; her heart was fluttering like a mad thing, not beating heavily but almost too fast to count.

He slipped the book beneath him and sat upon it. In rising to do so he managed to turn the chair in a seemingly accidental fashion, so that he would neither be constrained to face her nor yet have any difficulty in doing so. "I don't know what you mean, I'm sure." He stared directly at her with his icy green eyes and she felt a shiver of fear run through her.

Often as a child, when she had been in the right and a grown-up in the wrong, she had smarted at the unfairness of their superior strength and authority; they held all the cards. Now she was beginning to realize it had never been as simple as all that. In her present situation she held many more trumps than her father, yet somehow he continued to radiate that same old air of superiority; victory in anything was no longer a reward for his efforts, it had become a right of his very character, whether he deserved it or no.

She had to find some way of overcoming her own defeatism before she could even hope to tackle him. What would lift her beyond that barrier in her own spirit? Anger? Reason? Some feminine wile of which he would have little business experience? Each was tempting in its way; none offered more hope than the rest.

"We could talk about honesty for a start," she suggested.

He stirred in his seat and his even gaze faltered for a moment. She thought the ledger he was sitting on was making him uncomfortable. And then she realized it was, indeed — but not in the purely physical sense. When she said they might speak of honesty, she meant to reproach him for his dishonesty in saying he had no idea what they might talk about. But he had obviously assumed she was referring to his secret account book. Even more, from the way he had given a start at her words, he thought she was threatening to blackmail him!

Therefore he feared that blackmail — as a weapon in her hands.

Therefore her obvious course was to use it — or, at least, to turn the unintentional threat into a deliberate one.

But she was learning to distrust the obvious course. She racked her brains for something beyond it, instead.

It came to her all at once. And, all at once, too — before she could analyze it to shreds — she said, "If you're worried that I might try to exploit any discrepancies between your pencil accounts" — she gestured vaguely toward his chair — "and the ones you keep in ink, you may set your mind at rest. I have no need to descend to *that* level." She managed to make the word equivalent to 'your.'

"*You* have no need?" he echoed in surprise.

At first she did not understand why he stressed the 'you.' Was he contrasting her and himself — implying that he had no need of such blackmail, either? Then she realized: He was contrasting her and *Frank!* He still did not realize that the Helston Power Co. was *hers!* He would have expected her to say, 'Frank has no need to descend to that level.' Or, at best, 'We — that is, Frank and I — have no need …' Of course, he knew she had *some* part to play, but he must be thinking she was just in it for a lark. He had convinced himself that Frank was the prime mover!

The more she considered this possibility the more certain it seemed to her. And who could blame the old man? It would be consistent with everything the family had always know about Frank — that he never did openly what could be more enjoyably done by stealth.

How should she exploit this delusion of her father's? Kill it or feed it? What would *he* do? What would Frank do? No, no — they didn't matter. The only question was: What should *she* do?

She watched her father watching her. He was, she saw, beginning to realize he had said something revealing — something she had not known before. She knew that if she gave him much more silence, he'd work it out. She also knew that if she tried skirting around the topic, probing here, testing there, until she was absolutely sure of her ground, she'd lose more than she'd gain. He was a passed master of the probing-testing skirmish.

The alternative was to lay all her cards on the table. Show him the strength of her position — and the utter weakness of his. After all, a gunboat might be wise to camouflage itself from another gunboat, but when it's sent to frighten the natives it's best to steam boldly into harbour, dressed overall, guns charged and ready aimed.

The drawback was that her father was not the equivalent of some backward native. He would never dream of believing anything she told him outright. He'd pretend to believe it, of course, but he'd use it merely as a basis for all sorts of annoying and tedious provocations aimed at discovering the real truth. However, that might be an actual advantage to her. She could get on with her business while he wasted his time in a fruitless search for something other than the truth that was under his nose all the time.

What clinched it for her, though, was the thought that, if she told him the truth now, he would never be able to complain that she had lied to him. He would feel no shame that he had actually expected her to lie; he would simply gloss over the fact. Business is business and ordinary morality has no part in it. Behind this thought lay another, which she only dimly perceived at the time: She did not actually want to defeat him, or not so absolutely that they could never be on amicable terms again. She did not want to break him, merely to bend him to her will. He, on the other hand, *would* want to break her — because he would see that as the best way to bend her to his will.

There were three votes for truth, then.

She put her fingertips carefully together, one by one, as if each were a support in a complicated structure. When her little fingers met she looked up at him and said, "I see no need for a fight, Father. If we can agree sensible terms, I would consider letting you and your friends have up to a quarter of the shares in the Helston Power Company."

He laughed and said he had no idea what she was talking about. "Honesty," she replied. "I'm still talking about honesty — as I said just now. Cards on the table. You and your friends got the idea to build a generating station to provide the town with electrical current. But when you started looking for a site and canvassing for custom you found I'd got there first ..."

He shook his head impatiently. "Who are you really talking about, maid?" he asked. His tone was kindly, suggesting that he could take a joke as well as the next man — but that this joke was now spent.

She continued as if he had not spoken. "You have a number of very good people among your associates, some of whom have already undertaken similar projects in other Cornish towns."

"How do 'ee know that?" he asked — and then remembered to add: "Assuming I've got any associates or am looking to do anything so daw-brained as cut the throat of my Gas Company, that is."

Jessie was, of course, guessing that he'd hardly go into such a project without involving at least one director of a similar company in a nearby town. But there were too many to choose among for her to risk guessing a name now. So she answered him by sidestepping onto safer ground. "And you have the support of prominent local business-men, too. Mister Giles Curnow, for instance."

She knew that for a fact because Curnow himself had expressed surprise when Walter Blackwell had canvassed him for custom — since he'd naturally assumed that, as a shareholder and director of the company already, he'd be automatically signed up and would get his current at a favourable price. However, he'd passed it off with a laugh, saying that Barney Kernow, his namesake but for the spelling, had always been happiest when people's right hands had no idea what their left hands were doing.

The fact that she knew the name of at least one of his associates clearly shook her father. She followed up her advantage: "All these people have valuable contributions to make. You most of all, I think. It would be a tragedy if we all fell out over a little matter of wounded pride. A tragedy not just for the town but for us, too. We would all suffer. I would suffer more than I can ..."

Her voice trailed off as, without a word, he rose from his seat and walked toward her. His expression was inscrutable. For a moment she thought he was going to turn his lifelong verbal threat — which until now had never been anything other than verbal — into a reality, namely to 'give her a good fist between the eyes.' She steeled herself not to flinch; the reproach, already in her eyes, was her only defence.

He saw it and said grimly, "I shan't hit 'ee, maid. I'd no more hit 'ee than I'd hit any mechanical contraption." And, to her bewilderment, he put a hand gently on the nape of her neck, and bent her a few inches forward while her ran his other hand up and down the top few inches of her spinal column, rather like a doctor.

"What *are* you doing?" she asked crossly, trying to shake herself free of his touch.

"Must be somewhere," he muttered, letting her go and turning away. "I was looking for the key he used for winding you up."

"Aargh!" She sprang to her feet with a cry and ran two steps to him — and only just managed to pull an angry punch on his back, in the same region where he had touched her — his stiff, stubborn back. "I am *not* speaking for someone else," she shouted.

He gave no sign of having felt her touch, but he changed direction and made for the door. "Frank!" he shouted as he opened it.

There was silence in the house.

He took a step out into the passage and shouted the name again.

Still there was no sound. He walked along the passage to the stairwell and shouted down it, "Frank! Do 'ee come up here, boy!"

Jessie saw the pencil-account book pressed into the chair cushion — a simple, ordinary notebook with blue-marbled board covers, small enough to slip into one's pocket. Wearne's, the stationers in Meneage St, sold them by the dozen. In fact, come to think of it, Frank had bought a handful for himself only last week; she remembered his showing them to her. It gave the the idea for a jape to play on her father; at that stage it was no more than a jape.

Where had Frank put them?

Her eyes scanned the room frantically, searching for a hint of blue-marbled paper. They weren't in the small bookcase beside the fireplace — the only place where there were books of any kind in the room. As a last resort she went to the whatnot between the two windows and opened the little glove drawer at the top.

And there they were! All three of them. She picked up one and riffled the pages, making sure it was unused. Then she went swiftly back to the chair where the old man had sat and swapped them. She popped the original swiftly under her bodice and pressed the replacement into the dent it had left in the cushion.

She was only just in time. Her father must have remembered the account book for he came racing back to his chair, where he snatched it up and turned suspiciously toward her; she was by then standing at her brother's bookcase, pretending to read from a book of Dryden's poems. He actually riffled through the pages of the notebook, just as she had done, but, for some curious reason, he had his gaze on her as he did so. To make sure he kept it there she said, "You didn't find Frank? Dear me, I was hoping you would. I've quite run out of instructions. I wouldn't know *what* to say next."

"Whose is that trunk on the landing?" he asked. "That's my old father's, isn't it? You tell Frank he mayn't keep 'n."

She put the Dryden back on its shelf and said, "I brought it here, Father. I'm taking the set of chambers on the floor above. I'm moving here with Clarrie — that's why I'm here now, in fact."

"Eh?" was all he could say.

"We're up to the roof trusses," she explained. "I must be on hand."

"Frank!" He bellowed the name now.

Even Jessie began to wonder what had happened to her brother.

"Also, we're starting to run our cables into the town from next Monday. We'll be going right past Kernow and *Son* (ha ha!) — if you're interested in subscribing?"

He went toward the door and yelled Frank's name yet again, this time just as the man himself entered the room, out of breath and lightly perspiring. "Why do you women need so many clothes?" he asked Jessie accusingly. Then, turning to his father, "What may I do for you, sir?"

The old man, caught between them, turned from one to the other like an animal at bay. "It's true, then," he said incredulously.

"I keep saying it, Father," Jessie responded. "I've told you nothing *but* the truth all this time." She explained to Frank: "He imagines I'm a mere automaton of the Helston Power Company, speaking for you — or persons unknown."

Frank just smiled pleasantly and said, "Ah!" — as lightly as if she had said something trivial, like 'Dinner will be at eight' or 'There's black spot on the roses again.'

"This has gone far enough!" The old man was trembling with anger. "You play all the games you want — the pair of ye! Have your fun while you may. But mark me, now, and hearken carefully — I shall have the last laugh. You tell your fine Yorkshire gentlemen they'll be lucky to escape with the coats on their backs."

He strode toward the door, thrusting Frank aside. Jessie raced after him, catching him up at the stairhead. "Father!" she called out.

He did not even pause in his descent, much less turn his head.

"I don't want to fight you," she continued. "I know you can't win — not by fair means, anyway. But I still don't relish the prospect of ..."

He was at the foot of the stair by then, just about to pass out of view. He turned and smiled up at her, a smile that made her shiver. "Fair means, is it?" he said. "I'll fight by any means going, maid."

She dipped her head in sad acknowledgement of the challenge and said, "Then may the best man win."

"The best man?" He laughed harshly. "The *only* man, you mean."

s the front door (which was actually the side door) slammed behind their father, Frank said to Jessie, "What did you say to put him in such a good mood?" For reply she merely grinned and pulled out his pencil-account book. "I've given him the chance to turn over a new leaf," she said. "In fact, a whole book of new leaves. He'll discover it soon enough. Come on!"

Pausing only to tell Clarrie to make some scrambled eggs before she unpacked or made up the beds, she led her brother back into his sitting room and locked the door behind them. "I owe you one of these notebooks. Or," she said, taking another from the drawer, "two."

"He'll never forgive you for this," Frank warned her, in an oddly admiring spirit.

"It's exactly what *he'd* do if the situation were reversed."

"But that's *why* he won't forgive you."

"You heard what he said — or perhaps you didn't? I told him he couldn't beat us by fair means. We're too far in front. And he said he'd use *any* means." Her words began to drag out and her tone changed to one of bewilderment. "This can't be the right one," she said. "This is all petty cash." She passed the book to him.

He perused it page by page, running his eye down each column.

Disappointed at his lack of response she started pointing out certain items: "Ten pounds ... seven pounds, four shillings ... six pounds, nine, and fivepence farthing ... There's nothing there over twenty and most are under ten. Is he risking prosecution and disgrace for sums like that?"

"Yes but every one is cash, Jess. No trace is possible. No record but this." He tapped the book against his open palm and held it to face her. "And look at the frequency of the entries. I'll bet these dribs and drabs add up to five hundred a year. You can buy a lot of public servants and county officials for a monkey. Actually," he went on in a more thoughtful manner, "it looks as if you can buy just a few but many, many times over. I see old Walker's name here on almost every page. And Field's."

She opened the virgin notebook and sat herself down at his writing desk. "I'll copy them out one name per page," she said. "Then we'll see who his best friends are. It would help if you stood beside me here and called out all the Walker entries, then all the Fields, and so on."

They ate — but hardly tasted — the scrambled egg when Clarrie brought it down on a tray. One her way back, when she heard them lock the door once again, she tiptoed into Frank's bedroom and stared at the bed.

It was just a bed, rather narrow, four foot wide, too narrow to stay in all night. Good thing perhaps. Good thing definitely! She could feel no connection between me-here-now and me-here-tonight. He said she could still say No. When she thought of herself and the little world she had always known, she believed she would say No; but when her thoughts strayed toward him and the larger, unknown world, a Yes seemed more likely. At the moment, the greatest luxury of all was not having to say either. She returned to the little alcove-kitchen in Jessie's flat above and made her own scrambled eggs.

"This is so grubby, Frank," Jessie complained, though not until they had almost finished.

"I warned you," he reminded her. "You'll be far happier if you just stick to ..."

"I've gone too far," she interrupted.

"The old man would certainly agree with you there!"

"I mean too far to turn back. I shouldn't have mentioned Curnow."

"Eh?"

"Sorry — that was two separate thoughts." She closed her eyes and shook her head. "Everything's crowding my mind at once." She described the conversation with her father (which took less than half a minute!) and the circumstances in which she'd mentioned Curnow's name. "I must go and see him before I do anything else," she said. "Lord knows what poison the old man will pour into the ears of his associates. I'll bet he's sending out telegrams this very moment, calling them to a meeting tomorrow. It'll be a council of war, too."

She spoke more to herself than to him. He just stood and watched her in a kind of affectionate amazement. Strong passion in others always fascinated him, for he could hardly ever raise his own feelings to that pitch. Simple passions like anger and lust were less interesting — because so universal; but more complex ones, like the passion that now ruled his sister were utterly engrossing.

He had no doubt that Jessie loved the old man more than any of his sons did — perhaps even more than Cressida, whose feelings were strongly coloured by her physical need for him. But Jessie craved her father's approval with all the ferocity she could muster. And, Frank suspected, in his heart of hearts the old man felt the same toward her. He didn't *really* believe all those absurd notions about the place and rôle of women in life — or Cressida would still be the prim and innocent governess she was when she first came to Wheal Prosper. He just didn't like being crossed; much less did he enjoy being flagrantly disobeyed. If he had put his tactical thinking-cap on just now, he'd have told Jessie he'd been mulling over her behaviour and had come to see she was a real credit to the Kernow line, a truer daughter to him than any of his sons ... and so on. She'd have rolled over like a kitten and given him *three*-quarters of the company, then.

But, alas, it was as impossible for him to climb that far down the mountain of his own pride as it would be for her to admit that she craved his approval far more than she desired any commercial success.

Watching her now, popping the last of the cold scrambled egg into her mouth, not even knowing she was doing it ... chewing mechanically while her eyes focused on nothing and her thoughts raced, he realized that the struggle to make the Helston Power Co. a success was actually almost irrelevant. The real endeavour in Jessie's life was one to regain the old man's favour — but *on her own terms*. She'd never see it that way, of course.

Yet she was not so much blinkered as *sharpened*. She was a sword honed to its keenest edge for a single purpose, to hack a way through that forest of competing claims and interests out there and establish her as one of its local giants.

She had already left him, Frank, far behind; there was nothing he could tell her now, except to be cautious, and he doubted she'd even listen, though she'd pretend to, of course. He remembered the bright-eyed naïve who had boasted to her brothers of this venture, that evening on the landing at home; and even then there had been something about her that made it impossible to laugh, though the ambition was patently absurd. He regretted that he had not spent more time with her over the past ... what was it? Only five or six months since then? He would have loved to observe every little stage in such a momentous transition.

"It's funny," he mused aloud. "You're still my little sister in so many ways, and yet you've changed completely. What is it about you? Don't you feel it?"

To his surprise she blushed to the roots of her hair. "You've noticed," she said. "All morning I've been wondering if it showed. I was terrified the old man would see it …"

Throughout this semi-confession her bewildered brother looked at her with ever-sharper scrutiny, checking for all kinds of likely and unlikely alterations — a new style of hair, cosmetics, some chemical trickery with her eyes, newly pierced ears … But he found nothing. It was only when she concluded, "I wonder will it show in Clarrie tomorrow morning?" and grinned at him with a particular kind of archness that he finally twigged. Then it was *he* who blushed furiously — and she who laughed to see it.

"Didn't you mean that?" she asked when he had finished making a charade of fanning his face and pumping his shirt front like a bellows. "What did you mean then?"

He laughed. "It hardly matters now, does it! Not after *that* revelation!"

"Why? Why should it be any different for me than it is for you? You've been quite *un*blushing about your own desires — and yet you blush for *me!* Oh, you men are such irrational creatures!"

"Pax!" He held up both hands in a gesture of submission. "Well, er …" He cleared his throat. "Jolly good scrambled egg, wasn't it!"

"If I was Godfrey and made such an admission, you'd be saying tell me all about it and what was it like and so on."

He rolled his eyes and said, "All right — go on! There's no hope of stopping you, anyway."

"Oh, well," she said skittishly, rising and drawing on her gloves to go outdoors again, "if that's how you feel, I don't really have time, now." She turned from him and started to walk away. "I'll just say it was utterly wonderful."

"Jess?" His plea was the nearest he'd ever get to an apology.

She turned, skipped back to him, and threw her arms about him. "It was utterly wonderful," she said again, but this time in quite a different tone.

"I'm glad," he said, patting her back affectionately.

"You don't think it wicked of me?"

"Do you?"

"No."

"Then my opinion doesn't matter. For what it's worth, I happen to agree with you, little face — but that shouldn't matter to you. Even the old man's opinion shouldn't matter to you."

"*His* opinion!" she retorted scornfully. "I'd like to see that day when his opinion matters to me again."

*G*iles Curnow, rising forty, was tall and slim, with a strong, angular face; his curly hair, which Jessie remembered as chestnut, was now turning dove-grey. He was a landowner in a small way and a provision merchant in a large way — that is to say, wholesale. So there was none of a retail shopkeeper's aloof obsequiousness about him; in fact, he radiated a sort of patrician self-confidence. Jessie had the feeling he might have quite a temper if pushed into a corner. The only other thing she knew about him was that his wife, Laura, who was around the same age as Cressida, was widely rumoured to have been in love with some other man from Penzance; her parents, however, had forbidden her to see him and more or less forced her to marry Curnow, instead. The Penzance man had taken his broken heart out to the Cape and had died there. Still, she'd had four children by Curnow and, when Jessie had seen her at the Wheal Prosper garden party, she'd been carrying a fifth, so she'd obviously reconciled herself to the arrangement in the meanwhile.

Even so, Jessie could not help wondering, as she looked into Curnow's eyes, what it must be like to go about the place knowing that the one thing most people remembered about you was that your wife had once loved another and that she'd been forced into choosing you instead. Was his loquacious self-confidence, his open-hearted welcome, a response to that knowledge?

"It's very good of you to see me without an appointment, Mister Curnow," she said before she was fully seated.

He smiled and remained standing until she was comfortable. "We Curnows must stick together," he replied. "Even if we can't agree on the spelling. To what do I owe this honour — indeed, pleasure?" He sat down and closed the blotter on some letters he had been signing.

"I've come to clear up a misapprehension my father may have deliberately placed in your mind, Mister Curnow," she said calmly.

It wiped the social smile off his face at once and replaced it with a more businesslike wariness.

"But first," she went on, still with her own social smile in place, "how is Mrs Curnow? She must be very near her time?"

"She is," he agreed. "Fortunately she is no novice in that field." A wave of his hand dismissed the conversation. "I do assure you, your father has never said a word to me about you, Miss Kernow."

"Yes," she replied. "That is the misapprehension."

"Ah?" He leaned forward with interest; he was no longer the middle-aged gentleman preparing to be charming and tolerant to the daughter of an associate — for anything up to four or five minutes.

"He is not entirely to blame," Jessie went on. "I must shoulder my own share of the responsibility. When I conceived the idea of the Helston Power Company, I realized that if I went about the town and personally canvassed those parties who might be ..."

"I beg your pardon, Miss Kernow?" he interrupted. "Are you implying that the idea was yours in the first place."

She smiled sympathetically as if to show she understood his difficulty. "First and last, Mister Curnow. My father has no place in it at all. In fact, I have just parted with him after a most painful interview during which he vowed to break me and my company by all means at his command, fair or foul. But I was about to explain ..."

Curnow, though consumed with curiosity, remembered to say, "But, pray, why are you telling *me* all this, Miss Kernow?"

This time her smile merely warned him that false naïveté of that kind would not wash with her. "I was about to say that if I went up and down Helston myself, canvassing custom for the Power Company, I should either meet with incredulity" — she waved a hand vaguely toward him — "or ridicule. So when I recruited Mister Blackwell to canvass for me, and he mistakenly assumed I was an agent for my father, I thought it best not to disabuse him. Of course — and this is what I principally wish to assure you and your other associates — I did not then know that my father really *was* considering starting such an enterprise himself. So that my harmless imposture — as I thought it to be — has proved rather mischievous, instead. It was entirely unintentional, I assure you, and I want to apologize, most sincerely to you and your associates in my father's alternative venture."

He told her there was nothing to apologize for; he was not aware of any personal embarrassment as a result of it.

"If only my father had come directly to me the moment he heard of it!" she said regretfully. "He was so shocked when Mister Blackwell sought to rib him gently for sending his daughter out as a messenger for the new power company that he ... what do you business people say? He kicked for touch? What I mean is he allowed Mister Blackwell to continue enjoying the delusion while he himself considered what to do next."

"Ah! So your father knew nothing of your plans, Miss Kernow?"

She shook her head. "I had progressed far beyond mere plans by then, Mister Curnow. I had the capital. I had bought the site and ordered the generators — they'll arrive next Monday, by the way. I even have the blank turbine-log sheets printed already!"

"*Fait-accompli!*" he murmured.

She frowned, pretending not to understand him for a moment. Then she said, "Ah! From your point of view, you mean. Well ... yes and no, Mister Curnow."

He placed his hands together like a steeple and leaned forward, all ears; there was no longer any condescension in his attitude to her.

"I offered my father — and, through him, the rest of you, of course — a generous share in the Helston Power Company. The last thing ..."

She saw him draw breath to speak and she knew he was going to ask *how* generous — which was something she did not wish to tell him just yet. So she raised her tone a notch and pressed on: "The last thing I desire is open warfare between us."

"Oh, come-come!" He chuckled and waved his hands in good-natured protest. "Talk of warfare is altogether too ... I mean, I don't think any of us is likely to unlock his gun cabinet, you know."

"Not *you*, Mister Curnow, I'm sure. Nor, indeed, the others. But ... well, you know what my father is like when someone crosses him. And when that someone is his own daughter — whom he believed he had trained to do nothing but stab at fabrics with a needle and poke puddles of coloured water around on sheets of thick paper — well ...!" She laughed.

When he joined in she stopped and, grave again, completed the sentence: "... he ceases to act like a rational being. And my fear is not simply that he will scuttle his own best interests but that he will drag his associates along with him, willy-nilly. Of course, he will be full of remorse when the storm of his rage has blown itself out. He always is. But while the black dog rules him" — her hands sculpted huge, unspeakable disasters in the air between them — "who knows *what* he might not do!"

The tip of Curnow's tongue did a quick patrol! of his lips.

She added: "But that is all on the negative side. On the positive side, the Helston Power Company would welcome the addition to its board of such experienced men as yourselves. I realize it will be a pitifully small undertaking to begin with, but Helston is the natural centre from which the entire Lizard Peninsula will draw electricity. And Porthleven. And the whole countryside out to Porkellis ... Nancegollan ... Breage ... Gweek ... all this side of the Helford ... We may start by generating fewer than fifty thousand units a year but by the end of the decade we could well be selling fifty million! Alas, I think pride will prevent my father from ever joining the company. But I, with all my inexperience to hinder me and nothing but enthusiasm to spur me on, would surely come a cropper without the guidance of such experienced men as you — *principally* you, indeed, which is why I have come to you first, of course."

"You intend canvassing the others, then?" he asked.

"Do you think that would be unwise?"

"Who's next on your list?"

"I thought I'd go and see Mister ... oh! Stupid me! Name's on the tip of my tongue." She clicked her fingers in exasperation. "The other power-company man ... oh, how embarrassing!"

He knew very well that she was fishing, of course, but he had seen enough of her to be impressed. She was a chip off the old block, all right; and, though he could understand old Kernow's reservations about involving a daughter brought up as a lady in the rough, tough world of business, the arguments to overcome them were all here, sitting not six feet away. He was a man used to making swift decisions. He held up a finger to show her she could stop pretending and, taking up his pen once more, he wrote a complete list of his co-directors' names, which he then blotted and folded.

Before he passed it to her, however, he said, "You mentioned an offer of shares just now?"

"Three percent," she said at once — in a tone people usually reserve for speaking of world records. "I know you'll think me dreadfully rash to go so high."

He laughed. 'Rash' was not at all the word that had sprung to his mind. "At *five* percent I might start to show an interest," he countered.

This was very like one of half a dozen imaginary conversations she had run in her head on the way up here from Cross Street. She stared out of the window, furrowed her brow, and counted slowly to ten. Then, with the greatest reluctance, she said, "If you join my board, Mister Curnow, I'll give you three percent no matter what happens. If your associates in this other ... ah, *unfortunate* company, let's call it ... if they do nothing to oppose the Helston Power Company, you shall have four percent. If some of them join us and give us the benefit of their knowledge and experience, *then* I'll gladly make it five."

"*Which* other directors?" he asked at once, holding up the list, which was still folded.

"I'll tell you when I've had a chance to look at that." She pointed at his piece of paper.

"You think your father might not have chosen wisely?"

"I think my father may have chosen one or two people merely to repay obligations to them — obligations which I have not inherited."

He laughed heartily at that and said, "By Harry! You've inherited everything else, though!" — and was surprised to see that his compliment displeased her. It brought him back to earth with a bump.

"Is my proposition acceptable, Mister Curnow?" she asked coolly.

"Let me first ask one very workaday question, Miss Kernow," he replied. "There's no doubting that you have the vision, the dedication, and — I'm sure — the working knowledge to carry this project through. But tell me — what d'you think will be the principal change in your company's operations if you do, indeed, expand from fifty thousand units to something very much greater?"

The question was not one that had featured in any of those imaginary conversations. Why had he asked it? What did Giles Curnow, wholesale grocer and Italian warehouseman, know of such matters? Clearly he had done some reading into the subject since her father had first approached him; the more she learned of this man, the more eager she was to have him on her side. In some way, then, her answer to this puzzlingly vague question would tip the balance. She racked her brains for it. Something Riddoch had told her ... he had said something about small undertakings and large ones.

Then it came to her. She spoke as if she had been spending the time assembling the answer rather than desperately scrabbling for it: "Naturally, Mister Curnow, my thoughts have been consumed, night and day, with establishing a *small* electricity undertaking. Without wishing to sound boastful, I think there is little I could not now tell you about it. And I know that almost all my efforts have gone toward keeping the capital costs as low as possible. Capital and labour. At this stage the cost of fuel is less important. I mean that any time I spend looking for ways to cut capital and labour costs pays far better dividends than if I were to spend the same amount of time looking for cheaper fuel. However, as we grow larger — which we will — I'm sure that control of fuel costs will be more important than the cost of labour."

He passed the sheet of paper to her without further delay. "There is no shortage of people who can dream up grand schemes, Miss Kernow," he said. "But people who can flesh them out in such detail as you have just furnished are like hens' teeth."

"Thank you." She ran her eye down the list. "I think we can do without Mister James Gordon but I'm glad Mister Jim Kenney is there. Tell me how much to offer each of these gentlemen." She smiled sweetly and added, "By 'how much' I mean, of course, how *little!*"

*I*t was like a cathedral, Jessie thought. True, there was no roof yet, and even when there was it would be of humble corrugated iron; and the walls were of common red brick, not hand-carved stone; and there were no soaring pillars to erupt in a burst of delicate fan vaulting; and the windows were square-topped, not arched or pointed; and it was no larger than the average parish church. And yet it was the most cathedral-like non-cathedral that had ever taken her breath away. It was *her* power station.

So far she had seen it in hasty and surreptitious glances from the gig, when driving by into Helston; even at its nearest point the main road came no closer than a furlong, and from that distance it had seemed disappointingly minuscule — a little toy of a building. Close-to, no one could call the twenty-foot walls and two-foot-deep window openings toylike. Those who knew her had long since stopped thinking of her project as an absurd dream but for Jessie herself the moment when it finally became real for her as well was that moment when she stood for the first time in the as yet doorless doorway of the generating house and touched the soaring wall.

Cornwallis watched her in affectionate silence. "Did I exaggerate?" he asked at length.

She shook her head, too choked with emotion to say what thoughts the building evoked.

"That area to the side there is the hard standing for the crane, for when we lift the three generators in," he went on. "The turbine can come through the door in three parts, fortunately."

These down-to-earth details enabled her to find her voice at last. "And the trench?" she asked.

"It's for the high-pressure-steam line. It'll be covered over in steel plate eventually, and bolted down. That's the escape run if it blows a leak." He indicated a continuation of the trench beyond the turbine bed. "The furnace house is round the back. Hayle Foundries have promised the furnace and boilers for next Thursday — by which time we should have the turbine and generators bedded if not actually connected. The holes in the wall — in case you're wondering — are for the cable conduits."

It was all there, as in a dream — or a dream come true. Jessie looked around the building with a wonderment that was perpetually renewed as her eyes lighted on new details at every glance. Beneath the conduit holes he had spoken of she saw two 'electricians,' as they were called, building the switchgear and distribution boards beneath a temporary roof, to be dismantled when the permanent one was in place. So many little details — all coming together, one by one, each at the right moment; now that she saw it all, no longer in her mind's eye but there before her actual eye, she realized that if she had not had the ready-made plans from Mr Riddoch in Hunslett, she'd still be fiddling around with a ruler and dividers and wondering if glass insulators were better than porcelain.

"We've cheated," she said aloud and then laughed.

"Eh?" he responded.

"We've made an off-the-peg copy of a bespoke generator. We've saved six months. We've cheated time."

"Oh — yes — that. For one awful moment I thought you were confessing to having cheated the rival company, your father's crowd."

She grinned at him and said, "What company? What crowd? By Monday, I hope, our good friend Giles Curnow will have broken it up and brought all the ones we want on board." She told him briefly of her interview with Curnow the previous afternoon. "I've learned one very useful thing about being a woman in a man's world," she added. "There have been so many things I couldn't undertake myself that ..."

"For fear of ridicule?" he asked.

"No, I don't mind ridicule — or not any longer — though before all this got under way that was my greatest fear. It's just that it would take too long to convince people in general to take me seriously. So I had to concentrate on persuading just one or two — Walter Blackwell for the canvassing and now Giles Curnow to recruit a good board ..."

"And Frank to do the legal work and me to supervise the building," Cornwallis added.

"I said *persuade*," she reminded him. "And d'you know what I've found out about persuading people? *How* to persuade them?"

He took her arm and led her into the power house. "Tell me," he said, steadying her while she took a long stride over the trench for the steam pipe. "You can't make them *all* fall in love with you — I hope!"

"There was one summer when we were children when we often went over to the sands at Godrevy. And one game we used to play was to throw tennis balls into the sand dunes. We each had our own ball and we had to stand with our backs to the dunes and throw them over our shoulders, so we couldn't control where they landed. Then the trick was to try and get the ball back down to the beach without touching it. You had to dig a track and let gravity pull it downhill. You couldn't dig it straight because the dunes were all up and down, so you had to follow the lie of the land quite carefully. Well, persuading people to do things they might not otherwise do is a bit like that. Let people see an easy path ahead and they'll follow it."

"What takes the place of gravity? I mean, I presume you're not talking about getting Blackwell and Curnow to come physically rolling down Coinagehall Street to the market place?"

She dug him in the ribs with her elbow. "Self-interest. Blackwell can get free electricity for five years if he's very good. Curnow saw my father's company was just a waste of money — but that's only reason not to go on with it. To make him join me I had to put five percent in his path. Negative and positive — our trade!"

After a pause Cornwallis said, "And don't you imagine the same is true of your father?"

She thought it over a while and then said, "Sometimes you'd throw a ball into the dunes and it would land in a sort of natural crater. You *could* get it to move, of course, because it was still ten or fifteen feet above the level of the beach. But you'd be digging a day and a night to take away the rim of the crater on one side. It just wasn't worth it."

"And then?"

"You'd concede one point and have another throw."

"You can't do that here, though — can you!" he said quietly.

There were times when she could gladly hit him. She curbed her anger and said, "Let's go and see how they're doing with the poles."

*I*t was a full moon that night, or else Cressida might not have awakened when Barney drew apart the curtains. She opened her eyes to see him standing in the bay, leaning his forehead against the window frame. From where she lay she could not see whether his eyes were open or closed. If open, was he watching for something? Or someone? A vain watch for Jessica's return ... or a purposeful one for some clandestine visitor up to no good? If closed, were the lids slack and weary from lack of sleep, or puckered tight and trembling in some battle with his emotions? He stood there, carved in rock; one could not tell.

Jessica's departure had shattered him, not only the fact of it but also her reasons for going and her behaviour to him at their only meeting since then — on the very day it happened. He would never admit it, of course. Rather he masked it with his anger. 'Sharper than a serpent's tooth ...' and all that. He was using it to cloak his equally bitter disappointment at Harry's defection, too. He could not cope with both at once so he had somehow cancelled out his son's desertion with this cock-and-bull story about giving him a sabbatical, so as to get the artistic nonsense out of his system. He had told the tale to so many people by now, and fed his vanity with the glowing picture it painted of the indulgent, understanding father, that he had probably come to believe it himself. And any gnawing acid of disbelief went into the ocean of bile that now drowned his former love for Jessica.

Cressida slipped from the bed and went to him, carrying his dressing gown ready to slip over his shoulders. He did not turn his face to her until she actually touched him. "Can't you sleep?" she asked.

"Go back to bed, Pym," he said, accepting the dressing gown as a cloak, draped from his shoulders.

She tried to put one of his arms into its sleeve but he jerked away.

Outside it must have rained earlier, for everything was wet and sparkling and there was that characteristic aroma of wet fungus spores that comes with rain after a warm, dry spell. However, there was not a cloud in the sky now. The moon was over Nancegollan, in the last quarter of the sky, so it must be around half-past three, Cressida realized — a mere hour and a half to sunrise.

"You'll do no good just standing here," she said. "Shall I go down and make a pot of tea?"

"Tea," he replied tonelessly.

"Is that a Yes?"

His breathing clouded the pane. "Where has she got the money from?" he said.

Cressida felt a little squirt of panic hit her stomach.

"I asked Trelawney," he went on. "He promised me 'twasn't his family — which I can well believe, considering the state they've got theirselves in. But he wouldn't say who 'twas. 'Tis from Yorkshire — I do know that. But 'tis all damn nominees — men of straw. Who are the men of substance, eh? She never said nothing to you, I s'pose?"

Cressida tried a little laugh. "Really, Mister Kernow! I was with her practically every minute of our stay. If she had organized a meeting of Yorkshire financiers and persuaded them to part with a thousand pounds, I rather think ..."

"A thousand?" he retorted scornfully. "'Tis ten times that at the very least."

"Ten thousand, then — I know nothing of such matters — what I'm saying is that I think I might have noticed. Anyway, it's absurd to believe that a girl of her age — or a woman of *any* age — could persuade a group of financiers to part with money on that scale."

" 'Tis absurd to think a maid that age could build a power house and sign up two hundred customers in a tight-fisted town like Helston. But she has."

Cressida took his arm in hers. "It's not so absurd," she murmured. "She's Barney Kernow's daughter, after all."

"She's no daughter of mine," he said bitterly.

"All of Helston would dispute you there."

"She's turned the whole town agin me, then."

Cressida leaned her head against his shoulder. "You stubborn, stubborn man!" she said.

"That Giles Curnow!" He sucked at a tooth. "And old Jim Kenney, too. 'Course, Curnow never liked me very much. But what was Jim Kenney afore I took 'n to see Sir Hector? Nothing! And see how he repays me!"

"They're businessmen, Kernow, just like you. How often have you told me — there are no friends in business! You'd do the same as they've done, if your pride wasn't hurt. Come back to bed, now."

"I can't sleep. I haven't slept proper for … I don't know how long."

"You'll only get run down. And then you'll start making mistakes … some would say even worse mistakes than the one you're already making …"

"How? What? Who says?" He turned on her belligerently.

"I do, for one. You coped splendidly with Harry's departure. That could have been dreadfully embarrassing for you, but you've turned it into a little triumph. Why can't you do the same with Jessica? That wouldn't be a *little* triumph, either."

His breath whistled in and out of his nostrils, stertorously on each exhalation. "I would have," he said at last. "I was all ready to. The neck was bowed, the knee half-bent — and then she went and stole my account book."

"*Stole* it! Didn't she send it back within the hour?"

"Ha!" he sneered. "After she'd made a full copy. Now she's got me tied hand and foot. What daughter would do that to her own father, who never wished a morsel of harm to her and never wanted anything but her own good?"

"Say what you will, I can't believe she *stole* it. You should be ashamed to make such an accusation against your only daughter. You simply forgot it, that's all. And that's what I mean when I say you'll start making stupid ..."

"Forgot it?" he echoed angrily. "I leave a half-full account book on the chair. I come back to it a minute later — less than a minute — and it's been replaced by a blank book of the identical pattern — which I don't discover until I get back to the office — and an hour later she sends down the original. And no one else in the room all that time but her! 'Tisn't *me* that's accusing her, maid, 'tis the facts theirselves."

"Next thing, you'll be saying she came armed with that blank book because — by some magical process — she knew she'd find you there and — by some even more magical process — she knew you'd be writing in precisely that account book! And she *made* you forget it there. And she *enticed* you to go outside and leave her alone there for thirty seconds."

"So she did," he muttered reluctantly.

"If you heard anybody else going around saying such things about his own daughter, you'd scorn the man. And if he insisted, you'd suspect his sanity. You should think very carefully before you say such things."

"I don't say them to anyone but you. And Frank. And I should say them to her face if we chanced to meet, too."

"You should be careful even about thinking them. If you get provoked enough, you'll go and blurt them out. Then people will start whispering that you've become unhinged."

"Let 'em," he said morosely.

"Anyway," she went on in a more encouraging tone, "you quite obviously *don't* believe she's out to ruin you, or you wouldn't just wander about the place whining for pity. You'd *do* something. You say she's made a copy of your secret accounts, but you've got no evidence of that. The real truth is that it's very convenient for you — it's a convenient reason for doing nothing. And the reason you want to do nothing is that part of you is very proud of what she's done. Only Barney Kernow's daughter could have pulled it off — you must know that in your heart of hearts. But you've got this stubborn outer shell that won't admit it — so no one can see your heart of hearts. Except me." She thought of adding something about the full moon and its association with lunatics but realized it would be too literary for him.

"Whose side are 'ee on, maid?" he asked petulantly.

"Yours, of course — as always. It's a pity you're not there with me. You are your own worst enemy sometimes."

He shrugged off his dressing gown and tossed it over her shoulder. "Nobody's asking you," he said gruffly.

"*You* asked me," she pointed out. "And I answered."

"No! I do mean, nobody's asking you to stay. Harry's gone. Jessie's gone. You might just so well go, too. I don't need any of 'ee."

She slipped the gown back around his shoulders and said, in rather a brittle tone, "You should be careful, Kernow — saying things like that. One day somebody's going to take you at your word."

He snatched the gown off his shoulders yet again and flung it across the room to the bed. "Except you've got nowhere to go," he sneered. "You've burned your boats good and proper, Pym! Who'd have 'ee now!"

The jibe stung her sharply, especially as she knew it wasn't true; and yet her heart went out to him in his misery. For it was misery that made him lash out like that and hurt his nearest and dearest. A prisoner of her love for him — even though she felt that love dwindle with each passing day — she merely said, as she returned to her own bedroom: "Have it your own way. You never did otherwise in all your life — why should you change now?"

"Talk-talk-talk!" he snapped. "You've always got to have the last word."

She closed her door behind her and leaned against it, staring at her own as yet unruffled bed. Not for years had it seemed so desirable — her own inviolate castle.

What if she just stayed in it tomorrow night ... and the night after ... and all the nights after that? Would he eventually come to her? Head bowed and on bended knee — as he would no doubt put it? Yes, he would — it might take anything up to fifty years but he'd do it at last, just as he would eventually come round to accepting Jessica again.

The trouble was, Cressida thought, she could not wait even a single year. Once again she felt she had thrown her life away. The chance to recapture it, or what was left of it, was getting smaller by the week. If she did not grasp it soon, there would be nothing left to grasp.

*W*hen Harry had been in St Ives for two weeks — the longest two weeks of her life, Cressida thought — and there was still no word from him about sending on the rest of his things, she packed them into a trunk and set off to deliver them herself. It wasn't just any old trunk, either; it was the one Frank had used in March when he moved to Cross St, just as Jessica had used it at the beginning of this present month, and for the identical purpose. Whose clothes would be the next to be folded into its capacious maw, she wondered — Godfrey's? Her own? She suspected it would be her own but did not wish to speculate as to when or how. Or whither.

She always seemed to arrive at the studio when it was deserted. This time, however, she felt less squeamish about entering uninvited, because half of it was now Harry's, after all. Again she luxuriated in the intoxicating aroma of turps and linseed oil, which had become the smell of spiritual freedom to her. She wandered over to the pile of canvases leaning against the wall and flipped them one by one against her knee. Unsurprisingly, they had not changed, not even in their order, since her previous visit. The painting of Miss Pawl was also leaning against the wall but was set apart — presumably because it was still not dry enough to stack with the others.

Cressida lifted it onto the easel, which was empty, and stood back to admire it. She knew it was only paint, but she had to keep reminding herself of the fact; by contrast, the fact that it was also, in some mystical way, a nude Miss Pawl needed no such reminder. The young woman was alive in every vibrant brushstroke. It was curious — the way you could see the brushstrokes, for this was no *tour-de-force* of photographic realism, and yet see it as living flesh, too, in one and the same glance. She wondered what went through Peter Fisher's mind as he worked. Miss Pawl had obviously been his mistress as well as his model; did artist and man fight for top-dog in his consciousness as he worked? Had the man relished the flesh while the artist luxuriated in the paint? Was the canvas a kind of peace treaty in which the two obsessions were reconciled?

Now there's a sight for sore eyes!," Fisher said from the door. "You'd turn every painter in Saint Ives green with envy if you'd only consent to pose for me, Miss Pym."

She had been so absorbed in the painting — or he, alerted by the sight of the gig outside and the trunk marked 'Kernow,' had crept upstairs so stealthily — that she had heard nothing of his approach. "Oh, please forgive me," she stammered. She could actually feel the colour rushing to her neck and ears. "But I do admire it so."

He crossed the room to stand at her side, frowning as if he thought she must be admiring some more worthy painting. "The neck's a bit out of drawing," he said sourly. Then, more brightly, "Even so, better painters than I have suffered from that. Gainsborough could never sit a head properly on its shoulders. But, of course, he's a *great* painter — so people don't notice."

His voice was dark and gravelly; it seemed to make the side of her near him tingle. "You mean they pretend not to notice?" she asked.

"No, I think they genuinely don't — until someone actually points it out. Once people know an artist is a *great* artist, they only look for marks of his greatness. That's why I always make a point of telling people how great I am — or will be one day."

She laughed. "And does it work?"

He shrugged. "It will one day. If you've come to see Harry, by the way, you're out of luck. He and Miss Pawl have gone on a sketching holiday, walking the cliffs from here to Land's End and sleeping in a tent as they go. You wouldn't recognize him, though. He has two weeks of beard and stands six inches taller. You may smile, but it's quite true."

"Is he honestly happier?" she asked, forcing him to be more serious, or at least less flippant.

"He is," he said. "Did you think he wouldn't be?"

Fisher stood rather closer to her than was usual in polite society; it made her nervous, and that made her talk in a livelier, more animated fashion than was her wont. "He's very fond of his family," she said. "It's amazing really that we haven't heard from him at least once every week ..."

"I don't think he gives two hoots about them," Fisher interrupted amiably. "Painting requires a sort of dedication that almost precludes family ties. We're like monks and nuns — except in one rather obvious sense, of course."

"Yes," she laughed, greatly daring. "I don't suppose monks and nuns go off on camping holidays together — sleeping in the same tent, what? Eh?"

He leaned even closer to her and murmured, "Does that bother you at all?"

"No." She wished she couldn't hear her own breathing, that it were more regular, that she could find the courage to look him in the eye.

"I think it does," he said sympathetically, as if he were going on to suggest a cure for the condition.

"Did you mean it?" she asked quickly. "What you said about posing for you?"

He stepped back to a more normal distance. "Every word. Would you honestly consider it?" His tone was completely matter-of-fact now — pleased but not at all suggestive; or, if his manner suggested anything, it was that of a painter making a find rather than a man making a proposition.

"A portrait?" she said quickly. "In these clothes, perhaps? Or I have something rather grander." She wanted to make it clear that the choice was between different styles of clothing, not between clothes and nude skin.

He just stood there and smiled and let her flounder — until she began to feel foolish. He, the artist, had made an artistic proposition; she had responded to him, the man — so she was the one with the prurient mind. "I'll pay you, of course," she added.

"I'll do a portrait of you as well," he suggested.

"As well?"

"You know what I'm talking about, Miss Pym," he replied. And just in case she didn't, he poked a finger toward the painting of Miss Pawl. "I'm very quick but also very competent. I'll do a portrait of you in three days that most people will believe took a month. I'll *give* you the portrait if you'll give me your body."

He meant to paint. Of course that's what he meant! She wanted to say as much. Or she wanted him to say it without any prompting from her. She wasn't going to prompt him. It would sound so crass. Also, it would suggest possibilities that were better left unexpressed.

"I can't imagine you have any friends with nasty minds, Miss Pym," he added. "But if there are just one or two, I can guarantee that even they will look at the completed portrait and wonder how it was done in only a month."

"How can you do that?" She was skeptical but amused.

"Very easily, with your help. If you'll just sit there for half an hour now, I'll sketch in everything on the canvas except your head. Or just the outline of your head. Then, if you'll kindly leave me that blouse, which I'll drape it over a lay figure, then everything except your head will be completed by the time you arrive for your supposedly first sitting! You can take one of Miss Pawl's blouses to go home in. Have no fear — she is a scrupulously clean young lady. Her father is a member of the aristocracy, you know." Almost to himself he added, "The fact that he is also in gaol at the moment does add a certain chiaroscuro to the overall picture, I must admit."

Later, Miss Pym told herself it was that fascinating aside which finally caused her to agree; after hearing it she just had to know all about Miss Pawl. She owed it to Harry and to his father — to all the Kernows, indeed.

*M*onday, the third of September, in the year of Our Lord nineteen hundred ... the date reverberated in Jessie's mind before she even opened her eyes. In fact, she hardly dared open them at all. There was a touch of golden light beyond her firmly closed eyelids, which meant that the sun was getting up; for the past two days the rising sun had transformed the colour scheme in her bedroom by shining aslant the window and painting a narrow band of tangerine on the wall that ran perpendicular to it. Soon the clock would strike six. She ought to be up already — today of all days. Not that she could *do* anything, but it was easier to fret standing up fully dressed than lying in a feather mattress that only wanted to hug you and keep you warm and give you a hundred reasons for not getting up at all.

Monday, the third of September, in the year of Our Lord nineteen hundred — 3:9:1900. Another day in the history of the world. The dawning of new triumphs and tragedies for its untold millions. Would it be remembered as the day of the Great Cornish Earthquake? Or the day when some great ocean liner, bound for Southampton, mysteriously foundered off the Lizard in clear light and calm waters? Or — more credibly — as the day when disaster befell one of the mines between Camborne and Redruth. She shivered and exorcized the thought with a small prayer. In the world at large there would be no great military victory to commemorate this day; Roberts had taken Johannesburg last Friday and the Boer was on the run. So, whatever memorable event 3:9:1900 might bring, the one thing it would *not* be remembered for, she felt sure, was as the day on which the Helston Power Co. first steamed and tested its new boilers and turbines. Yet that was the reason for which it would be forever engraved in her memory. It was also the cause of her reluctance to rise and face it. She wanted it to be evening already, when she would either be drinking champagne with Cornwallis and Frank or telling Cressida how dreadfully sorry she was for throwing away all that money.

Where was Clarrie?

Cressida once said it made her feel especially virtuous to be up and about and fully dressed before the maids came stumbling and yawning down the back stairs and began their daily running arguments in whispers in the kitchen. Cressida would!

You'd think nothing was easier than to run a household that consisted of only one servant. There'd be no bother about status. You'd each know where you stood; you could both relax. But when the servant was also the mistress of *her* mistress's brother, who lived under the same roof ... it started to become a little complicated. And when the servant and her mistress were of the same age, and were both enjoying the pleasures of a conjugal alliance for the first time, and were dying to share their experiences with someone who would understand, well then their formal relationship became a knot inside a tangle wrapped up in chaos.

And somewhere lost in that chaos would be Clarrie's excuse for not bringing Jessie her kettle of hot water. Actually, cold water was better for the skin. Jessie extruded one wriggling foot into the chill September morn and drew it back again quickly. She opened her eyes at last and focused on the tangerine bar on the wall; at least the gay colour took some of the chill away. She braced herself and threw off her topsheet and eiderdown. The shock of the cold was briefer than she had expected; the morn — or at least the room — was not as cold as her foot had found it.

She rose, drew off her nightdress, and surveyed herself in the long glass in the wardrobe door. No difference. The simpering little idiot who had worried about not using belladonna to enhance the mystery of her eyes for the Centennial Ball and this successful (so far, touch wood) female entrepreneuse of the Cornish power industry, a young woman who had, moreover, crossed the great Rubicon in life, were outwardly identical. It wasn't fair. No wonder people still didn't take her quite seriously. She went to the washstand and drowned her chagrin in icy water. That was something no scientist had ever explained — how water could stand in a jug in a room all night and still end up ten degrees colder than the air around it.

As she dried herself she caught sight of her image once again. This time she fell to wondering if Harry's friend, Peter Fisher, would paint her portrait, too, after he'd finished Cressida's. Something to hang in the company's boardroom — when the company had risen to anything so grand. 'Miss Jessica Kernow, Founder of the Company' on a brass plate on the gilded frame. Or Mrs Jessica Trelawney? No. If actresses could keep their maiden names, then so could the founders of companies. Everyone was putting on an act, anyway. She was beginning to wonder if there was such a thing as a *real* grown-up in the whole wide world; she wasn't sure she'd met one yet. And should it be founder or foundress? Instigatrix, perhaps? It would make people stop and think, anyway.

Not that it was making *her* stop and think. Quite the opposite — it was stopping her from thinking, especially about steaming up the boilers and running the turbine.

The clock struck six at last. Barney Williams, furnaceman, and his son Tony, the stoker, should be kindling the fire at this moment. And she should be there to encourage them — or to give them tongue pie if they were late.

Cressida's portrait was taking an age, even though she went over there two or three afternoons a week. Also there was something slightly furtive about her whenever she spoke of it; she rather *over*stressed that she was really doing it just to keep an eye on Harry — purely out of duty to the family. Calls of duty did not often make Cressida's eye sparkle with such relish. Jessie had even wondered if she was not posing secretly for a nude picture, the sort of thing Fisher had painted of Miss Pawl — though she could not imagine Cressida, who buttoned everything up to the neck, agreeing to such a pose. However, there were many things one could not imagine Cressida agreeing to though she did them nonetheless.

Jessie was dressed as far as her underwear by the time Clarrie came bustling in with a kettle of now unneeded hot water. Her face fell when she saw her mistress already so far ahead of her. "I should have remembered," she said. "Today's the day."

"As long as there's boiling water down at the power station, the rest doesn't matter, Clarrie. Go back and turn that into a pot of tea. Then come and do my hair."

When the maid returned, with the welcome brew on a tray, she was surprised to see her mistress wearing the skirt of the clerical-gray suit she normally wore to funerals. She was about to ask if someone had died when Jessie explained: "I've just decided that from now on I shall dress as soberly as any man. I shall wear only suits of dark gray, all severely cut and tailored. And no flowery hats, either. Just those Tyrolean ones for ladies ..."

"What? The ones that look like men's hats?" Clarrie asked her mistress in amazement.

Jessie put a finger to her grinning lips and said, "Ssh! And a gray silk or chiffon square round the neck. And no colouring. And d'you remember the gold-rimmed spectacles I wore for *Iolanthe?* The ones with plain glass in? I think I'll take to wearing those, too, if you can put your hands on them. You can do my hair in a bun now. D'you remember that very metallic-looking bun Miss Pym used to wear? I want one just like that if you can manage it, Clarrie."

"No colour at all?" the maid asked as she began to comb out her mistress's hair.

"Hmm." Jessie stared at her reflection in the dressing-table looking glass, imagining how she would appear when she was dark gray from ankle to neck and her hair constrained in a bun that, if Clarrie got it right, would look more industrial than human. The maid had a point. She would seem like a woman trying to efface herself; even a nun would appear more feminine. "I shall wear a single red rose," she said. "Every day. We'll place an order with Hyatt at Trenethick Nurseries and you may collect it from his shop when you buy the vegetables. Yes — a single red rose." She patted the spot on her collarbone over which it would be pinned.

Clarrie giggled. "It'll be your trade mark, Miss."

Jessie clapped her hands. "Perfectly put!" she said. "You've hit the nail on the head, Clarrie. That's what these changes are all about — trade. Before long I fear I may be looking at other Helston ladies in their flowery prints and brocades and feeling just the smallest twinge of envy." With hardly a pause she went on: "I don't suppose there's much point in asking what delayed *you* this morning? More a question of *who,* eh?"

Clarrie merely blushed. Then a frown darkened her brow. "Oh, I meant to tell you, Miss. I met Master Godfrey up Meneage Street last night — about eight o'clock."

"And? I'm surprised he didn't call on Frank and me. He usually does when he comes into town."

"He has other fish to fry, Miss."

"Still? Is it still that whatsername girl ... the scullerymaid at the Angel? Tillie something?"

"Tillie Lambton. Yes, Miss. And you know what he asked me? He said how did I think Rachel and cook and Mrs Shaw would take to having that Tillie come to work at Wheal Prosper?"

"As scullery maid?"

"No, Miss. That's not his idea. As a replacement for me! He dared ask *me* that — Tillie Lambton replacing *me!* How I kept a civil tongue in my head I don't know!"

"What did you say?"

"I told him never mind what Rachel and the others might say, Miss Pym was the one who'd put her foot down over any such nonsense." Jessie was exasperated. "He's so self-reliant. One is apt to forget how juvenile he still is."

"Well, Miss ..." Clarrie bit her lip uncertainly.

"What? Go on."

"He gave me a sort of pitying look — as if to hint that he could take care of Miss Pym very well, thank you. He didn't say as much. He just waved his hand like that." She gave a dismissive waft of her fingers. "And then he asked me again about how would Rachel and the others take it. So I told him in no uncertain terms. Are you sure you want this bun quite so tight, Miss?"

Jessie tilted her head experimentally this way and that before agreeing that the maid could loosen it a bit. "I can feel it stretching the soles of my feet," she joked. "Was Godfrey at all downcast?"

"Never, Miss! He said Mrs Hodgson wasn't the only cook in Cornwall, nor Rachel the only housemaid. And by the time they'd been replaced maybe Mrs Shaw would see which side her bread was buttered. So there now!"

"The little tinpot Napoleon!" Jessie sneered. Then, thoughtful again, she added, "I wonder what he meant by waving the threat of Miss Pym aside like that?"

She already had a good idea of the answer, though. Godfrey must have gone over to St Ives to see Harry and had stumbled on something there, something Cressida would rather the rest of the family didn't know. *And, being a Kernow* ... she thought ruefully.

"I'll put a stop to that," she said with every show of confidence. "We can't have things like that going on, can we — ours is a respectable family and Wheal Prosper is a respectable house!"

*I*t was heat, of course, but you didn't feel it as heat, you felt it as pressure — an almost intolerable tension in the very air. Every boilerhouse disaster you ever heard about came to mind. You looked at the great pressure-vessel and you were sure one of those rivets would pop. You heard the water boiling inside with that peculiar muffled pinging it makes when the pressure is above a hundred pounds per square inch, and you're sure it's malevolent enough to find *some* way out. You look at the gauges, with their comfortable maximum of a hundred and fifty before the frighteningly ungraduated red of the danger segment, and you wonder if they haven't got stuck; you stare long and hard at the safety valve and you're quite sure it has.

Jessie's trouble was that once, when she was young, Harry had brought home a copper float — really just a hollow sphere of copper. It no longer floated because it had filled with water through a tiny pinhole. He had shaken out all but a thimbleful of it but then, his arms being exhausted, he had hit upon the wheeze of boiling the rest out over a gas ring in the company workshop; it couldn't explode, after all, because the pinhole would relieve the pressure. Ha ha! It had taken months of his pocket money to replace all the glass. The workshop foreman said if the half of the sphere that did all the damage had gone just ten inches farther to the right, Harry would have had no face left. Jessie, who had been standing beside him, would have suffered the same fate if it had gone a little farther to the left. Ever since then she had had a holy dread of anything to do with boiling up high-pressure steam. Using it was fine.

She jumped when Cornwallis touched her arm. "Are you all right?" he asked.

"Steam," she replied. "I'll explain later. I'll be fine when we get back to the turbine room."

"Cressida should be here for this," he went on.

Jessie shook her head. "I asked her but she said the risk of being seen by the old man was too great. I told her he wouldn't come within a mile of the place, but even so ..."

"Ah, well she's right and you're wrong, I'm afraid. I saw him lurking in the shrubbery as I arrived."

"What shrubbery?"

"Figure of speech. I mean he was walking up and down the Porthleven road with a couple of his men. They had a theodolite and chains and were pretending to be doing a survey. Surveying *us*, actually."

"Watch us blow ourselves to bits!" she said ruefully.

"Go on! We've been up to a hundred and twenty-five before now. This is the most absurdly over-engineered plant in the kingdom."

"It won't be when we're doing a quarter of a million units a year," she replied.

He lifted his hands as if to say he wouldn't run through that old argument again. "Anyway, he's out there watching us," he said.

Even that brief conversation had helped relieve her tension. It had also made it doubly difficult for her to go back to staring at gauges and wondering about the safety of rivets and welds. "I know the real reason why Cressida's not here," she said. "She's up to something over in Saint Ives."

Cornwallis stared at her in amazement. "With Harry?" he asked in tones of disbelief.

"No. With his chum Fisher. Peter Fisher."

Cornwallis couldn't respond because Barney Williams came round to check on the pressure gauge beside them.

"I hope they're all telling the same story," she remarked.

"Couldn't slip a fingernail between them, boss," he replied.

"Boss!" Cornwallis echoed when the man had gone back to tend to his furnace.

"He's called me that from the beginning," Jessie said. "He'll get a special bonus at Christmas. Men have gone straight to heaven for less. Actually" — her tone hardened — "this could be a good moment to slip out and have a word with the old man. If he's got two of his underlings with him, he can hardly spin on his heel and stalk away."

"You just want to get out of being blown to smithereens here," he said with a grin.

She laughed. "Yes, there is that, too, of course," she called out over her shoulder as she left.

"Shall I come, too?" he shouted after her.

"Best not."

She strode up the drive, which was new-laid with gravel now that the heaviest part of the building work was over. For part of the way she was screened by trees, then by the filter house at the sewage works. He did not see her until she gained the Porthleven road — between him and Kernow & Son. He looked swiftly all about him; his gestures showed he was thinking on exactly the lines she had described — and that he reached the same conclusion, too. He turned to face her squarely when he saw he had no choice.

"That was a stupid thing I did, Father," she called out when she was just within earshot and before he could say what was on his mind.

If anything was on his mind, her words silenced it until actual conversation became possible.

"When?" he asked suspiciously.

She gave a self-deprecating laugh. "Every day of my life, probably. But the day we last met, in particular."

"You got some nerve," he hissed. "After what you've done to me in this town." He was shivering with anger — though from his easy stance and the smile on his face his men would never have suspected it; they'd have to be standing as close as she was to realize what a fixed and ghastly grimace it was.

"We're steaming-in the turbines," she told him. "If it goes well, we'll put up a bit of load. Do come and join us?"

He stared at her as if unable to believe his ears; in truth, he was unable to believe his eyes, as well. The sweet little child he'd dandled so often on his knee — and chastised with the flat of his hand more than once, too — his darling Jessie, the apple of his eye, now stood before him, a ruin of all that he'd loved and struggled to preserve in her — that delicate flower of her femininity. "Steaming-in turbines!" he sneered. "Put up a bit of load! Lord have mercy upon us!" He searched her face, first peering deep in one eye, then in the other, as if at least one of them must divulge the secret of her lost whereabouts. "How are 'ee wearing spectacles now, maid?"

"Will you join us?" she repeated. "In every way, I mean? You remember I promised you twenty-five percent? I've managed to keep my commitments to Giles Curnow, Jim Kenney, and the others down to twelve percent in all. So there's still thirteen left for you. You'll outvote them all."

There were sudden tears in his eyes. He turned away to blow his nose. She thought he was softening. But when he turned back to her he said, "If I had a hundred percent of your shares, maid, I'd give them all to ... to the Camborne—Redruth Labour Party" — he named his greatest hate in the world, and then remembered one yet greater: "No! I'd give them all to the Income Tax Inspectors — just to get my dear li'l Jessie back."

The harshness of his words stung her into saying something that would never have occurred to her in a brace of lifetimes: "And I'll *give* you that hundred percent — or all that's mine to give — if I can just have my rightful place beside my dear old dad. So there!"

"What? ... How?" he asked, barely coherent.

"Take down that *Kernow and Son* — which is never going to earn you anything but ridicule and scorn — and put up the one that belongs there, instead: *Kernow and Daughter.*"

Before she was half-way through this little speech she could see he was preparing to say something utterly crushing. So she saved him the bother. She turned on her heel and flung the concluding three words over her shoulder.

The other reason was so that he should not see the tears streaming down her cheeks. "Stupid, silly, obtuse, stubborn, bull-headed, feeble-minded, addle-pated, old ... old *curmudgeon!*" she fumed as she stalked away from him. Surely there was a stronger word than 'curmudgeon'?

As he watched her go storming off a small voice in his head — which sounded remarkably like Pym's — told him he was making a complete fool of himself. Not only had he just turned down an offer of shares in what was obviously going to be the nearest thing to a goldmine Helston would ever have, he had also made a determined rival out of the best potential business partner he was ever likely to get. He actually drew breath to call her back before his pride regained enough control to silence him.

Jessie was quite calm again — outwardly, at least — by the time she returned to the furnace house.

"Not coming?" Cornwallis asked with a smile.

"He said another time, perhaps," she replied.

*T*he high-pressure steam line from the boiler room to the turbine room had been tested with compressed air but never with living steam; today was the day for that — and for the turbine it fed, and for the generators it powered. Barney Williams went to the door that linked the two rooms and shouted, "Steam gate off?"

George Blight, the chief engineer, who was stationed at the turbine end of the pipeline, raised his hand portentously and called back, "Steam gate off."

Williams returned to the pressure vessel and donned a pair of thick leather gloves. He put both his hands to the valve handle — a disc of metal, perforated to dissipate the heat — and turned it slowly in an anticlockwise direction.

The needles on the gauges dipped and there was a high-pitched shriek from inside the bulbous body of the valve — so high-pitched, indeed, that the older men there heard nothing, though Cornwallis gritted his teeth and Jessie had to put her hands over her ears. It broadened and died away as Williams continued to open the valve. After two full turns he went back to the door and shouted, "How's she doing, boy?"

"Brave," came the reply.

The furnaceman returned again to the valve and opened it fully. He kept his hands on the device, though, in case the call came to shut down again. They waited for the telltale hiss of escaping steam but there was none; apart from the subdued roar of the furnace the place was eerily quiet.

George Blight came through to the furnace room and gave his colleague a nod of satisfaction before turning to Jessie. "We'll have a look along the line now, boss?" he said, making it half a statement, half a request for her permission.

She went to join him for the brief walk along the line of the steam pipe. Cornwallis and Williams followed. The concrete trench that housed it had not yet been covered over with the steel plates. The pipes were in six-foot sections, made of cast iron and lapped in welded steel. The joints were between half-inch flanges, milled and polished, with high-pressure gaskets of asbestos fibre and boiled linseed oil. Blight spent a minute or more at each junction, listening for the smallest hiss of a leak and confirming its absence with the back of his hand — exactly as one would test the pneumatic tube of a car tyre for the draught from a puncture. He had a small mirror on a stick, which he put under the pipe while his assistant, Phil Pask, lowered an acetylene lamp into the trench beside it.

"If he was to leak down there, boss," Blight explained, " 'twould be dripping water by now — condensed steam on a cold pipe, see? That'll have an inch o' water in 'n afore he's up to temperature. When we'm sure he don't leak nowhere, us'll pack insulation in around 'n. Bits of moss and tree bark and such — 'cos that condensation, see, that's all wasted coals."

She nodded. "Now I understand why you tightened the bolts round those flanges with such care."

By the time they reached the turbine-inlet valve, at the downstream end of the line, she could feel the heat radiating from it — BTUs going to waste in all directions! Not for the first time she became aware of the prodigal rate at which industry operated. To someone accustomed to placing individual lumps of coal on a fire, it was breathtaking to see the stuff being shovelled into a furnace by the hundredweight. The level-headed woman of business in her wanted this test to be over and done with as soon as possible, so that they could put out the fires and save the fuel for when the generators started in earnest, tomorrow, when four days of line-testing would begin. But a more romantic, heedless Jessie reveled in the prodigality of it all; she would have invited the whole of Helston to a feast among the whirring machinery — if, indeed, it was going to whir today.

"That's our first big worry out the way," Blight said when he was satisfied there were no leaks.

"And the next?" she asked, turning eagerly to the turbine.

"We shall just have to make sure no birds haven't built their nests in any of the machinery, that's all," he joked.

She expected him to start opening the valve to the turbine at once, but instead he crouched down and opened a little tap on the bottom of the steam valve. The condensed steam, though it was turned back into water, was still well above boiling point; only the high pressure in the pipeline kept it liquid. It reverted to steam the moment it escaped into ordinary atmospheric pressure; soon they could hardly see one another in the dense clouds of swirling vapour.

"That's a lot more energy going to waste, surely?" she said.

" 'Tis too much condensate, boss," he explained. "There's always a bit, of course, 'cos you can't have a line like that without some loss. But a little bit is tol'able, see? It do pass straight through the high-pressure stage and does useful work in the medium-and low-pressure stages." He stooped and shut off the tap again; the air began to clear. "But that was too much for the high-pressure stage to handle, see?"

He, too, drew on thick leather gloves and put his hands to the turbine-inlet gate valve. "Say your prayers!" he remarked and drew a deep breath. To young Phil Pask he called out. "Is she decoupled?"

"Decoupled, sir," the lad called back. For want of anything better to do he was lifting the spring caps on the oil 'rezavoys' and giving each an extra — and quite unnecessary — squirt from his oilcan.

"Stand back!" the engineer cried and gave the valve a quarter turn.

Nothing happened. Jessie glanced nervously at Cornwallis, who responded with a reassuring smile — not that he had any greater cause for reassurance than she had, but she blessed him all the more for that.

Blight gave it another quarter turn, and now they heard the expected shriek of high-pressure steam. The turbine responded at once, though the only sign of it was a flick of the rev-counter and a sudden blurring of the splined shaft where it was decoupled from the generator train.

Keeping a wary eye on the rev-counter, the engineer opened the valve slowly; the high-pitched shrill of steam faded away to be replaced by a subtler whine, also at the upper limit of human hearing yet somehow more solid and musical — the whine of the turbine itself. As he heard the transition, Blight relaxed and smiled at the two onlookers. "We'm over the second hurdle, boss," he shouted.

Suddenly there was a muted clattering sound from the farther end of the turbine. Jessie's heart leaped up into her mouth, but Blight seemed unperturbed. Indeed, he cocked an ear toward it and nodded with satisfaction. As it dwindled, Jessie nudged him, pointed toward the pipe that seemed to be the source of the sound, and shouted, "What was that?"

"More condensate," he shouted back. "Turbine's cold, too, see? He's settling now, though."

"What *is* that pipe?" Cornwallis asked her.

She drew him aside and explained that the exhaust steam from the turbine, though it lacked enough energy to do any more work, still held useful heat. So, rather than simply vent it to the atmosphere, 'that pipe' conducted it back to the boiler, where it heated the feed water before condensing and itself topping up the feed tank. "Nothing wasted here," she concluded with pride. "Not if we can help it."

Blight meanwhile had removed his heavy gauntlets and was now carrying out a curious manoeuvre — placing a long, thin pole of wood against various parts of the turbine casing and pressing his ear to the other end of it — as children lay their ears to telegraph poles beside the road. Jessie went to him and asked to listen, too. He pointed out that the top of the rod was hardly clean enough for a lady's ear. Cornwallis took out his breast-pocket handkerchief and wrapped it round the rod. She laid her ear to it and heard a sound rather like a church-organ note when you pull out *Octave* and *Diapason* and all those stops that add extra harmonies when all you press is a single key; it was remote, though, as such a note might be heard from outside the church and from some distance away.

"Sweet!" he shouted and, taking back the rod, continued inspecting every journal and bearing it could reach.

Finding nothing to worry him, he put on one gauntlet, went back to the valve, and shut it down half a turn, until the note just began to drop. "We'll let 'n get up to full working temperature for a bitty while," he explained, "and see if he do stay so sweet and well behaved as what he is now."

For the next ten minutes they watched the temperature gauges on each stage of the turbine climb inexorably into the pale-green segment that marked the upper and lower limits of the preferred working temperature. And for the ten minutes after that they watched them *not* climbing any higher.

"Next hurdle over?" Jessie asked cheerfully.

Blight nodded with a diagonal dip of his head and said, "Now for the big one, boss!"

He put on both gauntlets and shut the valve down completely. Then he gave a wave to Barney Williams, who was standing in the connecting doorway. Barney went off to do whatever he had to do. Jessie made a mental note that they needed something like a ship's engine-room-to-bridge telegraph; otherwise one or other of them would always have to be running to that doorway — or standing in it, waiting for a wave from the other.

The whine of the turbine fell rather slowly through the octaves until it reached something between tenor and baritone. Blight nodded to his assistant, who took hold of a lever and pulled hard, rather like a signalman changing a railway signal. It was obviously a brake, for the baritone note dropped swiftly to bass and then to silence.

The two engineers walked the full length of the machine, flipping up the oil-reservoir lids to check on the consumption so far; only one appeared to need a squirt from Pask's ever-eager can.

"Now!" Blight exclaimed, giving his assistant and the two spectators a tight, nervous smile.

He took a small, square key from the breast pocket of his overalls and bent over the power shaft that linked — or soon would link — the turbine and the gear train to the three generators. He inserted the key in the head of a grub screw that held a splined sleeve firmly in place on the static side of the drive. As soon as the point of the grub screw no longer held it to the shaft, he moved the sleeve up along the corresponding splines — or what Jessie had called 'fins' before she knew better — at the ends of the drive shaft and the driven shaft. They were, of course, butted to within a hairsbreadth of meeting, so that when the sleeve slid up and covered the break, the two shafts became as one. This time he tightened two grub screws, one at each end of the sleeve, until not even his most strenuous efforts could make it budge the smallest fraction of an inch.

Yet again he donned the gauntlets and took a grip on the inlet-valve handle.

"When this place is working fully he'll be taking those things on and off all day," Cornwallis commented.

But Jessie pointed to a lever behind the valve, at present secured in the vertical position with a small padlock, and explained that it would normally be horizontal — whereupon the inlet valve became self-governing, opening and closing with variations in the generator load. "We've thought of everything," she said grandly — crossing her fingers and hoping it was true. Then, to placate the gods of chance, she added, "Except a ship's telegraph."

"I was just thinking that," he told her.

"Ready?" the engineer yelled.

The furnaceman appeared in the doorway and gave a cheery wave.

"See what I mean!" Jessie said just before the inlet-valve opened and the noise made further conversation impossible.

This time the turbine was slower to respond, for it had the inertia of one generator to overcome as well. They were so intent upon it that no one noticed Frank's arrival until he touched Jessie's elbow and shouted, "Is it safe here?"

She gave a start and then threw her arms about his neck and put her lips close enough to his ear to tell him it had all gone pretty well so far.

"Why is only one of those machines turning?" he asked, pointing to the middle generator.

"Because it's not eight o'clock on a December evening," Cornwallis said laconically.

Jessie elbowed him aside and said, "Pay no attention to him — he thinks we should simply cut unimportant customers off at eight o'clock on a December evening. I say better five hundred units too much capacity than fifty too little. The reason the other two generators are idle just now is that we're going to test them one by one before we run all three together."

"I say — are we going to see sparks and hear bangs and things?" he asked eagerly.

"I hope not! There shouldn't be anything to see at all, except hands moving on dials. Look!" She pointed to a dial in the centre bank of the control board on the wall behind him, where the hand stood rock steady at the figure 110. VOLTS, the dial also said.

He stared at it in fascination, then at the generator at the far end of the hall. "You mean that that machine over there is moving this dial over here?" he asked. "Amazing! I'll never get used to it."

"I'll tell you something even more amazing. You could disconnect that voltmeter from the board there, carry it right up to the end of our line, which is beyond the workhouse in Meneage Street, reconnect the terminals up there, and it would read exactly the same as down here. The slope of the hill makes absolutely no difference!"

"Amazing!" he said again. "Nothing can change it, eh?"

"Oh yes. If someone switched on a light or a heating coil or something."

"And then?"

"The voltage would drop a little bit. If it was only one light you wouldn't even see the needle move but if everybody started drawing current at once ... well, that's what we have to test over the next few days. We're going to put various resistances across the ends of our lines — in Saint John's, in Church Street ..."

"Can we turn on our electricity at home tonight?" he asked excitedly.

"No!" Her eyes raked the ceiling. "For heaven's sake — that's what I'm explaining — or trying to. We've got to put these different resistances across our lines in Wendron Street, Meneage Street ... and so on — and see how much the voltage drops. The resistances duplicate the effects of different loads."

"People aren't going to wait, you know," he warned her. "I passed Harvey Stevens at the Blue Anchor on the way here. He said he'd noticed the smoke from the power-station chimney and he'd been turning his lights on and off all morning but nothing was happening."

"Aargh!" She shook her fists at the ceiling. "They just don't listen. Nor read. We've visited every single subscriber and explained it to them — and left a leaflet saying the same thing all over again. Testing all this week — connecting everyone up over the week end, touch wood — and full service starts next Monday, a week today. What could be simpler?"

"I'll tell you what — they could just creep out and connect themselves up," he said. "All the house wiring-up is done. It's just a matter of connecting the two, surely? Six foot of copper wire and some thick rubber gloves. I'll bet a lot of them are thinking like that up there." He nodded in the general direction of the town.

Jessie's lips almost vanished and the rims round her nostrils whitened with anger while she thought the matter over. Then she crossed the room to where Blight was standing, doing his pole-to-ear test on the one working generator. "Can we vary the voltage?" she asked him. "What's the highest we can go — safely — I mean, without producing flashes of lightning and starting fires?"

"You mean now? While no one's connected?"

"While no one *ought* to be connected." She gave a savage grin.

He caught her drift. "You mean they're already trying it, boss?"

"Probably. My brother says some of them are bound to before the week's out."

"We could go up to two hundred and fifty, I s'pose."

"What would that do? Kill anyone?"

He shook his head. "Not if we just went up and down in three or four seconds. That wouldn't hardly kill no one — but it'd kill every lightbulb they had switched on at the time!"

She laughed with delight. "That'll teach 'em! We'll raise the voltage like that a couple of times every hour from tomorrow on, once we load up the distribution lines."

As she returned to Cornwallis and her brother she thought back through the dozens of copies of stuffy trade journals and pompous papers she had read on every aspect — or so she thought — of building and running a power company for a small town. Not one of them had mentioned the infinite capacity of the consumer to put a stick through the spokes and reduce any orderly operation to chaos. Her vigilance — like these generators from next Monday morning onward — would have to be unceasing.

*J*essie and the two men stayed until all three generators had spun and all had produced a stable voltage within the required range. The load test was crude but effective. George Blight connected the positive cable to an iron bar, which he then lowered into a bucket of water, taking care it did not touch the sides or bottom. Then he connected the negative cable to the bucket itself in three or four places, evenly spaced apart. Then a nod to Pask, who closed the switch. Blight increased the revs until the voltage reached the required hundred and ten, and within a remarkably short time the water in the bucket was boiling vigorously. The schedule called for this test to be repeated half a dozen times on each generator. After which there would be a tiresome and repetitive process in which a ten-thousand-volt static charge was placed on each winding to see if it held. If it didn't, there must be a breakdown in the insulation and that particular winding would have to be stripped and rewound by someone from the manufacturer.

The endless, careful testing was all very tedious but to Jessie it was the stuff of life itself; she wanted to stay until evening, by which time it would all be completed. But Frank managed to persuade her that she could employ her time better on matters beyond the competence of Blight and Pask. As they strolled up into the town, hoping to find at least a bowl of soup and some cold collation still being served at the Angel, she told him and Cornwallis the full story of her meeting with the old man that morning.

Frank looked worried when she came to the bit about promising him *all* her share of the Helston Power Co. in return for a painted board saying *Kernow and Daughter* over the farm machinery depot.

"But good heavens, I only meant it rhetorically," she protested. "As one might say, 'I'd give my life for an ice cream this minute' — you know, that sort of thing."

"Let's hope the old man sees it that way, too," her brother replied dubiously. "He's apt to remember stray remarks like that and throw them back in your face when it suits him best and you worst."

Then she remembered Clarrie's bit of news — how Godfrey had questioned her on the best way of infiltrating the Lambton girl into Wheal Prosper. "Cornwallis, my dear," she said as they went into the private bar at the Angel, "would you agree that the Helston Power Company has been a splendidly cooperative venture between the three of us?"

"Watch out, boy," Frank warned. "She's up to something."

Cornwallis eyed her warily. "That would be one possible interpretation," he replied.

"Give me another, then."

They ordered soup and ham sandwiches.

Cornwallis said, "I could also argue that the 'splendid cooperation' has been between Frank and me to ... how shall I put it? To sweep the corners you cannot reach — or could not reach until you revealed yourself in your true colours to your father."

Since either interpretation suited her purpose she did not quibble. "The main thing is that your earlier fears — namely that, if you played *any* part in the company's business, Helston people would think it was your venture, not mine — that fear was groundless. Yes?"

Frank watched his sister in fascination and thanked heaven that the legal profession was closed to women. Vosper Scawen, one of the town's older lawyers, had told him that if he needed to get a witness boxed in just where he wanted him, go out into the fields and watch a good sheepdog at work. Here was that advice in action.

Cornwallis realized something of the sort, too. He knew she was nudging him gently into some corner where she wanted him, so he considered every word carefully.

"That fear was groundless, wasn't it?" she repeated.

"Not at the time," he said. "Perhaps now. Certainly there's less and less to fear as time goes by. I mean, people are becoming increasingly aware that you are the leading light."

"Don't say so much, old man," Frank advised. "Just answer yes or no. Make her do the work."

Jessie gave him a withering look. "This is serious," she said. "It's about Godfrey."

Frank hit himself on the forehead. "Of course it is! What an idiot I am!" He turned to Cornwallis. "She hasn't mentioned Godfrey so far — therefore it's *probably* about him. She hasn't mentioned anything remotely connected with anything in which Godfrey is remotely interested — therefore it is *certainly* about him. Don't worry, you'll soon get the hang of it. The main thing is, you may now relax. All these penetrating questions about *you* and the company mean that you are actually the last person on her mind at the moment." He turned back to Jessie with a smile and offered her centre-stage again.

"Have you finished?" she asked coldly.

"Yes — by which, as *your* brother and a true Kernow, I of course mean no."

She ignored him and turned back to Cornwallis. "The way Godfrey comes into it is that he's embarked on some machiavellian plot to get a little tottie he's taken a shine to ... Well, you remember the girl, of course — the night he drove her home to Wheal Dream in your car!"

"Tillie Lambton," Cornwallis said.

"He even remembers her name," Frank said admiringly.

"A rather plain little girl, and yet oddly appealing," Cornwallis went on. "Lovely hair. Can't blame the lad. What's the machiavellian plot? A fake wedding with an actor dressed up as a priest?"

Walter Blackwell entered the bar at that moment, following the maid with their soup and sandwiches. "The ale is on the house," he said expansively. "Today, Miss Kernow, I signed up my hundred and fortieth subscriber to the Helston Power Company — which, I think, will ensure me free electricity for the next five years."

She looked all about her in consternation, as if he had just blurted out the most dreadful secret. Almost in a whisper she told him it was almost three times the number who had subscribed directly with the company — so he certainly deserved free current. Then she promised him faithfully the no one — absolutely *no* one — would *ever* hear of his good fortune from her or any other servant of the company.

He frowned, being unable to see why the whole world shouldn't know how clever he had been.

"One or two of them are bound to work out that their bills will be padded to make up the deficit," she explained. "It could rather strain the smile with which they greet the news of your good fortune, don't you imagine?"

He left looking more thoughtful than when he had entered.

Jessie relished a sip of the ale 'on the house.' As she put the tankard down she said to the others, "Does he really think the price of that pint came out of his own pocket? Amazing!"

"Tillie Lambton," Frank said. "Cornwallis Trelawney. The Helston Power Company. You were about to weave them all into one grand design that would make Machiavelli look as amateurish as Mine Host here at the Angel."

"This is excellent soup," Jessie said pleasantly.

"Well?" Cornwallis prompted.

She sighed. "I was merely pointing out that your participation in the company ..."

"Complicity?" he suggested.

"Whatever you like — it hasn't caused people to suppose that you are its leading light. And you yourself said that the likelihood of it is diminishing with each passing day. I was then on the point of saying how valuable your contribution has been and that I hoped you would be contributing even more now that your initial fear has proved groundless. You might then have responded that the farm would demand an increasing amount of your time now that you have to run it commercially, yourself — rather than treat it as a property to rent to someone else. Whereupon I would have mentioned this absurd proposal of Godfrey's to blackmail Cressida into taking Tillie Lambton on as a chambermaid at Wheal Prosper ..."

By now the two men were staring at her, open mouthed.

"A chambermaid?" Cornwallis asked.

"Blackmail?" Frank echoed, rubbing his hands with glee. "Is it possible? What deep, dark secret of the Surface Angel's has the young devil discovered?"

Jessie chuckled. "You mean could our sweet little brother be smarter than the rest of us — since we only know one, and it's hardly a secret?"

"He is marvellously observant," Cornwallis pointed out. "In the field of natural history, anyway."

"That's probably what we're talking about," Frank said glumly. "He's also off his chump. The other servants would just walk out."

"Godfrey's quite prepared for that. He's discussed it with Clarrie, which is how I got to hear of it. He says let one or two of them carry out their threat. The rest will think again. He seems quite confident he can force Cressida into doing it, too. I'm sure he's discovered something about her visits to Saint Ives — something she'd rather the old man didn't know. It doesn't take much imagination to guess what!"

Cornwallis laughed drily. "Nor does it take much imagination to guess what your solution is — now you've linked me with it!"

"She'd make an excellent dairymaid, darling. We both remarked on how clean she was — especially when you think of her origins and situation. Clean fingernails. Clean ears ..."

"Clean underwear," Frank added provocatively. Then, when they rewarded him with the appropriately shocked response, he explained how he had 'happened across' Godfrey and the girl swimming at Bullion Cliffs back in July.

"Anyway," Jessie pressed the point, "she'd train up very well as a cheesemaker and if you got in a few hundred pullets, she could manage the egg side of the business, too. She'd leap at the chance. It'd be a great step up for her. And it would put at least a bit of distance between her and the little devil. So" — she smiled sweetly — "why don't you slip out the back after you've emptied that tankard and have a quick word with her?"

One of the generators proved incapable of boiling a bucket of water in ten seconds — at least, having done so six times, one of its windings would not hold a static charge for the required length of time. Jessie's policy of ordering too much of everything — on the same principle that mothers adopt when buying clothes a size too big for their fast-growing children — was vindicated.

"As the Irishman said," she told Cornwallis: "If you smell a rat, nip it in the bud. Otherwise it will burst into a conflagration so vast, it will flood the entire countryside."

She thought she had covered every possible contingency — with the Helston Power Co., with her father, with Godfrey and his madcap ideas ... with the whole chaotic, scheming, indifferent, random world. Nothing could now go wrong — or, if it did, she had a solution ready for it. Or so she hoped. By the weekend, when her linesmen started connecting up the subscribers, her hopes were beginning to turn into something more like certainties. Out of several hundred glass insulators only two had proved defective — which Jim Kenney said was a better figure than any other power company he knew of had achieved. Those insulators, together with the slightly imperfect generator, were the only setbacks in the entire operation. She began to wish she had planned an opening ceremony with more flourish to it — indeed, any kind of ceremony at all would have done, for the start-up George Blight had arranged was strictly functional.

There were circuit breakers throughout the supply system, so that blocks of it could be isolated without shutting down the whole of Helston. As Blight had planned it, the town would be electrified block by block. He would begin with Coinagehall Street at quarter past seven — which was half an hour after sunset — and end an hour later with the block at the top end of Wendron Street, between the old gaol and the railway station. The town was lit by gas, of course, but a temporary electrical light had been set up at each circuit breaker, to be switched on when the circuit was closed; so any subscriber living between that point and the next circuit breaker could look out of the window, in most cases, and see whether or not his section had been electrified yet.

This piecemeal illumination of a dozen or so temporary street lamps was the only element that might be called 'public ceremony,' so Jessie and Cornwallis spent the Monday afternoon going about the town prevailing upon the Helston Silver Band and those members of the G&S they could reach to make up an impromptu parade that evening, singing and playing a selection of suitable songs — *Now the Night is Over ... Oh, End this Darkness, Drear and Dread ... Bright! Bright! The Merry Eve ...* and so on.

But by five o'clock the strain of the last few days finally told and she realized she simply had to get home and rest. Cornwallis drove back to Wheal Dream to make sure Tillie Lambton was coping. Five second-hand henhouses had been delivered on Saturday and she was supposed to have spent the day scrubbing them out with carbolic and ammonia. He'd be back well before the parade began.

When Jessie arrived back in Cross St and shut the garden gate behind her, she leaned against it — for it was, in fact, more like a door than an openwork gate — and closed her eyes. What bliss it was not to have the smell of coal and steam in her nostrils, nor of hot oil and that oddly acrid smell of electric sparks. And to hear birdsong again instead of the whine of the turbine. And just to luxuriate in the Indian-summer warmth of this September evening. The idle rich could enjoy this sort of thing day and night, of course — except that they wouldn't have any cause to appreciate it. She herself wouldn't have appreciated it like this even three months ago. People have to find *something* to fret about. The idle rich would fret about the next meal ... and would the dyspepsia caused by the previous meal have gone by then?

It was so pleasant out of doors that she wondered if she even needed to go inside. Probably not. She'd only lie in her darkened room and find something to fret about ... running through the evening's arrangements for the hundredth time. She could stay out here. Not leaning against the gate, of course, but she could spread one of the deck chairs and stretch out in it. And watch the bees passing from flower to flower. And the birds flitting from shrub to shrub. And just listen to the town, the sounds of the town, with night coming on. The night that would change for ever the ... No! She'd permit herself to think of anything but that. How long could she empty her mind and think of absolutely nothing? She decided to spread a deck chair and find out.

She opened her eyes and found herself staring directly at her father. He was standing about twelve paces away, gazing at her, his expression quite inscrutable. Their eyes met and locked. Neither flinched.

How long had he been there? How long since she herself had arrived, come to that? Three minutes? Five? Not more than five, anyway. Had he been there all that time? She hadn't heard him come out of the house — which is where he must have been.

Had he come to see Frank? Or her? Perhaps he'd come to declare *pax* on this day of all days. Or to claim her share of the Helston Power Co., as Frank had warned he might.

"Did you come to see me or Frank?" she asked.

"Who are you?" he replied.

She closed her eyes again and shook her head wearily. "Oh, Father — that is just so childish." She fixed him with her stare once more. He had not budged. "Are you going to join in our celebrations tonight? Please say yes."

'I want to go out that gate," he said gruffly.

She stepped off the path, up to her waist in the shrubs beside the gate — ceanothus, escallonia, and hebe.

He walked toward her, eyes fixed on the gate. She wanted to step forward again and hit him as he passed — anything to make him take notice of her.

She wanted to shout, "You'll lose all of us if you go on like this, you fool! You don't know how close you are to losing even Cressida. Ask Godfrey! Even Godfrey knows!"

She did neither of these things. In fact, she did nothing at all; and she said nothing, either, until she heard his footsteps receding down the hill. Then she just whispered, "Fool! You dear, darling ... old *fool!*"

*W*hen the power was switched on in Coinagehall St, the effect was immediately apparent to all. It was not that the whole place was suddenly ablaze with light, turning night back into day again; but shops and dwellings that normally had one lighted window, or at most two, now had several. And even those where there was no light directly in the room that faced onto the street had some degree of indirect illumination through fanlights and open doors. As a result, almost every window in each of the buildings was visible. It was enough to raise a cheer from the ad-hoc chorus of the G&S and put more heart into their rendering of Lambert's *Night has a Thousand Eyes.*

People came out to listen and applaud. But when they looked at their own and their neighbours' houses — those that had the new electricity and those that had still had gas — they were somewhat disappointed to observe so small a difference. Of course, they knew that the main distinction was invisible, anyway — namely that the walls would not turn yellow with the fumes and the air would not grow unbearably fuggy as the evening wore on. All the same, they felt there ought to be a more visible contrast, too.

And yet there *was* a difference, a subtle one, which nobody could quite put a finger on. Not until they had gone round half the town, cheering the switch-on, singing appropriate songs, and being cheered in return, did Jessie realize what it was: The *position* that people had chosen for their electric lights was different from the one for the old gas lighting. Most gas lamps had been installed before the invention of the incandescent mantle — back in the days of the old fishtail burner with the smoky yellow flame. Because they shone with only a few candlepower, the old gaslights were usually placed quite low down and often over the mantelpiece; since people chose to sit near the fire for its warmth, that was where they wanted the best illumination, too. But the brilliance of the new electric light bulbs made them uncomfortable down near eye level, so people had generally gone back to putting them where the old chandeliers, with their three or four dozen candles, had hung — up near the ceiling in the middle of each room.

"D'you notice something," Jessie said to Cornwallis once she had spotted the difference. "Each room with electric lighting looks from out here as if it's got no ceiling and the sun is shining straight in. It's not just the fact that it's brighter, it's that the light's shining downward, as it does from the sun, not horizontally, as it does from a gaslamp."

"Bottled sunshine!" he replied. "That's what we're really selling. I'll bet we could get another fifty to sign on with that slogan."

Jessie laughed at his fancy — but she took the first chance of a break to talk to Michael Vestey, one of the wealthier citizens who had so far failed to subscribe to the Helston Power Co., and draw his attention to the advantages of 'bottled sunshine.' He did not sign up on the spot, of course, but there was a sort of thoughtful look about him.

An hour after their parade had begun, when the whole of Helston was glowing with bottled sunshine, those who had not signed the pledge or joined the Band of Hope finished up in the bar of the Angel, where there was a pint of best bitter or a glass of brown sherry for each — by courtesy of the Helston Power Co. Walter Blackwell had every light in the house switched on.

"He's trying to rub it in," Frank said glumly. "You've stopped him from boasting to all and sundry that he's getting it free, so he's going to rub your nose in it, instead."

"Oh, Frank!" his sister laughed. "You're a fine lawyer but you've no head for commerce at all. This place is our best advertisement — don't you see? Look how bright and welcoming it is. Pick up any of those newspapers. Stand wherever you like. You can read it without strain. Just compare this with the miserable gloom in those bars where they haven't subscribed to us yet. Hold up your pint and see how it glistens. The whole town knows what a cautious man with the money old Blackwell is. *They* don't know he's gettting it free, of course — because I made jolly sure he'd keep mum about it! They're going to say to themselves, 'Well, if old Blackwell is willing to splash out on it like that … there must be something in it.' Even if he hadn't slaved like a Trojan to sign up everyone else, I'd probably have given him a discount to light the place like this anyway. In fact, just between ourselves and don't tell anybody" — she lowered her voice and drew him closer — "I went to old Wakeham last Saturday, and offered him four hours free lighting for his shop windows, every night from now until next April. Not Sundays, of course. So, what with the Angel here and Wakeham's across the road, this central part of Helston is going to be a blaze of electrical lighting. I'll bet more than half the shop windows will have their own lights before Christmas. What did the old man want with you this afternoon, by the way?"

The question took him so much by surprise that he put a hand to his stomach, as if she had winded him there.

"Was it professional?" she suggested.

He shook his head. "As a matter of fact, he wanted to know if I'd seen Cressida. Did he say anything to you about it?"

"He asked me who I was."

"Oh." He pulled a face.

Jessie and Cornwallis left the crowd soon after that; she had earlier sent a couple of bottles of champagne down to the power station and she wanted to share the toast with the men of the two shifts, which were changing over at ten.

They strolled arm in arm down Coinagehall St, picking out the houses that had electricity and shouting, "Bravo!" at them. There were enough for them to grow tired of the game before they were halfway down. Then, more soberly, Cornwallis said, "You know how you can stand on the bridge in Saint John's and look at the Cober and say, 'That's the Cober,' even though the actual river — the water itself, I mean — flows away and is never seen there again. Not those actual molecules. So what *is* the river? It's not the water itself, because that's different every second you look at it."

"The banks?" she suggested. What else was there?

"No, because if you dammed the water or diverted it some other way, people would point at the banks and say, 'There *used to be* a river here.' In short, a *river* is neither the water nor the banks. So what is it?"

She laughed. "I don't know. Why ask me now? Why tonight?"

"Because there's a similar puzzle about electricity. D'you realize that from tonight onwards — for *ever* — or at least until the end of civilization, Helston will have electricity."

"Except during emergencies and breakdowns."

"Yes. Well — rivers run dry from time to time, too. But what I'm getting at is that the present power station may be pulled down one day — vanish off the face of the earth. The Helston Power Company may be swallowed up in the Cornish Power Company — or the West of England — or the All-England Power Company. These overhead cables may all go underground, just like the gas and water pipes. The wires in the houses may all be replaced. Fifty years from now there may not be a trace of anything connected with tonight's great event. Yet for every second of every minute of all that time — barring emergencies — Helston will have a continuous supply of electricity."

She saw his point at last. "You mean that everything we've built and installed is really just like the water in a river. It'll all be swept away. But electricity itself, like the river itself, will always be there. Golly!" The awesomeness of it made her shiver.

"It's as near as we get to anything eternal," he added. "And you're the one who's done it. *You*, my darling, have lit an eternal flame in Helston tonight and ..."

"Oh, come!" she protested. "I've had lots of help. You. Frank. Cressida. John Riddoch. The list's as long as ..."

"But the *vision*, love! The vision is yours and no one else's. I was watching poor young Frank just now when you were explaining why old Blackwell's lavish use of electricity is exactly what you want of him. Frank's a lawyer. He thinks like an accountant. He saw your point the moment you explained it, of course, because he's not a fool. But it would never have occurred to him on his own. Whereas you — I'll bet it was the *first* thing you thought of."

Her cup ran over. They had turned the corner into Monument Road by now, where Bullock Lane led down to the power station. She drew him into a gap between two houses and raised her lips hungrily to his. "I'm tired of being an immoral woman," she said when they broke for breath. "Can you think of any reason why we shouldn't get married at the first opportunity?"

He stood as still as a statue.

"Eh?" she prompted.

"Give me time," he said. "I'll think of something."

She punched him playfully and ran ahead of him down the lane. He caught up with her just short of the power-house entrance, where they paused a minute or two to get their breath back.

"Talking of immoral women," he said, "what about Cressida? D'you suppose she's bolted?"

Jessie shrugged and shook her head. "It doesn't bear thinking about. Nothing we can do about it now, anyway."

They went into the generator room, where, between them, they described the excitements of the evening up in the town. Down there at the heart of it all, the men most responsible had seen nothing but the flickering of needles on gauges and heard nothing but sudden changes in the hum of the machinery as each new block had come onto load. There was more cheering as the champagne corks popped and solemn toasts were drunk to the best company in the whole of Cornwall. When Jessie and Cornwallis left, around eleven, the load had dropped and the stoker was banking down the furnace to the point where the turbine could run on its low-pressure section alone, all night long until tomorrow's dawn.

The moon, two days past the full, was almost directly overhead as they stepped outside again. It glistened on the slate roofs of the town above and shimmered with an almost supernatural pallor on the whitewashed walls of the houses along St John's. Here and there an electric lamp was burning still but most of the town was bathed in the dim glow of gaslamps, which fought a losing battle against the brilliance of the moon.

"We have far to go before we may compete with you," Jessie murmured to the great silver globe above.

The sky seemed black until they saw it through gaps in leaf-laden branches of oak and sycamore; then it turned to the deepest, most royal blue. And when the branches obscured the moon, the two of them saw that the sky was full of unsuspected stars.

"So many!" Jessie murmured. "I don't think I've ever seen so many."

"Jealousy," Cornwallis assured her. "They can't believe what they're witnessing down here tonight."

They strolled on in silence past the cattle market, past the gasworks — where they valiantly resisted the temptation to shout out taunts and insults — and so drew level with the premises of Kernow & Son. The traction engines looked like toys in the moonlight; their bright reds and blues and greens were muted and only appeared as coloured because the shadows were so intensely black.

"It seems like a lifetime since I drove that fellow." Cornwallis pointed out the machine he had hired. "When was it? Only March!"

Jessie said nothing. He turned to see what might be distracting her and found her peering hard at the office. "Something up?" he asked.

"I'm sure I saw a light there," she replied. "Yes — there it is again. Someone's striking a match."

"Burglars?"

She shook her head. "They won't find much — unless they're expert safebreakers, too."

Whoever was striking matches, and whatever they were trying to light, they seemed to give up, for no more flickering lights were seen. Jessie continued to watch and, a moment later, a figure came to the window. As soon as the full moonlight fell upon him Jessie recognized her father.

So did Cornwallis. He prepared for her to stiffen, to make some slighting remark, to step out more briskly in that see-if-I-care manner her father always brought out in her; but she did none of these things. She simply stood her ground and stared back at him — for the second time that day.

Did he recognize her? Cornwallis wondered. Could he even see her up here among the higgledy-piggledy of hedgerow, trees, and steep, boulder-strewn fields? If he did, he gave no sign of it.

After a silence she said, "Would you mind going ahead, darling?" "I'll wait along by the bridge."

"No. Go to Cross Street. Tell Frank. I have an odd sort of premonition about ... I don't know. I may not go home tonight — or not to the apartment. I may go to Wheal Prosper."

*T*he gate to the depot was wide open, which alone would have caused them to investigate. Cornwallis again suggested he should wait for her, just in case. He could not say in case of what. Again she declined the offer and asked him to go on to Cross St, to let Frank know what was happening here. Reluctantly he consented but even so he loitered at the corner by the toll house until no screams or cries of murder were heard. As he walked on he reflected grimly that whether those half-expected cries had been in Jessie's voice or her father's, neither would have surprised him.

The gate was visible from the clerk's office but not from her father's, as Jessie now realized for the first time. It struck her as odd that a man like her father could sit comfortably in his office when every socialist in Redruth or every tax inspector in Cornwall might be entering by the gate. Perhaps she did not know him as well as she supposed? What, for instance, might have brought him into Helston at this hour, only to stand in a darkened office, occasionally striking matches, occasionally staring blankly out of the window? It was not the behaviour of the man she thought she knew.

As she walked down the broad, well-flattened lane between the ranks of ploughs, harves, mangold slicers, corn kibblers, and the rest, she tried to cast her mind back over the more memorable occasions of their lives, or her life in his house; but somehow they would not fasten there. She could think of them in words — almost like picture titles: 'The Day I Fell from My Pony and He Carried Me Home' ... 'The Night of Harry's Twenty-First when I Got Tipsy and He Tried Not to

Laugh' ... and so on. But they merely reminded her of the littleness of her life so far — all those belittling constraints from which she had been so desperate to escape; they formed a composite picture entitled 'The Life that Drove Me to This!'

Thinking of her father now it was a composite of a different kind that came to her mind's eye without effort. No grand occasions. No memorable events. Just little vignettes of Barney Kernow being himself. Barney Kernow holding Alderman James's sleeve, lightly pinched between finger and thumb, telling him something secret or scurrilous, fixing him with his twinkling eye, watching every nuance of the man's reaction ... Barney Kernow at a point-to-point, glasses trained on a rider he'd backed, ears peeled for the conversation going on behind him ... Barney Kernow in the interval of a G&S performance, murmuring something slightly risqué into the ear of Mrs Stour, making her laugh with shock and then stare at him with mock-reproach ... Barney Kernow returning to the table and complaining that his meal had been ruined, while a man whose whole life had just been ruined by him walked away down the drive, thinking of suicide ... Barney Kernow, warts and all — the most damnable, hateable, lovable man she was ever likely to know.

She did not go in by the door but sidled along the wall toward the window where she had last seen him — the window she had once jokingly said he would have to block up now that it afforded a view of her power-station chimney. She paused for a moment to look across the Penzance road and the marshy waste between it and the Porthleven road and she saw that the chimney was even more prominent than she had imagined it might be. It brought no feeling of exultation, though.

When she reached the window she was surprised to find him standing there still. Oddly though, he seemed not at all surprised when she suddenly came into view out there. They stood so, two feet apart, staring blankly at each other for a long silent time. Once, when he'd found Godfrey standing at a window, having seen him at the same window fifteen minutes earlier, he'd advised the boy never to be so foolish again — to offer a perfect target to all his enemies out there. The memory of that little jest fed her surprise now.

At last he put his hand to the casement stay and opened the window. "She'm gone," he said blankly.

"I don't think so," Jessie said. "Not for good, anyway." The calm of her voice was another surprise — or would have been if she had not passed beyond all surprising by now.

"I shan't take her back," he said.

"You will," she replied soothingly. "You're only saying that."
There was a long pause while he gazed blankly at the hillside opposite. "How?" he said at last with a sigh. "How has it all happened?"
"Come on out of there," she told him. "I'll go home with you."
He did not move.

"What made you come in here?" she asked, though she could guess — it was the last place left him where the old order still prevailed.

"I shan't sleep," he said.

"We'll walk all the way. We'll both sleep then."
He continued to stare at her. At least he wasn't saying a flat No.

"And tomorrow," she promised, "I'll go over to Saint Ives and tell Cressida not to be such a fool. It's only a gesture on her part." Shyly she reached through the window opening and touched his arm. "You force people to make gestures, you know. We'd rather not but you leave us no choice."

His eyes strayed toward the power-house chimney.

"Yes," she added. "Some of them are quite permanent, too."
The first flicker of a smile twitched at the corners of his lips. "You did it, then, maid," he said.

"Come on. If you don't want to walk home, we'll go up to Frank's."
He gazed at her sharply and she realized it was because she had called it 'Frank's' rather than 'my place' — something she had done without thinking. "Cornwallis will drive you home," she concluded.

When he still did not move she pushed the window shut and tapped the glass by the catch in a peremptory, schoolmarmish manner.

He closed it then and withdrew into the darkness that still shrouded the room. She sauntered back to the entrance. When she saw how he fumbled with the keys she realized suddenly how old he had become. He could still walk back to Nancegollan if he wished. He could still put in a day's work that would exhaust most other men his age. He could probably still outsmart anyone who challenged him in business. But in little gestures like putting a key in a lock, or stepping down two steps, he was old.

Perhaps he knew it? Perhaps he had known it for some time but had pushed all such thoughts aside — only to have tonight's events bring them back in spate. She pictured his life like an arc across the sky. Like the moon above their heads now, he was being nibbled away. Parts of him that shone last year were now darkened. The time would come when he'd wane to a mere outline of himself, and there would be no waxing phase to follow, no reprieve, no prospects.

At the foot of the steps he paused and stared up at the town. Now

the only electric lighting that was visible was the temporary array of
street lights, one at each circuit-breaker, rivals to his ancient gas
lighting. "You've done it, then, maid," he said again.

"Only because people thought I was acting as your agent," she told
him. "I wish I had been, too."

He turned to stare at her — in disbelief, she thought, until she saw
an odd sort of smile twisting his lips.

"What were you doing down here, anyway?" she asked.

He continued to stare at her, and his smile broadened. "Sketches,"
he replied.

"What?" she asked in amazement; the only sketches she'd ever seen
him make were little matchstick men, to amuse them when they were
children. And that was a long time ago.

To prove it it fished a crumpled piece of paper out of his pocket. He
walked to the moonlit face of the building and flattened it against the
wall. He held it there between his two flat hands, almost as if he were
shoring up the building, and, looking back over his shoulder, said,
"Come-us on — have a look! Say what you think."

From a distance all she could see was a number of crudely drawn
rectangles. As she drew closer she saw writing upon them. Another
pace and she saw that some was in severe Roman lettering, some in the
sort they use for playbills, some in the kind favoured by circuses and
traveling fairs. Only when she was right behind him did she realize
that all of them spelled out the same three words: *Kernow and Daughter*.

He waited until the incredulity showed in every line of her face
before he added, "He's looking a bit bare up there, see." And he
nodded toward the roof.

Still in a daze, she raised her eyes and saw that the old sign saying
Kernow & Son — she called it *old*, though it had not been there a year —
had been removed. She drew breath to speak but no words came. Her
throat was choked with words that would not come. Tears prickled
behind her eyelids. Her lip trembled. Overwhelmed at last she put her
arms about him and hugged herself awkwardly against the stubborn
bulk of him. She heard him swallow heavily and his adam's apple
bobbed up and down near her ear.

At last he slipped his arms around her, too, and almost crushed the
life out of her. "Kernow and Daughter," he said in a voice gruff and
salty. "I don't s'pose 'twill ever sound what you might call fitty-like."